# THE FALLEN PART TWO

## THE WATCHER SERIES BOOK FIVE

## ROBIN WOODS

Second Edition

Epic Books Publishing





Lead Editor: Beth Braithwaite
Additional Editing: Tamar Hela

Cover Design by Vera Walker.

Summary: Betrayed by the person she trusted most, Aleria breaks away from the safety of the Watchers only to become more entangled in the endgame of the Fallen. But fallen angels aren't the only threat. As Aleria's visions become something else entirely, mutiny threatens the new king of the French Coven, jeopardizing the delicate truce between vampire and humankind.

Now separated from Aleria, desperation pushes Gabriel to join forces with an unlikely ally as he tries to manage the chaos within his own ranks.  But he must remain focused on one objective: stop Semjâzâ before he can enslave the world. The stage is set for an all or nothing battle to defeat the Fallen once and for all.



[Fiction-Fantasy, Fiction-Young Adult, Fiction-Paranormal, Fiction-Vampires]

ISBN-10: 1941077072
ISBN-13: 978-1-941077-07-8

CONTENTS

*To my editors and friends—*

*Tamar and Beth*

ALERIA

"Vengeance is in my heart, death in my hand,
Blood and revenge are hammering in my head."
from *Titus Andronicus*

—William Shakespeare

---

GABRIEL

"It is a characteristic of wisdom not to do desperate things."

—Henry David Thoreau

1

---

RECKLESS

We soared past a road sign that said, "Welcome to Hell." Well, maybe not. It said either "Welcome to France" or "French Border." Same difference.

Bowen's voice was subdued. "Tyran, we'll stop in the next city."

"Are you sure you don't want to continue home?"

"She isn't ready. We can't return with her like this. The moment we walk through that door, a clock starts ticking."

"God, I hadn't thought of that."

"You should have," Bowen clipped.

I wondered what they were talking about, but I didn't bother asking. It didn't even upset me that they kept speaking like I wasn't in the car with them. I just didn't care. I'd retreated so far into my head that I did little beside breathe, blink, and follow basic commands.

Here I was, free to run into Bowen's arms like Joshua had

accused, yet I shied away from his touch and remained disconnected—broken.

What Tyran had tried to do for years, Joshua had done in seconds.

I kept turning Josh's words over and over again in my head, reliving what I'd sensed through the blood bond. *"It's your fault Sebastian is dead! It's your fault Peter is gone...and Leslie and Gentry! All of it. You leave a trail of bodies everywhere you go...If you weren't so damned intent on sacrificing yourself, then Sebastian would be alive...you had to go and serve yourself up on a platter to Moloch...I can't trust you anymore!...I can't be with someone I can't trust...I can't take it anymore. Love isn't enough to take this kind of abuse. True love shouldn't require this much suffering!"*

There was a phantom handprint on my face from his slap that seemed to both sting and make me numb, even now. And the result: I was petrified to let Bowen in, fearful not of being hurt, but that I would ruin him, too.

The chill of an oncoming vision pricked at me, but this time, I felt something else seeming to piggyback with it. I hadn't recognized this the last time.

Panting, I grabbed Bowen's hand as blood started to pour out of my nose. I felt his hands on my shoulders and saw a flash of worried, blue eyes. Then, my eyes rolled back into my head, and blackness squeezed out the light.


GABRIEL

Three days had passed since Aleria had chosen to leave with Belenus and Taranis. *Driven out* may have been more accurate. She had been a husk, walking woodenly out with them. It was difficult to look at Joshua now.

My phone rang, and I pressed it to my ear. "Speak."

"She's with Blackthorne right now," replied Samael, his voice hushed.

"Follow her. Remember, she is the most dangerous thing you have ever tracked."

"I know. She took me out before I knew she was there during our last encounter, remember?"

"Be well, my friend."

"Be well," Samael replied as I tapped the red button ending the call.

Pressing the phone to my forehead, I wished that the mystery of Ana would reveal itself. *Friend or foe?* After Ali had departed, I had revealed everything I knew to Samael, needing his help. He had inferred more than I had realized, but still was angry that I had not confided in him earlier.

"Ian, kick Joshua out of bed. Sun sets in five. I want to be on the road in seven."

"Yes, sir," replied Ian. Even in the worst of times, Ian had used his humor to power through, but silence had closed around we few who were left.

Light faded as the sun went to rest for the day. I packed the last of the electronics just as Joshua appeared with his bags.

"May I help with something?" asked he, his voice low.

"Just get into the van. Take your stuff."

He met my stare for the first time, raging winds behind his eyes, but dipped his head in acquiescence as he whispered outside using vampire stealth.

I thrust my fist in the air, squeezing it shut until it felt as if my knuckles would split, willing my anger back into place. Seeing him now brought to mind the look on Aleria's face the moment after he had raised his hand to her. Exhaling, I shook my hands out, allowing calm to fill my chest and ease the muscles in my shoulders.

Ian strode into the room. "Final sweep. Place is clean. Ready to depart."

"Meet you outside." My voice was neutral once again.

I took one more breath, making one last visual check before I slung my bag over my shoulder and exited.

While Samael tracked Ana, I had my own prey. Phineas had been holed up in Luxembourg for forty-eight hours, and now he was on the move. I was going to find out what role Phineas had in all of this. He had been a pawn before, but now, I feared he was a player—a *key* player.


ALERIA

I woke and found myself in a bed, with bloodstains down the front of my shirt. Looking around, I spotted a fresh dress on a hanger hooked on the top of a simple armoire.

When I moved, I realized my pants were gone. I had no idea how long it had been, so I grabbed my disposable cell off of the nightstand and checked the time.

Seven hours of my life were missing, and there was nothing of the vision left in my brain, no matter how hard I tried to remember. The same blankness I'd had before, but this time, there wasn't even a remnant.

"My brother said that you usually wake not long after having a vision," Bowen said from somewhere in the room.

I was startled, but didn't move or even look at him. I hadn't spoken in days and still didn't really want to.

Samael's voice about my codename was on repeat in my head: "Do you know what Cassandra means…'she who entangles men.'" I had reduced Joshua to a paranoid, screaming mess who blamed me for the loss of everyone he'd cared about in the last three years.

I glanced at Bowen for a millisecond, more to see where he was located than anything else. He was in a chair in the corner and looked exhausted. I steeled myself. I couldn't let him get close; I had to keep my defenses up, lest I drag him down too.

"Is that correct?" he asked when I didn't comment.

I felt as if I was swimming to the surface from beneath leagues of water, trying to find my voice. I drew in air. "Minutes, usually."

"You *are* in there."

I turned my head and looked out the window, avoiding eye contact, but I couldn't see anything except the reflection of the room and Bowen in a chair in the corner with a book propped in his lap. I focused my eyes on the bedspread, feeling his desire to come closer.

"I need to return to the castle tomorrow evening. Morpheus can't stave off the wolves any longer. I will have Tyran wait here with you until you are ready. We are about two hours from home."

"That won't look good for you." A statement, not a question. It had been three weeks since I'd departed the coven with Tyran, and four days since leaving Gabriel and the others. Returning to the coven without his new bride would weaken his position.

Bowen paused and walked to the bed, sitting at the foot, a few inches from my toes. I pulled my feet away, wrapping my hands around my knees. I peeped at him; his face remained passive, but my retreat had bothered him.

"No, it won't," his reply plain.

I bit my lip, trying to rouse some sort of feeling. Squeezing my eyes shut, I fought with myself for a moment. "I'll come."

"Not until you are ready."

"I am or will be tomorrow."

"You won't. You can't even look at me right now."

I opened my eyes, but had to psych myself up to make eye contact. "I'll be ready. I'm at your disposal."

He screwed up his face. "What does that mean? 'At your disposal?' You aren't chattel or a tool for me to use."

I could no longer take the eye contact, my voice sounding dead. "I'm whatever you need me to be."

"The way he treated you—he isn't worth mourning. You shouldn't give him a second thought! Where are you in there? I want the girl with fire in her belly, ready to defy a queen and face off with a god!"

My voice was still empty when I replied, "I'll do whatever you want. I won't undermine your reign. I'll stand by your side and smile and nod and be whatever you need." I kept my voice even as I uttered the worst thing I could possibly conjure to push him away. "You want a lover? Go ahead." I flipped the covers off half my body and allowed my bare leg to fall open. "You can complete your conquest—consummate the marriage. I'll lie still. I won't resist."

He couldn't hide the disgust on his face. He flicked the covers back over me, stood, then whirled away from me.

"You aren't just some *conquest* to me, and you know it. How dare—" he stopped abruptly. He stilled, looking at the ground, his anger close under the surface. He didn't say anything else; a scoffing sound escaped his lips.

A moment later, a door shut. It wasn't slammed, but almost.
*Well done.*

Tyran entered a minute later, slowly clapping. *"Bravo.* So, is this rock bottom? Or do we still have a ways to go? Any more collateral damage, sissy?"

I met his hard stare and blinked, keeping my mouth shut.

He flopped on the bed next to me and propped his head up with his left hand. The covers came partially off with his weight on the bed, but I froze and didn't recover myself. He ran his fingers up my right thigh, and when they drifted a little too close to the inner part of my leg, I flinched.

He narrowed his eyes and leaned closer. "Not so ready to throw your body away, are you?"

I started trembling.

"What would you have done if he had taken you up on your offer?" He made a small circle on my knee over and over with his index finger.

"Please stop," I whimpered.

Tyran smiled and rolled onto his back. "You knew he wouldn't. So why did you do it?"

I slid farther under the covers, pulling them up to my chin, wishing they were a magical shield to keep Mr. Probing Questions out of my head.

"I'm a terrible person. Let's just leave it at that. Please leave. I would like get some extra sleep."

To my surprise, Tyran got up and sauntered to the door. Then, he laughed. He turned and hung his hands from the top of the frame, leaning into the room.

He laughed again. "You truly believe that, don't you? That's why you did it." He really started laughing then, and I had to listen to him as his voice echoed all the way down the hall.


GABRIEL

Joshua was on a run to purchase batteries for the comms. He still was not acting as I would have expected. I turned to Ian. "If you truly believed that your wife had been cheating on you, and you had driven her away, how would you be feeling just four days later?"

Leaning back in his chair, Ian pondered, "I think I would still be running on anger. Justifying my actions."

"Does Joshua seem angry to you? Has he uttered one negative comment about Aleria?"

"No. He seems…"

"Anything but angry. Subservient."

"Guilty," offered Ian.

"I am missing something."

"You don't think, I mean, what if Ali? I don't want to doubt her, but the dude is a king and wanted to be all up in her business. If I was a chick, I would've been all over *that*."

I raised my brows at him.

"I'm man enough to say it. The dude is hot."

I suppressed the rare urge to roll my eyes.

"Then again, Joshua isn't a slouch. I would probably do him, too."

"I am glad to see your humor has returned. May I now have my Lieutenant back?"

Ian rubbed at his sore shoulder from the Strigoi bite. "Yes, sir. What would you like me to do?"

"Test the tracker one last time. We tag Phineas tonight."

2

———

CURSE

When I woke, I became aware that the sun had set and that Tyran was pressed against my side. His breathing was slow and even. It jarred memories of him sleeping next to me while I'd been dying of Aurora. I was surprised that Tyran would sleep when there weren't any sentries safeguarding us. It made me wonder where we were; I couldn't sense Bowen in the vicinity. I'd been delivered to this bedroom unconscious and hadn't left it since.

Feeding and bathing were high on my priority list. I yawned and stretched; Tyran was instantly alert. It was apparent that he'd been sleeping next to me in order to keep track of me while he rested.

He looked around the room, and then at his watch. "Damn it."

"What's wrong?"

He didn't answer, but instead virtually vanished from the room. He was back seconds later. "He never came back."

A balloon of I–deserve-to-be-tossed-in-an-active-volcano rose up. "This is my fault."

"Yes, it is."

*And there's the gut punch.*

"I'm foiling your little plot to drive him away the second he returns. Your actions are not protecting him. They are hurting him."

"If you tell him why I pushed him away, then I will have hurt him for nothing. I am a curse. Can't you see that?"

Tyran dropped his snarky routine to speak in earnest. "Your ex was right about one thing: you are too ready to sacrifice yourself for others. You can have my brother and a kingdom to spare, yet you choose to live in some self-imposed prison in an attempt to protect him from your vast evilness."

Suddenly, his face was inches from mine. "You want to know how I have survived centuries without going insane or walking into the sun to end the tedium? I. Drink. In. Life. I take whatever I can get and revel in it. You want him? Take him—but do it the *right* way. Be honest with yourself, for once, and let go."

"What if I am cursed?" I protested.

"Then we can all be cursed together, as if we aren't already! You are not weak, so stop living in fear. I won't allow it!"

"You aren't the boss of me!" I shouted.

"Maybe I should be!" he growled back. Then, almost as if he couldn't help himself, he added, "If you knew the things he has done for you!"

"I know what he's done for me!" I retorted.

But then a memory surfaced. I looked away, trying to lock onto the thought. After we had captured the Strigoi for the delivery, Tyran had covered our escape. Afterwards, he had caught up and said something before passing out.

I looked at Tyran again. "He did something I don't know about," I stated, louder than necessary. "In the truck in Romania, you said 'he took on my punishment.' What did you mean by that?"

Instantly, the anger drained from his face and was replaced with something unreadable. "Nothing." His voice went out for a moment. "You choosing your ex has been punishment enough. You should never have left with the Slayer after the sacrifice had been stopped."

"That is not what you meant," I accused. I knew he was lying. His expression became stone, and I quickly realized that pushing him now wouldn't help me get the info in the future.

A little more nicely, he said, "You will fix things with my brother."

Needing to get away from him, I crawled out of bed, feeling angry—mostly because he was right. The thought of being with Bowen terrified me—more than terrified me. It had never occurred to me just *how* deathly afraid of it I was.

I realized I was pacing back and forth in nothing but a t-shirt and underwear. When I turned back to Tyran, he was looking at my face and not my undies, which surprised me almost as much as the fact that he was giving sage advice. Advice I intended to follow. But when I thought of speaking to Bowen, embarrassment crept up my limbs, filling me with galactic-level dread. I didn't know if I could face him again. My impulse to run overcame me.

*Fight or flight.*

"Flight" was blaring in my head like a siren attached to a Broadway sign on top of a carnival.

Tyran must have seen something in my expression. "Oh, no you don't." He jumped up and ripped the hanger from the edge of the armoire, then started shoving me and the dress towards the bathroom. "Shower. You stink of dirty laundry and dried blood. You'll feed when you get out."

"Tyran—" I started to argue.

"I would be happy to scrub you down." His expression became wolfish as the surly side of him surfaced.

I grabbed the clothing from his hands.

"Do I need to guard the door so you don't sneak out? Or can I find you someone on which to feed?"

I hung my head. "I won't go anywhere."

He patted me on the head patronizingly. "Good little sissy. I'll be back shortly."

I took a long shower, part of me wishing I could wash myself down the drain with all the suds. Afterwards, I tugged the dress over my curves, the fabric clinging to my still damp skin.

At that moment, I heard the door in the hallway. Dabbing my dripping hair with my towel, I opened the bathroom door. "Tyran, I—"

Bowen was sitting on the edge of the bed resting his elbows on his knees, hands dangling, head bowed. His shirt was rumpled.

I swallowed hard.

"After I pulled you out of that dungeon, in all of the months we spent together, have I ever *once* been reckless with your heart?"

Petrescu had accused me of being reckless, but that had been an act. What I'd said to Bowen had been calculated for optimum effect—and it *had* been reckless, in a way.

"Never," I finally choked, my heart thudding painfully in my chest.

"Then I ask you not to be reckless with mine."

I stood there, feeling too many emotions to move.

Bowen rose and headed for the door.

"Wait," I implored breathlessly.

He stopped, but didn't turn to look at me. In fact, he hadn't looked at me since he'd returned.

"I'm scared," I admitted, without any sort of preamble, half-surprised it had popped out of my mouth.

His shoulders shifted just enough that I knew he'd heard me. After an uncomfortable silence, he spoke. "I am aware that you are hurting and that you are afraid of getting hurt aga—"

"That's not what I am scared of. I mean, I *am* hurting. And I'm not exactly rushing to trust someone like I had Jo—" I stopped short of finishing his name. "I...I know I can trust you. That's not what...I...you..."

Bowen turned, his brow furrowed with confusion.

The words hung in my mind a moment before I could latch onto them. "You terrify me."

"I would nev—"

"Not like that. The thought of you. You're so...I...We will never date. You will never buy me popcorn at a movie or talk to me on the phone until I can't hold my eyes open any longer. This isn't simple. You are a king. We are already married, even though I don't feel like we are! There was no minister and no you!"

I threw my hands up, exasperated. "It's all or nothing. Do you have any idea how intimidating this situation is...and *you* are? Even among vampires, you stand out." I had to gulp down air to continue before I lost my nerve. "But more than anything, I'm afraid that I will destroy you. Everyone close to me gets hurt. Look what I did to Jo—," I gulped air, "*him*."

There was a flash of anger in his eyes. "*He* did that to himself. You had done nothing wrong."

"I told your brother that I am a curse. I meant it. I'm beyond petrified that I will ruin you. Ruin—as in, cannot ever be repaired."

Bowen stood in front of me, looking lost. "Isn't that *my* choice, and not yours, to make?" he asked as he cautiously approached me.

I felt raw. As if I had flayed myself open.

He tucked a strand of dripping hair behind my ear.

Something in the energy between us changed; I held my breath as he slowly leaned in and gently brushed his lips across mine. Then he kissed me so softly, I wasn't sure if it had happened.

I felt conflicted.

Guilt surfaced, from letting someone else, besides *him*, touch me. As well as the guilt over *how* I'd pushed Bowen away. I think Bowen could feel it too.

He pulled back and looked me in the eyes, examining me. After a long moment, he said, "I spoke with Morpheus while I was out. We will wait another week before returning. You are in mourning, and I want you to be as ready as you can be."

Tears pricked at my eyes. I was so thankful. "I'm so, so sorry for hurting you."

"I forgive you." Then he pressed his lips to my ear, "And *when* I do bed you, you will not be lying still. You will be pleading with me *for more*."

I looked at him, half-shocked.

He gave me a grin, more seductive than I'd thought possible, and kissed me once again before striding from the room. It was feather soft, and not much more than a peck, but it had warmed me.

I stood there, trembling and scared...

and part of me...

wanting more.


GABRIEL

I red-buttoned the call, then ran my hand through my hair simply for the movement. There were too many pieces that did not fit. "Phineas told Blackthorne that he is still in France."

Ian furrowed his brow, his confusion reflecting my own. "You didn't tell Blackthorne that Phineas was lying?"

"No."

"I thought that if Phineas was up to something, Blackthorne would be behind it."

"Agreed."

"Or Rousseau trying to get back in on the action."

"You did not see her after the meeting with Ali and Ana. Whatever hole they dropped her in, she is changed. She wanted to meet with Ali alone. I denied her request."

"You weren't curious?" questioned Ian.

"Ali did not need to relive past betrayals. She had enough on deck to think about. I wanted her to have a clear head."

After a moment, Ian stated, "I miss her."

My regret of the way she had left had been my constant companion. I wished that I had spoken to her and offered her some solace.

I was moving our small band to southern Belgium. The borders of both Germany and France were close, placing us strategically. It seemed most of the persons of interest were moving in the northern region of continental Europe and London. I wondered for a moment if I should call them "beings" of interest since few were actually human. Then I realized that

Ali had made that quip over a year ago. She was not dead, but certainly part of me was mourning.

With precision, I marked the map with all of the locations in which we had tracked Phineas in the last two days. He had been a busy boy.

3

---

# VIOLATION

ALERIA

I timidly wandered into the living room of our suite with that awkward feeling you have after a fight with someone. We'd talked, but I wasn't really sure if I was wholly forgiven.

Bowen reclined on a couch, while Tyran was perched on a captain's chair. There was a reporter on television, spouting on about the shift in economies across continental Europe and the world. I closed my eyes, not wanting to hear anything remotely negative. But then I remembered something that Tyran had said to Gabriel.

"Has Switzerland closed its borders?"

"Yes, they are open now, but they were for several days," Tyran answered.

Bowen added, "Dubai, London, Hong Kong, Toronto, Paris, Tokyo, San Francisco, Singapore, and New York have all gone on an alert of some sort due to threats."

"That's a lot of cities," I commented. "Do you still think that this has to do with the Fallen? Or terrorists?"

Tyran shrugged. "I believe I have said this before: control the money, control the world."

"If the Fallen can unify the world against a common enemy, it would be much easier for them to seize power," Bowen mused.

"Do you believe they are puppeteering a terrorist organization to take the fall?" Tyran questioned.

"How would anyone orchestrate something that large?" I asked, not really expecting an answer. It was overwhelming. I'd been so focused on what was going on with me, that I'd lost the bigger picture. Someone was playing chess while I was still playing tic-tac-toe.

"We start with what we can control," Bowen stated.

"And what is that?" I asked.

"Our coven."

*Our.* I was part of his coven whether I liked it or not. I sighed. I was keeping him away from the very place he needed to be.

I moved towards the couch, but before I could sit, the chill of a vision came over me. As I dropped to my knees, I felt hands on me, but the blackness devoured me before I could register who had me.

---

I was standing in an open field. Trees rose up, splitting the ground in a large circle around me. And as they did, the sky darkened, and the air stopped moving. A light came shining from above, and I had to cover my eyes. When I looked again, there was a gigantic moon hanging just above the trees. I was no longer in a clearing—I was in a graveyard.

Ancient monuments stood all around me as a reminder of the long dead. I started to walk, but as I did, I didn't seem to make any progress towards the trees. A breeze began to pick up, the air scented with smoke and incense.

An ornate mausoleum rose up directly in front of me from a series of flat gravestones, much like the trees had moments before. Ivy quickly sprouted and raced up the building's columns and onto the roof. But as soon as it covered the roof, all of the color faded from green to grey and the ivy began knitting together to form something.

After a few more seconds, the shapes appeared to be gargoyles. I wanted to run from their horrific faces. At that moment, the ground began to shake, and some of the cement fell away to reveal beautiful, stone angels beneath. I stared up at them in awe. They were exquisite. Then their faces twisted in anger, and to my horror, one took flight. His terrible wings were so wide, they almost blotted out the moon.

He seemed to hover there for a moment, suspended in terrifying beauty, before diving straight at me. My legs wouldn't work. I was stone-still, just like the statuary in the graveyard. The angel knocked me on my back, and he straddled me, wrapping his large, stone hands around my neck.

I tried to call for help and to throw him off, but I couldn't move, though I didn't stop trying. So, I attempted to gather details and memorize his face, but it was somehow blurry. Vines began to spring from the ground. They encircled my wrists and ankles. After I was shackled by the growth, one continued to travel across my palm until it perfectly circled my wedding ring finger and turned to stone, weighing my hand down.

The stone angel's face was still indistinct; though I had the impression he smiled. He released my neck, and the vines immediately constricted my throat. With renewed zeal, I tried to break free.

His hands then went to my stomach. He placed them side-by-side, and when he did, my belly began to swell as if I was with child. Panic surged through my veins.

He spoke, and to my terror, he sounded like there were many voices all at once. I listened, but I couldn't understand a single word he uttered.

I felt hopeless.

The moment I stopped struggling, the vines around my neck eased enough that I could raise my head. I stared at my swollen belly, and then everything on my body began to crack. A great reddish light shone from beneath—it looked as if it was lava beneath a thick crust. A debilitating, burning sensation surged through me. I cried out just as my body was consumed, and I turned to ash.

---

I woke, gasping in Bowen's arms. I wrenched myself away and skittered into the corner like a fearful, wild animal. My eyes darted around the room as I tried to control my breathing, but I couldn't. It was like an irrepressible spasm.

My hands flew down to my belly. It was flat, and there was nothing wrong with me. Suddenly, the ring on my finger felt confining. I desperately tugged it off and throwing it onto the carpet a few feet in front of me.

Bowen made a move to come closer, and I shrieked. "Get back! Don't touch me!" I knew I was being irrational, but there was just no containing it. Everything was closing in on me. I could still feel the vines around my wrists and ankles, and the ring turning to stone on my finger.

Tyran got onto his knees in front of me. His voice was completely calm. "Ali, I need you to tell me what you saw." I tried to remember if he'd ever called me "Ali" before. It seemed to jar me from my hysteria.

I pressed my palms to the flooring and concentrated on calming my body. My sprinting heart began to slow. I closed my eyes, and as I'd done a hundred times with Gabriel, I recounted the vision. When I was finished, I opened my eyes. Bowen met my gaze, but the emotion on his face forced me to look over at Tyran. His face was composed.

"Was anyone altering your dream?" Tyran asked. I realized he was framing his questions just like Gabriel in order to help me. I had to make myself not think about Gabriel and how much I missed him.

I thought for a moment. "No, no one was in my head this time."

"Have you ever had a vision quite like this?"

I shook my head. "Not in the form of a vision that overtakes me. Nightmares. Prophetic nightmares, yes. When I was still human, and the Oneiroi were injecting themselves into my dreams, that scene was no worse." I thought about the nightmare about the subway car coming to life and all the people melting into the ground like candle wax, leaving pools of blood. Then I continued. "But they weren't in this dream. I am being warned about something."

I took another cleansing breath as if I was doing yoga, then leaned against the wall. I felt like an idiot. I noticed the ring on the floor, but couldn't even think about putting it back on again; I rubbed at my finger as if it were burning.

"You turning to ash could simply be from your recent sun exposure. You fought Ananiel in a cemetery. Much of this can be explained, sissy." Tyran's tone was soothing, and he was being very rational. But there was more to this.

My thoughts started to clear, and I realized part of the reason

I was so rattled. "The child. It was a violation. I don't know any other way to describe it."

"Like you had been forced to bear a child?" Bowen's voice was uneven.

I swallowed. "I don't know. I need time to decode this." I stood up. "I think I just need to be alone for a little while. I...I'm sorry." I couldn't look at Bowen as I left.

As soon as I was in the safety of my room, I curled up on the bed, hugging a pillow.

My own words kept repeating in my head:

It was a violation.

GABRIEL

"Gabriel," Ian called me from the other room.

"You have the traffic cam footage?"

"You won't believe what I found!" hollered Ian.

Sliding the tablet away from me, I quickly trotted into the den. Ian was positioned in the corner and had the curtains pulled shut over both windows.

"Phineas was meeting with someone all right."

Ian clicked play. The traffic cam caught Phineas slithering into an alcove next to the front of a building in Germany. Ian punched fast forward. Several minutes later, someone stepped into the alcove with him for a total of thirty-six seconds. When the person left, my blood cooled.

"Can you get a close up of his face?"

"I wish; this isn't the movies."

I shot Ian a disapproving look.

He raised his hands. "Sorry, I wish I could. I tried, but the resolution is too low, and it became too pixilated. If the light was better, maybe, but dusk is difficult. And whatever, we still have important info just from that."

"We do. Whoever he was meeting with was not human."

"Yup, way too big for human, unless he has taken up meeting with Danish bodybuilders."

"Danish?" I questioned, almost afraid to ask.

"Aren't the Dutch the tallest people on the planet? I thought they were. Maybe not."

"Keep at it. I am going for a run. I want for us to have time to spar before lunch."

"Soooo, you want to kick my ass for being so charming the last few days." He winked. Ian had been extra mouthy, but even more efficient and dutiful.

I grinned. If I had wanted to kick someone's ass, I would have asked Joshua to spar. Since driving Ali off, he had been the example of perfection in his duties and manners. Doing everything I had asked and more. Always ready with a please and a thank you. But he had not said a single word in regards to his behavior from a week ago. I still felt as if I was missing a piece, and I was not alone in those thoughts. Ian had confirmed as much.

ALERIA

The sun had risen during my hours of solitude. I was still curled into a ball on the bed, hugging a pillow, and had hardly moved since retreating to my hotel room. It took hours, but I'd been able to work my way through the sense of violation that had been so oppressive after the vision. I had left the door open the entire time I'd been in here, partially so I could hear, but also because I felt scared.

Bowen's presence outside the door interrupted my musings;

he'd just been speaking to someone on the phone. It was a relief to feel him near me. I didn't really want to be alone anymore, and had debated on slinking back to the other room, but I felt like an idiot for my reaction after the vision.

"You can come in," I offered.

My back was to him, but I didn't move. He walked around the bed and came into view. His emotions were tightly controlled.

"I just wanted to check on you."

I patted the empty space on the bed next to me. "Will you stay?"

He seemed to deliberate a moment, and then sat on the bed with his back to me. I wished I could see his face. The set of his shoulders seemed burdened.

"Was that Morpheus you were speaking to on the phone?"

"Yes."

"Do we need to go back today?"

"I promised you another week. We have six more days."

"I know you pro—"

"Aleria." He said my name like a caress. "You aren't ready... and after what I saw in the other room..." His back was still to me.

I stretched and put my hand on his forearm. "I'm sorry."

He turned his head and looked at my hand. "You always apologize for things not your fault." He paused. "You had so few visions the months you stayed with me. You woke from nightmares, but after what you have gone through, I would have expected nothing less. Is this what your life has become?"

Tyran had had the same question not long ago.

"Five weeks ago, I had control. I would lose consciousness, but most of the time, I managed to do no more than drop to a knee. I recovered in minutes. Gabriel or Jo—" I swallowed, "would talk me through them, just as you saw Tyran do. Tyran had seen Gabriel help me. Before the sacrifice, my visions increased in volume and intensity. My guess is that this is the same. Or maybe I'm defective."

Bowen finally turned a little more to see my face. I managed to smile a little. He exhaled. I pulled my arm back when he rolled so that he was on his side facing me. It felt quiet and intimate and nice.

The corner of his mouth quirked up. "Defective?"

"Yeah, you may have been married off to a faulty model."

His brow furrowed, and the humor drained from his face. There was something deeper bothering him.

"You can ask me anything," I prompted.

"Were you holding something back in regards to your vision?"

"No, I told you everything I could remember," I answered, confused.

He seemed to hesitate. "Was it about me? Is that how you feel about our marriage? Trapped and violated?"

"No," I replied, remembering that I'd ripped off my ring and threw it away from me. "No. You have never once made me feel unsafe—ever. I mean, after the evil twin thing was resolved and everything."

"But do you feel trapped?"

I reached out across the bed and took his hand. He laced his fingers through mine and waited expectantly. "By the situation, but not by you. Please don't question how much I care about you. I know I joked that I was defective. Truth is, I'm broken, just not in that area. I don—" I stopped when he squeezed my hand.

It was apparent he was choosing his words carefully. "I have never seen anyone dismantle someone who they cared about with such...precision. I have witnessed unbridled cruelty and experienced it myself. Yet, I cannot comprehend what I witnessed." He paused. "I want you, but I would never have wished for you to be hurt in this manner."

I pulled his hand to my face and pressed it to my cheek. Bowen always made me feel comforted and wanted. "Thank you," I murmured against his palm.

Now that he was in here with me, I realized how tired I was. I'd been afraid to sleep. The vision had drained me, and I had been in here, obsessing over every detail for hours—forcing myself to replay it over and over again. The absolute horror of it had made me feel very human and almost afraid to doze off.

"The sun is up. I should let you get some rest." He started to pull his hand away.

"Please stay."

He looked at me cautiously.

"I know I needed space, but I really hate being alone after visions like that. *Please...*"

He nodded, but didn't say anything. He had the same cautious look on his face from moments before.

I readjusted and scooted closer, resting my forehead against his chest. He reached around and rubbed my back in slow circles. It was hard to believe that with being unconscious for all of those hours that I wouldn't be wide awake, but I felt exhausted. My body started to relax, and Bowen's breathing became more even.

"You always smell so good," I murmured into his shirt, my voice heavy.

He didn't say anything as he kissed the top of my head. I pressed myself a little closer, and the hand rubbing circles on my back slowed. I could feel his fatigue.

Barely above a whisper, I said, "I think you still owe me a story."

"I do?" he breathed.

"When we were in that basement, infected with Aurora, you told me that *when* I survived, you would tell me a story from when you were younger."

"I remember now. I believe the next time we were alone enough to talk, we were in that cave, and you tried to kill me."

"Does that mean you take it back? What's a little attempted murder between friends? In my defense, Dagan's blood did cause temporary insanity. That would've been my defense anyway."

A single, tired chuckle came out of him. "I will tell you any story you would like to hear. You did earn it back when you saved my life soon after."

I listened to him breathe for a long while, then I asked for one more thing. "And I would like to know what punishment you took for me."

There was no response. It was then I realized that Bowen had stopped breathing altogether. He'd heard me just fine.

4

I WILL

ALERIA

When I woke, I could feel it was still daylight. Bowen was no longer asleep next to me. I sat up, trying to shake the bleariness from my eyes, when I became aware that there was a hushed, yet heated conversation going on in the next room. I listened for a moment, debating what to do.

Bowen admonished, "...She wasn't to know—ever."

"I did not tell her. I give you my word."

"She knew enough to ask. She spoke of the 'punishment I had taken for her.'"

Before, I may have stayed in here and listened, but feelings of betrayal crept in, and I refused to succumb to them. I got out of bed and walked to the living area of the suite. I leaned in the doorway and waited for them to notice me. Tyran had said something I didn't hear; it must've been a denial of some sort.

Bowen was angry. "You and Morpheus *both* promised me."

I kept my voice even. "Promised not to tell me what?"

Bowen froze for a moment. "I thought you were sleeping."

I felt like saying something snarky, but I refrained. I simply let my gaze go between both Bowen and Tyran until one of them spoke.

"Tell her."

Bowen gritted his teeth. "No."

My instinct to run was kicking in. If it wasn't still daylight, I might've grabbed my bags and set off on my own.

I tried to think, despite the charged air in the room. "Do I have a right to know this?"

They replied simultaneously.

Tyran: "Yes."

Bowen: "No."

"Does this have to do with me?"

Bowen answered, "Yes, but it is not what you think." He glowered at Tyran and cursed, "Damn you."

I placed a shaky hand over my heart. "I can't. I can't take any more betrayal." I spun around to leave the room.

Tyran blurted, "*Succedaneum.* (Latin: substitute)"

I stopped, but kept my back to them.

Tyran continued, "When you were human, and he pulled you out of that dungeon, there was a price to pay. Our mother whipped the flesh from his back."

I slowly faced them.

Bowen sounded defeated. "Taranis, *please.*"

Tyran glared at Bowen. "He endured it three times in order for him to keep you with him and away from me. If you hadn't been turned with his blood, he would have had to continue every single day after you went to sleep until he couldn't endure it any longer."

I looked at Bowen. "I thought you were with me the whole time."

He said nothing.

"Morpheus guarded you while he was away. Mother used

Pyralis on him to prevent him from healing too quickly. He had to bear it and feel it as a human would."

"Pyralis?"

"A version of the blue liquid you were made to drink in order for the branding not to heal for the sacrifice. It is saved for only the worst criminals."

"Why? Why would you do that for me?" I asked Bowen as I searched my memory, wondering how I'd treated him then. I closed my eyes. "When you pulled me out, hadn't I just told you that I'd spent months hating you?" I leaned against the wall and slid down until I was sitting on the floor. The weight of this was too much.

Tyran smirked. "I think my job here is complete." He bowed, making a flourish with his hands. "Now, I will return to bed after being so rudely awakened."

Bowen scowled at Tyran as his brother strutted from the room, but I think that Tyran was genuinely upset about something. The set of his shoulders was stiff. Bowen sat on the couch straight across from me and stared at the coffee table instead of making eye contact. I could still feel his anger as clearly as my own heartbeat.

"Why did you keep this from me?"

"There are many, many reasons."

I waited.

He sighed. "I have never wanted you to feel obligated to me. If you came to love me, I wanted it to be for *me*. Not because you felt guilty or indebted due to my protection."

"And?"

He finally looked up at me, his blue eyes bright. "I hadn't admitted it to myself at the time, but even then, I loved you. Need I have another reason?"

Both reasons were valid. I couldn't dispute that.

He stood, walked over, and sat down next to me on the floor. "Aleria, I saw into your very heart within those first two weeks. If you had known, guilt would have driven some of your decisions. You are impressively good at guilt."

I laughed softly. He did know me. I looped my arm through his and leaned my head on his shoulder. "Thank you. Thank you for so many things."

We sat there for a long while.

Finally, I got on my feet and offered Bowen my hand. "You should probably get some sleep—since you were just pretending before in order to ambush your brother."

He smiled tiredly. "Did your Watchers not teach you the definition of ambush?"

"Testy when you get called out for fake sleeping," I teased while he pulled himself up.

"The definition of ambush is?" He grinned and headed towards his room.

"Bowen?"

"Yes?"

I hedged a moment in the doorway to mine. "Would it be selfish of me to ask you to stay with me? To hold me? I still don't want to be alone."

He didn't reply, but walked towards me and took my hand, leading me to the bed. Both his expression and emotions were unreadable. He stopped, expecting me to lay down where I'd been before, but I circled to the other side of the bed and crawled under the covers. He hesitated.

"You like to sleep on your left side," I explained, answering his unasked question.

A wisp of a smile passed over his face. He stood there for a moment longer, then crawled in with me. I rolled so that my back was to him. He slid his left arm under my head and wrapped his right around me, his breath warming my neck.

Bowen whispered into my ear, "I promise not to fake sleep this time."

"Do you promise to be here when I wake up this time, too?" My heart beat unevenly when I asked.

"I will," he murmured against my hair, but it felt like he was saying much, much more with those two words.


GABRIEL

I dropped the binoculars onto my lap. "I want to know what Phineas purchased in that shop."

Ian grinned. "Did you see the dirty look she gave him when he left?"

"Yes."

"That's my in," replied he. Ian rolled his sleeves to above his elbows revealing his sleeves of tattoos. He flipped the visor down and disheveled his hair. "Loan me that?"

I removed the leather cuff I wore over my Slayer tattoo.

Ian snapped it onto his wrist and stuck a piece of gum into his mouth. "Be back in a few." He hopped out of the van and jogged down the stairs of the parking garage and into the electronics store from which Phineas had just vacated. The store had a glass front and an exit in the rear of the building.

Raising the binoculars once more, I scanned the street to make sure Phineas' cab was not returning and checked the rest of the street for someone tailing him, then focused back on Ian inside the store.

He was speaking to the female clerk behind the counter. She leaned against the rear shelving, with arms crossed, listening. Ian appeared to be distressed. After a moment, he leaned in closer; his grin widened as her arms dropped to her sides. She was no longer defensive.

I quickly scanned the street once more for unfriendlies, then focused back on Ian's op inside the store.

The clerk ran her fingers over the design she had inked on her collarbone. She leaned her head back when she laughed at something he had said. She was exposing her neck when she did so: basic biology; she trusted him.

After he spoke to her for another ninety seconds, he ran his hand over the counter next to the register and tapped it. She nodded, and her demeanor changed. He had her.

She pulled a receipt from the register and allowed Ian to see it. He leaned on his elbows, speaking as if it were a secret. She pulled out a pen and wrote on his palm. He spoke for a moment longer, and then exited the store, his pace quicker. He turned to the left, taking an alternate route back. I scanned the street and the garage behind me in the monitors while I waited.

Ian swung the passenger door open. "He bought a thumb drive *and* some decryption software. The kind you get on the black market. The owner of the electronics' store is a hacker. And the worst news: Phineas was in there over a week ago and purchased something. She didn't help him, so she had no idea what he got." Ian shut the door and strapped in.

"Good work." I briefly examined the GPS and proceeded towards Phineas' next location.

"You don't want to know how I got her to tell me?"

"You were the Romeo."

"I am dead sexy, but no. That wasn't my approach. I told her Phineas was dating my sister, and I thought he was getting her into something he shouldn't. Then, I played Romeo to seal the deal."

"As I said, good work."

"Sometimes, I don't think you appreciate my awesomeness, Gabriel."

"I should have said you were a honeypot, rather than Romeo, with all your girlie whining."

Ian coughed and got back on topic. "Do you think he got something from a member of the Fallen that he needs to decrypt?"

"That is a distinct possibility."

Ian was quiet for several minutes. "If Ali was here, she would say I just channeled my shiny shirt from the club and would then give me crap about it."

I squeezed the steering wheel and concentrated on the road. I hated the hole her absence had left; I prayed we would have her back when this was over.


ALERIA

"You aren't sleeping," Bowen whispered.

"I did for a little while and neither are you." I rolled over and pulled a pillow under my head so I could see his face. There was just enough light from the hall to make things visible. If I'd been human, he would barely be a silhouette. "I keep running that vision through my head over and over."

"You will find clarity soon."

"And what is keeping you up?"

"Kingly duties," he answered vaguely.

It took me a minute to work up the courage to ask him something. "I know your favorite color and your favorite music through different ages. I know that you love Russian literature, which I think is boring, by the way. That you value human life, even though most of our kind doesn't. And even that you prefer O positive blood."

After too long of a pause, he prompted me, "Are you working up to some type of conclusion?"

"How many times have you been married?"

A gentle smile upturned his lips.

"What?"

"I have waited for you to ask me that for a long time. You never did in all of those months."

"It seemed…"

"I know why you didn't. You avoided all topics having to do with romantic entanglements."

"You never asked about Josh," I countered, forcing myself to say *his* name.

"You were in mourning. I didn't want to ask for something you weren't willing to offer. The answer is twice and close to a third. Two for duty, and the third would have been for love."

I was quiet for a moment. "I can't imagine an arranged marriage. Did you love them?"

"I was twenty years of age when I was first wed to Belisama."

"Her name was Belisama and you, Belenus?"

"She had been born for me; the name was tribute. The arrangement had been made before she had been conceived."

"What was she like?"

"She was striking and clever. Even though we were betrothed, I still courted her, making grand gestures and I fell for her completely."

"She must have been crazy about you."

"I thought so, but less than a year after we were wed, her true nature surfaced. She was trained to be a royal—the ruthless variety. We had our own lands; she was seen as a bright star who loved her people, but then she started secretly enslaving them. She kept it hidden, even from me, for longer than I care to admit. The maze beneath my mother's castle was inspired by her actions. It was the warlike part of her deity.

"She pushed, and her cruelty increased until there was a revolt. Hundreds came. The peasants turned out to be more intelligent than we had given them credit. They waited and watched, logging all of our movements, our numbers. We received a distress call from a fortification a half night's ride away. We sent riders to assist. When our numbers were depleted, they came. It was one for the storybooks. Pitchforks, fiery torches, crossbows—it was a bloodbath."

"But you survived."

"We could have all escaped. There was a tunnel through the catacombs. She didn't even care about our own guard. She had said it was 'their duty to die for her.' It disgusted me. It felt like dishonor, but I left. She and all that had aided her in her tyrannical deception perished that night.

"I vowed never to be so naïve again. Consequently, I have hated the politics that come with the throne ever since. Yet, I have studied them as to never be taken advantage of."

"What did you do afterward?"

"I returned home. My mother sent an army the next night and slaughtered every human that they could find for ten miles around the fortress. There was a rumor that those who instigated the plan escaped. But there was no proof.

"I wanted to go to ground. Sleep for a few decades, but Queen Mother had other plans. Another marriage was arranged —a princess from the Italian Coven."

"How long until you were married again?"

"Weeks."

"How did you feel about that?" I asked, trying to understand.

"I was bound by duty. It didn't matter how I felt. Concordia and I were together for two decades. Her sister had a child, so she went to her homeland to visit. The caravan fell under attack during daylight. After the raiders had taken all of the valuables, they burned everything. My wife, her attendants, and her vampire guards burned to ash from either the sun or the flames. A few of the human guard escaped and returned with word of the attack. I hunted the raiding party down. I killed them—all of them."

"You loved her," I stated.

He exhaled. "We respected one another. She was a good companion, but she wasn't the first thing I wanted to see in the morning. When she traveled, I missed her, but I wasn't urgently yearning for her return. I cared and was grieved when she was killed."

We quietly looked at one another for long enough that I could have drifted off to sleep. "And the third?" I finally asked.

"She was human."

I blinked.

"My mother had left me alone after Concordia. I swore to her that if she tried to force me into another marriage that I would disappear. Taranis had lost his fiancé while I was with Concordia. For once, my mother didn't try to control us. I met Amée a century later. She was everything that I had never experienced. After a year, I proposed and wanted it to last forever."

"What happened?"

"There was a terrible plague. I was so fearful that I would lose her to sickness, I convinced her to let me turn her." He paused, his voice rough. "She didn't survive the transformation. She died in my arms and it was entirely my fault." I felt a wave a grief from Bowen in just recounting the story for me.

I sat up, suddenly wide awake. "People don't always survive being turned?"

"No. You didn't know that?"

"No!" This fact somehow rocked my world. It made me feel even luckier to be alive. Then my empathy kicked in, and I remembered the incapacitating grief I'd experienced when I thought Joshua had died. I focused on that sense of shared loss and not my break from Joshua. This wasn't about me; Bowen was reliving his heartbreak for me. "I am so incredibly sorry that you went through that." My words felt insufficient. I released a halting breath, then laid back down beside him.

He started to speak. "When..." I felt another surge of emotion from him. He closed his eyes. "When you were turned, it was so horrific. I knew that you would lose your human life, but I had feared that I was going lose you entirely."

Hesitantly, I moved closer and placed my hands on both sides of his face. He didn't open his eyes. I could feel him still trying to mask his emotions. I wanted to comfort him further, and suddenly found my lips on his.

He didn't react at first, but then his lips parted, and I felt his arms encircle me. His raw emotion was all encompassing, as it too, surrounded me during that kiss. Afterward, he pressed his forehead to mine for a moment, then gave me three soft kisses. He readjusted, so that my head was tucked against his chest and his arms around me. I realized he was once again being kind and not pushing me to do anything more.

Bowen murmured against the top of my head. "You have a power over me that I have never allowed anyone else. I don't understand it."

"And you are married once again and didn't get to choose it."

"I chose you a long time ago."

# 5

# DENIAL TO DEPRESSION

ALERIA

"Aleria," Bowen whispered.

He was still curled behind me. I smiled. "Mmm hmm?"

"I need to get up, but I promised I would be here when you woke. I told Morpheus I would call thirty before sunset to check in."

I rolled over to face him. His t-shirt was wrinkled, and his hair a mess—I liked it. Part of me had had this tortured, bad-boy prince on a pedestal. The entire time we were in the castle, he had gotten up earlier than me and had been fully dressed. "Thanks for letting me know."

Even after the openness and intimacy of our conversation last night, I wasn't ready for more, and I shied away from kissing him.

He pressed the back of my hand to his lips, holding it there. After several seconds, he kissed and released it. Then I blinked, and he was gone. I didn't even sense his weight leave the bed.

Once alone, I stretched and lay there, trying to ignore the desire to retreat back into my semi-comatose state. Depression wasn't good on me, but the moment no one was around, it was all I'd felt. I was struggling with the want to simultaneously pull Bowen closer and push him away.

I sat up and thought about changing into real clothes. But second my feet hit the floor, I noticed a yellow light flashing from a small LED bulb in the ceiling. I hadn't noticed it was there before. It reminded me of the emergency lights that flashed during the fire alarms at my high school, except they were yellow.

I flew into the living room and realized lights were flashing in every room.

Tyran had his phone to his ear and held up his hand to keep me quiet. "Bridget, darling, do we need to worry?...How many?...Are they inside the hotel?...Human?... Yes...Yes." He hung up.

"Watchers were spotted a few hours ago in a café across the street. An assault team of unknown origin has breached the building. Thermal readings were inconclusive. It is unknown whether the two are connected or whether they are here for us. There are royals from Egypt here, but my instincts say they are after us. The team disconnected the video feed, so we have no clue where they are." He looked to Bowen. "Stay or go?"

"How many?"

"Ten or more."

Bowen and I answered in unison, "We go."

I was dressed in seconds. We ditched most of our luggage. We kept the money, weapons, and travel documents. Clothes could be replaced.

Tyran led the way to a back stairwell labeled "twelve." I had no idea we were that many floors up. The curtains had been closed when I'd finally gotten out of bed. We sped down two cases, and just as I passed the door on the ninth floor, there was a small explosion that blew off the door and tossed me over Tyran.

I landed on my back on the next landing. I was instantly on my feet, with Tyran at my side. Despite a few singe marks on my clothing, I was fine. I glanced up at Bowen; he hesitated, gave his brother a nod, then disappeared through the doorway.

Tyran put his hand around my bicep, but I shrugged him off and watched the doorway. Bowen reappeared sixty seconds later. He paused to pull a four-inch blade from his ribcage, but then kept moving. As he passed by me, he handed me the blade. It was a small Durateus throwing knife, which could mean only one thing: Watchers. He was rubbing something between his index finger and thumb afterwards.

"There are three more groups, five to a team," Bowen informed us. We started down the stairs again, but this time with caution, not speed. "They waited until the security system was down for the other teams to enter."

Tyran asked, "Human? Vampire? Slayer? Or…"

"Human, but…"

Tyran stopped and grabbed his brother's hand, smelling the substance Bowen was still rubbing between his fingers. Then Tyran immediately looked at the wound in Bowen's ribcage. "Damn it. Do you want to try for the car or head for the sewers?"

"Sewers," Bowen decided. We started descending the stairs again.

"Should we just hide and wait for sunset? It's not that long. Or should I try to talk to them?" I offered.

"Sissy, it's not the Watchers. They coated that blade with Pyralis. They have weaponry from both sides."

"Could they be herding us into the sewers?" I wondered.

"Possibly, but we won't come out where they would expect us," Bowen whispered.

At that moment, I heard the distinctive click of an assault rifle on the stairs a few stories below us. Bowen winked at me, and then jumped on top of the railing. He drew his arms in, crossing them over his chest, then dropped down the middle of the stairs, landing at the bottom without a sound.

Tyran grinned and flashed in the direction of the gunman—I followed. But when we arrived, Bowen was spinning around, taking out the last of the hit team. I stood amazed—Bowen was faster than Tyran. Part of me wished I'd witnessed more, and the other part of me wondered why we needed to run if Bowen could take out two of the teams with such ease even when wounded, but I trusted his instincts. Bowen had also used deadly force, and knowing him, there was a reason for it. He didn't kill humans without reason.

We didn't more than pause; Tyran picked up one of their earpieces as we continued to the third floor. We waited at the door for a moment while Tyran listened. "They know you killed the second unit. They must be monitoring vital signs. They expect us in the parking garage any second now. Unit coming from above to drive us that way." Tyran took off the comm and tossed it to the ground.

I looked at him questioningly.

"It went dead," he explained, answering my silent question. "They must have shut down the slain team's communications."

We slipped through the third floor exit, and Bowen quickly led us to a utility closet. Once inside, Tyran and Bowen moved as if their minds were linked. Bowen stripped off his shirt and pants, tossing them into the utility sink. Tyran had grabbed bleach and dumped it over the clothing. Bowen grabbed a rag, wet it with something, and wiped his blood away. He then swiped some duct tape from the shelf.

When he was about to tape the knife wound shut, I asked, "Do you want me to seal it shut?"

"No. Pyralis. I don't want it in your system. We just need to rid ourselves of anything that smells of blood in case they have trackers." He quickly taped the whole section of his ribcage. "Do you smell blood?"

I sniffed. "No."

"No clothes, brother." Tyran grinned at Bowen. "It's a nice look."

Bowen raised a brow at his brother while he stood there in his fitted boxer briefs, socks, and designer shoes.

"Want me to search one of the adjacent hotel rooms for clothing?" Tyran asked.

Bowen shook his head. "Let's go."

I was thankful I'd never had to escape somewhere in my underwear. Fleeing in Petrescu's dress shirt and boxers was more than I ever wanted to experience again.

Tyran pulled a shelving unit away from the wall. The whole thing moved like it was on hinges, along with the plaster wall, to reveal a ladder going down into the darkness. Tyran started down. Bowen urged me onto the ladder, and within seconds, he was above me and had shut the secret access panel.

We descended in utter blackness. When we reached the ground, Tyran took my hand, and soon after Bowen took my other hand. We crept along, and I was glad they seemed to know in which direction to go.

We came to a stop, and Tyran let go of me. There was the faintest clunk and a sliver of blue light that infiltrated our space. The light disappeared, followed by another clunk. He spoke softly in the suffocating darkness. "They are waiting at the south junction for us."

Bowen commented just as quietly, "Above, they had two sets of powder-coated restraints with them. They wanted to capture at least two of us. One of them had a tattoo in the language of the angels. I assume whatever they have waiting out there and in the parking garage is a little more formidable."

"Powder-coated?" I whispered.

Tyran explained in a voice so low only we could hear, "The shackles the Seekers used on you to fulfill Cadeyn's bounty. It is a version of Pyralis that makes the bonds too painful to break."

I thought back to the torrent of pain when I'd tried to free myself. Bowen had to be feeling that in his ribcage right now, but he was acting unaffected.

Bowen whispered, "We need to go deeper and get to the junction under the Opera house."

"I will draw them away," Tyran responded.

"No, we stay together. You know we would normally face them, but there is something unsettling about this. Too many unknowns."

"Better I draw them away, then."

"No. Need I make it a command?" Bowen countered.

I felt Tyran's hand on my arm; it slid down until it enveloped my hand. He started tugging me forward. Bowen still had my other hand. We walked along a long passageway in the pitch black. Sometimes it became narrow, and we had to squeeze through. Other times, it sounded like the space was wide.

Tyran dropped my hand as we came to a dead end. At least, I *thought* it was a dead end. There was a corner that I could feel with my free hand where I groped in the darkness. I wasn't sure how Tyran and Bowen were navigating this place with such confidence and speed. The grind of metal echoed, followed by the smell of fresh water.

"I doubt the humans have scuba gear," Tyran reassured.

I groaned a little, memories of evacuating the Academy into the maze beneath London resurfacing. Before thinking, I asked Tyran, "Do you know how close you were to catching me in the sewers beneath London?"

"I felt you were close."

Bowen squeezed my hand.

"A few more feet, and you would've walked right into Gabriel, Peter, and me. We had three Slayers with us, but things would have ended much differently." At just the mention, I realized that I missed Gabriel so much it made my chest constrict. I shoved the feelings away before I started thinking more about Joshua.

"Are you strong enough for this, brother?" Tyran asked.

I wished I could see him. I didn't know how much of a toll the Pyralis was taking on him. I remembered feeling the closest to human I'd ever felt.

"Keep Aleria with you. I will be fine."

I felt Tyran's hand on my shoulder. "We will have to swim a long way. We are going with the current. I want you to hold onto my belt. It will be just wide enough for the two of us." He paused. "What happens to your heart when you don't breathe for a long while?"

"It stops." My voice had a slight shake.

"And…"

"It makes me want to panic, but I can handle it."

Tyran's voice was softer. "Just don't let go."

I nodded, then realized that he couldn't see me. "I won't."

Bowen still had my hand. He let go and slid his hand up my

arm and didn't stop until he cupped my face. Then I felt his lips on my forehead. "It won't take long. I'll be right behind you."

Tyran pulled me towards the sound of the water, and Bowen let go. He stepped down into something, and I followed, but I tripped when my foot struck a ledge. I realized we were stepping into a large pipe—or maybe it was a duct. I eased my legs inside, and the rushing water was halfway up my thigh and icy cold. The current wanted to pull me the rest of the way in.

Tyran placed my hand on his belt. "You ready?"

"Yes," I replied a little breathlessly, trying not to feel claustrophobic. A loud clank rang out in the distance. Tyran immediately tugged me beneath the water.

The current took us briskly through the pipe, but Tyran was still swimming. I followed suit, but panic started to tunnel its way through my body.

Clenching my teeth, I closed my eyes as I held onto Tyran's belt. That was my point of concentration. My heart strained, and I bucked, knocking my head into the side of the pipe.

Tyran kicked harder, occasionally striking me in the shin. I didn't know if it was the lack of air, the all-encompassing darkness, or the closed-in space, but it was triggering a vision.

I grabbed onto his belt with my other hand. When I did so, he grasped my wrist and pulled me up so that he could hug me to his chest. He must have sensed something was wrong. I felt his arm wrap around me just as my consciousness slipped away.

---

It was as if I was inside an insect zooming around. I flew low through a modern city with its residents bustling through the streets. When I reached the edge of the city, I came upon an angel standing at the edge of the developed area. Behind him was a wasteland. Wind blew, stirring up dust into eddies. He spread his black wings wide and raised his hands. Dark, grey twisting vines shot from his mouth and eyes. They dove into the earth and cracked it apart as they spread wildly, porpoising through the surface, spreading like a root system from some insane plant.

When the roots reached the pavement of the city, they seemed to move even faster. The people in the city stood in horror, but did not move. When the vines reached the first people, they wound around their legs, holding them in place. Then additional roots lurched from the ground, latching around their wrists. They were tugged forward, until they fell to their knees, as if they were falling prostrate before a god.

Suddenly, everyone in sight was shackled to the ground, bowing before this angel of destruction. The angel appeared to be drawing energy from the hundreds, or maybe thousands, of souls it had bound in the roots. Then, the angel grew and grew until the ground cracked beneath his feet.

At that moment, I observed that I was in a white dress, standing at the town's center on top of a circle of grass. The grass shriveled and died. When I glanced down at my body, I noticed a speck of red just above my bellybutton. The spot spread until my entire belly was dripping in blood. I tried to scream out, but only the sound of wind came rushing from me.

The vines reached the circle of grass, and before I could take another breath, they had overtaken me and pulled me into the earth.

I choked and spit up water as I woke. Then I was being hugged —Tyran. I was jarred when he let go, held my face, and kissed me briskly on the lips. "Stay here; don't move. I'll be right back."

Nodding, I watched him as he trudged through knee-deep water to a deeper pool where larger ducts were all spewing water. Cool, blue evening light filtered down from the grates above. I was so relieved to have light. Tyran had left me lying on my side on a stone shelf a couple of feet above the waterline. I sat up, my feet dangling into the water.

A moment later, Bowen came head first out of the highest duct. Tyran pulled him from the pool instantly, saying, "I was afraid you hadn't made the turn."

"Barely."

Tyran smiled and hugged his brother. I didn't think I'd ever witnessed that type of affection between them before.

"Come on."

Tyran trudged through the water towards me, and I hopped off the ledge with a splash, falling in step behind him and next to Bowen. I took Bowen's hand, partially for comfort and partly because he looked especially pale.

Bowen looked piercingly at me. "What happened while we were in there?"

"Another vision."

"Do you remember it?"

"It was symbolic, like the one yesterday. In a nutshell, it was an angel of destruction enslaving an entire city—like, the *whole* thing."

"We will stop them."

"There's that optimism I remember so well." I grinned.

Bowen grinned back. "It isn't optimism. It's a promise."

"Says the man in the sewers in nothing but his boxers."

He just smiled and held my hand a little tighter.

After walking for what seemed like forever, we came to a new junction with three sets of ladders leading upwards to different locations. We climbed up one level. Pipes ran down the walls, and it was filthy, but dry. We walked down a few more passageways and up another ladder, then came to a steel door. Tyran opened it, and we entered a dark room. It was quiet, like there was something absorbing the sound, maybe fabric. After a moment, dim lights blinked on.

We were in a storage room with props. Very faintly, I could hear music above.

"Stay here. I'll see what I can find in the dressing rooms," Tyran instructed. He was gone before either of us had responded.

I walked over and sat on an oversized wooden box that was mounted on casters. It rolled a little. Staring at the floor, I spoke. "Bowen, I don't think we should wait another five days. I think we should go back to the coven tonight."

He approached me slowly; I glanced at his face. He appeared to be weighing something in his mind. I kept my eyes on his shoes, which made me want to laugh instead of feeling creepy for staring at his abs or at even worse things. *Is it hot in here?*

"I think you need another couple of days, at least."

"We hardly got out of there. What if you guys hadn't had a secret escape route?"

"Three more days," Bowen bargained.

I finally looked at him. "Why? I thought you wanted to go back?"

He hedged. "How honest would you like me to be?"

I narrowed my eyes. "Overly."

He pushed the counter-high box I was sitting on a few more inches until it was pressed against the wall. He leaned forward, his hips between my legs. He took both my hands in his, and I hoped he didn't hear my heart pick up speed.

"Aleria, I'm worried. You have not cried once. You are not dealing with this. Joshua was important to you." I flinched at *his* name. "This was not a fling from which you could recover quickly. He was part of your family since childhood *and* your lover. This was more than a normal relationship."

"I'll be fine," I protested, but it came out hoarse.

"You went straight from shock to depression. You haven't dealt with anything. There has not been anger or bargaining—"

"You sound like a textbook."

"For good reason."

"I can do this. As your brother keeps telling me, I am a queen now. I need to take responsibility. I...I can't be this selfish. We can return, and you can let me ease into my duties, if that will make you feel better. You can keep me out of sight while you play Superman. *Please.*" I touched the bare skin above his taped ribs. Just touching his skin made heat spread in my belly. I knew that I loved Bowen, but this wasn't love. I wanted to touch him to forget, which was purely physical.

The reservation that had been on his face a moment before was gone, and suddenly his lips were on mine, heat flooding my body. My hands inched around his waist, feeling the hard muscle moving beneath his skin, as he twisted his hands in my wet hair and pulled me closer. Involuntarily, a soft moan escaped me as the kiss grew ravenous. I wrapped my legs around his hips and pulled him even closer, the void inside me wanting more.

His breath uneven, he broke from my lips long enough to murmur, "I have longed to kiss you freely for almost three years." Then he seemed to catch himself. He took a long look into my eyes, reading something. "I'm sorry, I shouldn't have done that." He quickly backed away and turned around, his control suddenly back in place. I couldn't feel any of his emotions or see his face.

My heart was beating hard, and I felt a little dazed and desirous. I sat there, still feeling the warmth of his lips, though he was across the room. I realized that that had been my dream, slightly altered, from a few weeks ago. I thought back to the dream.

*For a long moment, Bowen had stood silently in front of me, looking lost. Something in the energy between us had changed; I held my breath as he slowly leaned in and gently brushed his lips across mine...once...twice...three times. Then he really kissed me. His lips were soft, and I was barely able to keep my knees from giving out. My hands inched around his waist, feeling the hard muscle moving beneath his skin as he twisted his hands in my hair and pulled me closer. I ached for more. Involuntarily, a soft moan escaped me as the kisses grew in intensity.*

*His breath was uneven, and he broke away from my lips just long enough to murmur in my ear, "I have longed to kiss you freely for the last three years."*

I hadn't been able to tell if it was prophetic or not. But this encounter had happened sooner. Like the timetable had been pushed forward. After another moment, his quick retreat made me feel a little stung.

Tyran arrived with his arms full of clothes. "Some performers may have to go home in ridiculous costumes, but *we* will leave in style." He dumped the clothes on the prop of a pushcart and started shucking off his wet shirt. He looked between the two of us. "Did I miss something?"

Bowen turned profile to me. "We return to the castle tonight."

"We do?" he replied, surprised.

I looked at Bowen. "Thank you."

# 6

## WIPED

ALERIA

When we stole out the back door in our pilfered clothes and trotted down the alley to the main street, I was shocked at our location.

"When you said 'the opera house,' I didn't know you meant *The Opera*...or *Le Opera*. Isn't Paris totally out of the way?"

We started walking towards a cab as Bowen answered, "We wanted to be within two hours of the castle. There are several vampire-run hotels here with security."

"Obviously their security wasn't what it should've been," I griped.

"It will be investigated," Bowen assured.

We took a cab across the city where I could only glimpse places I'd dreamt of seeing. The driver dropped us in front of a market, and then walked the rest of the way to our destination.

Tyran punched in a code and disabled the alarm. We ambled through the house; all of the furniture was covered with white sheets.

"Who does this house belong to?"

"It's mine," Tyran answered. I must've given him a look. "What, sissy?"

"You just don't seem like the house-in-Paris-type." I shrugged.

We continued on into an immaculate kitchen with quartz counters and custom everything. *Kind of a waste for a vampire.* Tyran rummaged in a drawer and pulled out car keys and two disposable cell phones. He tossed one of the phones to Bowen.

I'd almost forgotten my comment when he asked, "And what do I seem like?"

"Eh, evil slumlord, human trafficker, gatekeeper of hell. You know, something stab-worthy," I quipped.

He just shook his head, grinning. "Garage is this way."

We followed him to the garage. Once inside, Tyran sat behind the wheel of a black Mercedes.

I felt a sudden jab of fear at the thought of returning to the coven—maybe for good. I tried to think about butterflies and rainbows, but it did nothing. After a moment and a few deep breaths, I crawled into the back passenger seat. Just when I was ready to slide the buckle into the clasp, the door next to me opened.

"Would you mind scooting over?"

I slid to the other side, surprised for some reason that Bowen wasn't riding in the front.

Tyran immediately pulled out and started heading in the direction of the castle. I leaned my head back and watched the stars through the sunroof for a while; clouds were rolling in, and it appeared that we were driving towards a storm. When I could no longer see the stars, I rolled my head to the side to look at Bowen.

He had his head reclined and had been watching me. "You

nervous?"

I nodded.

"I won't leave your side when we get there."

I smiled, but I knew it was a wisp of one. "I know." He took my hand, and I moved closer to lean my head on his shoulder.

Two hours later, my breath came out in a shaky rush as we pulled onto the circular drive leading to the castle entrance. Members of the coven were ready to receive us on the steps. Even though Bowen had held my hand the whole rest of the ride here, he'd remained reserved with his affection. After that kiss in the Opera basement, I was off balance—a chaotic mix of fear, desire, and sadness all battering my brain at once.

Tyran smirked at me in the rearview mirror. "You'd better put your game face on, sissy. I smell blood in the water."

I glanced ahead at the crowd. Zahra was standing, with arms crossed, glowering in the direction of our car. The desire to murder her slowly swelled inside me.

"Hey," Bowen said softly, getting my attention. "Eyes on me." He placed his fingers under my chin, turning my gaze from Enemy #1 on my hit list.

I took another shaky breath.

"I think you will need this." He opened his palm, out of the view of our awaiting entourage to reveal the wedding ring I'd tossed away after my horrifying vision. I leaned towards him, and he discretely slid the ring onto my finger.

"All you need to worry about is me. Keep focused on me. You understand? They don't exist." Then he kissed me, his lips molding to mine.

It was an unhurried sort of kiss that stretches out time in front of you and blots out all reason. Before I realized it, I found my hands were moving from his chest to his waist so I could pull him nearer.

His hand was up the back of my shirt, caressing the skin between my shoulder blades and sending shivers through my whole body.

I was a sail caught in his storm.

Tyran cleared his throat. "Should I get popcorn, or do you actually want to go inside and maybe do this in a bed later?"

When Bowen stopped kissing me, it felt almost painful. He grinned. "Can you think of that and not those in the crowd?" He'd been holding back in the Opera—even now he was.

I nodded, not sure I could speak.

"Eyes on me," he murmured one last time, his lips brushing my earlobe.

A member of the Royal Guard opened the door. The night air carried a biting chill from the fresh coat of snow that delicately veiled the landscape. Bowen stepped out and offered me his hand. I slid out of the back, and the moment I was on my feet, he pulled me in for another kiss in front of everyone, as if they hadn't just seen us in the car. But this was a statement. Doubters could clearly see both Tyran and Bowen. Any conspiracies as to the validity of our marriage were dispelled.

Everyone parted like the Red Sea, allowing us to pass, each of them bowing slightly or curtseying as we proceeded inside. It reminded me of all the movies I'd watched with my mom growing up—but this was *me*. I still didn't feel like a queen or married to Bowen, for that matter.

The imposing front doors swung open simultaneously, and we paraded inside. Morpheus fell in step with Bowen.

"Good to have you back, my liege."

"Good to be back. Where are our guests?"

Morpheus scowled. "The throne room."

Bowen's face became cold, the glacial blue of his eyes piercing. He released my hand and calmly walked past the grand staircase towards the throne room. He spun abruptly towards me, but looked over my head.

"Brother, would you take—"

I stepped forward, grabbed his hand, and squeezed hard, making him look at me. I didn't want to argue with him in public. My parents had always put on a united front; this seemed like a good idea in this situation. I knew he was about to send me away. If he wanted me to rule with him, he couldn't protect me. I needed to be by his side. I stared in his eyes, pleading for him to understand my silent communication.

He exhaled quietly, keeping my hand in his, and continued towards the throne room. The Royal Guard was outside the doors and opened them wide.

There were six members of the Fallen inside. The desk Agrona had kept at the bottom of the steps leading to the throne was now covered in food, like a Viking banquet table. Fruits and gargantuan chunks of meat were heaped on plates. One of the Fallen stood over the feast, stuffing his face.

In the past, I'd thought them so civilized, but I now understood that not all angels were alike. We were looking at foot soldiers, except for the one sprawled on Bowen's throne. He had one leg over the ornate arm and was examining his nails. I was sure it was a pose he'd struck the moment he heard the doorknobs turning.

He looked familiar, and then it came to me. He'd been the light-haired angel with Semjâzâ when they'd dug up the artifact in my first vision, and he might've been at the first exchange. He was definitely in Semjâzâ's inner circle. I stared at him for a moment.

His skin was golden brown, and his hair was an odd color; it had both whitish blond and strawberry streaks that didn't match his eyes. It seemed they should be blue, but they were almost black; they were unnervingly dark and shrewd. His nose was wavy, like a boxer's nose that had been broken repeatedly.

But what drew my attention most were the tattoos skirting the right side of his face. They were different from the ones on Ana's partner. Three circular tattoos were connected by elaborate lines, reminiscent of crop circles. A circle was on his temple, under his cheekbone in front of his ear, and just under his jaw. They were dark blue and charcoal grey in an odd sheen that made them appear as if they were giving off light, but that didn't seem possible. It was then I realized I was looking at Batariel, Semjâzâ's general of sorts.

Chuckles under the breath of the two that had closed in behind us pulled my attention away from him. I glanced around and noticed that everyone in the greeting committee had fallen back, with the exception of Morpheus.

Not even Zahra had the boldness to enter, though maybe she was hoping we would be taken out so she could glide onto the throne herself. Apparently, she didn't realize that there might not be a throne at all if the Fallen took over. I never spotted Cadeyn, Icelos, or Phantasos.

"I see you have been made comfortable," Bowen commented, magically keeping his voice even.

Batariel replied smoothly, "Yes, your cousin, Morpheus, and some of your guard have kept us quite entertained. Though, we were growing impatient waiting for you."

"I apologize. I needed some time with my new wife, as I am sure you have heard."

"Yes, the timeline has been *interesting*," Batariel mused. "I see your brother has returned with you." He eyed each of them suspiciously, probably wondering which one of them they'd imprisoned.

"One happy family," Bowen clipped.

I let go of Bowen's hand, giving myself space to move, feeling cramped. We four were now completely surrounded; the Fallen behind us were circling back and forth like predators assessing their prey—sharks, maybe. I guessed there *was* blood in the water.

One of them had a long staff and let it pound on the floor with each step. When Tyran had told me to put my "game face on," that had been an understatement.

One of the Fallen grazed my backside as he strolled by me. I dug deep and put on my "touch-me-again-and-you-will-not-belong-for-this-world" face.

The one with the staff scraped by me this time, and I turned, jerking the staff from his hands faster than he expected. He looked like he was going to come at me.

"Stop," the leader boomed.

"Batariel," he implored like a spoiled child.

"This is not how we treat our hostess. Do you not recognize the Queen in her casual attire? You were witness to her outside the gates of the castle." Batariel's voice was pleasant, but clearly a warning.

Staff Boy's small, beady eyes widened with recognition, and he immediately stepped back and gave me more space. I returned the favor by taking a slow step towards him, cocking my head to the side, and looking him up and down. I tossed away the staff to the corner of the room.

The temper in the room shifted when the rest of them realized that I'd killed one of them. I thought it would've stirred a need for revenge inside them, but it seemed to have instead earned me respect.

Bowen interrupted our standoff.

"Batariel, I would like you and your underlings to leave," he stated bluntly. "We have demonstrated goodwill and shall continue to honor the agreement. I respectfully ask that you afford us the same deference."

Batariel shot off the throne and stood nose-to-nose with Bowen. A wicked smile spread across Bowen's face, and he stepped forward a few inches, nudging Batariel with his chest. "I trained regularly with Dagan. I know your weaknesses. The blood of angels runs in my veins, as well as my wife's, as you know. Are you truly seeking a challenge? Is this what Semjâzâ desires?"

There was a spark in Batariel's eyes as he reached up and smoothed the front of Bowen's shirt and dusted off his shoulders. Bowen stood like stone, keeping his sneering coolness. Batariel wasn't afraid of the challenge, but it was obvious there was a leash, even if it was a long one.

"I look forward to our next meeting." Batariel turned on his heel and walked towards me, looking me up and down and groping me with his eyes. "And you, I will count the minutes until next I see you." He made a guttural sound that I had to force myself to ignore. He was trying to rattle me. Batariel whistled through his teeth. "We return home."

In a flash, there was a flutter of wings. The front doors of the castle burst open, and they were gone. I turned and realized that the entire greeting committee was still standing in the great hall outside the throne room. They had witnessed everything.

I found Zahra in the crowd and stared her down. She slithered back into the congregation and disappeared. A moment later, I caught the first sighting of both Icelos and Phantasos—their stormy grey eyes watching. I observed as their heads of short, black hair skulked in the same direction Zahra had fled.

We had the castle. I just wondered how long it would last.

The second the main hall had cleared, Morpheus shuffled us

into an octagon-shaped anteroom behind the throne. It was furnished as a library. It had high-ceilings and shelves so tall that they required the ladder that was attached to a track running around three-quarters of the room. It smelled like old books and leather and made me feel oddly at home.

Tyran moved to one of the leather chairs and lounged across it. I expected Morpheus to sit, but he slowly circled, looking nervous. I'd never seen him that way before.

Bowen tiredly sat in another chair, and I eased onto the side of it. He looped his arm around my hips and locked his gaze on the unsettled Morpheus. "What happened?"

Morpheus stopped moving. "Those creatures became restless and started meddling with members of the coven. Batariel placed no limitations on his men. Cadeyn found some of them in the quarters of our female familiars." He stopped, exhaling slowly. "They did unspeakable things to the humans. Cadeyn lost his temper and gravely injured two of them. Batariel arrived at the fight before we did. He has a power I have never seen and used it on Cadeyn."

Bowen leaned forward a little. "Is he alive?"

"Yes, he's fine, but it would be easier to show you."

"Summon him."

Morpheus proceeded to the entrance and whispered to someone outside the door.

We didn't speak while we waited for Cadeyn. My heart started to race, nervous about seeing him again. He'd promised to end me for killing his brother. I had only killed Gareth in order to protect Joshua and get to Peter after the sacrifice. I'd had no choice.

Bowen broke my reverie when he pulled me off the arm and onto his lap and kissed my temple. Leaning into him, I made a pillow of his shoulder, trying to calm my nerves.

There was a knock at the door. I stood, then moved to the chair next to Bowen. Sitting on his lap probably wasn't going to make me appear very queenly.

"Come," Bowen answered.

Cadeyn entered with a pleasant expression fixed on his face. "I am pleased you have returned."

"It is good to be back."

Cadeyn smiled and held out his hand to me, his odd yellow eyes bright and clear. "I am honored to meet my new Queen. I feel odd that we haven't met before."

With a cautious smile, I stuck out my hand. He bowed and kissed the back of it, but I felt like this was some sort of joke. Though, there didn't seem to be any sort of aggression or deceit emanating from him.

"Is there anything you require of me? I was finishing the adjustments on the duty rosters now that you have returned. I have added a contingent for the Queen and the Prince. I have not been comfortable with the guests we have been entertaining."

"No. Thank you, Cadeyn. Please, continue with your duties."

Cadeyn bowed reverently and departed.

Once the door shut, Tyran was the first to comment. "What was that?"

"Batariel can wipe memories from anyone. Cadeyn has lost five years," Morpheus informed us.

"Five years?" Bowen breathed.

Morpheus continued, "I had to tell him of your mother's death. He has no memory of Aleria. I didn't inform him of his brother's death. I wasn't sure how you wanted to handle it. Since this incident, we have given Batariel and his men a wide berth."

"That was wise."

"There's more. The only thing that seemed to keep them

entertained was the games in the maze. I know you have forbidden runners unless they volunteered, but we ran out. That is when they attacked the women."

Bowen frowned. "I understand. Thank you, Morpheus. Are there any other immediate concerns?"

"No, Sire." He paused. "I did ask Batariel to remove the memories of the attack from the familiars. They don't remember any of it. I realize you may see this as a violation, but I felt it would be for the best. Celeste was among them."

"Thank you," Bowen responded calmly, but anger was rolling off of him.

Morpheus bowed and exited.

Celeste had totally slipped from my mind. She was the exotically beautiful familiar that Zahra had poisoned trying to get to me. When I'd fed on her, unwanted visions had flooded my mind. I still wasn't in balance and was having a hard time managing my emotions. Jealousy took hold of me. She'd seduced Bowen not long after the sacrifice. I'd seen it, and the way that Morpheus had just said her name, it was obvious Bowen cared for her.

Tyran, Bowen, and I sat silently for a long while.

Tyran let out a sort of chortle and startled me. "You seem to have won the lottery, my dear. Cadeyn was bent on destroying you."

"Until one of you tell him." I coughed. "He's going to find out."

"He doesn't need to know," Tyran contested.

Bowen remained quiet.

All I could think was that when things arrived wrapped in tidy packages, they never stayed that way—ever.

7

TRUST

I woke, barely able to breathe, my heart sprinting like an Olympic runner. It had been a nightmare—unless three-headed demon dogs were in my near future. *I pray not.* I sat up, wiping the tears from my eyes. I hadn't cried, but they were watering profusely.

It was lonely in here. I'd chosen to sleep in the queen's private bedroom off of the main sleeping quarters. It was common in many castles to have his and hers bedrooms, bathrooms, and dressing chambers off of the shared royal bedroom.

I thought it was crazy at first, and then I realized I really needed the time alone. Bowen had been gracious when I asked him if he minded me sleeping in the other quarters. I was suspicious that he'd expected me to ask, even though he'd spent the previous night holding me.

After Tyran had chastised me, I was determined to do things right. So, I fought with my urge to go and crawl into bed with

Bowen. I didn't want to run to the other room like a scared child after a nightmare.

I continued to rest, but my thoughts were loud.

Swinging my legs out of bed, I made a decision. If I couldn't sleep, I would do something with my time. Tickling in the back recesses of my brain, I recalled Bowen telling me long ago about a library on this floor. I walked to the closet and opened the door wide. A motion-activated light came on, illuminating a closet half full of clothes in my size. I dragged myself into some yoga pants, a long sweater, and slippers.

Once in cozy clothes, I crept into the shared bedroom, but Bowen wasn't in here. I glanced at his private bedroom and noticed that there was light spilling from beneath the door.

Not wanting to bother him, I headed for the main doors and quietly opened the one on the right. Two guards snapped to attention. I shut the door as silently as possible, so as to not alert Bowen, and looked at the taller of the guards. "Would you show me to the library on this floor?"

He bobbed his head. "Of course, my Queen." When he turned on his heel, I followed him. We traveled through three hallways and came to a set of intricately carved wooden doors. He opened them and held his arm wide, bidding me entrance. "I will wait here to escort you back."

"Thank you." I shut the doors and leaned against them, taking in the room. The entire perimeter was lined with cherrywood bookshelves at least fifteen feet high with sliding ladders to reach the higher shelves. The remaining wall space was covered with wood paneling and hung with paintings done by masters. The ceiling was covered in a mural with chubby, cherubic angels, and three massive, crystal chandeliers were centered over three large tables.

But my favorite features of this room, as with all over the

castle, were the windows. They were coated in a substance that protected us from the harmful effects of daylight. And this room was fitted with three large stained glass edged panes and built-in window seats with custom cushions and pillows. I took a deep breath, enjoying the safe sunlight. I had forgotten how much I'd missed being able to see the landscape in daytime.

I walked around the room, my fingers drifting over the spines of the books as I strolled. After I found that I'd walked around the room several times, I decided on a book of poetry and settled into the window seat on the right of the trio of windows.

With the book open in my lap, I stared out at the ocean. The water was a dark greyish-blue and quite choppy. Small whitecaps could be seen far into the distance. I watched as seabirds dove into the water and disappeared for longer than I thought possible, then pop up fifty yards away with fish in their mouths.

Josh would have loved the view. As soon as I'd thought it, I froze, taking in a startled breath. I had managed not to think of him for an entire day, and the moment I did, it felt as if I'd been pulled under those cold waters outside. I willed the tears away, but couldn't help hearing his last words to me, yet again.

*"It's your fault Sebastian is dead! And Peter...and Leslie and Gentry! ...You leave a trail of bodies everywhere you go...I can't trust you anymore! ...I can't be with someone I can't trust...Love isn't enough to take this kind of abuse. True love shouldn't require this much suffering!"*

I stuck the tip of my thumb into my mouth and bit down, trying to thrust his voice from my head. Then, as much as it hurt, I realized that I needed to think about him. When he'd screamed at me, completely unhinged, I'd only felt anger, betrayal, and hatred through our blood bond.

There'd been a few occasions I'd managed to mask my feelings from Tyran by thinking of something else so that he had sensed a different emotion. But I didn't know if Joshua was capable of that type of deception.

Bowen's words rose to the surface: *"I have never seen anyone dismantle someone that they cared about with such...precision."*

That was the problem. Josh knew exactly how to hurt me, and he'd done it without mercy. He had preyed on my greatest vulnerabilities. I didn't know if I could ever trust him again. He had to have had a reason, but even if he did, it meant he truly didn't trust me. If he had, he would've told me and let me make my own decision.

But maybe it wasn't an act. Was it possible that he had been *that* jealous of Bowen? Had I driven him to some sort of psychotic break? I knew that I'd hurt Josh, but when I'd fallen for Bowen, I had thought that Joshua was dead. It wasn't fair to anyone, but I had done my best to keep my feelings for Bowen in a box buried deep.

Guilt rose up in me again; I slammed my book shut and pressed the leather cover to my forehead. It all came down to trust. If Joshua had broken it off because of Bowen—he didn't trust me. And if Josh had ended us because of some other reason —he didn't trust me.

*Could I go back to someone, who deep down, didn't trust me?*

"I'm surprised you came back."

I jumped, losing my grip on the book pressed to my forehead, but before it could hit the hardwood floor, Morpheus had caught it.

"I apologize; I didn't mean to startle you," Morpheus commented.

I sighed. "I didn't expect to be back either." It didn't surprise me that Morpheus had sensed my original intentions.

He sat on the large table two yards away and curled his fingers around the edge, placing his right foot on the seat of a chair. "I am glad that you are."

"Are you?" I asked, surprised. Then I realized that I sounded a little rude. "I mean, your brothers hate me—and Zahra. I thought it might've been a relief for you that I was gone."

He didn't reply right away. He looked out the window past me, contemplating. "Belenus is a good king. He shouldn't be alone."

"I'm sure there are many more qualified people to help him rule."

"If you take wise council, in time, you too will be a good ruler," he answered, his grey eyes sympathetic.

"You think people will accept me?"

Morpheus cocked his head to the side. "Why did you come back? Do you not love Belenus?"

"I do. You know I do. It's complicated."

Morpheus pressed his lips into a thin line, but didn't say anything. We sat there for several minutes in silence.

I stood up awkwardly. "I think I am going to go and try to sleep again. I'll let you have the room to yourself."

"Sleep well." Morpheus paused. "You will make a good queen."

I gave him a tight-lipped smiled and nodded. The second I entered the hallway, the guard bowed a tiny bit, then led me back towards my room. When we arrived outside, I noticed that the guard that had been left behind looked a little nervous. He put his hand on the doorknob, but I stopped short.

"He knows that I left, doesn't he?"

"Yes, my Queen."

I motioned, and he opened the door. Bowen wasn't in our

room, but his light was still on in his private quarters. Then I realized that Morpheus hadn't happened upon me in the library. I was pretty sure that Bowen had sent him—he knew I was upset. He was trying to give me space, so he sent someone less annoying than Tyran. I smiled faintly; it was kind of him.

Moving silently to my room, I shut the door and changed back into pajamas. Once I was snuggled in under the sheets, my thoughts drifted back to Joshua. The bed was cold, and I'd grown so used to his body tangled in sleep with mine.

All I could think was...

....he didn't trust me...

...he didn't trust me...

...and it broke my heart all over again.

GABRIEL

I pulled my phone from my pocket when it vibrated. It was Blackthorne—again. I red-buttoned the call and shoved it into my pocket.

"Blackthorne?" asked Ian.

I nodded.

"You sure you want to ditch his calls?" Hastily, Ian added, "Sir."

"Aleria has left us for the French Coven. If he does not know already, he will soon. I do not care to have any extra scrutiny while we are looking into our own people."

My phone vibrated again. I checked the screen. It was a different number, but my gut told me it was Blackthorne on another line. When I did not answer, Ian's phone rang.

"Blackthorne?" I asked.

Ian stared at his phone. "Yup. He's never called me."

I gritted my teeth and stared at the map. We were going to have to move quickly, or we were going to have people coming at us from three fronts, and vampires and angels were already enough. I peered over at Joshua researching on a laptop. I only wished my team was whole.

8

TIME

ALERIA

I woke for the second day in a row in a terror. Another three-headed demon dog had been chasing me. The tension slowly drained from my limbs, and my heart slowed. Pushing my hair from my face, I sat hugging a pillow, not ready to try sleeping again.

Bowen had worked all night, so I'd spent my time in the library I'd found the day before. Though actually, I had done more staring out the window.

The only thing I'd accomplished was the drawing of one very painful conclusion: I could never go back to Joshua. Even if I could forgive him for hurting me, I couldn't get past the fact that he didn't trust me. No matter the reason.

A lump developed in my throat, and I flopped back onto the bed. There was something very final about my feelings, and it made me uneasy.

At some point, I'd drifted back to sleep, but I woke with my heart sprinting once again. I sat up and squeezed my eyes shut, holding back a whimper. It wasn't a demon dog this time; it was a bird of prey with glowing red eyes and blood dripping from its talons.

I settled back between my pillows, and my mind drifted to Bowen. I thought of the weeks we'd spent together in California and what it had felt like when he'd pulled me out of the dungeon. He had brought me back from oblivion. He had kept his promise after I'd been turned and had never let me take a human life. But more than anything, he'd been my friend. That was exactly what he said he'd hoped to be, even though I knew that he'd wanted more.

My mind lingered on the moments I'd watched him sleep on the couch across the room from me. When my grief had no longer choked me, I'd fallen crazy in love with him.

Slowly, a realization unfurled inside me. There was no denying it—I *wanted* Bowen—and not because I was sad or alone. I wanted to breathe him in and feel the healing of lying next to him in sleep, to hear our breathing synchronize.

My heart picked up pace again, urging me to get out of bed. Taking a deep breath, I padded to the next room; he was in bed. I traversed the few steps up the platform and just stood there. He looked so serene. All of the stress and pressure I'd seen since we had returned to the castle was merely a memory.

He seemed so at peace, I decided I didn't want to disturb him. He'd hardly slept; he was always needed for some sort of kingly business. I eased down a step.

"Aleria, are you all right?"

I froze. "I'm sorry. I didn't mean to wake you."

His eyes opened. "Can I do something for you?"

I hesitated. "I..."

"Anything," he whispered, and my heart fluttered.

"Can you...I...I'm..." I took a breath, feeling flustered. "Would you just hold me again?" I hoped it didn't sound as pathetic as in my head.

Bowen held the covers open, and I crawled in next to him. He rolled on his side and wrapped his arms around me. I nuzzled into his chest and nestled my leg between his. He was about three inches taller than Joshua and his shoulders broader. We fit differently.

When I made the comparison, my eyes welled up. Before the tears had a chance to go anywhere, I found Bowen's lips on mine, like he knew where my thoughts had just wandered, and he was distracting me.

It was a lazy kiss. Like a stroll on a Sunday afternoon when there's no hurry because the only plans you have are to be together. He pulled me closer, his tongue parting my lips, and I became liquid in his arms. He smelled of soap and safety, and it made my heart ache.

He ended the kiss and pressed his forehead to mine. "I am here for you. If you want to cry—cry. There is no judgment. I feel your heart still breaking, and it breaks mine."

I knew Bowen loved me; I had no doubts in that. But I couldn't stop thinking about Celeste. I wanted to ask him about her, but couldn't work up the nerve.

"What is it?"

I struggled for a second. "Do you love Celeste?"

He remained very still and didn't answer right away. "I care for her, but I do not love her. I have never claimed her as my familiar."

"Claimed?"

"When you claim a familiar, they are yours alone. No one may touch them without permission. The familiar must consent, and you must feed on them *before* the claim can be made. It is not taken lightly. Few here have claimed familiars."

"Why not?"

"You vow to provide for them until their human life is over—truly dead or turned. Violation of this law is serious and carries harsh punishment."

I mulled that over for a little while, and eventually, my thoughts returned to Celeste. "She's really attached to you."

"She wants to be turned. She's ambitious." He sighed. "I know your moral compass doesn't understand this, but she felt good—that is all."

"You don't have to explain."

"I never took her into my bed, and I never kissed her. It seemed too...intimate."

"But you had sex."

He kissed me and ran his fingers across my cheek and tucked some of my hair behind my ear. "This is intimate. What I did with her wasn't."

I knew Bowen was being truthful, and realization dawned. I'd seen Celeste push Bowen until he'd succumbed to her charms, but the latter part of what I experienced in the vision wasn't Bowen at all.

It was Tyran. I suddenly recognized the difference between the kisses. I cringed, wanting to wash my brain out with nuclear waste. I made a disgusted sound, and Bowen went absolutely still again.

"Oh, no, no. I am so sorry. I am not judging you. I have no right, and that is not at all what I was just thinking. Your brother was sleeping with her after you'd left. When I was in her head, I was seeing *him*. She made it into your bed and a whole lot more. She thought she was inches from the throne."

"Of course, he did." Bowen released the breath he was holding in an ironic gust.

"I didn't intend to inquisition you when I came in here. I'm sorry. I really didn't have a right to ask. I shouldn't have—"

"You do have the right. Whether you feel like it or not, you are my wife. I want no secrets. You are different, and it's not just the Lux blood in your veins calling to me. I want to be better for you. I don't want what I have had in the past."

"No pressure." I swallowed. "I think *you* are thinking too highly of *me* this time. I don't feel like I deserve this." It wasn't low self-esteem talking. It was humility.

"You are worth the wait."

I watched the soft expression on his face, and had a moment of absolute clarity. I had buried my love for Bowen deep when I'd discovered Joshua was still alive, but the last of the walls I'd built to protect myself from him were crumbling.

Consequently, by allowing that barrier down, all of the other emotion I'd been holding back crashed in on me. It was then that I felt the rage. I was so angry with Joshua for crushing my heart like I had no value.

Bowen had said it worried him that I hadn't cried. I was about to, and it wasn't going to be the pretty sort of crying.

When the first sob came, it racked my body almost convulsively. Then the tear-flood came in epic, Noah-sized proportions. I wailed, feeling the ugliness of everything—anger, betrayal, pain. I wished I could go back and change something so that none of this would've happened.

I wondered how Joshua could change like that overnight. How love could turn to hate in an instant. His blaming me for Sebastian and Peter and Leslie and Gentry's deaths drove me into a deeper spiral. I'd given him everything that was *me*, and he didn't want it.

He didn't want me. I felt like everything he had ever said to me was a lie, even though I knew that it wasn't true. Something had taken root and twisted him.

Bowen encircled me with his arms, helping me to weather the storm, and it wasn't the first time he'd done so. When I seemed like I was going to come apart, he held me tighter and let me sob with abandon.

I cried out with so much pain that I heard the guards open the door and Bowen wave his arm to call them off. But I couldn't stop. I felt the loss, betrayal, and humiliation in every cell of my body. A small piece of me wondered if I would ever be whole again. The moment I wondered this, Bowen pressed his lips to my forehead, and that hopeless part of me settled down.

After the tears had stopped flowing, I rested with my head against Bowen's chest, his arm still around me. He was asleep.

I realized that I'd only told him twice that I loved him. Once, after he'd given me the antidote to Aurora. He'd forced me to tell him my feelings, and it'd made me angry. I hadn't realized it at the time, but he'd needed to hear it out loud before he had tried to kill his own mother to save me from the sacrifice.

The other was when that attempt had failed, and he was chained to a pillar. I was being taken to the altar to be sacrificed, and had fought my way to him. It was there that I had told him, but I wouldn't have if I hadn't thought I was about to die.

I gently hugged him, so as to not wake him.

"I love you," I whispered.

Maybe tomorrow I would have the courage to say it while he was awake...

...maybe.

GABRIEL

"If I requested leave to go back to the States for a while, would you let me?" asked Joshua.

I was taken aback and stared at him, unmoving. Waiting for him to give some indication of what was going on in the recesses of his brain. I felt a scowl replace my neutral expression. "If it did not compromise a mission," I answered finally, when he showed no signs of continuing to speak.

"Thank you."

"Do you have a time in mind?"

"As soon as you don't need me—soon."

My frown deepened, and I nodded, dismissing him. He left the room in a whisper.

Ian entered. "Did he just ask to go back to the U.S.?"

"Yes."

"Has he ever asked before?"

"Not since Ali."

I reclined into my chair and perused our command center work wall. It had been two weeks since her departure, and we had been very busy. We had posted surveillance photos of Phineas, Blackthorne, and Ana, as well as a color-coded map with their movements. I had sent another Slayer, Hermah, to put eyes on the Fallen stronghold in Germany. They had taken out one of the cameras, but two were still live.

I made a decision. We needed to test Ana in some way. Joshua could sense her intentions like any other sentient entity. I needed his skills. If her people had been meeting Phineas, trusting her was out. But what did she desire if she was subverting Semjâzâ? I stared at the wall, praying for something to reveal itself to me.

My eyes landed on Ali's sketches of the artifact. I needed to see what Uriel had discovered thus far.

I punched in her number and waited for her to answer.

"Yes," she answered.

"Can you speak?"

"Wait." There was a long pause. "I'm clear. I was going to call you today. I know what the artifact does and the consequence of trying to destroy it."

## ALERIA

I sat, feeling that hollow feeling after spending way too long crying. Bowen didn't want to leave me alone for the day, so he'd asked me to take my throne next to him. Apparently, he thought boredom would help.

I'd been given a crown fashioned from platinum and gems and dressed in an elegant gown by my new handmaidens. I wanted to be in jeans and a soft sweater, curled up with a book in the anteroom behind the throne. But apparently, this was the glamorous life of a queen.

Who knew being a king and queen could be this tedious? Vampire after vampire after familiar after another vampire sought their audience with Bowen to seek his judgment in their squabbles.

One vampire accused another of stealing his intended spawn. He had bitten someone, but the blood of the other had turned the girl. I knew this one—blood trumps bite. But with others, I was clueless. So many of the disputes were petty, and I couldn't believe they were being brought to the king. It seemed I had two millennia of etiquette to catch up on. I tried to fix my face with an expression of concern. I didn't want them to think that their new queen didn't care—but I had a hard time focusing.

A vamp, dressed in an exquisite suit with a satin sash draped across his chest, entered the throne room in a flurry of motion. His pointed beard and collar-length hair reminded me of Renaissance paintings. I could feel his irritability from here.

Bowen sat even straighter. "Special Envoy Pierce, it is a pleasure to see you."

"I would say the same, King Belenus, but the King and Queen of the Southern Realm are not pleased with you."

Bowen gave him a patient smile. "And how have I offended my fellow monarchs?"

"Many feel mistreated. You, who have not taken a wife in centuries, have done so in private! Such things are not done. It is an affront to tradition."

"I apologize if this has offended the Consortium. We have plans in motion to have a grand coronation to make amends with all who would have liked to have attended the wedding."

"Some thought perhaps you were hiding her. There are questions about her loyalty."

Bowen's posture became completely rigid, and he stood, descending from the throne, coming face-to-face with Special Envoy Pierce. "And *who*, may I ask, is questioning her?"

Pierce took a half step back. "Rumors and whispers, Sire. Nothing definite, but I thought you should be made aware." His face had this faux-humility that made it seem as if he had walked through fire to deliver this information.

"I thank you for the consideration."

Pierce bowed with a little extra flourish, then started backing away.

"You can tell the others that formal invitations will be

delivered within the week. As with tradition, we will hold it forty days after the return from our wedding tour."

Pierce stopped and smiled, but it looked more like he was in pain. "I will inform everyone."

"I am sure that you will," Bowen replied pleasantly. I had the feeling that this Pierce could spread gossip faster than a junior high mean girl.

Bowen held up his hand to Cadeyn. "That is all for today."

Cadeyn urged his guards into motion, and after a minute, the doors were shut, and we were left alone, with the exception of Tyran, who'd seated himself at his mother's old desk and was working at something.

"Is my word good?" Bowen asked Tyran.

"Of course, brother. I am taking care of everything. I have an entire team starting preparations."

"Good."

Bowen turned towards me. I was still sitting awkwardly on my throne, not sure what I should be doing. He ascended from the dais, with almost a skip in his step, and grabbed my hand, pulling me towards the anteroom.

Once inside, he sat down on the arm of one of the leather wingback chairs so that we were at eye level. He pulled me close, his face serious.

"I wish there wasn't a time limit, but barring an international incident in our world, I need to ask you something before we send out the invitations for the Coronation."

"I didn't know there was going to be a Coronation."

"I apologize. We knew this was coming and tried to get ahead of it." Bowen took a long look at me, weighing his words. "I need to know that this is what you want. I fear that you are here because you have nowhere else to go." He paused and seemed a little nervous. "I need to know you chose me."

For some reason, his thinking I had nowhere else to go surprised me. "I do have somewhere to go. I have many friends in the Watchers and have had offers to go elsewhere." I grinned. "I'm kind of a rock star."

He shifted and dropped my hands, putting his on my hips; a shadow of a smile passed over his lips, but then he looked away.

I cupped his face, making him meet my gaze. "I'm still terrified and want nothing to do with the throne."

He opened his mouth. "I und—" He was upset, and I felt it surge through me.

"Let me finish." I took a deep breath.

"You don't ne—" he said, hurt now on his face.

I glared at him. "Stop and let me speak." His emotions were ruffling me, but my voice came out strong and clear—not a trace of doubt in it. "Thank you for giving me a couple of weeks. I know it wasn't easy for you. But I have made my decision; I refuse to be a coward. I'll take all of it—the throne and everything—if I can have you. *You* are worth it."

He stared at me, his brow still clouded.

And then I said it: "I love you." Then, *I* kissed *him*.

The question that had plagued me for the last couple of weeks was whether I would have chosen Bowen if the situation had been different—if Joshua had died rather than ripping out my heart and throwing it away. I always came up with the same answer.

A sudden feeling of relief washed over me when I realized that my decision was sound. I could feel warmth spreading throughout my body and the deliciously calm feeling of knowing that I'd made the right decision. It had been a crooked and treacherous path to get here, but I was in the right place and had made this decision for the right reasons.

I felt him smile against my lips. "Say it again."

I grinned back. "I love you," I murmured against his lips.

"You don't say those words very easily. I should probably hear it a few more time before you forget how to say them again." He was really grinning now.

I grabbed his hair and leaned his head back, wanting him to see the seriousness of my face. "I love you. I said it to you last night, but I was too chicken to say it while you were awake." I kissed him again and was demanding; he met me with equal fervor. The burn in my belly for him was steadily increasing.

He pulled away and smiled until the edges of his beautiful blue eyes crinkled in the corners. "I have somewhere to take you."

"Where?" I asked cautiously.

"You don't feel married to me."

"Huh?"

He didn't clarify; he simply led me out into the night air, determined to surprise me.

## 9

## CHERISH

GABRIEL

I summoned Ian and Joshua while plugging in the secure cell to the external speaker. "Uriel, you are clear to speak."

"Long version or short?"

"Short, please."

"Understood. When someone tries to destroy the artifact, it doesn't just kill the person attempting the destruction. It kills everyone in their family and leaves them alive to mourn. If they are a vampire, it will kill everyone in their sire line. So, as an example, if it was someone like Belenus, potentially thousands of vamps could fall dead."

"Including Aleria," added Ian.

"Yes, but Aleria would die anyway." Uriel hesitated. "She is his wife now. She would die, as well as her parents, brother, and your daughter, Gabriel. All immediate family."

Ian inquired, "So, why a whole sire line?"

"Direct blood relation. Spawns more than three generations

down are eliminated. Anything above that is like a great-great-grandchild."

"Is destroying it an option?" I asked.

"Besides the death toll, I'm not sure. I'm still working on it."

"What if the one destroying it has no family—or spouse?" wondered Joshua.

Uriel paused again, knowing full well what Joshua was asking. "I quote: 'Then the destroyer shall be destroyed.'"

If Joshua tried to destroy it, he would die—and no one else.


## ALERIA

I had never realized how expansive the grounds of the castle were. We walked along a path, the cliff's side on our right and lightly forested area on the left. The Royal Guard was keeping a safe distance away, at least giving us the illusion of privacy.

"Aren't we safe on the castle property?" I inquired.

Bowen was quiet for a moment. "There have been some threats. It's a precaution. There was an attempt on the lives of the ruling family in Egypt. We are pulling in members from all over the world to increase security for your Coronation."

"So, no weekends away?" I teasingly asked.

Bowen glanced at a couple of the guards. "We did just have over a month on our tour."

I smiled. *Yes, our "wedding tour."* I peered off of the cliff, taking in the dark waters made even darker by the moonlight reflected on the rippling surface, all the while hearing the waves crash far below us.

We ambled around the next bend in the tree-lined path, skirting an outcropping of trees to reveal the curvy shore of a large, natural pond. Not far behind it stood a church—well, actually, a large Gothic cathedral. It had flying buttresses, one of the few architectural things I remembered from World History.

This church, with its ornate spires, looked as if it were from the Middle Ages. Mammoth stained glass windows that narrowed to points adorned each wall, but in the moonlight, it was too dark to discern what was depicted on them from the outside.

"We keep it in good repair for ceremonies. It's where we will have your Coronation."

"Does it seem weird that vampires have a church on their compound?"

"Castles used to be the center of village life. Many had churches within the walls. The outer wall runs about a kilometer inside the property line and stretches the entire distance—it was added during the Renaissance. The wall is almost ten kilometers long. We have had to work hard to keep tourists and historians away. A barbed wire and chain link fence with private property signs is on the actual property line."

I looked around. "Is there a road leading to the cathedral?"

"Guests will arrive and be housed in the castle. Horse-drawn carriages will bring them out here—a tradition that hasn't been broken for marriages and official ceremonies of state."

"Until our secret marriage," I corrected.

"Yes." He bent and whispered so the guards couldn't hear. "I wish I had been there."

We approached the door, but Cadeyn was suddenly in front of us. "Permission to clear the building, Sire?"

"Granted."

Cadeyn disappeared inside for about two full minutes, and then returned. "Clear, my King. I will hold the men outside, as requested." He bowed, and then backed away, taking his station a few yards from the entrance.

We walked through the double doors that were at least fifteen feet high. The floor plan was in the shape of a cross, like most medieval cathedrals. I could see the alcoves on the left and right two-thirds of the way through the sanctuary.

I jumped when I looked upward towards the ceiling. There were statues of angels with their wings spread overlooking the entire cathedral. There were dozens of them, either looking at the sanctuary, the altar, or towards the heavens. After I realized they weren't moving, I was amazed at their beauty, and wanted to figure out how to get up there and examine them more closely.

Bowen placed his hand on my upper arm. "Spectacular, aren't they?"

"Yes, I can't even..."

"I thought you would like them. You had told me about the stained glass windows in Ireland. I had hoped you would see these someday."

The clink of metal at the front of the church drew my attention. Lighting candles on the altar was a priest—or maybe a monk. I wasn't sure if they were the same thing. He had on a dark brown robe tied at the waist with a cord.

"Jean Michel," Bowen called out.

The monk-priest turned, and his face lit up. "*Votre Majesté,* (Your, Majesty)" he bowed.

"*Avez-vous reçu le paquet que j'ai envoyé avec les instructions?* (Did you get the package I sent with the instructions?)"

He patted the pocket hidden in his robe. "*Je vous attendais.* (I have been waiting for you)"

"English, please," Bowen urged.

The monk-priest put his hand over his mouth as if embarrassed. And judging from the adorable blush on his cheeks, he was.

"Aleria, I would like you to meet Jean Michel, our resident priest."

"A human priest. Here?"

Jean Michel addressed me. "I was taken from a small monastery in the South. His Majesty saved me."

Bowen explained. "Before I outlawed kidnapping runners for the maze. Jean Michel was awaiting his turn in the cages. I liberated him and gave him a parish of sorts. He is safe here on holy ground. And he has found that many visit to speak with him. He gives good council."

"I am honored, Your Majesty." His hazel eyes were almost tearful.

"And you didn't try to run?" I queried.

Jean Michel pulled up his robe and held out his ankle. It looked like an ankle bracelet for prisoners. "If I leave the grounds, I die. But, I would choose to stay."

"He wasn't compelled to forget everything before he was brought in. Icelos never lets the priests survive. He has a particular taste for monks. After many long talks, I gave Jean Michel the choice to live here with the bracelet or be turned and become one of us."

Jean Michel dipped his head reverently. "I prefer to keep my soul."

There was sadness in my voice when I responded, but no bitterness. "Some of us didn't have a choice, whether it was an accident or we were born into it."

"I am sure our heavenly Father will take that into consideration. I have seen His Majesty's heart."

I smiled at him politely, but I didn't know how to respond.

"I will return in just a moment; I need my Bible. Please, excuse me."

My eyes followed Jean Michel as he darted across the altar and through a door behind the podium area in the rear.

"Aleria." The tone of Bowen's voice made my heart stutter.

"Yes?" My reply came out in a breath.

"I realize that everything is backwards—that you should have had more time to heal. I should have had time to court you properly—to woo you—even though you have known my feelings all along. I love you. I am glad we are married." He got on one knee. "Will you marry me again? Right here—now. With both of us present." He grinned. "With as close to a reverend as I can provide."

I would've liked to have been wooed and to have had more time to get over Joshua. But I did love Bowen. I'd never stopped; I'd just tried not to think about it.

Bowen continued. "I just need to hear, one last time, that you choose me. That if Joshua regains his senses and begs for your forgiveness—that you choose *me*. That you will stay with *me*."

As I stood there, gazing into Bowen's sky-blue eyes, I knew my decision was sound. Joshua didn't trust me on some level, and he'd cut me to the heart without mercy. When he had cast me aside, I had felt nothing but distrust and anger through our blood bond.

I leaned towards Bowen. "I love you. I choose you."

Jean Michel returned at that moment. He spoke for a minute with Bowen in French again, forgetting that I couldn't speak it. I could only pick out what I thought was the words "traditional," "wife," and maybe "rings."

With a shy smile, Jean Michel arranged us facing one another on the steps of the altar and stood at the top with his Bible. He took a deep breath and exhaled, ruffling the pages of scripture.

He began our private ceremony with a blessing over each of

us. Then he handed Bowen a ring made of white gold. Bowen slid it onto my finger, and it fit perfectly with the cushion style engagement ring I'd been wearing.

Jean Michel then prompted Bowen. I let out a shaky breath, feeling emotion swell inside me. Bowen repeated the vows while looking into my eyes and holding both my hands tightly. My heart raced, and my throat choked.

"I, Belenus, take you, Aleria Elizabeth, to be my beloved wife, to have and to hold you, to honor you, to treasure you, to be at your side in sorrow and in joy, in the good times, and in the bad, and to love and cherish you always. I promise you this from my heart, for all the days of my eternal life."

Jean Michel then turned to me, and I repeated the same vows to Bowen, as prompted. Jean Michel was about to say something in closing, but there was a knock on the main door, and it swung open a second later.

Cadeyn got on a knee. "I am sorry to disturb you, my King. You have a visitor at the castle. Batariel is back."

I squeezed his hands. "I'm coming with you."

Bowen looked at Cadeyn. "I'll be there in ten minutes."

"I will let him know, Sire."

We headed to the doors, but before we exited, I pulled him to a stop. He looked down at me, his thoughts obviously back at the castle.

"Thank you," I smiled.

"I had hoped to continue with the wooing."

I grabbed his collar and pulled him down to kiss me. "You forgot to kiss the bride. I may have to punish you for that later."

He looked at me, surprised—and a little hopeful.

I smirked and walked out ahead of him towards our "guest."

GABRIEL

Joshua, still as the dead, sat with his hand on either side of the blueprints and stared without blinking.

"I did hear you correctly," said he, finally breaking his silence. "You want me to steal this gemstone."

"Yes."

"Steal."

I drew my mouth to the side. "Borrow. You will temporarily replace it with this." I held up a replica between my thumb and index.

Joshua pressed his fingers into his temples. "When would you like me to do this?"

"Tonight. Ian rigged the furnace to shut off. He is there 'fixing it' and getting into their security system as we speak. I have the rest of the schematics here." I pointed to the black duffle in the doorway. "All of the tools you will need are in there."

"Okay. I'll memorize them now." Joshua picked up the plans and returned to the room in which he had been staying. Not once did he ask me why we were breaking the law. Not once had he asked what I was to do with the stone. The closest he had come to questioning me was his confirmation of "steal." This troubled me.

Joshua was automatically my first candidate for the job due to the fact that he would not set off the heat sensors. A vampire's skills and stealth made them perfect thieves. My mind had gone to Sebastian, wishing I had him here to help me plan all of this.

When I thought of Sebastian, it had reminded me of his grandfather being set up by vampires to take the fall for a series of heists. His grandfather had won the court case after over a year and retreated into the Watchers. Once he had recovered from the ordeal, he had become one of the greatest strategists we had ever seen.

This remembrance led me to what Ana would want—one of the gems for the artifact. She was willing to risk Aleria's life for half of the disk. Giving her one of the real stones was an unacceptable risk, not that we had them. But Petrescu had given us specific information on them.

This stone had the right shape, clarity, and color. A simulated stone would be found out too quickly. I needed a genuine stone to attract Ana. Deciding my approach to her was proving difficult—even more difficult than planning a heist.

I yelled down the hall to Joshua. "I am going for my run."

He poked his head outside his door and looked towards the sliver of fading light through the taped-off window.

"A short run."

This was the first time Joshua had questioned me since Ali had left us. Though, I understood his worry, it was light out and he would be powerless to help me. We had sequestered ourselves from most of the Concilium, not knowing whom we could trust. We had needed the extra caution.

I examined the security camera feeds and the traffic cams we had hacked before venturing out. Shutting the front door, I pushed myself immediately, still checking my six in the reflection of windows. My feet pounding on the pavement brought the needed clarity for the missions ahead.


ALERIA

We were walking back, holding hands, and I felt almost giddy. I was trying not to think about the probable confrontation ahead with Batariel. We passed the edge of the pond and a shrub exploded with activity. At first, I thought they were bats as they took to the sky. But the telltale caw of crows startled me. I turned to Bowen. "Are there normally crows out here at night?"

His lips formed a thin line. "No." He patted my hand. "I'm sure it's nothing."

I nodded, but still felt unsettled.

Bowen nudged my shoulder with his arm a moment later and smiled down at me. "It's nothing," he reassured.

I exhaled, releasing the tension, thinking myself a little silly. Then I felt something like a raindrop hitting my chest. I looked up only to see stars spilled across the heavens as far as I could see.

Then blood began to gush from my nose at the same time that frost threaded its way through my brain.

All I could think was that this was so much worse than the other times.

I felt my body twisting, arching backwards, and the night sky sprinting away from me.


## GABRIEL

At precisely midnight, Joshua casually walked down the street, hands shoved into his pockets, a beanie tugged low on his head. We rolled up next to him, and he slid into the backseat, hardly breaking his stride.

"Got it," said he, as we pulled away from the curb.

"Any problems?"

"No. Your plans were perfect. They won't notice unless they check the jewel itself."

"Good work."

As a precaution, we pulled into a parking garage a few blocks away, wiped down the sedan, and switched vehicles. We had a few hours' drive to get back to southern Belgium.

Joshua made a small sound under his breath. I examined him in the rearview mirror for a moment. He was suppressing a reaction to something. He could not hide that from me.

"Tell me," I ordered. I was not going to play.

Joshua glared back at me in the rearview. "She was happy for the first time since she left."

"You have been sensing her emotions since she departed?"

"Just glimpses. Enough to know she is safe," Joshua's voice was hoarse. He turned his head and scowled into the darkness outside.

*He is worried whether she is safe.*

My grip tightened on the wheel, and I turned my concentration towards Ana. She was to meet Blackthorne tomorrow, so I knew the where. Now, I simply needed the how.

Joshua leaned forward and moaned. "She's having a vision," he gasped. "But something's wrong—very, *very* wrong."

10

SIDES

ALERIA

It felt as if someone had packed my brain into the garbage disposal, scooped it out, and then crammed it back into my head through my nose. I tried to remember what I'd been doing. A cathedral—having something with my Coronation—maybe. I had the same sensation that memories had been blotted out.

The doorknob made the faintest of clicking sounds. Someone entered. A vampire. It didn't smell like anyone I knew. They were moving closer. I wanted to move, but I also wanted to know what they were about to do.

My nerves were screaming, and my heart had picked up pace. If they could hear it, they would know I was awake. I could feel them standing next to the bed. Somehow, I managed to keep my breathing even.

I didn't move until I felt a needle press against the skin of my arm.

GABRIEL

The meeting should have been completed by now, but I could still see Ana's figure through the window. I sat on the roof across the street. I had good sight lines in all directions. Ian and Joshua were positioned down the street. There was a flash of movement on the top of the building in which the meeting was taking place. I remained still, keeping behind the vent I had been using for concealment.

It was Ana's cohort that Ali had described: a dark-haired male with a circular tattoo on his left temple. Basing my measurements on the architecture of the building, he was my height, except he had more girth. His wings quivered, and a section of them retracted into his body between his shoulder blades; the rest seemed to lie absolutely flat against his back, ending at his waist. Judging from the grimace on his visage, the transformation was painful. He concealed what was visible of his wings with a long coat he pulled from a satchel. If I had not witnessed it, I would never have believed.

My focus was so transfixed on Ana's male accomplice that I lost track of her. This was not like me. The lights were out. Making a sweep with the binoculars, I tried to locate everyone from the meeting. Blackthorne exited with two bodyguards and was shuffled into an awaiting car.

"Ian, do you have eyes on Ana?"

"No. Security feed shows that she never got onto the elevator."

I glanced back at the rooftop. The male was standing on the edge of building staring straight at me. It was then I sensed something alight behind me. I cursed silently at myself.

"Gabriel, I was wondering when we would meet again. What a delight."

ALERIA

I grabbed onto a wrist and squeezed, feeling bones crush in my hand. I opened my eyes, and using the vamp's arm as leverage, swung my body out of the bed. I held his arm and twisted it behind his back, landing hard on his spine with my knees.

He cried out in pain, but I didn't relinquish my grip. I carefully plucked the syringe, still full of its contents, from his captured hand.

"What is this?" I questioned.

He grunted.

I twisted the wrist I had broken, feeling another pop. "What's in the syringe?"

"I don't know."

"Who sent you?"

"I don't know."

At that moment, both Tyran and Bowen burst into the room. I held up the syringe, and Bowen relieved me of it. He smelled it, then handed it to Tyran, who did the same.

"What is it?" I asked.

Tyran pointed at the vamp I was pinning beneath me. "It wasn't possible for *this* one to have staked all four of the guards outside unaided."

"No, it wasn't," Bowen agreed. "Are you all right?"

I nodded. "Fine."

"You can let him up. He's not going anywhere."

I stood, sticking my knee into his back a little harder than necessary. The intruder was a young vamp. He rolled and stayed on his backside, scuttling backwards like a crab until he hit the wall. He cradled his arm, looking like a wounded alley cat.

Bowen pulled me close and cupped my face, his brow

furrowed. "I'm sorry I wasn't here. I didn't know you were awake until I felt your alarm."

"How long was I out?"

His eyes darkened. "It has been a day."

"Like, twenty-four hours?"

"Yes."

Morpheus and Cadeyn had entered seconds after Bowen and Tyran had arrived, stepping over the bodies of my staked guards.

Tyran handed Morpheus the syringe. "Do you know what this is?"

Morpheus sniffed it, and his stormy grey eyes flashed with recognition as he went still as a statue. He looked almost unsteady on his feet. "I will look into this, if you permit me, Your Highness."

"What are you not telling me, Cousin?"

Morpheus' voice was heavy. "Please, let me investigate before I cast doubt on someone."

"I am only allowing this because it is you."

"Thank you, Sire." Morpheus bowed lower than I'd ever seen him, and he backed from the room, almost tripping on one of the guards. Something had seriously shaken him up.

Tyran dropped to one knee in front of the prisoner. "That isn't healing properly, is it?" Tyran seized his wrist and yanked it, snapping the bones to reset it—roughly. The neophyte whimpered, barely suppressing a scream. "I would like to start my questioning with a clean slate." The sadistic gleam in Tyran's eye made me shudder, and it wasn't even aimed at me. He dragged the vamp to his feet, holding his upper arm in a vice-like grip. "I'll take him to be interrogated."

"No." Bowen stated.

Tyran looked at him inquisitively.

"*I'll* question him."

Tyran raised both his brows and chuckled, looking at the intruder. "You will wish you'd had me."

"Cadeyn, prep him. I'll be along shortly. As Captain of the Guard, this was your responsibility."

Cadeyn bowed and whisked off the prisoner, feeling the full weight of Bowen's words.

Bowen turned and kissed me. "I don't want you left alone anymore."

"I defended myself just fine. I'm not exactly helpless."

"No, you aren't. But if he had arrived an hour earlier while you were still unconscious, what would have happened? I thought four guards would have been enough."

I had no answer.

"Did you have a vision? Do you remember anything?"

I shook my head. "No. I remember going on a walk with you, and you showing me the church where the Coronation will take place..." My voice trailed as I searched my memory. I finally stated, "Then nothing."

"You don't remember..." Bowen stopped and was clearly holding back dark emotions, but putting on a brave face about something.

I tried to reach into the blackness of those missing hours. Tyran's voice jarred me. "Stop!"

Bowen leaned my head back as I felt the blood pour from my nose. I hadn't even sensed it.

Tyran stripped a pillowcase from a pillow and handed it to me as he spoke to Bowen. "Semjâzâ is somehow responsible for this. Over the last several weeks, if she tried to access a vision where Semjâzâ was present, this is what would happen. We almost lost her once. She had blood coming from her ears and eyes—everywhere. It was horrific."

"This feels different," I interrupted. "The visions were still in my head before, but fuzzy, as if they were being blocked. These are just...gone." I looked at Bowen, contemplating. "And apparently, I lost more than the vision this time. My actual memory is gone, isn't it?"

"You are missing about a half hour prior to the vision." There was the flicker of hurt again—maybe hurt wasn't the right word.

My nose stopped bleeding. I stepped away from Bowen and eased onto the bed, feeling lightheaded.

"I want you to stay here with her. Don't you dare leave her side for any reason." Bowen started heading for the door. "And get her someone to feed on—not Celeste." He shot Tyran a dirty look, then was out the door.


GABRIEL

Ana pulled the pin from her fiery hair and shook it out. She tilted her head to the side, a coy grin displayed on her face. She was seductive when she wanted to be. Her black wings flapped slowly, creating a rhythm that reminded me of a cobra swaying back and forth, hypnotizing its prey right before it struck. *She* was not snake-like, though.

Part of me wanted to succumb to her. Realization hit me. She smelled sweet and inviting, and her wings were wafting whatever pheromone she was releasing towards me.

It all became clear: she could lure men. She had Blackthorne caught in her trap. I wondered what he had divulged to her. Once I had identified the threat, I forced my head to clear.

She realized her seduction was not working. Her wings became motionless, and she shrugged. "You are a strong Slayer, aren't you?" she cooed.

Her flattery fell flat, and I could see that my original plan was not going to work. I altered it and decided to be direct. No games. "What do you want with the artifact?"

"Semjâzâ wants to tear apart the veil between our worlds and bring Hell to Earth. He plans to merge everything onto this plane of existence and rule over all of it."

"I thought it had resurrection abilities?"

She smiled and stepped a little closer. "It does. It restores powers that have been stripped away. Most of my kind were stripped of all our heavenly powers before we were cast into the abyss. We are still stronger and faster, but we only have a fraction of the power we once had."

"Whose side are you on?"

"It is said that there is only one that can see the weakness of the master."

"Is Semjâzâ the master? Why does he want 200 vampires to sacrifice?"

"Blackthorne has no idea who I am, does he? Why haven't you informed him?"

"What happens if Semjâzâ does not sacrifice the 200?"

"Are you off on your own? Not knowing who to trust? Your leader potentially compromised."

"How close are you to completing the artifact?"

"We have the dagger, if that is what you are wondering."

"Are you on Semjâzâ's side?"

She took a step back and fully extended her wings.

"For right now, let us say that I am on the winning side." She was airborne in the blink of an eye. The male joined her, and in seconds, they were nothing but dots in the distance.

I spoke into the comm. "Did you hear all that?"

"The one that can see the weakness of the master. Do you think that's Ali?" asked Ian.

"If it is, then she is in more danger than I had originally imagined."

"And they have the dagger," said Joshua.


ALERIA

Tyran stretched out on the bed beside me.

"You could hang out over there, you know." I pointed to the chaise and oversized ottoman in the corner of my private bedroom.

He moved closer. "He said not to leave your side, and besides, your bed is so much more comfortable." He grinned.

"I don't think he literally meant *by my side*."

"On the contrary."

Exasperated, I threw my arm over my face and closed my eyes, avoiding his scrutiny.

"So when are you going to open your legs for my brother? He is getting rather cranky."

"*Excuse* me?" I lifted my arm.

He shrugged and rolled on his back.

I sighed. "Do you know what happened to me? During the half hour before my vision," I clarified.

"You really don't remember?"

"No."

"He had told me that you didn't feel married, and he had been cheated of the experience. He intended to fix that. I assume he took you to that priest he keeps in the cathedral. He wouldn't let me come, so I can't be sure."

"You think he married me in a church?"

"Did I set your heart a pitter-patter with the romance of it?"

I found a stupid grin on my face. "I'd told him there had been no church and no pastor, and that it'd bothered me."

Tyran rolled his eyes. "Oh, the sweetness of it—and yet, you're still locked at the knees."

"Please, don't." I wasn't in the mood for his being crude.

"If you are worried about your skills, I could practice a few things with you."

I frowned, but for some idiotic reason, something totally honest popped out of my mouth. "I am a little nervous. I..."

Tyran looked at me a little surprised, and I punched him in the ribs in one swift movement.

"Stop being an ass," I growled.

He held his rib, which I was pretty sure I broke, and coughed a laugh. "I wasn't serious about the practice, but I was about the marital bed."

"I know what you're serious about." I swallowed, changing the subject. "Was that boy trying to kill me?"

"I don't think so. The smell reminded me of a sedative, but I can't be sure," Tyran mused.

"Does Morpheus think his brothers are involved?"

"Perceptive, aren't you?"

"When I'm not being naïve," I quipped, reminding him of his jab from weeks ago.

"You are sometimes."

"I'm twenty-one and like to think the best of people. Sue me."

"I just don't want it to get you killed."

"Well, I don't really want to die."


GABRIEL

Upon our return, we started creating cards to add to our wall. I examined the column we had compiled for the artifact and crossed off "dagger" in red marker. They possessed three-fourths of the disk and the dagger. We had one quarter. Two stones were outstanding. Two gems holding off Armageddon.

I held the card with the quote, "One who can see the weakness of the master," tapping it on my palm.

Before bringing up Ali, I hesitated, but I needed information from Joshua. "When you felt Ali have a vision yesterday, you said something was wrong. What was it?"

Joshua looked thoughtful, though his shoulders did tense. "The recent visions where she was unconscious for extended periods of time were more painful. This was unlike any that I have sensed before. It was debilitating and even more invasive. When she loses consciousness, I lose her, but that vision was over a minute long." He grasped for words. "It was like hot torches were searing her mind."

"Like damage was being done?"

"I'm only guessing. Maybe she stays unconscious for so long because that's how long it takes to repair the damage?"

The room was silent for a long while—our band of three staring at the wall of evidence, praying for clues to reveal themselves.

"We have some questions on which we need to focus: If Ali has the ability to figure out how to defeat Semjâzâ, we need to figure out if he wants her alive or dead. If he wants her alive, where does he want her? With us, with the French Coven, or with him? What happens if they do not sacrifice the 200 immortals? And, where are the two gemstones for the artifact?"

"Also, what side is Ana really on?" added Ian.

I turned towards Joshua. "I wish you could sense intentions over the comm. I wanted you with me when I spoke to Ana."

"I'm sorry." He paused. "We are forgetting someone. Where does Phineas fit in with all of this?" asked Joshua.

"Where *is* Phineas?" I asked.

Ian opened a minimized window on the desktop. "France. A few miles from the coven."

"I do not like it."

"There is nothing in this situation *to* like," breathed Joshua.

My phone rang. "Speak."

"There is sudden movement in covens across the globe. Security forces are being reinforced everywhere. Something is up," reported Samael.

That seemed to be an understatement.

# 11

# PENANCE

ALERIA

I was curled into a chair, reading in my favorite place in the castle—the anteroom behind the throne. Even Tyran sitting next to me wasn't spoiling my mood. Cadeyn ushered Morpheus into the room, and Morpheus looked as if he could barely stand.

"Morpheus? What's wrong?" I put my book down and jumped up, guiding him to one of the chairs.

He sat heavily. After a long pause, he finally spoke. "My brother, Phantasos...he had something to do with what has been happening to you. He has sided with those demons against his own coven. Against *me*." The grief in his voice was so great that it made me forget this was partially about me.

"Does Bowen know?" I asked.

"Yes, a tribunal has been called. He has removed himself from judgment since he is our kin."

"Is that good?"

"A tribunal is made up of members from other covens. They

don't know him and have had no interactions with Batariel or Semjâzâ," Morpheus explained.

I looked at Tyran. He shook his head. Phantasos was as good as dead. As good as that was for me, I didn't like seeing one of my few friends here in pain. I couldn't imagine losing my brother, and one I'd been with for centuries nonetheless.

I hated to push him, but I wanted to know what had been happening to me. I sat on the love seat and turned towards him. "What did Phantasos do, specifically?"

"He has been keeping himself in tune with you. For weeks, he has watched all of your dreams and visions. He recently teamed with Batariel. After several attempts, he was able to piggyback Batariel into your head. There are similarities in their powers.

"Batariel would watch your vision. If there was something that would hinder Semjâzâ's plans, he suppressed them at first; then later, when he learned how, he wiped them from your memory.

"As you know, there is always a backlash when you alter a dream. Phantasos would lose his memory of the event, too. He has no recollection of what he has seen. Batariel has fled. Icelos is under guard, though it is believed Phantasos was acting alone."

"What about the boy with the needle?"

"It was a sedative that would have knocked you out for weeks and kept you in a dream state. It wasn't an assassination attempt. But they would have had free reign in your head for as long as it had lasted. None of your memories would have been safe."

I sat stunned, feeling so violated I wanted to curl up into a ball. I must've also looked like it. Tyran moved next to me and put his arm around my shoulders.

"I'm sorry, Morpheus," I offered.

His eyes met mine, but there were no words.

## GABRIEL

Praying before dialing the number, I held the phone to my ear, only to listen to the message that it was not in service. I had already tried to reach Ali via secure email. She had cut everything off—or it was cut off for her.

There was one last option, short of risking my life and walking to the front gates of the coven itself. I wrote a cryptic message to be read by either Aleria or Belenus. I did not care who. I needed to speak to one of them. They needed to be warned, and I hoped they could supply some of the missing pieces.

## ALERIA

I woke, gasping for breath after running from another demon dog in my sleep. I was petrified of sleeping—afraid that Batariel would figure out another way into my head without the aid of Phantasos.

Tyran was asleep on top of the covers next to me. Bowen hadn't come to bed yet. I missed him. I slipped from bed and tiptoed to the bathroom. When I came out afterwards, Tyran was standing in the doorway, and I was too startled to scream. I punched him in the ribs.

He spoke through gritted teeth. "Wake me if you are going anywhere."

"The bathroom! I didn't leave my room. I didn't even venture into the main bedroom. You are worse than Gabriel ever was when I was human!"

"You are in more danger now!"

"Really? *You* were pretty dangerous."

Tyran rocked back on his heels. "This is what you lived like when I was after you?"

"We had to move around more, and the beds weren't as comfortable—if I had a bed. Also, Phantasos wasn't the only Oneiroi in my head back then."

Tyran didn't say anything. Instead, he simply looked at me with a blank expression. I wished I knew what he was thinking.

"Are you worried that Icelos is involved as well?" I asked.

"Yes." Tyran rubbed at his chest and walked back to the bed. "I..."

"What is it?" He turned back.

"I think Icelos was just in my dream. I think he has been posing as a demon dog and chasing me. When I do sleep, I'm being chased. I'm so tired, I can't think straight."

He sighed. "My brother needs sleep, too. I will call him and get him back here. I'll go and sit with Icelos and Phantasos to make sure you can get some real sleep. I could use a break from the broken ribs." Tyran winked, then left. I had *not* broken his rib—this time.

Bowen came in after a short while. He had dark circles under his eyes and practically fell into bed. Being in his arms felt healing. Part of me wanted to stay awake just to enjoy being with him.

Knowing Tyran was keeping the Oneiroi from my head allowed me to fall deep asleep without worries of monsters and demon dogs—at least for a few hours.

---

I woke and stretched, feeling good for the first time in weeks. Sunset had arrived, and gorgeous, amber light streamed in through the protective windows. Besides Bowen, that had been the one thing I'd missed about the castle—seeing the sun. I'd been sleeping in a brightly lit room just because I could. Tyran had grumbled when I forbade him to draw the curtains.

Bowen was still asleep. I watched his profile as he took each slow and steady breath. His eyes darted back and forth beneath his lids, his lashes looking like spun gold. He was so beautiful.

The memory of the first time I'd seen him in the coffee shop resurfaced. I remembered blinking up at him and thinking that there was no way someone that gorgeous was talking to me. But, that was quickly trumped by the thought that he was not okay in the head. It'd taken me a little too long to realize he was offering to save me from my ex's harassing friends.

I was suddenly having a hard time keeping my hands off of him. His full lips were making me a little crazed, but I managed to control myself. Twenty or so minutes later, he woke. I immediately wiggled as close as I could get and gave him a greedy kiss. He smiled halfway through it, and I ended up kissing his teeth.

He laughed. "I like waking up to this Aleria."

"I have been waiting for you to wake."

He rolled so that I was on my back, and he was on his side. He propped his head on his hand and looked down at me, clearly pleased. He ran his foot from just above the inside of my knee down to my ankle while his hand went from my hip to rest just below my breast. My heart started racing.

I lifted my head from the pillow to capture his lips again. His tongue slid into my mouth and teased mine. My right hand worked his t-shirt upwards, wanting to feel more of his skin.

"This needs to go." I tugged at his shirt again. He reached behind his collar and yanked it from his body, making a show of tossing it on the floor.

His mouth was on my ear. "I like this you very, very much." He smiled again, resting more of his weight on top of me. I ran my hands under his waistband and over his backside; he arched a little, pressing his hips into me harder, his breathing coming faster.

His lips went to my neck, his tongue running down the pulse point, lingering there.

"Do you want to taste me?" I asked.

"Yes," he breathed. "I want to do a lot of things to you at this moment."

"I want you too."

His teeth immediately sank into my neck, and when the rapture of the bite overtook me, everything was heightened. I moaned and pulled my nightgown up to my hips, wrapping my legs around him.

He sealed the bite and continued kissing down my neck, collarbone, and chest. I felt trapped by the thin fabric of my nightgown and pulled it off my shoulders bending towards him, wanting his mouth everywhere. Just as his lips were almost where I wanted them, he pulled back abruptly and gazed at me feverishly. It took a second for him to regain his composure. He looked out the darkened window, then back at me.

"How long did I sleep?"

"A long time. I didn't want to wake you."

He reached for his watch on the nightstand. "Delegates are arriving in ten minutes for the tribunal. They will be prompt."

"I don't suppose anyone else can greet them?"

"No. It would be seen as an affront."

He crawled back towards me, a wide grin on his face. He straddled my hips, but stayed on his hands and knees. Dipping down, he kissed me, his lips soft and persistent. Then he playfully nipped at my neck. "I need to go take a very, *very* cold shower."

Tyran walked in right as Bowen left. Bowen must've called him before he got into the shower. I quickly grabbed my robe.

"You look a little disheveled." Tyran eyed me suggestively.

"I'm going to take a nice long bath."

"I'll be here, ever your humble servant." He dramatically flopped onto the bed. "Unless, of course, you would like me to scrub your back?"

I paused before entering the bathroom. "How long does it usually take the tribunal to pronounce judgment?"

"Three days at most."

"You were close to Phantasos?"

The smile from his face faded. "He's my cousin."

GABRIEL

"I am done trying to figure out what Phineas is up to. We will pick him up tomorrow," I growled.

"On or off the books?"

"Off."

Ian shrugged.

I had needlessly prepared for his protest. "Will there be a problem with that?"

"Never liked the dude," responded Ian. He swiveled back in his chair and continued to scan through video footage.

Joshua made no comment. He did not need to. He had no love for Phineas, yet had always treated him respectfully.

*The boy who always treats everyone respectfully, even Phineas, had slapped Ali across the face.*

I was almost done waiting for Joshua, too.

## ALERIA

When I sloshed out of the tub and entered my room, there were four handmaidens waiting to dress me in a beautiful gown. I tried not to sigh. It seemed *modesty* and *queen* were diametrically opposed.

"Tyran, you mind?" I asked, wanting him to leave the room.

"Not going anywhere." He scrutinized my handmaidens suspiciously and strolled towards the window. He turned his back, but his body language said he was not going anywhere.

"So, for what am I being dressed for?" I was trying to sound regal, but I think I had only accomplished awkward. Pretty sure I'd used the word "for" twice for no reason.

"There will be a cocktail reception after opening statements in the tribunal. His Majesty has requested your presence," one of my handmaidens answered.

"Of course." I held out my arms and allowed them to primp, powder, prod, and poke me. In the end, I was in a crimson, floor-length beaded gown, with a slit halfway up my thigh. It was off the shoulders with inlaid meshy material that covered some of my cleavage, making me feel a little more comfortable. Then I was draped in jewels and a crown that rivaled anything shown at Oscar time on the red carpet.

Once the handmaidens had finished, they stood there, but Tyran shooed them away. "I will escort you to the door; as soon as you are with my brother, I will clean up, then return and meet you at the reception."

"You are taking the 'don't leave her side' rather seriously, aren't you?"

He put his thumb under my chin and tipped it up so I would

look at him. He had the same blank expression that always made me wonder what he was thinking. "Not seriously enough. Are you ready?"

"Why do I have a terrible feeling about this?"

He held that same expression. "Do not trust any of them. And know I am not belittling you. Play the part of the submissive wife and smile. They will bait you. And..." he dropped his hand. "Sharing blood between vampires is not done lightly. It is saved for mates."

I stopped breathing and took a half-step back, feeling like this was way too intimate. "So..." I stopped when I wasn't sure which direction to take my questioning.

Tyran sighed and looked uncomfortable. "Our circumstances are uncommon, but acceptable in our world. I wanted you to be aware in case one of the delegates pushes you to use your ability. Under no circumstances should you come in contact with their blood. Having a connection to you would be a political advantage."

"How? If they don't drink from me?"

"*You* would feel connected to *them* and that could compromise your judgment. You know the connection is much stronger between vampires than it is to humans. You can drink from a familiar and never regard them again unless you *want* to. There is no comparison. Think about it. You have hated the connection you've had to me after trying to kill me. You still hate it." Tyran smirked like he did whenever he had some sort of insight about me.

He wasn't wrong. I searched the floor while I framed my next question. "Did you force-feed me back then because you needed to save me for the sacrifice? Or was there a drive to complete the connection with me?"

Tyran's eyes became harder. "That doesn't matter now. I

simply wanted you to be made aware. Let us go." He held out his arm for me to take. *Hot-cold-hot-cold-hot-cold.*

I took his arm, but I squeezed it, feeling frustrated. We walked into the main bedroom, though just short of the doors, he stopped and spun me around, holding me by the upper arms. "Do not walk in there and do something reckless because you are angry with me."

"I won't," I replied, but my voice came out petulant and haughty.

Tyran stared at me for a long moment, then seemed to wilt a little. His voice sounded rough. "You are my penance. That is all I will say."

My mind was swimming with questions, but it was clear he was done speaking. He dropped his hands from my arms and opened the doors. The guards snapped to as we passed.

I concealed my sigh. "Just a party," I repeated to myself —*more like a den of poisonous vipers.*

Shoving down my nerves, I took Tyran's arm, nicely this time, as we walked into what felt like my doom.

12

ADDRESS

ALERIA

Pageantry was the only word that could describe what I saw the moment the ballroom doors swung wide for me. I was announced, and every head turned, every eye on me. Stepping into the crowd, I fixed my face with a mess-with-me-and-I-will-smile-while-I-stand-on-your-corpse type of grin, nodding to all the onlookers as I passed them by. I tried to keep my air of confidence steady as I desperately searched for Bowen in the crowd. I felt like I'd been dumped into a tank of eels, and they were slithering all around me—all whispers and touches.

When I found him, he was already moving towards me, and I was immediately steadied. Bowen was dressed in a tailored suit that looked turn of the last century. He wore a blue sash with the coven crest embroidered on it that intensified the color of his eyes.

He took both my hands and leaned in to my ear. "You look stunning."

I smiled shyly, feeling awkward. "Thank you. You look..." And then my desire got the better of me; I wished we could finish what we'd started a little while ago. I looked at his neck and wanted nothing more than to taste him right here and now. My heart was a drum beating against my ribs. I licked my lips, and Tyran's words sank in.

All I wanted was to close the loop and taste his blood. I had only had Bowen's blood twice, and both times I'd been on the cusp of death. Once, when I'd been turned, and the other when I almost died of Aurora. The more I desired intimacy with Bowen, the more I wanted to share blood, as well as my body. This spark, or more like inferno, made me realize how little I knew about the vampire world in which I was suddenly a queen.

Bowen narrowed his eyes and simply whispered, "Yes." The single word dispelled my nervousness and drew me in again, only to be shattered by the realization that I was standing in a room full of people, most of whom were sizing me up. When he put his hand to my cheek, I leaned into it.

At that moment, a gentleman standing a little too close crooned a little too effeminately, "Oh! Do you see how in love they are?! I had heard the rumors! Fabulous! Wunderbar!" He was holding a handkerchief over his mouth, and then he fanned it as if holding back emotion.

He had wavy, dark hair combed forward like one would see in the Napoleonic era. In fact, his coat with tassels and cords reminded me of just that. He wore dark slacks instead of the knickers and tights from that time period. His large hazel eyes raked over me and told me that he was very intelligent, despite his foppish show.

Standing next to him was a severe-looking woman in a sheer white gown with golden embroidery. Her lavish hairstyle was embellished with feathers and pearls on strings that were woven in dizzying patterns. She flipped open a fan and stared at us as if we weren't standing five feet away. "She is adorable, but it's a pity he didn't accept the offers of marriage. She's young and can't have much value."

"You didn't hear?" A tall man with a hooked nose and the sharpest cheekbones I'd ever seen leaned to her ear and spoke in a stage whisper. "She's a Seer. The last of the Lux Casta that Agrona had scoured the planet for."

The severe woman turned back and reassessed me. "She is a new poppet then, isn't she?" She ran her tongue across her lips as if salivating, making me squirm.

I took a step back, placing Bowen between me and the grouping.

Each of them spoke as if I couldn't hear them, and no one approached. I felt Bowen's fingers breeze over my cheek again. My eyes met his. He gave me an encouraging look. "Focus on me," he murmured.

I took a deep breath, steeling myself to the fishbowl I was standing in. As quietly as possible, I asked, "When someone calls for a tribunal, do they normally come so quickly?"

A woman interrupted, "Of course not, darling. We are here for *you*." She stepped up and ran her icy fingertip up the back of my arm and played with the sheer material at my shoulder, touching the farthest edge of my collarbone.

She had full lips that were painted red and a hint of olive tone under her pallor. She was all soft curves and sensuality. The sides of her dark hair were shaved short, and the top section was longer and wavy and tied into a knot that accentuated the short sides. Her black gown had streaks of color the same shade as her green-blue eyes. I couldn't decide if she looked artsy or fierce.

"Tamara, this is my wife, Aleria."

"Yes, nice to meet you." She grinned at Bowen. "She looks simply delicious. Did she really keep her powers after she was turned?"

Bowen's posture straightened. "I thought you had stopped participating in tribunals and other political affairs?"

"How does it work? Do you need to touch me? Do you need to look deep into my eyes?" Tamara fluttered her lids suggestively.

"This is not the time or place," Bowen warned.

She pouted. "But I'm already bored, and all I have heard are the opening statements. And look at the familiars you have provided. None of them look as good as you." She motioned to the corner of the room. There were over a dozen familiars all dressed in white with red ribbons tied around their wrists or necks.

I watched as a vamp filled his champagne glass from a fountain and motioned for a familiar. She offered her wrist, and he sliced it with a blade, draining her blood into the sparkling wine in the glass. Once it had reached his desired mixture, he sealed the wound with his tongue. Others were feeding very openly on the Victorian-style chairs and couches.

Tamara ran her fingers down my arm, and my attention snapped back to her. Bowen's face was pleasant, but it was evident that she'd been pushing him while I'd been staring at the familiars.

"Come on, darling. Oh, it's blood, isn't it? Just take a little taste and tell me my fortune." With preternatural speed, she had cut a small slice on her wrist and offered it up to me.

I stepped back. "Ummm. Thank you, but I can't."

Bowen opened his mouth, his face no longer a mask of patience, when Tyran arrived. He stood behind Tamara and kissed her neck. "I'm afraid you can't treat my new sister like a parlor trick." She melted a little when his hands slid around her waist.

"I was hoping you were here," she purred.

"You should have told me you were coming," Tyran teased and scolded, his lips on the hollow behind her ear. She arched backwards towards him, and I wondered, because there was so much heat between them, if her clothes were going to spontaneously burn from her body.

Tyran glanced up at Bowen. "I assume I have the evening off? I have some...catching up to do with old friends."

"Of course," Bowen replied.

"Come on, I'm hungry. Then I think you need to be spanked...or something." Tyran shot me a devilish look as he hurried her off towards the familiars.

"What just happened?" I asked Bowen.

Bowen was shaking his head and grinning. "He was protecting you, but I don't think he is suffering very much. When Tamara sets her sights on something, she usually gets what she wants. Be careful of her."

Tamara was right about one thing: everyone was here for me. As I listened, I found almost every conversation was about me and not the trial. I caught snippets of rumors: "she is a Watcher spy," "I want to keep her as a pet," "she is bedding both of those brothers," "Lux blood is the most desired substance, imagine how she would taste now," and the list went on and on.

Then I felt the chill of an oncoming vision. Fear shot through me. "Bowen, one's—"

I heard Bowen shout Tyran's name, and Tyran became nothing but a blur leaving the room.

Then everything went dark.

The lights were flickering. I was flat on my back, the side of my head throbbing. I felt someone grasp my ankles and start climbing up my body, clawing me as they did so. I raised my heavy head, feeling woozy, and watched two glowing green-blue eyes get closer. The lights flickered again, and I could see that it was Tamara. She had a giant axe lodged in her back and was dragging her lower body like her spine had been severed. There was a trailing river of blood behind her—she was bleeding out.

She grabbed my hair and yanked, making my neck available. "It's either you or me, girlfriend," she said. Then she bit into my neck so hard that tears came to my eyes, but I couldn't fight her. My heart started to strain, but she didn't care—she was going to take it all.

## GABRIEL

"Dude is stronger than I thought he would be," remarked Ian.

Phineas was strapped to a chair and dosed with truth serum in the next room. His sweaty, black hair was plastered to his skull, and there was no sign of him breaking any time soon.

"We need to switch the meds. I suspect he has been made immune to what we have been giving him." I did not like giving him anything stronger, but I was certainly committed at this juncture.

"He knows you took him. He doesn't think you'll cross that line."

"*I* will," Joshua spoke quietly from the back of the room. His eyes had not left the surveillance screen since we had brought in Phineas.

I chose my next words carefully. "Do you have recent concerns about Phineas?"

Joshua's eyes went from the video, to me, then back to the video. There was not a single tell in his posture. "I will question him. If you like."

## ALERIA

My eyes opened, and I flailed. I heaved a breath and realized it was Bowen restraining me. I stopped fighting and smiled up at him, so he released me.

Blood was dripping down my face and under my chin. I was on the floor, in Bowen's arms, in front of everyone, but I didn't care. There'd been one instance that felt as if my dream was being invaded, but then it stopped abruptly.

Despite the terrifying vision, I couldn't help but feel joy when I looked up at him. "I remember."

"You saw something," he confirmed.

My eyes roamed the circle of the room. Staring didn't begin to describe it. All eyes were glowing, and locked on me. Glasses of blood wine hung halfway to lips. If I hadn't been so disoriented, I would've felt self-conscious. I wanted to speak with Bowen without everyone listening in. "Can you get me out of here?"

Without a word, he stood with me in his arms and headed for the doors. I started to straighten my body; I could walk on my own, but he squeezed me closer.

Tamara approached and reached out with a handkerchief she'd pulled from her black beaded bag. "Let me help!" she offered in a gracious tone.

Bowen angled me away from her. "Thank you, but I have her."

Her hand dropped to her side, and she looked as if her prize had been snatched away. Then I realized it had been—my blood. Her eyes followed the trail of it down my cheek and my chest.

When Bowen reached the doors, he turned to the crowd. "I trust all of you will have a wonderful evening. I will join you tomorrow afternoon for the proceedings. Good night."

Cadeyn closed the doors behind us.

"Cadeyn, summon more familiars. Have them bring more wine and anything else our guests may need. And get my brother in there. No one disturbs us for the rest of the night."

"Yes, King Belenus," Cadeyn answered as he bowed his head.

Once we were out of earshot, I whispered, "It doesn't take me that long to recover."

He grinned, but kept his eyes straight ahead. "They don't know that."

"Won't that make me look weak?"

"Give them something to chatter about."

There were no protests. I liked the thought of having him completely to myself for a whole night. He'd been constantly working, trying to put out all of the fires from his weeks away.

When we entered our room, he gently eased my feet to the floor, but I kept my arms looped around his neck.

"Is my blood that different from other vampires? The way everyone was looking at me..."

Bowen closed his eyes, as if experiencing it again. "Yes," he replied, his voice rough. When he opened them again, they were glowing. "Imagine the difference between human and vampire blood. That—tenfold."

GABRIEL

Joshua sat across the table from Phineas with the ice-cold calm of a seasoned interrogator. He had been asking Phineas questions for five hours. Phineas was finally showing the first signs of cracking. His hands were cuffed in front of him, and he sat with his shoulders hunched in the chair.

Joshua asked again, "What did you do, Phineas? We know you are working with someone outside of the Watchers."

Phineas smacked his lips when he moved his parched mouth.

Joshua stood abruptly and left the room. Phineas flinched at the sudden movement. It was then that I realized that Phineas feared Joshua—I wanted to know why. Phineas had never feared him before.

Joshua entered the command room. "He's almost there...I think."

"You are doing well. Keep pushing." I tossed him a bottle of water from the cooler, water droplets flying. Joshua nodded and returned to the room.

Phineas' eyes were fixated on the water. Joshua opened it and acted as if he was going to take a sip. Halfway to his mouth, Phineas rasped, "Please."

Joshua placed it on the table, just out of reach. Phineas stared at the condensation leisurely dripping down the side and smacked his lips again.

Joshua pushed, "Give me something—anything."

"You will kill me," Phineas choked flatly with his dry throat.

"I won't."

"You will," retorted Phineas who stared at the video camera that was providing me the feed.

I stood in anticipation.

Ian spoke. "Gabriel, I have a bad feeling about this."

I glanced at Ian. "Me, too."

Phineas finally said, "An address. I gave them an address."

"What address?" asked Joshua.

"You know the one."

The moment recognition set in on Joshua's face, I ran for the interrogation room, hoping I would not be too late.

13

VOW

ALERIA

I stepped out of my bathroom in a towel. My handmaidens had been here. My bed was turned down, and there was beautiful lingerie spread out on the duvet: a black, lacy baby doll with a knee-length matching robe.

At this time of day, I would've normally been in my "daytime clothes," but it seemed that the rest of this particular evening was going to be different than normal.

Once I was dressed, I wrapped the robe around me; the baby doll top barely reached the top of my thighs and didn't cover my underwear. I took a deep breath and opened the door to the shared bedroom. Bowen had damp hair and was bent in front of the fireplace, coaxing the fire to life, dressed in a t-shirt and pajama pants.

My stomach did a little flip-flop. I was suddenly nervous—really nervous. Yesterday, somehow waking up next to him and getting physical had felt natural. Now, I'd had time to get anxious. He placed the stoker into a holder and turned to see me standing silently in my doorway.

He smiled, but his eyes were so sultry that the only word in my vocabulary seemed to be: sex. He embodied it at the moment. It was coming off of him in waves. Sex. Sex. Sex.

I was afraid that my brain had spontaneously developed Tourette syndrome, and I was going to blurt out the word. Suddenly, my knees felt like they were going to give out, and I clamped my hand over my mouth.

He looked a little amused and way more at ease than me.

"Yesterday made me feel like you are ready. Am I correct in assuming this? I won't push you."

My heart picked up the pace, and I broke his intense gaze. "Tyran said that you took me to the church the other night for reasons other than to show me the place of the Coronation."

"I did...and yes." He slowly walked towards me like a predator on the prowl, but this time I wanted to be caught. Although, a little piece of me was really freaked out, and it made me want to bolt back into my bedroom and hide from the all-too-beautiful boy in front of me.

He ran his fingertips over my cheek and down my neck, and I shivered. All thoughts of hiding in the other room vanished.

"What did you show me?"

The playfulness left his eyes, and he looked at me quite seriously. "You said you wanted to be married in a church with a pastor. I wish you remembered." The seriousness was replaced by a hint of sadness.

"We were married by a pastor?"

He shrugged a little. "A priest. The best I could do."

I stood on my tiptoes and pulled him down to kiss me. "What type of vows did we exchange?"

"I picked something traditional that I thought you would like."

"Do you remember any of them?"

He kissed me again and pushed the robe from my shoulder. "I remember all of them; would you like to hear them?"

I nodded mutely.

He kissed my shoulder again. "I, Belenus, take you, Aleria Elizabeth, to be my beloved wife, to have and to hold you."

Pausing, he pushed the robe off my other shoulder and trailed kisses to my neck. "To honor you, to treasure you, to be at your side in sorrow and in joy."

He pulled the tie on the robe, and it slid down to the crooks in my elbows. "In the good times, and in the bad, and to love and cherish you always." He took my hand and placed it on his chest. "I promise you this from my heart, for all the days of my eternal life."

My breath came out shaky. "That's beautiful."

He grinned. "I found it on the Internet."

I cough-laughed. "Way to kill the mood." I pushed at him, and he stepped back and chuckled.

He puckered his lips, thinking. "I almost wrote vows, but I was surprising you. I didn't want you to feel..."

"Angry that I hadn't had time to write mine?"

"Yes."

"What would you have said?" I inquired.

He scooped me up and sauntered over to the fireplace, stepping over the abundance of pillows and blankets and soft things on the floor. He dropped my feet onto the hearth so that I was standing eye level with him.

"I, Belenus, vow to love you for the rest of my days. First for your mind." He framed my face with his hands and tilted it so he could kiss my forehead.

"For your spirit and for your heart." He ran his hand up my back, parallel to my spine, and arched me backwards, pressing his ear to my heart, his breath uneven.

After a moment, he righted me, and had that same feverish look on his face that I'd seen yesterday. He picked me up again and stepped into the ring of pillows on the floor.

I swallowed. "The vows?" I urged.

"I swear to worship, every curve..." He stripped off my robe and tossed it to the floor. He bent and kissed the little freckle between my breasts. "And every freckle..."

I grabbed the bottom hem of his t-shirt and helped him with it over his head. I wrapped my arms around his torso and pressed my cheek to his bare chest, breathing him in. He smelled like soap and desire. I knew my eyes were glowing; I wanted to close the loop and drink from him so badly, I couldn't think straight.

He pulled me down onto the pillows. "I vow to be completely yours."

And at that moment, he offered me his neck. I kissed him first, sliding my tongue into his mouth. He kissed me back urgently, and then offered his neck once more.

And that was when I finally bit him. The taste of his blood was like unlike anything I'd ever experienced. I had tasted him twice before, but I'd been dying—literally—in both instances. This was different.

This was for bonding, but it seemed there was more to it. I didn't know if it was because he was my sire or half-angel or... or...I drank deeply, unable to think about anything beyond how amazing it felt.

His hands were on my thighs, his fingers pressing into them almost painfully, but still I wanted more. Once I was done, I offered him my neck, and he immediately rolled us over and drank from me.

Trailing his tongue down my body, he stopped every few inches to kiss whatever patch of flesh he was exploring. He pushed up the baby doll and kissed above my hipbone. I gasped. Liking my reaction, he kissed his way to my bellybutton, then stopped. His warm breath spilled across my skin. He ran his hands up the insides of my thighs.

Rolling me onto my side, he kissed the backside of my hipbone. I started trembling. Then, he rolled me onto my stomach and kissed the small of my back, his lips lingering on my birthmark. He proceeded to kiss the dimples on my lower back. "I vow to love every dimple," he breathed.

Still on my belly, he slowly ran his hands up my sides and eased down on top of me. He reached up and folded his arms around mine, taking my hands in his as he nestled his face next to my neck.

"I pledge to make you my partner and share my heart and body with you as your friend, your lover, and your husband until we cease to exist on this earth."

I turned my head so I could see his face in my peripheral. "I love you." It sounded like a lame offering after everything he'd just said.

He allowed me to roll on my side, our faces so close I was breathing his air. A sigh escaped his lips that seemed like relief.

"What?" I asked.

"I love hearing you say it."

"I promise you will hear it a lot more. I won't clam up," I joked, referencing his comment yesterday. I wrapped my arms around his neck and kissed him so hard, it felt as if I might break him.

There was a trace of worry in his eyes. "What else am I not remembering?"

He closed his eyes and exhaled. "I had asked you one question. The same one I have asked you in the past—if you chose me. That if Joshua arrived at the door and begged for your forgiveness, you would still choose me. I am offering you everything. My soul is damned, so I don't have one to offer you, but everything I do have is yours. I lay myself open for you."

I looked at him and how painfully vulnerable he was being. He made it look easy, but now, for the first time, I could see that he was being open for *me*—not because it was his nature. He was different with me, and I hadn't noticed it until now.

I placed his hand on my heart so he could feel how steady it was beating when I said the words, "I choose you—no matter what. I choose you. I will love you completely until I am nothing but ash."

He kissed me then, withholding nothing.

The power of the ocean was unleashed, crashing over me.


GABRIEL

I could hear Joshua before I entered the room.

"Why? Why would you do it? They are innocent!"

I jerked the door open. Joshua had Phineas against the wall, feet dangling.

Phineas snarled, "Because you are his spawn! He killed my parents!!"

"I didn't ask for this. I didn't want to be turned. I was helping a stranger, and I paid for it with my life. I hate Tyran!"

"Joshua, let go of him!" I ordered.

Phineas was frothing at the mouth, his anger very thick. "I will see all of you leeches burn. Including your bitch ex-wife. All of you!!"

Joshua made a motion with his hand, and Phineas instantly fell silent and went limp. Joshua dropped him to the floor.

I started. "What d—"

Joshua looked at me, and the hatred in his stare stopped me

short. "You don't understand what he did. He couldn't be trusted ever again."

"We do not kill our people! That is what makes us different!" I ran my hand through my hair and paced. Never had I allowed something to get so out of control.

Joshua gasped, and his gaze became distant. He staggered backwards a couple of steps. It was clear that this was not about killing Phineas.

"What is wrong?"

Joshua's face was in torment. He rubbed at his eyes and laughed ironically. "He finally has her in his bed." He heaved a few breaths, his eyes darting around the room. "It's over. She committed herself to him."

"What did you expect? You served her up to him on a platter!" I retorted, incredulous.

"I'm going out." Joshua stormed towards the door.

"Where are you going?" I barked. "You just—"

"Out!" cried he, arms flung wide as if cursing the sky. As he fled, he ran into Ian, who it seemed had purposely gotten in Joshua's way. Joshua shoved past him and sped into the night.

I stood in the silent room, listening to my breath and Ian's.

"I'm surprised she lasted weeks," commented Ian.

We both turned at the same time and stared at Phineas' crumpled body.

"He drove her out; why is he this upset? And what address would push him to kill Phineas?" Not waiting for Ian to comment, I headed to Joshua's room.


ALERIA

The door burst open. "Good afternoon, brother." Tyran's grin was wider than usual.

Bowen pulled the covers over both of us and looked at me in our hiding place.

"I see it's a *very* good afternoon."

Bowen was annoyed. "Proceedings don't begin for another hour." He pulled me closer, nuzzling his face into the small of my neck.

I whispered conspiratorially, "If we pretend we aren't here, maybe he'll go away."

Tyran jumped onto the end of the bed. "I would love to let you two continue canoodling, but King Vladimir decided to show his face late last night. It seems he is in a tizzy about something."

Bowen flipped the covers down to look at Tyran. "Do I know what he is upset about?"

"The Strigoi."

"Why is he *here?*"

"I suppose he is covering his bases since he let the infestation get out of control—of course, we don't know that. You are on the council of elders. He will need to have support from some of you, but also, you have married a Watcher. He was complaining about an increased activity of the Concilium on his land."

Bowen sighed and turned his head to look at me.

"Do you want me to go with you?" I asked.

"Let me see what he really wants. I'll send for you if I need your expertise." Bowen got up and walked shamelessly to the bathroom. I, on the other hand, tucked the blankets tightly around me since I was being left alone with Tyran once again.

Tyran grinned like the Cheshire cat. "Sooooo. You look well-sated. Last n—"

I cut him off before he could make more comments I didn't

want to hear. "Did Phantasos try to break into my vision during the reception last night?"

Tyran's grin vanished. "Yes."

"He risked it even while imprisoned?"

"Yes." He got off the bed and wandered over to the fireplace and stared at the ash.

"Why?"

"He has nothing to lose. He's dead. If you ever end up being called before a tribunal, make your peace. They are a formality."

"What am I missing? Why would he risk it?"

Tyran met my gaze, and there was no mask to his pain. He was going to lose his cousin. "I can think of no reason great enough to risk what he has. I am sorry."

He rested his hand on the mantel and seemed to sag under the weight of his sudden grief. I sat there on the bed, feeling the depth of his torment through our blood bond.

I pulled the sheet from the bed and draped it tightly around myself two times, then tossed the excess over my shoulder, effectively making the sheet a toga. I approached Tyran slowly. When I reached him, he turned his face away so I couldn't see it.

Biting the inside of my lip and cursing myself a little, I ducked under his left arm and wrapped my arms around his torso. Part of me couldn't believe I was consoling him, but he was about to lose some of his family.

When I squeezed him, he shuddered, and then I felt the sob in his chest reverberate in mine. The thin control he had failed; he hung onto me and grieved, his tears expressing sorrows I had not thought him capable.

GABRIEL

I made a quick survey of Joshua's room and was not sure as to what to look for—something to explain his erratic behavior. When nothing was obvious, I divided the room up into a grid and started systematically searching. Then something rose in my memory: the exact moment to which I could attribute Joshua's behavioral difference. It had not occurred to me until now.

I began tossing the room, searching for the small padded envelope not much bigger than a postcard that Joshua had received when we met Samael in the penthouse. I recalled the look of confusion on Samael's face when he had discovered it in his bag. I searched the mattresses, pillowcases, air vent, inside shoes—every possible hiding place.

I sat on the bed, defeated, staring at everything I had strewn over the floor. Joshua had departed in such a hurry, he had left his jacket behind. Dropping on a knee, I combed through the interior pockets. I freed a minuscule thumb drive and folded postcard. On the blank side of the postcard, the word "silence" had been written. I flipped it over and felt as if my blood had gone cold. It read: "Visit Historic Campbell, California." There was a collage of pictures: a historic home with the thatched roof, a quaint shot of downtown Campbell, and the water tower that loomed over the whole downtown area.

Taking the flash drive that had accompanied the postcard, I immediately headed for one of the laptops. In under a minute, I had pulled up the video file.

Shaky footage from within a car began. I froze; I recognized the house. I had spent thirteen days hovering in and around this home—Aleria's family home. Ali's mother walked outside to pick up the mail. She stood there and rifled through the envelopes, then strolled back inside, unaware that she was being filmed. Then the scene cut to a soccer field. It did not take me long to identify Aleria's younger brother. He had grown considerably.

At that moment, an electronically altered voice began speaking over the images. "If you want to save her family—*your* family—release her. Put her on the throne. Tell anyone—they die. Tell her—they die. If there is any hint that she knows—they die. She has two weeks to take her place with the Andraste. You have twenty-four hours to break off your relationship, or there will be consequences."

There were images of Aleria's parents at the grocery store, at their jobs, and every other aspect of their lives. Whoever this was, they were thorough.

Ian cursed from the other room.

Clenching my fist around the postcard, I swiveled around to look at him through the open door.

"Gabriel, when Josh left, I may have..." Ian held up Joshua's phone connected to his laptop. That explained Ian stepping in Joshua's path as he tried to leave.

"What made you do that?"

"When Josh returned from dropping off the Strigoi, it took him longer to get inside the van than it should have. I didn't think much of it at the time. But then I remembered that he watched something on his phone, and I swear he lost the color in his face, if that's even possible. I shouldn't have lifted it, but..."

"He just executed someone without explanation. It is fine. Have you found anything?"

"I pulled everything off the phone since we were in Romania. There are two encrypted files. I'm cracking them now."

Ian's computer beeped. I joined him in the other room and

stared down at the laptop. It was the older of the two files. Ian hesitated with his finger on the mouse.

"Do it," I ordered and sat down next to him.

"I think this is what he watched in the van right after the exchange." He opened the file. Footage of a soccer field came into view. The field flooded with players. The video clicked, and we were suddenly seeing everything through a rifle scope, yet there was still sound. The cross-hairs were locked on a jersey marked with the last name "Hayes." Aleria's brother ran the ball back and forth, warming up.

The altered voice we had heard on the last video spoke, "You were warned."

The gunman fired, and Aleria's brother twisted awkwardly and fell into a heap on the ground. I stood, feeling adrenaline surging through my veins. The marksman shot the next kid who went to Cameron's aide through the leg and then again at someone else.

A coach was screaming, "Run!! Run!!" and thrashing his arms. He grabbed onto Cameron and dragged him behind some benches. He ripped off his sweatshirt, and it looked like he was giving medical treatment.

The voice came on again. "Tell no one. Put her on the throne." Then the screen went black.

Before I could open my mouth, Ian was online with the search window reading: "School shootings California."

A dozen articles popped up about a shooting a couple of weeks ago. Three injured. No deaths. I dropped into a seat, feeling overwhelming relief.

The encryption program beeped again; the other file was ready. "This was two hours later. So, he watched it right before we got back to the penthouse," said Ian, his voice shaky.

He double clicked the file. It was a dark room—a hospital

room, and Aleria's mother was curled asleep in a chair next to the gurney. A pistol with a silencer was raised into the frame. The intruder pushed some hair back from her face with the barrel. The video went dark for a split-second, and when it came up, I feared my heart would stop. Video was being taken through a telephoto lens. Uriel was walking back and forth through a room with my daughter fast asleep in her arms. Uriel rubbed the baby's back, appearing to be singing.

The voice came on again. "There will be no more warnings." The screen went black.

Instantly, I had the phone at my ear. "Uriel, you need to get out. Your location has been compromised. I am sorry. I should not have contacted you."

"I'm already in a new location. We're fine. External security sensors were tripped after we talked. I'm not taking any chances. Be well."

"Be well."

She disconnected.

I sat stricken, unable to process all of the directions in which I needed to run.

# 14

## LOGICAL

GABRIEL

Sitting in a midnight room, I waited.

The door silently opened. He must have sensed me waiting in the dark. Joshua paused in the darkest shadow and leaned against the wall.

"You waiting up for me?"

"Yes." I leaned forward in my seat.

He stepped into the moonlight. There was blood on his shirt. "Did she live?"

His expression became clouded, and then he examined his collar. Joshua's exhale came in a burst. He turned towards the door as if thinking about leaving. "I fed. I didn't kill anyone." Then he became deathly still. After sixty seconds of listening to the wall clock ticking, he approached and dropped into the seat across from me. His footsteps were uncharacteristically heavy. "You know."

"You should have trusted me."

"I didn't believe the first message, and I got Cameron and

those other boys shot. Ali would've never forgiven me if he'd died. I wouldn't have forgiven myself. I couldn't risk it."

"She deserved to know."

"She would've been on the first plane to the States."

"Or she would have returned with Belenus and pretended until we rooted out those responsible."

"Whoever this is has both Watchers and members of Bowen's coven in their pocket. Ali's files are sealed. Most everything on the Internet about her has been scrubbed or purposely falsified to mislead. They got to Phineas, one of the few people outside our circle who knows where she came from.

"I realized that making it look like she was a traitor and having an affair was their first attempt to ruin my marriage and send her back to France." His voice became hoarse. "When that didn't take, they went for our family," he choked, "I have gone over and over this. They would've known if she'd been faking it —they would've known."

I had no false hope to give him.

Tears streaked down his cheeks, and he did not bother to wipe them away. "Part of me is so angry with her for believing that I would turn on her like that."

"You were convincing."

"Then I think of the look on her face after I'd slapped her. And that the last thing she did was leave *me* here with you so *I* wouldn't be alone. She was more than hurt when she left—she was terrified of going to that coven."

"Terrified?"

"She was having nightmares. She spoke in her sleep. She said, 'Don't make me go; death is waiting for me.'"

"She told you that the dream was about the coven?"

"No. She told me the dream was nothing. But I tasted the fear in that dream, and it was the same fear she had every time anyone spoke of the coven. The same fear she had when she left."

"She will be fine," I uttered, yet it was more of a prayer than an assurance.

Joshua stood abruptly and took three measured steps towards his room. He paused, yet did not turn towards me. "I say this because it's the logical choice, not because I have lost her. The artifact. I'll do it. Find out how we destroy it, and I will take care of it. You have a daughter. Ian has parents and a brother. If either Bowen or Tyran try, it could kill Ali and countless others. We have run out of candidates. I'm the logical choice."

"No."

Joshua turned to meet my gaze. "You will agree with me soon." Then he was a blur of movement as he exited.

I sat alone, listening to the clock in the midnight room once more.


ALERIA

The water had gone cold in my bath, but I hadn't bothered to drag myself out of the tub. The bathroom was my only refuge. When Bowen wasn't with me, Tyran was. Occasionally, Morpheus would stop by, but I felt completely isolated.

My mind drifted to the reception and how ethereal and graceful all of the delegates were. I wasn't one of them, and I didn't know if I was capable of ever fitting in. I was genetically different. Maybe it was just time. Maybe I would wear down like sandstone until my sense of compassion was dulled. But the way everyone reacted to me seemed to imply that I *was* different.

The tribunal had started a week ago. Bowen had said the outcome was obvious, but the delegates were stalling. I knew he was anguished about all of this, but he was keeping those emotions wrapped tightly. He spent time with Phantasos every evening, both wanting time with his cousin while he still could, and hoping that it would give him some clarity about the situation. But there was nothing.

I sat up and reached for my towel. Just as I was raising my body from the water, a vision aggressively tunneled into my brain. I gasped from the chill of it and slipped soundlessly beneath the water with no more than a gasp and the horrible realization that Batariel had once more found his way into my head.

Opening my eyes, all I could see was red, red, and more red. Then I realized I was under perfectly still water, and I'd been here awhile. My heart wasn't beating, and the absence of the sensation was excruciating. Before I could move to figure out *why* I was under water, hands plunged through the surface and fished me out.

I was naked and folded over someone's arm when I began to vomit the water from my lungs.

"Let it all out," Bowen urged.

A little bit of my mortification melted away until I heard the next voice.

"I'm sorry, brother. I didn't sense her distress."

A sob welled up inside as I expelled the last of the liquid. Most of my panic was because I feared losing the privacy of the bathroom, too. I wasn't safe anywhere—not even in my own head.

A towel was wrapped around me, but I felt too weak to lift my arms. I must've lost a lot of blood.

"Was he in your head?" Bowen asked.

I wasn't sure if he meant Phantasos or Batariel, so I simply answered, "Batariel and someone else." I had thought Phantasos' incarceration would've stopped him, but I couldn't be sure it was even him.

"What is the last thing you remember?"

I thought for a moment. "Waking next to you at sunset and you leaving for the tribunal."

"It is almost sunrise."

I closed my eyes, feeling violated all over again. "What don't I remember?"

Tyran chimed in, "Just my charming company. You also may have confessed your undying love for me."

"So, *nothing* in other words," I replied deadpan, but I felt like he was both relieved and upset by something I'd forgotten.

"Ouch, I'm wounded." He put his hand over his heart, but it didn't mask his genuine concern. "I'll leave you two." He stepped outside and shut the door, the last expression on his face puzzling.

I sat propped against the tub, swaddled in towels while Bowen started wiping up my blood from the bathroom. It seemed odd to see him doing something as mundane as cleaning, but I guessed he had lived much of his life away from castles and servants.

"You don't want to have someone else do that?" I finally asked.

"I don't want anyone else to have access to your blood."

I nodded. "Do you think that someone else has the Oneiroi's ability?"

Bowen stopped moving and stared at the bloody water receding in the tub. "I don't want to take unnecessary risks," he finally uttered, but he didn't meet my gaze.

He had the same look Joshua always had after there'd been a

close call. I swallowed, feeling guilty—like I was still an albatross, simply hung around someone else's neck.

"Are you regretting that you pursued me?"

His eyes snapped to mine. "No—never." His voice was soft but incredulous. He dropped the washrag into the gurgling tub and dropped on his knees next to me. "Do you know if it was Phantasos?"

"I'm sorry. I can't remember anything for sure."

"I want to know what they are trying to keep you from seeing."

"Maybe they are just messing with me. Keeping you unbalanced."

He smiled thinly and kissed my forehead. "Maybe," he uttered in response, but he didn't believe it.


GABRIEL

"Have you heard from Ali? Did that letter get through?" asked Ian, looking up from a pile of books.

"No. It was a long shot."

Joshua came up the stairs, his lips thin with a frown. He was back to saying nothing but what was absolutely necessary.

Glancing around the third floor research library of the bookstore in York, I heaved a sigh. This place was full of ghosts. Winslow, Peter, and Ali had been here with me on my last visit. Now Winslow and Peter were dead, as well as the clerk. I felt bad that I did not remember his name—Stephen? David? He was the reason Winslow had broken when Taranis had tortured him for information.

Rubbing my eyes, I pushed back from the table and paced the room, stretching my legs and wishing I had gone for a run today.

Ian stood. "Found it."

I quickly circled behind Ian and looked over his shoulder at the text. It was a clear sketch of the completed artifact. There was no mistaking it.

## ALERIA

After the bathroom had been cleaned and I'd showered the bloody water from my body, Bowen had summoned two familiars for me to feed on. I finally felt like myself again. I pulled over my head a long-sleeved jersey knit dress that brushed the floor as I walked in my bare feet. The fabric and fit were comforting.

When I exited my walk-in closet, Bowen and Tyran were talking in hushed tones in the main room. Bowen was angry. I stood and listened, even though I felt a little creepy about it.

"Yes, and you were supposed to be watching her. How could you let this happen?" Bowen spat.

"If you would like me to watch your wife take a bath, then just say the word. I am happy to oblige."

"You should have sensed something wrong."

"I don't have the link with her that you do. You are her blood sire. I haven't tasted her since she was human—unless, of course, you would like me to?"

Bowen fell silent.

The snark drained from Tyran's voice. "I desire no harm to come her way. Please believe me, brother."

"I do," Bowen replied after several bloated seconds had passed by.

I took a deep breath and pushed through the door and was stunned to see how visibly upset Tyran looked. He smirked and squared his shoulders, but not quickly enough. "So, there she is, your beautiful bride. I will take my leave."

"Tyran...I..." I wasn't sure why I stopped him or what I was trying to say. Some sort of encouragement. Suddenly, I was aware that he was as shackled to *me* as I was to *him*.

He nodded and gave me a knowing look, the smirk fading to a wry smile as he exited. Bowen and I were alone.

"You aren't going back to the tribunal?" I asked.

Bowen approached and brushed his fingers over my cheek like he always did. "No. While you were feeding, I requested a recess for the evening."

I exhaled, feeling relieved.

He bent and kissed me, slow and leisurely. The type of kiss that told me this was the first of many. I slid my hands up inside his shirt, wanting all sorts of things I wasn't thinking about thirty seconds ago.

Bowen started walking me backwards as he kissed me hungrily, his hands curved around my backside. When we reached the bed, his hands slid to my waist, and he picked me up and tossed me to the middle of the bed. I sat up, surprised and smiling, and bent my knees while leaning back on straight arms. He prowled forward on his hands and knees so slowly that anticipation bubbled inside me. I curled my toes and drew my legs towards my body, the skirt of my dress spilling in a circle around me.

When Bowen reached me, he grabbed my ankles and slid me towards him quickly. My arms went out from behind me, and I ended up flat on my back. He stopped and watched me for a long, quiet moment—his even breath and soft eyes speaking more than words.

He sat back and rested on his ankles, my feet on either side of him. With some ceremony, he unbuttoned his shirt *slowly*, and tossed it to the floor *slowly*. He took off his belt *slowly* and tossed it over his shoulder. Then he unbuttoned his pants and unzipped them *slowly*, letting them ride low on his hips. I ran my eyes over his body, my eyes lingering on his hipbones, and thought that if he did anything else *slowly*, I might burst.

He broke the silence. "I have been a trifle distracted during the tribunal proceedings. It seems that all I could think about was getting back to you."

He started moving *slowly* again, but this time, I didn't mind. He was pushing up the hem of my dress. He ran his hands back down my legs, and then up again. When his hands reached my inner thighs, I gasped. Then he stopped abruptly, his thumb moving in a circle on my left leg.

"What is this?" He looked confused as he pressed on the hard knot embedded in the muscle of my leg.

"Something I am keeping safe."

"In your thigh?"

I closed my eyes while I organized my thoughts. "I told you about my mission with Petrescu. I took an artifact. It's dangerous if it falls into the wrong hands. It was daylight, and I didn't want someone to find the whole thing in case I didn't make it. I pried the gemstone out and stuck it in my leg. Then I just left it. At first, I thought it might be safer if no one knew, but honestly, I just didn't think about it."

"You didn't tell Gabriel?"

"No. Not even Joshua or Ian. Just you."


GABRIEL

Ian flopped back in his seat. "So, this thing will kill more than the person who tries to destroy it? Whoever has the other missing pieces will die too."

"It appears that way. We can wipe out Semjâzâ without ever facing him."

"That is a win for us, but…"

Joshua spoke for the first time in a day. "Who has the other pieces? Ana has the dagger, but the gemstones are still out there."

"Collateral damage," I responded. "We cannot miss this chance to remove Semjâzâ."

"Even if an innocent is killed? What if someone in our organization has possession of the one of the stones?"

"Our people die to protect humanity all the time."

"Of course," replied Joshua, yet he did not agree.

Joshua had taken the life of an innocent when he was sick, not to mention Phineas a couple of days ago. It was weighing on him. It was also obvious he did not want to be responsible for taking another life unnecessarily. And that was why I had to find another way.

It was the logical choice, but I was truly not ready to let him do it. He had become my family as much as Aleria had.


ALERIA

I woke on my belly to the caress of fingers drifting over my shoulder, down my spine, and circling my birthmark on my lower back. I opened my eyes and took in a very contented-looking Bowen propped on one arm as he traced lines onto my skin. He hadn't noticed that I had woken.

He'd dimmed the lights while I slept. His hair was shining tones of muted gold, his lashes a fine fringe that reminded me of corn silk.

His eyes met mine, and a grin curled the edges of his mouth. "You dozed off on me."

"I sleep better when you're here."

"Tyran said you had been fitful the last few days."

"I haven't been a very good sleeper for a long time." I opened my mouth and closed it, chickening out.

"What is it?"

I pinned my brows together, already feeling his refusal. "I want to speak with Phantasos."

He looked at me blankly and said nothing. His finger stopped moving along my ribs.

"I have some questions only he can answer. I know he hasn't talked to you. Maybe…"

He didn't say anything, but got out of bed and stood there, running both hands through his hair. "If you must do this, let's go now and get it over with."

I scooted to the end of the bed and plucked my dress from the floor, which I had worn for about three minutes, and wiggled back into it. As I quickly padded to the bathroom, I glanced back. Bowen was still standing next to the bed, completely naked, with a far off look that made my stomach twist.

Phantasos wasn't being kept in the main part of the dungeon. He was behind a metal door that I'd passed many times, but never gone through.

We entered what was a more modern-looking area than the rest of the dungeon. Plaster walls in a bluish color and thick metal doors with small, reinforced windows lined the long passageway. They were strong enough to hold an aged vampire, and from the dead silence in the hall, they were soundproof. What looked like monitors were set in the wall next to each door, but were turned off. In front of each door, there were guards with earpieces that reminded me of the secret service, except there was also a high-tech-looking eyepiece over each of their left eyes. I wondered if it was a live feed from the room they were guarding.

Bowen went in to speak with Phantasos alone. While I waited, the vamp in the room to the left was screaming at me and banging his head against the square of glass in the door. Despite my preternatural hearing, I couldn't decipher a word, but I was thankful for that. When the glass became entirely smeared with the blood from his forehead, he stopped. My eyes went back to the square of glass in Phantasos' door. Bowen had been speaking to him for over a minute.

Phantasos got on his knees, crossed his feet, and sat on them. Then he laced his fingers behind his neck. The door buzzed, and the guard pulled it open, letting Bowen out.

"He's ready for you. If he moves, go for the door; don't engage. You are as strong as he is, but he is older. Never underestimate that."

"I won't." I kissed him, and the guard opened the door for me.

Phantasos and Icelos, being twins, looked very much alike. They were tall and slender with chiseled features. Their noses hooked slightly, large grey eyes, just like Morpheus', were their most striking feature. But unlike Morpheus, there was no shred of kindness in them.

I forced myself to be calm. Phantasos had had my blood when I was human and could sense my emotions to a point.

His grin looked more like a snarl. "I must say your visit is a surprise. And what may I do for my Queen? Besides die, of course."

"I don't wish you dead, but I do want you to stay out of my head."

"Not even a little dead?"

"This is the first time I've ever talked to you." I exhaled. He was driving me off course. "I would like to know why you've been in my head. I have the right to know."

His eyes narrowed. "But then it would all be for naught."

"You want to die for this?"

"You have no control in this. You have an empty throne in this matter. Do not pretend you have more power than you do."

"I am not pretending. I know nothing of the power I have. I didn't want it." *And still don't.*

Phantasos looked away.

"Please tell me why," I asked again, humility in my voice.

He looked back at me, but this time, there was pain in his eyes that hadn't been there a moment before. "I can't tell you... *can't.*"

"Would you answer something else then? Were you trying to harm Bowen?"

His voice was a rush. "No. Never. Zahra and Cadeyn's earlier actions were unsanctioned. We want you alive and on the throne. That is all I will say."

I stood there, dumbfounded, and didn't move until I felt Bowen's hand on my elbow.


They wanted me on the throne...

...they had me right where they wanted me.

# 15

## MERCY

ALERIA

"It's time," Bowen uttered, not much above a whisper.

"Are you sure you want me with you? Many of the people in attendance blame me."

"I *need* you with me."

I stuck my feet in black stilettos and smoothed my black dress, feeling nervous. Attending an execution may have been part of the culture, but I didn't understand it.

Over the centuries, crowds had gathered in the town squares to watch people hung at the gallows, be beheaded at the guillotine, burned at the stake, or shot by a firing squad. I would've avoided it, except for the way Bowen's voice broke a little on the word "need." His cousin was being put to death.

I took his elbow, and we walked solemnly away from our chambers. He pulled his arm back and took my hand instead, interlacing his fingers with mine. He squeezed hard once we arrived at the grand entrance of the castle. All of the delegates I'd met before were in attendance.

Phantasos had been given a choice of deaths. Apparently, most chose sunlight. After having experienced that, it would never be my choice. Phantasos opted for the maze. The condemned would face four vamps and various wild animals while being handicapped in some way. If he or she made it through the ever-shifting maze to the safety of the cages on the far side, he or she would be granted the mercy of a quick death and beheaded. Phantasos loved the maze; it didn't surprise me he'd chosen it.

We walked as a group to the dungeons. I was still staggered when the walkway opened up to the cavernous room entirely illuminated by torches and pyres; the maze itself was larger than a football field. Eight giant pillars kept the roof of the immense structure from folding in on itself. A haze caused by the black smoke from the fires surrounded the arena. Dark, chiseled stone walls, heavy with soot, towered four stories above. The damp walls extended into the distance, topped with a walkway that was interspersed with cages and prison cells. Moans and screams underscored the horrific feeling that permeated this place.

We rounded a corner and came to a sitting area with two thrones elevated in the back and a generous sitting area with couches. This was the exact location of my first meeting with Phantasos and his Oneiroi brothers when I'd still been human and imprisoned here.

Bowen and I took our seats. Each of the delegates clumped together with their attendants in excited groupings to watch. Familiars in the same white attire with red ribbons arrived carrying rose-colored champagne on silver platters. Bowen hadn't let go of my hand yet, though he'd been smiling and conversing with the delegates as we'd made our way to the dungeons. If he hadn't been holding my hand, I would've thought him unfazed. His emotions were tightly coiled, and he wasn't allowing me to feel anything through our blood bond.

I searched the gathering for Tyran. After a moment, I noticed him on the periphery, standing in the shadows. When he caught me looking, he slowly made his way towards us. He walked around the back of the thrones and stood between us, resting a hand on each throne. I didn't ask him how he was. He had the identical look Bowen wore.

The moment the last delegate was served a beverage, Phantasos appeared on the elevated slab at the beginning of the maze. He bowed to all of the delegates, then looked stoically at the maze. A horn blast rang out, and the slab slowly tilted towards the maze. Phantasos slid down on his feet with the skill of a seasoned snowboarder.

When he started moving towards the goal, I noticed he was traveling much slower than I would've expected.

I turned to Bowen and whispered, "Why is he moving like that?"

"He has weights on each leg—in the American system...over one hundred pounds on each. The cuffs are rigid and don't allow the wearer to bend the ankles very much. The weight alone wouldn't handicap him enough. Though, the collar on his neck will deliver an electric charge if he tries to jump to the top of a wall."

"Who comes up with this stuff?"

Bowen gave me a tight smile and tilted his head towards a group of the tribunal members. I nodded and shut my mouth. But a moment later, I realized Morpheus wasn't here.

"Where's Morpheus?"

Another gong went off. Bowen jut his chin towards the maze. Four figures emerged from a tunnel at the mid-mark of the maze. Morpheus, Icelos, Zahra, and someone I didn't recognize.

The gong went off once more, and there was a horrific cackling sound reverberating from the tunnel on the opposite side. Over a half dozen hyenas came pouring from the mouth of it, yipping and calling. I remembered from the Discovery Channel that a hyena could crush bone in their jaws.

The maze walls shifted and moved, creating a different set of pathways and dead ends. Phantasos lost some of his progress. He jogged as best he could when Icelos dropped in front of him. Icelos made a single swipe with a sword, then darted away. When Phantasos turned the corner, the entire front of his shirt was red with blood. My heart started hammering. I didn't want to watch this.

It happened again and again. Each time Phantasos turned a corner, there was someone there to take another swipe at him. He was moving slower and slower. The hyenas had picked up on the scent of blood and were howling. Their cacophony was setting my teeth on edge.

Shifting in my seat, it was all I could do to stay; I'd seen enough death in this maze. Bowen squeezed my hand, and I remembered the real reason I was here—to support him.

The maze shifted again, and it set Phantasos back a second time. He was only halfway, and the hyenas were close. He rounded a corner, and Zahra gashed his arm. Phantasos stumbled backwards, lessening the blow, but just as he recovered his footing, the pack of hyenas found him. Phantasos ran, dragging a leg slightly behind him. He flew around a corner and came to a stop. He looked up at Bowen, put his hand over his heart, and nodded. Phantasos had made a wrong turn and was at a dead-end.

He turned and faced the menacing snarls of the hyenas that were circling the only exit and charged them. He killed three before he was on his knees, chunks of flesh being ripped away.

The largest of them came in from behind and had Phantasos' upper arm. He screamed out and his arm went limp; the nerves must've been severed.

I looked away. Bowen squeezed my hand again. I knew it was for support and as a warning. He'd told me not to look away—to fix my face with ice. Queens could not be sickened by an execution.

My eyes returned to the maze. I set my sights a yard away from the action, hoping that no one was scrutinizing me enough to notice. I tried not to notice when the hyenas started pulling him apart and not to notice when he was still screaming. I prayed no one would hear my heart or notice that my throat was so choked that I was incapable of speech.

When my entire body was shaking and I felt as if I couldn't take another moment of the carnage, Bowen stood.

"I grant mercy. This is done."

I caught a glare from Tamara who seemed to be reveling in the bloodshed, but within two seconds, the screaming had stopped. Morpheus had ended his brother's torment. I wasn't sure if what Bowen had just done was protocol, but no one else seemed to have an objection. I gave each member of the tribunal a hollow smile as they filed by.

Bowen remained steady until the second our bedroom door was closed. Then he fell to his knees, and every bit of emotion he'd damned back since Phantasos had betrayed him was unleashed. The only thing I could do was hold onto him and be the lifeline he'd been for me so many times in the past.


GABRIEL

We stared at the color-coded map.

"These are the only locations left?" questioned Joshua.

"Yes," I answered brusquely.

Joshua bitterly snorted. "This is some sort of cosmic joke."

Ian was uncharacteristically quiet.

I continued, "There are not many intact churches left on original ancient settlements. The text indicated that it must be hallowed ground on the original lands established by one of the twelve ancient covens after they had left Israel."

"Dude, the one in Rome has to be the easiest?" said Ian, a question in his voice.

"That land is in the Vatican City; the Concilium would know. If there is a traitor besides Phineas, they could stop us and take the relic for their own purposes."

"I thought you said there was a mosque here." Joshua pointed to the map.

"That is what I was researching a few minutes ago. It was decimated during the conflicts in the 1990s. This is the only location we can go without Concilium interference."

"If I'm not killed on sight," commented Joshua.

"If *we* are not."

## ALERIA

I woke in a silent gasp, sitting up and tearing a hole in the sheet. I shook off the dread of my horrible nightmare, still feeling the rancid breath of the hyena on my face. Hyenas had haunted me in my sleep since the execution. Their yips, calls, and cackles had been the music to which I slept, and it was wearing me out.

The delegates had all left within two days of the execution. Some of them were still requesting to meet with me. Bowen begged off the requests and reminded them that they would be back in a few weeks' time for the coronation. And by that time, our family would have finished grieving and could resume our normal duties. They were promised parties and splendor.

I prayed that the invasion of my head would be over. If not, I was still vulnerable. We weren't sure if Phantasos was responsible for my bathtub incident. He'd appeared to have been sleeping at the time.

After dressing for the day, I parked myself in silence and read books while Tyran was doing something on a laptop. We spent hours this way.

Finally, tossing the book I was reading onto the ottoman, I stood abruptly and set my sights on Tyran. "You are getting me out of this room. I can't take it anymore."

"And where, Your Queenship, am I supposed to take you?"

"On a walk or...or something. Out. I need out," I sputtered.

His eyes narrowed. "How about the training room? I'll even let you try to punch me."

"Try?"

He raised an eyebrow.

"Game on. Challenge accepted," I grinned.

"Go change. I'll rummage through my brother's closet. Do not set foot out that door without me."

I hoped when I left the room that I would leave the oppression of my hyena dreams behind. I ran to my room, so giddy at the thought of getting out, a small squeal may've escaped my lips. I stood by the door in the shared bedroom only seconds later in black yoga pants and a fitted long-sleeved t-shirt while twisting my hair into a messy bun.

Tyran reappeared in sweats and a blue t-shirt that matched his eyes. I jogged in place, holding my arms above my head triumphantly.

He raised a brow. "Maybe we can be dignified until we reach the training room? You are a queen, sissy."

"Am I? Yet, I mean. Before the coronation."

He grabbed my bun and tugged a little. "Close enough. Let us go." He swung open the door to six guards, two more than normal. There was a hitch in his step as we walked past.

I walked next to Tyran, feeling like a cauldron about to bubble over—a happy cauldron. And ignoring the fact that there were more new guards.

Two hours later, he'd knocked me on my back for the millionth time. I felt like the navy blue wrestling mats were my new home. The room was large, with white walls and wooden racks cradling various weapons. Tyran had chosen wooden swords that were dull and flat. He repeatedly smacked me on my backside with the flat side of the sword whenever I missed. What had started as playful had become charged.

"Stop thinking like a Slayer!"

"Why? I don't understand why what I am doing is wrong?"

Tyran turned his back to me, placing his hands on his hips. "A good fighter can switch styles. You've been trained well, but I want more." He turned, looking fierce. I was frustrated that I hadn't been able to land a single blow.

Tyran lunged at me and took a swipe with his practice sword. I spun and avoided the blow, and instead of spinning around to face him again, I backflipped. The moment I popped back up, I launched myself in the air, somersaulting over his head and landing behind him. When I jumped on his back to put him in a chokehold, he elbowed me so hard in the ribs that I knew at least three were broken. He really wasn't playing anymore.

I looped my arm around his neck and squeezed. This wouldn't work on a vampire since we didn't need to breathe; I would have to snap his neck. But the move would work on the Fallen, a Slayer, or a human.

Tyran staggered and fell to his knees when I crushed a vertebra in his neck. At the moment, I thought I had him, but then I felt the practice sword jam into my neck hard enough that I yelped. He would have severed half my neck if the blade had been real. Angry, I let go and fell onto my back, clutching my healing ribs. I glanced at Tyran; he was on his hands and knees, rubbing at his neck. He turned and sat cross-legged so he was facing me.

"You ready?"

"No! I am *not* ready. I want my ribs to heal before you pummel me again."

Disapproval shaped his mouth.

I exhaled. "What just changed? Why are you pushing me so hard? I just wanted to get out of the room for a bit."

Tyran scooted over and lay on his back next to me at arm's length. He had his thinking face on, so I waited and stared at the plaster that was peeling up in the corner of the room to reveal the stone beneath it.

After several minutes of silence, he finally spoke. "I realized that the Fallen have seen you fight. *They* know that *we* know their weakness. You need to be able to surprise them when we engage them again."

"Do you know something that I don't?"

His face looked pinched. "It's coming. Are you going to deny it?"

"Can we think about this after the Coronation? The thought of all of those delegates and a hundred more is almost more than I can bear. Maybe I should have you giving me vampire etiquette lessons. I think I would rather face gun-toting mercenaries."

He looked at me appraisingly. "You ready?"

I groaned. "You are worse than Gabriel." I stopped, rolling my lips inward and biting down until I could taste the metallic tang of my own blood. The ache of missing him seemed to snuff the air from the room. I stared at the ceiling, attempting to stave off all thoughts of Gabriel, Joshua, Ian, and everyone else I'd left behind.

Tyran was suddenly up and offering me his hand—he knew. "Put away your sword. I have some other skill sets to practice."

I nodded, trying to get myself under control again. I relieved him of his sword and took both of them to the wall. When I'd nestled them into their cradles, Tyran asked, "Do you want to call Gabriel? You aren't in prison. It's allowed."

My voice came out choked. "Not yet. I just..."

He paused, reading me, and then proceeded to the center of the mat. "All right, sissy. I want to go through some moves to help you with a larger and more powerful opponent."

"Aren't we already doing that? You have at least eight inches and eighty pounds on me."

"And Semjâzâ?"

I exhaled a shaky breath and prepared to have a few more ribs cracked before he was done with me, but not even broken bones could distract me from the aching loss of my second family.

# 16

# BURN IT

ALERIA

I woke, my nightmare interrupted. I realized that Bowen was in bed next to me. My dream had taken me to some dark place, and I was having trouble shaking it—shadows, metal, and screams. At least there weren't hyenas. My fingers found Bowen's arm under the sheets, and I rolled on my side so that I could watch him sleep.

His eyes were moving feverishly under his lids, and his breath was uneven. I'd never seen him have a nightmare in all the months I'd stayed with him as a human or since we'd been married. His chest heaved, and he started squirming.

"Stop...stop...stop..." he moaned.

I sat up and put my hand on his chest, trying to soothe him. Without opening his eyes, he grabbed my arm so hard that I felt something snap, and then he shoved me, propelling me off the bed and into the wall. It had been so abrupt, that in my groggy state, I hadn't braced or protected myself.

A moment later, Bowen flung the covers back and looked

around, disoriented. When his eyes settled on me several yards away on the floor clutching my arm, he was instantly at my side.

"Please tell me I didn't just do that to you."

"You prefer we have someone else in our bedroom throwing me around?" I tried to keep my tone light.

His eyes tightened even more. "I prefer not to hurt you." He sat back. "In my entire life, I have not hurt someone in my sleep before. Are you all right?"

"I'm fine. Just startled." I rotated my wrist, testing it. It had already healed. "See? Fine."

Bowen exhaled. "I am truly sorry."

"I know. You were dreaming." I crawled onto his lap and looped my arms around his neck, comforting him as best I could. "Was it just a nightmare? Or is someone getting into *your* head now, too?"

I felt a tiny tremor go through him as he recalled his dream. "We were held captive in a small room filled with metal furniture. Semjâzâ had them insert one of those metal creatures back inside me. When they made the incision to insert one inside of you...I..."

There was no need to hear anymore.

I decided to distract him. Grabbing onto his hair, I kissed him and touched my tongue to his lips. His lips parted, a coo escaping, and I could feel the agony of the dream receding in him. His hands were working my tank top up my back as I pressed myself to him even harder.

I pulled away slightly. "Just so you know, this is how I prefer to wake up at sunset."

There was a little bit of a growl when he picked me up and carried me back to bed. I tried not to think about the implications of his dream—I had shared it with him.

I had watched them cut Bowen and put another beastie

inside his belly. I had smelled my blood when they cut me. My throat almost felt sore from all the screaming. I wasn't sure if I'd unknowingly stolen into his dream, or if there were more sinister forces at work.

We had only a few days until the coronation. Dignitaries would start to arrive tomorrow. When the ceremony was completed, we were going to have to deal with the Fallen head on. Bowen had to be worried about it; this was the first sign of true stress I'd seen. Maybe it was a Post-Traumatic Stress Disorder type of response.

Bowen's lips were on my collarbone, and I pushed back the dread, instead concentrating on his lips on my skin and his hands exploring my body, wishing I could block out the rest of the world forever.

GABRIEL

The web of clues we had pinned to the wall seemed to mock me. Strategically, the only singular item they had in common was Aleria. We had not seen Ana since my encounter with her on the rooftop—she was one thread of which I was worried most.

My phone vibrated with an incoming message. I pulled it from my pocket and stared at the screen in disbelief.

It read: "I'VE BEEN THINKING ABOUT U ALL DAY. I'M BEING CORONATED IN 3 DAYS, BUT WON'T HAVE MY FAMILY HERE. I FEEL LIKE A BRIDE WITH NO ONE TO GIVE ME AWAY. I MISS U. —A"

My heart slowed, and I typed a response: "MISS YOU TOO, KID. ARE YOU ALL RIGHT? I HAVE INFORMATION YOU NEED."

The text immediately came back undeliverable.

Clenching my teeth, I stared back at the wall.

"Who was that?" asked Ian.

"Excuse me?"

"You just read a text, and the temperature in the room changed. Just wondering. Never mind." Ian waved a white napkin.

It was at that moment I felt the screen on my phone give way; I had crushed it in my hand. "Ali sent a text."

Both Ian and Joshua stared at me, waiting for more information.

"She is being coronated in three days."

"Did you respond?" asked Joshua.

"It bounced back. I doubt we will hear from her again for a while."

Joshua confirmed, "No, we won't. She lives entirely in the present when she is troubled. We will be nothing but a distant memory."

I glared back at the message through the spider web fracture on the screen. "No, we are heavy on her thoughts." I needed to think clearly. "I am going for a run."

Ten minutes later, the rhythmic pounding of my feet on the asphalt helped me to realign the contents of the wall of clues in my head. I pushed hard, feeling the burn in my legs and lungs, and welcomed the discomfort.

Events that were seemingly disconnected on the timeline were suddenly clear. I stopped, gasping for air; my eyes groped the dark street as a revelation emerged: Batariel.

Taranis had said that Batariel had taken up residence in the castle while he was with our team. I had to search the files for his ability.

I prayed I was not correct. If I was, everything made horrible sense.

ALERIA

I stood hidden behind a pillar and watched the first of the vehicles arrive. It seemed my life was in fast forward. I had lost three days to dress fittings, preparations, and nightmares. Bowen was busier than ever, and Tyran took me seriously regarding the etiquette lessons. He summoned Morpheus to help, partially as a distraction for Morpheus. He was drowning in grief from the loss of his brother, but I was beginning to see glimpses of the real him again.

"Your Highness, break is over," Tyran crooned.

I sighed and unhitched myself from the wall and strolled back inside. I had long skirts on over my yoga pants and had been running through a series of scenarios, many of them involving conversation while dancing. They were having me memorize lines of dialog. Much like Gabriel had before I had faced off with Semjâzâ. They wanted me to appear crafty and not naïve. The last thing we needed was another coven challenging Bowen's rule...and mine.

Something occurred to me. "Hey, can you teach me that throwing me back thing..." I held my hand out in front of me like I was Iron Man and made a pushing motion.

"Sorry, sissy. You were turned by the wrong brother for that. Besides, you can't use it if you are fighting more than one adversary. You lose focus on everything else around you."

Morpheus actually spoke. "You were turned by the right one. You have stealth. It is much more advantageous."

I grinned. "I sense a story in this."

Tyran looked irritated. "Back to work, little one."

Morpheus and I exchanged a look, then returned to training.

After about twenty minutes more of lessons, Tyran pulled his phone from his pocket and grinned.

"Look, Tyran is still capable of doing something other than scolding me."

Tyran ignored me and typed a text. "Morpheus, do you think you can handle babysitting my darling sister?"

Morpheus turned to me. "It is your decision."

"If we can stop with etiquette and go to the training room so I can hit something, you have a deal." I smiled sweetly and batted my lashes.

The corner of Morpheus' mouth curled upwards. "I don't care much for dancing. This way." He paused. "Your brother isn't going to be angry that you left her alone with me?"

"You are the only other person with whom he trusts her."

"Feeling like a piece of property," I muttered under my breath. Before he reached the doorway, I called to him. "Tyran, where are you going, anyway?"

"Tamara arrived and is feeling naughty." He wore his wolfish smile as he sauntered out of the room.

"Sorry I asked," I called after him, but there was something off about the energy rolling from him.

Morpheus started towards the other door, so I jogged to catch up with him. When we were out of earshot, even for Tyran, I asked, "Is something up with Tyran?"

"Why do you ask?" Morpheus evasively responded.

"With the exception of the last two minutes, he didn't make a single sarcastic remark over the last three hours *and* he seemed genuinely upset with me every time I messed up. *That's* why."

Morpheus glanced at me, and then back at the hall we were walking down. "Have any of your dreams been meddled with since—"

I quickly interrupted, not making him say his brother's name. "No, but I shared one with Bowen. I'm not sure how it happened. Has anything like that happened to you?"

"No. Although, you share a blood bond. It is not surprising."

"But it never happened with—"

Morpheus granted me the same kindness. "Belenus is also your sire. You have a stronger connection."

I nodded. We walked the rest of the way in silence.

The moment we entered the training room, I kicked off my heels and shed my long skirt. I preferred to be barefoot in yoga pants over a fancy dress any day. Morpheus shed his jacket and pulled his black hair back into a ponytail.

Quickly, I realized I had become accustomed to fighting tall opponents. Gabriel's six-foot-four frame and Tyran's six-two both towered over me. Morpheus didn't quite reach six feet tall. He was built like a heavyweight boxer with broad shoulders and bulkier arms. His center of gravity was different—a new challenge.

Morpheus was an elegant teacher. He didn't literally break my bones like Tyran had a habit of doing. But he did manage to smack my knuckles with the wooden sword so quickly that not even my eyes could see it.

When my block faltered, he rapped my knuckles again quite hard. I yelped and felt very defeated.

He bowed his head slightly. "It's been an hour. Do you need a break?"

I sat down on the mat and dropped the practice sword in front of me. "I need for people not to be lining up to kill me."

He grinned. "Some of them simply want to use you."

I smiled tiredly. "Can't forget that."

Morpheus looked thoughtfully at me and sank to the floor several feet away. "Ask what you have been wanting to ask for the last hour."

I frowned. "I don't want to upset you. It's not important."

He sat stock-still and stared me down with his stormy grey eyes.

I wilted and shook my head. My voice hesitant, I asked, "How could you hunt your brother?"

He had no reaction to my question, just sat there like granite for almost thirty seconds. "I couldn't have anyone else do it. I convinced the others, and we volunteered. We made sure the cuts were shallow, yet garish, and hoped he would make it to the cages swiftly."

"You are braver than I am." It made sense, but I didn't think I could have done that.

"You would have done the same."

I exhaled harshly, ready to protest, when I felt the comings of a vision. I attempted to say the word "vision," but I wasn't sure if it had actually escaped my lips.

---

I was in a darkened corridor, moving silently. Pausing, I slipped into the shadows as someone approached. Then I wasn't alone. I had a vial in my hand, and I pressed it into an eager grip —Zahra.

I whispered. "Get this into the cup, and you will have everything you want."

"Are you sure? If this doesn't work, I'll be the one running from beasts."

"I'm sure."

Zahra's broad lips twisted into a dreadful grin. A conversation could be heard in the distance. It was Tyran's voice. Zahra sped off, and everything went black.

When I woke, my head was swimming, and it felt nearly

impossible to open my eyes. I was confused and being carried in someone's arms—Morpheus. He always smelled nice, like fresh air and rain and a hint of leather. I realized I was drifting and forced myself to focus.

"I'm awake."

Morpheus stopped and dropped my feet to the floor. The moment he knew I could stand on my own, he stepped back. "Would you like to continue back to your quarters?"

I stood, blinking at him. Fear rose up inside me. My vision had been of Zahra, his sister-in-law. *How would he react to one of his family members betraying the crown yet again?* I swallowed a smile flickering on my face. "Yes."

We started towards my room again.

"Taranis has me paranoid. I felt as if you didn't trust me for a moment." The look on his face was pleasant, but he felt that my surge of fear had involved him.

"I know your limits. You are loyal to me as long as I don't ask you to stand against your family," I stated more bluntly than I'd intended.

He stopped, taking my arm. I looked at his hand, and he dropped it to his side. "Was I in your vision?"

"No."

"My brother?"

"No."

"Then there is no reason to fear me." Again, he was pleasant. He began walking again. When we reached my hall, the guards stood at attention and opened the doors.

Morpheus and I proceeded inside. Once the doors shut, he turned to me.

"You don't need to wait with me."

His eyes narrowed. "There it is again. If not me, what reaction in me do you fear?"

I pursed my lips. It irritated me that I was drawn to people who could pick me apart. Of course, the fact that he had had my blood when I'd been human didn't help.

Morpheus took a step back again. "I apologize, Your Highness. You are my cousin's bride and my Queen. I believe that makes you family. You are not what you were when we last spoke of my loyalties."

"True."

The doors opened, and Tyran stormed inside smelling of perfume and alcohol. "Did something happen, sissy? I couldn't sense you."

Grinning, I walked over and wiped the lipstick off of his cheek with my thumb, trying to cover my discomfort. "Was playtime nice?"

He tapped my forehead and slurred a little. "What did you see, love?"

"Don't call me that." I shoved him back.

Tyran laughed and sauntered over to the wall and pressed a panel. "I think I hit a nerve, eh, Morpheus?" The panel slid open to reveal a bar with beautiful crystal decanters. He poured two drinks and took a large swig while ambling over to Morpheus to hand him a glass. Morpheus accepted, but stood there stiffly with the glass, his eyes missing nothing.

Stepping forward, I asked, "I could ask the same of you right now. What's going on in your head?"

Tyran laughed again, harder than he should have. "All is well!" He spun around in a circle holding up his glass. "You will be crowned in two nights, and all will be perfection. We should invite Semjâzâ and all his friends."

He chugged the rest of his drink and sat it on the end table, but missed, and it fell to the ground, spewing ice cubes across the marble.

He closed the distance between us and grabbed my face and held it in his hand. "Maybe, once you are officially queen, Semjâzâ will reveal his plans for you. You know he has plans. You saw the way he looked at you. Like...like he is a dragon and you are gold. So when he has devoured you and my brother and everyone I care about, everything will be fine. Won't it, sissy?" Then he gave me a sloppy kiss on the lips.

I shoved away and wiped his kiss from my lips with my sleeve.

"What will be fine?" Bowen quietly asked from the doorway. His eyes were pinned on his brother.

"It seems Taranis has a roundabout way in which to question your wife," Morpheus calmly stated as if the tension in the room wasn't debilitating. He was still frozen with alert eyes and in the same position with the drink Tyran had given him.

"And why does she need to be questioned?" Bowen's eyes were still on Tyran.

"She had a vision and..." Tyran stood a little straighter as if sobering up. He looked at Morpheus.

Hesitantly, I finally admitted, "Zahra was in it. That's why I didn't say anything."

Morpheus flinched. "That stupid," he said under his breath.

Bowen finally looked my way. "Will you tell *me*?"


GABRIEL

I burst through the door. "Pack up. I know what they are planning. Ian, burn everything on the wall. Joshua, pack up the equipment. We leave in twenty minutes."

"It's almost sunrise."

"Wear daylight gear. You lay in the backseat. This cannot wait."

"Where are we going?"

"France."

Joshua and Ian looked at one another for a split-second, some type of communication passed between them, and then they sped into action.

I prayed we would not be too late.

# 17

# MERCY IS WEAKNESS

ALERIA

The entire time I sat in the throne room with Bowen, I kept thinking about the look on Morpheus' face the moment I'd admitted to Zahra having been in my last vision. Losing Phantasos had taken a toll on all three of the people I cared about in this coven.

The first time I'd seen Zahra, she was hunting in the maze with Morpheus. She was terrifying, fierce, and deadly. She loved hunting humans and fed off of their fear.

She had loved torturing me while I'd been locked away in the dungeon. Each morning and evening, she delivered my food, tossing it to the floor and making sure it slopped over onto the filthy ground. She always whispered atrocities, making me doubt myself and those around me.

During the sacrifice, she'd delighted in my impending doom. And even just a few short weeks ago, she'd tried to poison me using Celeste. But worst of all, she killed my friend Peter, just to hurt me.

I hated her with the heat of a quadrillion suns. I didn't see a single redeeming quality inside her. And yet, I didn't want Morpheus to lose someone else he cared about.

I was no longer needed in the throne room; Bowen was going to attend a meeting I didn't need to be at. So, I headed up to our room for some much needed alone time, at least until Tyran arrived. I convinced Bowen that I could walk by myself down the hall, up the main staircase, and down two more halls to our room. He'd argued, but caved. I wasn't sure what look I had given him, but I'd felt so caged today for some reason that I felt angry and ready to lash out. The Coronation was tomorrow, and I needed to get whatever this was under control.

Cadeyn shadowed me to the bottom of the stairs, then watched me go up. Every time I looked at him, I waited for him to remember that I'd killed his older brother, Gareth. But he still had no memory of it at all. It was kind of creepy.

Once at the top, I nodded to Cadeyn, and he returned to the door of the throne room. Halfway down the first hall, a door opened. I stopped in my tracks and waited to see who would emerge. When Zahra stepped out into the hall looking the other direction, I couldn't help but see the irony; I'd just been thinking about her.

When she turned in my direction, she froze. There was a long moment where neither of us moved, and I felt like we were two male Siamese fighting fish dumped into the same bowl, prepping to fight and prove dominance over the other. She would have fins of red and black for her auburn hair, and I would be lavender for my eyes. Somehow I could see our fins flaring and floating around us as we postured.

A smug grin twisted as her full red lips. "Did Daddy let you out of your crate?"

I narrowed my eyes at her.

"What? Baby girl doesn't have someone to speak for her, so she doesn't speak at all?"

I squeezed my eyes shut, and in my head I chanted, "Morpheus, Morpheus, Morpheus," trying to summon some type of control. I'd never once killed for revenge—only for self-preservation or in defense of another. I wanted to kill her with my own hands, even though I knew it was wrong. I could feel the Durateus blade I had strapped to my thigh calling to me.

I walked towards her, heading back to my room; I wasn't going to take the bait. I felt triumphant, like I had my big girl pants on.

As I passed directly in front of her, she whispered so low that only I could hear, "Enjoy your empty throne. It won't be yours for long."

I came to halt. "That sounds like treason."

Zahra scoffed, but kept her hushed tone. "You aren't my Queen, and Belenus won't be my King much longer."

I could stomach her threatening me, but threatening Bowen—line crossed. My hand shot out, and I grabbed her throat and rammed her into the wall so hard, the wood paneling cracked. I glanced down the hall to see if the guards would come from around the corner, but they didn't.

She laughed, and I realized she'd stuck a small blade into my side. I could feel my blood trickling over my hip and beneath my dress, but amazingly it didn't hurt much.

I leaned in closer. "Please don't do this to Morpheus. He just lost his brother."

"You are a usurper, just cleverer than the rest. I will see you stripped of the throne and enslaved," she sneered.

"What did I do to you?" I couldn't help but ask.

Zahra twisted the blade farther into my side, just as I heard Tyran's voice.

"Let go of the knife, Zahra." I felt Tyran's hand on my back as he reached around and grabbed Zahra's wrist. He twisted it upwards, relieving her of the knife, taking note of my blood on her hand.

"I don't need your help, Tyran," I bit.

Tyran held me with a murderous look. "To your room, my Queen."

I glared at him, but complied. Putting pressure on my wound as I walked, I glanced back and realized that Tyran was dragging Zahra along with us to my room. Once inside, he pulled her into the bathroom and washed my blood from her hand. Afterwards, he towed her into the room, practically tossing her onto one of the captain's chairs.

"Zahra, your stupidity astounds me," he spat.

"She has made you sick, like everyone else. The Oneiroi are immune, and I would be under her spell too if I didn't have Icelos' blood in my system. You don't see what she is."

Tyran shook his head. "Your theory is invalid. Morpheus is immune, yet he trusts her."

Zahra crossed her arms—her mind was set.

"I'll summon Cadeyn to remove her."

"No." I swallowed. "Call Morpheus."

Tyran exhaled while staring at Zahra distastefully, then raised his phone to his ear. "Cousin, I need you in the main royal bedchamber...No...Come quickly, I have Zahra in here." Tyran glanced at the phone like Morpheus had hung up on him.

Not ten seconds later, he knocked on the door.

"Come," I responded.

Morpheus entered. If I'd thought his grey eyes were stormy before, now they were a tempest. "Taranis...my Queen." He bobbed his head. "How may I be of service?" he asked calmly, but the muscles in neck were twitching with tension.

I didn't know if Tyran would agree, but I addressed Morpheus. "Because I care about *you*, I am turning Zahra over to you. Do as you see fit. But I give you this warning: if she even glares at me in the future, I will kill her. You won't be able to stop me next time."

Zahra's head snapped in my direction. It was apparent that Morpheus had never told her about his intervention after she'd poisoned me. I'd had only one thought, and hadn't cared about the consequence. If Morpheus hadn't stopped me, either Zahra or I would've already been dead.

Morpheus walked to Zahra and put his hand around her upper arm, wrenching her from the chair. When they got to the door, Morpheus looked at me gravely. "Thank you."

I nodded, and they exited.

As soon as the door shut, Tyran turned to me, and was way too close. "*That* was a mistake."

"I couldn't do it to Morpheus, Tyran. I just couldn't."

Tyran was clearly displeased, but he turned his attention to the wound in my side. "Have you healed?"

"I'm fine." I took a half step back.

"You can't allow personal feeling to sacrifice your safety. Remember, Belenus had to call for a tribunal on a member of his own family."

"Mercy isn't always weakness. Sometimes, it shows strength. It took a hell of a lot more strength for me to release her."

"What did she say to you to set you off?"

I hedged. "I don't really want to say, but we need to keep a close eye on her. She may lead us to whomever she has been working with."

"What did she say?" But it wasn't Tyran asking, it was Bowen. He'd entered at some point, and I had no idea how much he'd overheard. It was the second time he'd done that. Then, I remembered that Bowen had the ability to mask his presence. I'd inherited that ability from him, but often forgot to use it.

"How long have you been there?" I asked.

"I came up as soon as I caught a glimpse of Morpheus escorting Zahra towards the dungeon. I knew it had to do with the agitation I felt from you." He glimpsed the bloodstain on my side. "Apparently, you are getting better at suppressing your emotions from me."

Both Bowen and Tyran were radiating anger. I walked over to the couch and plopped ungracefully onto it. I took a deep breath and spilled. "She said, '*You're not my Queen, and Belenus won't be my King much longer...You are a usurper, just cleverer than the rest. I will see you stripped of the throne and enslaved.*' The enslaved comment made me think about the dreams I experienced in Paris." I managed to repress a shudder.

"I will put surveillance in her room while Morpheus has her occupied. You are gambling with your life, sissy."

I disputed, "It's no different than the catch and release we did in the Watchers to see where they would go."

"This is different, and you know it—people guilty of treason die," Tyran reprimanded.

I opened my mouth, but Tyran shook his head and waved his hand. He didn't want to hear it, so he left the room.

Once the door shut, I looked at Bowen nervously. He walked over and sat next to me, very silently. I didn't think he was even breathing.

"Are you mad at me?"

He sighed. "What is done, is done." Then he looped his arm behind me and pulled me onto his lap so that I was straddling him. He framed my face with his hands and pressed his forehead to mine. "I finally have everything I want, and I'm afraid that it will be taken from me."

I grabbed onto his shirt collar. "I don't plan on letting *anyone* take me anywhere."

Bowen's hands glided up my sides and back down to my hips. He squeezed, holding me in place. I tried to sense his emotions, but he was withholding them.

"So, I'm gonna ask again: are you angry with me?"

"I *have* been angry with you before, but not now."

I'm not sure why it popped out of my mouth, when I said, "When I escaped the castle, without saying goodbye."

He exhaled slowly. "Yes, anger is *one* of the things I felt." He paused. "And, accidentally as it may have been, when you exposed me to Aurora, but you know that."

"And when I left after the sacrifice was stopped."

His brows pinned together. "Is there a reason you are bringing up these things? Are you wanting me to be angry with you?"

"No, I want to know how you are feeling. You've been really controlled. I don't know." I covered my face with my hands. "I don't know what I am saying. I'm just nervous, I guess."

Bowen pried my hands away. "I have spent many lifetimes learning how to deal with anger. It can lead to ruin." He kissed both of my palms. "My own mother tried to kill me at that sacrifice. Cadeyn, whom I considered one of my closest friends, held me in place, along with his brother, while she drained me of life. Do you think that that didn't make me angry or hurt?"

"I hadn't thought about that."

"Cadeyn chooses duty above all else. That is why he is Captain of the Royal Guard. It pained him to do it, but he did as commanded by his sovereign. I have to put everything in perspective." He raised his left brow. "Are you angry with *me*?"

"Nope."

"So you aren't using the female tactic of asking me how I feel, so I will ask you the same?"

"Not a hint, just a question." I chuckled humorously. "I think the only time I have ever actually been angry with you is when you forced me to tell you how I felt about you."

He took my hand and put it over his silent heart. "I have you and an entire kingdom to worry about. I haven't wanted you to worry, too."

"You aren't alone in this. I'm strong enough to share the burden."

"I recall someone wanting to 'ease into it.'"

"Bah, using my words against me." I waved my hand in the air as if to bat away his words.

He grabbed onto me and swung me onto my back, quickly lying on top of me. He stayed propped on his elbows. "And how am I feeling right now?"

I closed my eyes and felt completely connected to him. Love didn't seem like a strong enough word. He allowed the weight of his upper body to settle on me as his lips found mine again. I untucked his shirt and hooked my left leg around his thigh. "How long until you need to return?"

"We have a welcome reception to attend in four hours."

I wanted to sigh, but I didn't want him to feel bad. I smiled. "Good. I plan to distract you from your 'worries.'"

"And how do you plan to do that?" he asked, his voice growing more husky.

"Gratuitous sex."

Bowen coughed a laugh. "You never fail to surprise me, wife." A shudder ran through his body, and his eyes began to glow as his fangs elongated.

I offered him my neck, and when the hormone hit my

system, I moaned in pleasure, pushing away the Coronation and the Fallen and all of the other stresses.

GABRIEL

The line was filled with static. "Raphael?"

"Yes, Gabriel?"

"I need you to do something for me. I need you to quietly check on Ali's family in California—very quietly."

"Is there a reason?"

"Threats are to be eliminated with extreme prejudice."

It was quiet for a moment. "Understood. Does this have something to do with Blackthorne calling me and inquiring as to your whereabouts?"

"Yes."

"Are you about to do something I won't like?"

I paused before answering. "Be well, Raphael."

"Gabriel? Be well."

I hit the red button.

"I can still go in alone," said Joshua. I didn't realize he was there.

"We stick to the plan. I am going for a run." I pushed past Joshua and headed out for my last run before we attempted to get inside the French Coven.

When I returned, I would have one last piece of personal business—writing a letter to my daughter. I prayed it would never have to be delivered.

# 18

## LAST THING

GABRIEL

I clicked the comm unit, needing to know if Ian had hidden the artifact. In case this attempt to get to Ali and Belenus went wrong, I could not know where the artifact had been concealed. "Ian, did you finish your task?"

"Affirmative."

"No matter what happens, do not engage. You hear me?"

There was a long pause. I had given him his orders several times. Ian was not one to disobey, but he was uncomfortable sitting this out.

Joshua clicked the remote, and the car sputtered to a stop. He thrust himself from the front seat, looking under the hood.

"I can still go alone. You sure?" whispered Joshua over the comm.

I replied through my teeth, "You went over the surveillance reports. How many uninvited guests get in?"

"None," admitted he. Through the gap under the open hood, I could see Joshua peering at me over the engine.

"How many mercenaries with prisoners?"

"Almost all of them, but I still think they may recognize me."

"Your disguise will work. They *will* recognize *me,* and that will draw focus. We will get through the gates and find a friendly."

Joshua slammed the hood shut. He pulled an assault rifle from his back and leveled it at me as he opened the rear door.

I eased out of the backseat, keeping my shackled wrists raised in front of me. He kicked the rear door shut, then pushed me against the sedan and searched me one last time. I could feel eyes on us from a kilometer away.

Joshua pulled the tactical mask over the lower part of his face, concealing it while he said, "Ian, I'm tossing the comm in a moment. I will activate the tracker as soon as we are safely inside."

"This is when I wish both of you had vital signs for me to monitor," replied Ian.

"Ian, this will work," I encouraged.

"Be well, Josh, Gabriel...I..."

"We will see you in a few hours, buddy," I reassured.

Ian paused, his voice rough. "See you both at the rally point." The transmission disconnected.

Joshua shoved me forward with the barrel of his rifle in my back. A breeze picked up and brought the scent of at least two vamps on our three o'clock. I could sense more on our flank. I controlled my breathing and pulse as we walked at a measured pace.

At 250 meters from the outer gate, a spotlight bore down on us. With my heightened hearing, I could make out radio transmissions between the guards, calling for an alert.

Panels slid open on the towers on either side of the road, revealing machine gun turrets. *That was not on the surveillance.* I skidded to a stop and made Joshua push me forward; they couldn't know that we *wanted* inside.

The gate was defended by an entire platoon of guards. That included the six closing in from the rear and sides. There were six more on the gate, four on the turrets, and another eight at intervals on the road to the castle. I exhaled, trying to slow my heart once again. I balled my fists, and then relaxed my hands.

We were closing in on the main gate...200 meters...150...100...50...I kept my head bowed as we approached.

"Halt. Identify yourself."

Joshua's voice was clear and commanding. "I am here to collect the bounty on this Slayer."

One of the gatekeepers slowly approached. Other vamps were shadows behind each of his shoulders. "You do not have clearance to be here."

"I have a bounty to collect from Prince Taranis himself. This is personal. He wants *this* Slayer."

The commander laughed. "The Prince spoke to *you* directly?"

"Yes. I have fulfilled my obligation. Please let him know that I have arrived."

He laughed again; the others behind him joined in.

I straightened my shoulders and stood at my full height, raising my head. The laughing stopped.

"Is that—?"

"Yes. Please contact the Prince."

The commander glanced from side-to-side, suddenly nervous. "You expect us to believe you captured him alone?"

"The rest of my team is dead. Call Prince Taranis."

The commander stared at me for a long moment, and then his eyes went over my shoulder to Joshua. He spoke into a comm on his wrist. "Put a line through to the Prince." He walked back to the guard station, and the phone rang a moment later. I heard him say "yes" several times, and then he uttered my name. Within moments, the massive gate opened, and we were motioned forward; Joshua shoved me from behind with the barrel of his rifle again.

The commander addressed Joshua. "I need your rifle. You may keep your other weapons until you reach the castle. At that point, they will be checked in with the guard. You will not see the Prince until you do so. Understood?"

"Yes."

"Proceed."

Joshua took out a dagger and pressed it against my shoulder. "Walk."

I flared my nostrils and glared, reluctantly moving towards the castle. The guard fell in around us—two in front, two single-file on each side, and at least two in the rear, making it eight or more. They had us boxed in as we marched onward. Beyond the gate, the driveway was about 800 meters.

As we walked, we edged to the side of the road as a vehicle passed by. I concentrated on my breathing again. Additional lights came on at the castle.

The smell of car exhaust cleared after another 50 meters; there was a new scent in the air—I stopped in my tracks. Joshua shoved at me to keep moving, but at that moment, blood splattered across my face, accompanied by the sound of something moving at high speed. The guard on my left fell dead, yet his head still traveled towards the castle.

I pivoted towards Joshua, and he broke my shackles with the hilt of his blade. Semjâzâ's people were swooping in from above. A Fallen landed, grabbing at my shoulders. Joshua buried his blade into the angel's back, allowing me to break free. We sprinted towards the castle, but it was chaos. The men ahead of us were plucked into the air, leaving only screams in their place.

My legs were burning from my sprint. Events seemed to slow. Joshua was at my side, his hand on my shoulder as we ran. Then a figure swooped down from the sky, pausing for a split-second, his immense, black wings flapping. He folded them inward like a skydiver, and hit me, knocking me from my feet and propelling me backwards.

Joshua was instantly on the angel's back, tearing at his wings, the Fallen crying out in agony. I scrambled backwards, springing to my feet. A body of one of the guards hit me from behind, bowling me forwards. At the same time, Joshua and the angel came crashing back to the ground.

They rolled, and Joshua caught my eye for an instant, just as a different angel swooped in. I had seen that look in battle before.

"Noooo!!!" I boomed, trying to get to them.

Joshua continued fighting and screamed, "Run!!"

My trajectory didn't waver, but I could do nothing as I watched the new angel brutally slit Joshua open. Blood was everywhere. Then he grabbed Joshua by the head and rocketed upwards before I could reach them. I stood panting—helpless— as everyone around me was picked off one-by-one.

Someone started shooting, and it jerked me back to reality. I needed to move. With nowhere else to go, I ran with everything I had towards the castle. I was 400 meters out when Joshua's body was dropped from the sky, splitting the distance. He wasn't moving. I bellowed his name, and it felt as if I was trudging through mud in my need to get to him.

Before I made it 100 meters more, something hit me from the side with such force, I only had seconds before I blacked out. The castle grew small as the tunnel of darkness closed in.

I was being carried into the air, and there was no one left to carry my message.

## ALERIA

I was reading on a leather chair in the anteroom behind the thrones. Bowen was dealing with some local territorial squabbles in the throne room.

Tyran had been skulking about, pretending to read, and being fretful. But two minutes ago, he'd gotten a phone call, gave me a frantic look, then sped off without a word. I drew in a deep breath, enjoying being in a room by myself for once.

Then I felt a twinge. I clutched my chest and shot up out of my seat. "Gabriel...Joshua..." I looked around the room, trying to assess what I was sensing. They were close. And in trouble.

I dropped my leather bound book to the floor and stumbled towards the throne room. Gabriel was terrified. I couldn't recall ever feeling it this strongly from him. I continued rubbing at my now racing heart as I emerged from behind the throne, walking mechanically towards the doors.

"Aleria?" Bowen asked as I walked right past him.

Cadeyn looked hesitantly at me, then opened the door to the main hall. I gasped. Joshua was in pain—too much pain. I could feel it tearing through my own body, and for a split-second, stumbled to a knee. Then, I moved forward, instinct drawing me to the front of the castle.

Bowen's hand clasped my shoulder. "What's wrong, love?"

It took me a moment to focus on him. "Gabriel. Joshua. Something is wrong. They're close."

Gunfire shattered the night, along with screeches of inhuman pain.

Instantly, Cadeyn was herding us back into the throne room. "All guards report for duty. Secure the King and Queen."

"No." I resisted being pushed away from where I needed to go. I argued with both Bowen and Cadeyn for over a minute, and finally, wrenched myself free. "If either of you try to stop me again, I will…" My voice trailed. I didn't know what I would do. I stormed down the wide hall and picked up speed when I smelled Joshua's blood.

I didn't get very far; Tyran seemed to appear out of nowhere in front of me. I crashed into him before I could stop, and he grabbed my shoulders. Joshua's blood was all over him.

"What did you do, Tyran?" I accused.

His voice hitched, my question injuring him. "I tried to save him."

It felt as if all the blood flowing in my body had stopped. "Tried? He's…"

"I don't know. I sent him to the infirmary."

"Gabriel?"

A guard ran in from outside. Tyran turned to him. "Report."

"Seven dead, three missing, two more were sent to medical, not including the mercenary you already sent. Sire, there is no sign of the Slayer or Batariel and his accomplices."

"Continue to search the area in the armored vehicles in case they dropped the bodies."

"Yes, Sire."

"Dismissed."

Cadeyn spoke, "Your Highnesses, the infirmary is not in a secured part of the castle. Please allow me to move my men before you proceed."

Bowen put his arm around me, and it made me realize how hard I had been trembling. "We will wait in the library, Cadeyn. Please notify us when you are ready with our escort."

We backed towards the door, and I looked at Tyran. "You are coming with us. I want to know everything."

Tyran pinned his brows together, but then reluctantly followed.

Three hours later, I was allowed to see Joshua. His injuries had been so extensive, that they'd to perform surgery to put him back together. They'd pumped bags of blood into him during the process. The in-house doctor informed me that Josh would be weak but fully recovered within a day if they kept up the blood treatments, and that most of the scarring would disappear.

After surgery, he'd been moved to the high security section of the dungeon in which I'd seen Phantasos. That was a battle I would fight a little later; all I cared about now was seeing Josh.

Bowen hesitated. "Would you wait out here for a moment?"

"I should go in first," I disagreed.

"Please, humor me. Watch on the monitor."

I clenched my jaw and nodded. This was awkward enough.

Bowen stepped inside the cell, and I could only see his back. Joshua was awake—his wounds still angry and pink. He was on a cot, but his wrists were shackled to chains connected to the rear wall. When he saw Bowen, he popped up, knocking the cot over, and pressed himself to the back wall.

Bowen's voice was calm. "Joshua, do you know why you are here? Or why you would risk coming?"

Joshua's eyes darted back and forth, the full weight of his confinement seeming to sink in. "How did I get here?"

"What do you last remember?" Bowen asked in a reassuring tone.

Josh took a deep breath and exhaled. I could tell he had no intention of answering; his eyes became distant, and he peered at the floor. Bowen continued to ask questions, but Josh ignored them. He was relying on Watcher training now, disconnecting himself.

I turned to the guard. "Let me inside."

He nodded and buzzed me in.

There was only a flicker on Joshua's face registering my movement.

"Joshua."

He stared off in the distance.

"Joshua, it's me. Please look up."

His brow furrowed. A few seconds later, his eyes became keen once again, and he looked at me. Finally, there was some recognition. "Als?" he questioned, confused.

"It's me."

"You...you're..." The look of horror on his face was beyond comprehension. He didn't remember me being turned; my heart stuttered. Then his eyes slid back to Bowen, and Joshua lunged forward. "Did you do this to her, too?"

"Josh, no. This isn't Tyran; it's Bowen, his twin brother. You don't remember?"

"Remember what? He was in that alley. He was the one that did this to me!" Joshua kept tugging against the shackles until blood was seeping from beneath the fetters. "Why are you here? What did they do to you?"

"Josh, this is Bowen; he is my husband. His brother turned you."

"Husband? You're in high school! How can you be married?"

My eyes welled up with tears, and my voice became choked. I questioned him. "What is the last thing you remember? Do you remember Sebastian? Gabriel? Jess?"

He became agitated again. "How do you know them?"

The tears pooling at the edges of my eyes plummeted down my cheeks. "But you don't remember? You don't remember me since you were turned?"

"Als, what are you talking about?"

He stopped tugging, and his eyes went to the ceiling, as they often did when he was trying to remember something. "We went to Romania and returned to London." His eyes went to the floor, and he tugged at one of the shackles again. "I remember being worried. I'd asked Sebastian to... you... my journal. My picture of you was missing. I asked him to go to California. You were in danger." His eyes went to the ceiling again, but he shook his head as if trying to recover the memory anymore was useless. "That's the last thing I remember."

Bowen spoke, and I almost jumped. "It must have been Batariel who attacked him."

"Batariel?" Joshua asked.

I turned to Joshua, wiping away the tears that refused to stop. "He's a fallen angel that has the ability to wipe memories from his victims. He's done it to me, but only small snippets were stolen, not—" I cut myself off.

"How much is missing?" Josh asked.

There was a shake in my voice when I answered, "About three years." I knew the look on my face was tragic.

Joshua swallowed hard and stood up straight. After a moment, he righted the cot and sat down hard.

Bowen's phone buzzed, and he read a message. "Can I speak with you outside?" he asked.

I nodded and followed him out.

The door closed. "I need to go upstairs. Do you want to stay here?" I could feel that he was uncomfortable.

"Yes. I...I need to tell him about Sebastian, at least. He was like a father to him."

"And what are you going to tell him about the two of you?"

I frowned and thought for a minute. "That he was my best friend for the last three years, and that we dated, but now I'm married to you. Is that dishonest?"

"Yes and no."

"I'm going to unchain him. He isn't a threat to me."

Bowen smiled, but his eyes were anxious. "I know. He wouldn't have risked coming here unless it was important."

"After I finish speaking with Joshua, I'll meet you in our room."

"No, I'll come get you—or Tyran will."

"I am not weak."

"You are vulnerable if you have a vision, and it's obvious that Batariel is close. We don't know if he has figured out another way into your head. That is all, my strong wife."

I grabbed his collar and pulled his lips to mine. "I love you."

He grinned and looked at the guard. "Give her the keys to the constraints." He looked back at me. "You can show me how you *feel* in a few hours." Then he flashed down the hall and disappeared.

I took a deep breath and reentered Joshua's cell. How was I going to tell him that so many people he cared about were dead? Sebastian, Michael, Kez, and Amara were all gone. He might not remember Peter at all. He'd known Gentry before the California mission, but I wasn't sure about Leslie.

Stepping inside, I hesitated by the door. The light glinted in his green eyes as he looked at me expectantly, his expression both anxious and lost. I suddenly felt homesick. I could taste my heartache—hundreds of memories that he would never remember sharing with me crashed in all at once.

# 19

## CONVERGING

ALERIA

It had been twenty-four hours since the Fallen had attacked Gabriel and Joshua. I entered the anteroom in search of Tyran. I hadn't seen him since the immediate aftermath. He was sitting with a book open in his lap and a far off expression on his face that made him look very much like Bowen.

"I need to apologize to you," I said, my voice too loud in the quiet of the room.

Tyran looked at me with his unreadable face.

"I accused you of doing something to Joshua yesterday. I shouldn't have and I'm sorry." I hesitated. "I hope you can forgive me."

He gave me an almost nonexistent nod; somehow, he looked brittle.

"And, I wanted to thank you."

He pursed his lips, but didn't respond.

I continued, "The men told me that you ran outside after

Gabriel and Joshua, despite the fact that the Fallen were still attacking."

He remained very still when he finally spoke, "It was purely for information. He and Gabriel wouldn't risk coming here if it wasn't of utmost importance." His voice was a little cold.

"Well, thanks anyway. I...I guess I should go start getting ready—Coronation and all." I turned my back and headed for the door, feeling disappointed for some reason. I knew I still had hours to get ready, but couldn't stay.

When my hand was on the doorknob, Tyran spoke again. "And I did it for you." I turned, but his hand was shielding his eyes, and his nose back in the book.

"Thank you," I whispered once more and slipped out into the throne room to Bowen and my awaiting security detail. I stood tentatively next to the throne, and Bowen took my hand. I could see the backs of some coven members leaving in Daylight gear.

"Cadeyn, please take the guards outside."

"Yes, Sire."

The doors closed. My heart raced in alarm. "Did they find something?"

Still sitting on the throne, Bowen handed me a sealed plastic bag. Bloodied handcuffs were inside. I opened the bag just enough to smell the blood: Gabriel.

"They were located about two kilometers from the castle. My men also found a car on the main road. It had been torn apart. And they found this." He pulled a small earpiece comm unit from his pocket and handed it to me.

"How much blood was there where they found the cuffs?"

"Not much. There is still hope. Can you sense him?"

"No. But Gabriel is really controlled, so I rarely do. But, I think I would've sensed him die." I hesitated. "Do we have to keep Joshua locked up?"

"It's for his protection more than anything. After tonight, we will talk. Do you wish to see him?"

I pursed my lips. "This is killing you, isn't it?"

He didn't rush his answer. "He has been part of your life since childhood and is part of your family." He seemed to struggle for words for a moment, which I'd rarely seen him do. Then he pulled me onto his lap and tucked a lock of my hair behind my ear, closely examining me. "I know that you need to be there for him. You don't abandon the people you care about, and he doesn't remember what compelled you to leave him."

I frowned. "I still don't understand what happened. It's just so opposite his character." I stopped myself and closed my eyes before I blathered on. Bowen didn't need to discuss Joshua with me anymore than necessary. "I'm sorry." I opened my eyes when he affectionately ran his fingers up my spine. I wound my arms around his neck, pressing my forehead to his.

"I'll walk you to his cell," he said, but he didn't move.

After a long moment, I slid off his lap. He reached for me and threaded his fingers through mine, tugging me towards the door. We walked silently to the cells.

When we arrived at the hall, I stared at the security screen for a long moment. Joshua was sitting on the floor next to the cot with his head cradled in his hands while his wavy locks poked through his fingers like ribbon. His wrists were still in shackles, the chains draping to the floor.

Bowen turned to the guard. "Please report."

"The prisoner was agitated, but has been quiet for nearly an hour. No incidents. He fed this morning and never made a move to break free or harm the familiar."

Bowen released my hand, turning to me and framing my face

with his hands, his eyes roving my face. But he didn't say anything.

"Do you not want me to see him?"

"It's not that. I would like to speak with him alone for a moment."

"Okaaay?"

Bowen gave me a crooked grin. "I promise to be good." He reached over and turned off the monitor.

"King Belenus?" the guard protested. It was obvious he was nervous about questioning Bowen.

Bowen glanced at him, then disappeared into the cell.

I stood outside, my stomach churning. I knew they wouldn't physically hurt one another, but I wondered what Bowen didn't want me to hear. Fidgeting in a very un-queenly way, it was all I could do to keep from pacing. I stared at my feet and noticed that I needed to feed. I could see the veins in my feet disappearing beneath the edge of my flats.

When the door opened several minutes later, I exhaled in relief.

Bowen grinned at me again. He stood in the doorway and bent to kiss my forehead. "Your handmaidens will expect you in two hours. If I don't hear from you, I will come, or my brother will. Call me if you are ready before then." He glanced over his shoulder at Joshua, then I stepped around him and shut the door behind me.

I turned to Joshua. He was rubbing his wrists. Bowen had removed the shackles, but Josh hadn't moved from the floor. I slowly walked over to him and slid down the wall until I was seated next to him. I didn't say anything; I just sat there in silence, happy that he looked improved since my last visit.

Joshua let out an ironic sort of chuckle. "Just a little while ago,

I had this memory of you. Your mother had been helping me sort and pack boxes all day after my parents' funeral. I'd told her to go home. An hour or so later, it had started to pour rain; I pictured the rain flooding my house and pulling me under, and then you startled me out of my daydream. I can't remember if I'd actually jumped or not. You held up a plate of food and put it on the table.

"When I looked up at you, I thought, *If one more person asked how I am doing, I'm going to burst,* but you didn't ask. And you didn't look like you felt sorry for me. You looked like you were *with* me in my grief. I'd felt so alone, even though I'd been surrounded by people helping me, and at that moment, you changed that. I think you sat on the floor next to me for over an hour. Did you ever say anything to me?"

I nodded. I could still smell the rain and the damp cardboard from that evening. "I told you that I loved you...platonically," I quickly added.

He frowned. "We more than just lightly dated, didn't we?"

I swallowed. "What makes you say that?"

"Multiple reasons. One, I don't think we would risk our friendship if we weren't serious. And," Joshua tilted his head, appraising my reaction, "both times you have visited, your husband made sure that I saw him first. He was making sure that I know you are his. And..."

"And?" I finally prompted.

"I feel like I did that night after the funeral. That there is something huge I lost that I will never get back. And I keep thinking about the expression on your face when I told you the last thing I remembered." We sat in silence for at least a minute. "Are you going to tell me I'm wrong?"

I took his hand like I had before, but this time, I didn't kiss it, or press it to my cheek. "You are observant, as usual. I'm sorry;

maybe I should've told you more. I just thought maybe it would be easier. Maybe it's good you don't remember?"

"Did you dump me for him or something?"

I laughed. "Ummm, no. I was the dumpee."

"Really? I don't understand. Why is your husband being so territorial then?"

"Josh, I..."

"I need to know, Als."

"It was the only time in my entire life I've seen you be cruel. You weren't *you*. I don't know what happened, but after, we were done."

"I was *cruel* to you?" Josh said in disbelief, but his voice seemed to be stretching into his memory. It seemed like he believed me.

I paused, wondering what I should say. "I still love you, but just not like I did before. You are still part of my family, you always will be."

He sighed and put his arm around me, then rested the side of his head on mine like he had so many times while we were growing up.

"Your husband offered to let me attend the Coronation to represent your family. He said that you're alone here."

I smiled. That was why Bowen had come in alone. "It would mean a lot to me, but I understand if you don't want to take the risk. There are other vampires here that will not be friendly towards you."

"If you want me there. I'm there."

I squeezed his hand and nodded against his shoulder, feeling choked up.

Joshua paused. "I came here with Gabriel?"

"Yes. I never saw him, but Tyran ran outside to meet you

both, and he saw everything. Gabriel was carried off by one of the fallen angels that we've been trying to stop."

"Do you think he is still alive?"

"I think so. I think I would've felt it if he'd been killed. But I'm still worried—"

"You would've *felt* it?"

I sat up and squared my shoulders, releasing his hand. I scooted over so I was sitting directly in front of him. "I would, through a blood bond. I was accidentally poisoned, and he saved my life by having me feed on him." I pulled out my phone and looked at the time. "I have a little over an hour. You ready for an information dump? I can tell you as much as I can."

He sat up a little, sitting cross-legged in front of me. Our knees were almost touching. "I'm ready."

I started at the beginning—the evening I met Bowen in the coffee shop—and speed-talked my way through the past three years. He stopped to question me for details a handful of times. The only things I left out were him slapping me and what he said to drive me off.

Once I'd finished, he sat quietly for the remaining few minutes before my escort arrived.

I finally broke the silence. "Do you believe me? Do you have any questions?"

A ghost of a smile crossed his face. "I can sense intentions, remember? You had no other purpose than truthfulness and protection the entire time you spoke. I've never had cause to doubt you—ever."

"You'll still be at the Coronation?"

There was a knock at the door.

"I wouldn't miss it, Als."

Tyran stood before us, leaning on the frame. "Time's up,

sissy. Looks like you and loverboy are coming with me. This is a terrible idea, by the way."

I stood and walked towards him. "Huh. That's funny. I don't seem to care about your opinion."

Tyran smirked. "Sassy. We will drop you at your room, and the boy will come with me to shower and change. I have attendants getting him clothing."

I narrowed my eyes. "Tyran, I—"

"Tsk, tsk. I'm on my best behavior." He dipped down and quickly kissed me on the lips. "Well, *almost* best behavior."

I wiped his kiss away with the back of my hand. "I really hate you."

He tugged at my hair as if he was pulling a pigtail. He kept his eyes on me while addressing Joshua. "Come on, Son. Time to get pretty and watch your ex officially become your queen."

I glared and marched out, waiting at the end of the hall. The walk to my room surprisingly went by in a blink. I gave Tyran one last warning glare before he left with Joshua. Josh had an indecipherable expression as I smiled encouragingly and mouthed, "I'm sorry" as Tyran dragged him off somewhere to dress for the ceremony.

When I entered my room, it was bustling with activity. There were six handmaidens all prepping for me. I swallowed and entered, ready to submit myself to scrubbing and poking and primping and whatever other tortures they'd planned for me.

---

I stood in my room in a black and gold corseted dress, laced so tightly, I was glad I didn't need to breathe. My hair was up in a swirl of barrel curls with real gems stuck on bits of Velcro that adhered to my locks. They'd arranged it so the crown would nest perfectly once it was placed on my head during the ceremony.

They adjusted the train of my dress just as the doors opened to reveal Bowen standing there. His eyes widened with a pleased expression. "You look like the Queen. You are stunning."

I smiled nervously. "Thank you." It was an effort not to bat away or deflect the compliment.

He turned and offered me his arm. I took it, and my attendants scurried out ahead of us with the robe I would wear once we arrived at the church. It was almost fifteen feet long, so I wouldn't have to wear it on the ride over.

I moved forward, squeezing Bowen's arm. He was smiling and remarkably at ease.

"You ready?" he asked.

"Did you feel ready when they coronated you?"

He chuckled. "No."

"Then we had better get going."


## GABRIEL

"You fool!" Ana bellowed the moment I opened my eyes.

I scrubbed at my face, trying to clear the fog in my eyes. I probed a throbbing spot on my head, and my fingers came away with crimson flakes of dried blood.

Ana paced as she spoke. "I have tipped my hand. We have been looking for you for days. Not even your own people knew where you were. Michael is dead. Uriel has gone dark. You have sent Raphael to America."

She was listing Slayers in the bloodlines from the Angels of the Four Corners. Suddenly awake, I asked, "What do you want from me?"

She pulled out an ornate dagger. My blood pressure

increased when I recognized it as the blade to complete the artifact.

"There is something that only your bloodline can do."

I could feel all the lines converging. This was the path to which everything had been leading to for months. I readied myself to hear my fate.

20

# LEGITIMATELY

ALERIA

Cadeyn and another of the Royal Guard stood ready to open the doors to the cathedral. My handmaidens fastened the fifteen-foot robe to the pins on my shoulders. It had a fur collar in the tradition of many royal robes, but it was black fur, and the cloth was nearly see-through, entirely embroidered with black and gold and gems to match my corseted gown. I could hardly breathe from the clothing, not to mention my nerves. I smiled and tried to look regal, praying that no one could tell I was a mess of nerves. My attendants weren't consoling me, so I was assuming I was successful.

When Cadeyn put his hand on the door as if to open it, I put my hand up. He stopped.

"I just need a moment."

Cadeyn smiled reassuringly. "When you're ready."

"Late won't be fashionable in this case." I tilted my head in Tyran's direction as he appeared from around the corner. I felt an odd mixture of relief and aggravation at seeing him.

"I can't take you teasing me right now."

He shook his head. "It is not traditional to be escorted down the aisle in our ceremonies, but it would be acceptable for a prince to do so. I came to offer you escort. I understand if you would like to refuse."

I stood there, blinking, for the moment. This was the third version of Tyran I'd seen today. Part of me wondered how many more I would see before the end of the night.

Tyran's face fell infinitesimally. "I underst—"

"Yes," I swallowed, "thank you."

He sidled up next to me and bent his elbow. I placed my hand in the loop of his arm. We took one step forward, and he leaned to my ear. "You're trembling."

I squeezed his arm harder.

"Don't worry, I won't tell. But I may bring it up later."

I grinned a little. The doors swung open, and we slowly promenaded over the threshold. The aisle was much longer than I thought it would be, and there were at least a couple of hundred faces scrutinizing me.

I searched the front for Bowen. He smiled, and his eyes went to the front row on my left: Joshua. He was surrounded by guards, but he was here.

The three elders stood on the altar next to Bowen. Each had a physical item. One of the elders held the crown representing the mind and the decisions I would have to make for my people. The next had an orb that stood for the whole of the body and the sacrifice I would have to make. The last had a scepter, which was symbolic of the spirit and the heart I needed to have for my people. Bowen held a ring with the royal crest, symbolic of the power I would wield.

We took one step past the foyer, and I jumped slightly when I saw the statues of angels lining the entire perimeter of the ceiling—dozens of them—fifty at least, but probably more. Tyran placed his free hand on my own hand that was clutching the crook of his arm. I settled, and we continued moving forward. My gut was twisting in my belly, and I couldn't shake the sensation that something was wrong. My heart was beating so hard, it felt as if it was thrashing inside my chest.

As we reached the halfway point, I was completely focused on Bowen. He was smiling, but there was a hint of worry behind his eyes. I was sure he felt my anxiety.

We reached the three-quarter mark—almost there.

Then something small fell and tumbled down the front of my dress, leaving a dusty grey trail. Plaster from the ceiling, possibly? No one else seemed to notice, but I couldn't help but look up.

I stared at the statue on the ledge overlooking the altar as we moved forward, letting Tyran keep me on track. The angel's wings were spread wide, his expression fierce. I continued forward, thinking his likeness was familiar.

We were almost at the front when I heard the grand doors close behind us.


GABRIEL

Being direct was my only course. "If you are planning on killing me, do it now. Otherwise, return me to the castle. I need to warn them before your people execute their plan."

"I need you for *my* plan," replied Ana.

"What is it you need with *me*?"

"Your ancestors, the Angels of the Four Corners, were the ones who imprisoned us. Only those with the same bloodline can send us back, but we need two of you."

"If that is the case, then why has Semjâzâ not killed all of us?"

"Do you recall the attack against your genetics lab over two years ago?"

"Yes, they took something of mine."

Ana grinned. "After Queen Agrona's people, the Andraste, had stolen your seed from the lab, *my* people seized the opportunity and executed the Slayer Michael, not the team led by Icelos. My people watched you later in Ireland as you had the memorial for Michael at the riverside—the candles and flowers —touching. We kept our distance and made no attempt on your life at that time. Aleria was still human then and could have been damaged too easily. And, nothing could be traced back to us. After that, two attempts on Raphael were aborted and one on Uriel. That was my doing—I insisted they would have revealed our presence and that we needed to wait for better opportunities."

"Michael was killed over a year before the Hellmouths were opened," I pointed out.

"Dagan wasn't the only one who escaped the original imprisonment. Batariel and one named Armaros have secretly aided all those who have attempted to open the Hellmouths. The Andraste are the only ones who succeeded in opening it," explained Ana.

"And then Dagan turned on Moloch—or Azâzêl—and killed him."

"Yes, and we proceeded without either of them. Aleria has been under surveillance since our escape. Once our plans started to intersect with the fates of your team, Batariel was dispatched to ensure your girl's visions didn't spook Belenus from turning over more of his people."

"The blank spots in her visions. Ali bleeding from them...

that was not Semjâzâ?" I questioned for confirmation of my hypothesis.

Ana impatiently answered, "The lost memory was Batariel. The physical harm was Semjâzâ. He needs Batariel as a bridge. Batariel has erased far more memory from her since she has returned to the Andraste castle."

"If we are truly allies, then you need to get me back to the castle *now*. He does not want Aleria on the throne. Semjâzâ wants the coronation to occur. He wants to cull *all* of the Ancients at the same time. Royal marriages and coronations are the only reason the oldest and most powerful vampires would converge in one location. He has been pulling strings to unravel Ali's relationship with Joshua for months."

"He *does* want her on the throne. He plans to sacrifice both Belenus and Taranis and take her as a wife to become rightful king. She's strong enough to bear Nephilim children and has impressed him. He intends to rule all of the Shadow world first, and then conquer the seen human world."

"She will not agree."

"She will not have a choice." Ana's phone rang; she pressed it to her ear. "All of them are gone? Where?...Are any of us with them?...No, he must have already been suspicious of me...No... Yes...Go now."

"What is it?" I questioned.

"Our headquarters are empty—"

One of Ana's people interrupted us; a phone was pressed to his ear. "The Coronation has just begun."

I grabbed Ana's arm. "Get me there."

"We don't have another Slayer from the Four. I won't risk your safety until we do."

"Someone from Michael's bloodline is already there. Return me—now."

ALERIA

When we arrived at the front, I felt as if I had made it to base in some deranged version of tag and could make it through this ordeal. Tyran smirked a little when he bowed to me, then took his place in the front row a few spots down from Joshua. I glanced over; Joshua's eyes were anxious, but he gave me a thin smile.

My eyes flicked to Bowen; he nodded, encouraging me to take my place halfway up the steps. I did. The elders, each from different covens, approached and started the service. I listened and nodded and parroted just as I was supposed to do. My nerves were still electric, partly wondering if I was ready to be a queen, and also because I still sensed danger.

Of course, I had vampires behind me that wanted a taste of my blood so badly I could feel it. And I'd seen Zahra in my peripheral vision, glaring daggers at me. She'd been so quiet since our altercation in the hallway, it made me nervous.

The elders finally placed the crown on my head. Bowen stepped forward, sliding the royal ring onto my finger. Then I was handed the orb and scepter. I was announced as Queen. Just when I was about to turn and be presented to all the guests, I had an overwhelming urge to look upwards. My eyes settled on the same statue that felt familiar when we'd walked down the aisle.

I gasped, not turning as I should have. Semjâzâ. The statue was of Semjâzâ, and I could feel him. Then the unthinkable happened, and his eyes snapped open, plaster flaking away— none of them were statues. He crouched ever so slightly and fully extended his wings. Grey clouds of dusty plaster began to shower down as dozens of the Fallen shifted. I turned quickly to survey the exits. Fully armed Fallen dropped from their perches with heavy chains to bar the doors.

I had seconds. I filled my lungs with air and bellowed, "Take their wi—"

Semjâzâ flattened me, knocking the air from my lungs. His knee was in the middle of my chest; I couldn't see beyond his wings to find Bowen or Joshua or Tyran or Morpheus or...or...

I struggled under his weight, thrashing, but I couldn't free myself. Then, as it had in a much different version of my vision, the lights went out, and I was surrounded by screams.


## GABRIEL

The limits of my faith were being tested as I dangled between two members of the Fallen. The wind howled in my ears whilst we flew towards the Coronation. We were not far away, but it took several minutes for Ana to inform her people. Semjâzâ had managed to root out most of the dissenters and had left them behind.

Ana estimated that Semjâzâ's group was sixty strong; we would have just over twelve. There were possibly a half-dozen more that would join us from the inside. The rest of the 200 were scattered all over the world, laying the foundation for phase two of Semjâzâ's plans.

We landed a kilometer from the perimeter fence. Within minutes, all of Ana's people assembled.

A late arrival coming from the direction of the castle alighted on the ground next to Ana. "The Queen has been crowned, and I sense our people inside."

Ana bowed her head and murmured something in a language I did not understand. Then the voices of all of the others joined in unison, repeating the same statement. It was eerie.

A female with jet-black hair approached Ana with her palm outstretched. It was filled to the brim with what appeared to be white clay. Ana scooped some up and rubbed the substance between her palms, then proceeded to make streaks across her face like war paint. She continued making markings on her breastplate, arms, and finally, her wings, as she and the others continued to repeat the same refrain over and over again.

Glancing around, I noted that all of the Fallen were marking themselves with the white clay. When Ana was finished, the white patterns on the tops of her wings made it appear as if her wings were actually white and that the black lower half was merely shadow.

Ana approached me and used her index finger to make marks on my forehead and cheekbones.

"What are you saying?" I inquired, in a hushed tone.

"It is a prayer for forgiveness and a request for safety. We ask that our sins not blemish the world."

"And this?" I pointed at the white clay.

"More of the same." She paused. "We will make ourselves targets, or if the vampires join us, they will know which of us not to kill."

At that moment, screams reached out through the blackness of night.

Ana's eyes were both excited and fearful. "We are being summoned."

I turned, holding out my elbows, readying myself for flight. Seconds later, I was jerked off my feet and soaring towards the cries of pain and the sounds of war.

ALERIA

Semjâzâ's hands were crushing my windpipe while his right knee pressed so hard into my chest that I worried my sternum would crack. My fears spun wildly, not only for my own safety, but also for everyone else.

Neither Bowen nor Tyran had yelled that the wings were the Fallen's weakness. I couldn't remember if I'd told Josh or not; without that information, it could be the death of everyone.

Semjâzâ jerked forward, and additional weight pressed me into the stone floor. He released my throat and clutched the side of his neck, blood pouring from the side of it. I coughed, barely able to get air through my windpipe as it healed. I still couldn't yell. Semjâzâ fell to his side, but he managed to keep a knee and palm on top of me to hold me down, while his free hand was clasping his neck to staunch the blood flow.

It was at that point I could see that Josh had stabbed Semjâzâ repeatedly, but had just been pulled off by one of the other angels.

I moaned and realized I could speak again. Making eye contact with Joshua, I gasped, "Wings! Tear off their win—"

Something hard hit me in the temple, temporarily blotting out my eyesight. I blinked away the blur, trying to focus or move or do something just as the stained glass windows seemed to explode and rain down colored glass on us and all the thrashing bodies inside.

Semjâzâ's weight disappeared, and I rolled away from him, trying to put distance between us, but I still couldn't see straight. I struggled to my knees, my gown getting in the way. A hand reached under my arm and helped me to my feet.

A hushed female voice rushed, "Your Majesty, we need to get you out of here."

I was startled; it was Tamara. My eyes finally focused. She started dragging me towards one of the alcoves with a blown out window. "Call the guard from the castle," I ordered.

"Tried. They are jamming all communication," Tamara replied.

We pushed towards the window. I didn't intend to leave; I intended to get Tamara out so she could retrieve reinforcements.

The windows—I turned and realized that there were more Fallen inside the cathedral than a moment ago, but their wings and faces were smudged with white, and they were fighting their own people.

Somehow, Tamara and I managed to weave through the chaos, but a few yards from our planned exit, she stopped dead in her tracks and fell limp to the floor. I whirled around, expecting to engage a member of the Fallen, but that wasn't who I was facing—it was Zahra.

She made a large swiping motion in front of her with a dagger; I jumped back, but she clipped me under the ribs, slicing through the stays in my dress.

We needed to be fighting the Fallen and not each other. I scrambled for something to say. "Zahra, stop! This is treason." I felt stupid saying it, but it was the only thing I could think of— she hated me, and there was no personal plea she would've heard.

Zahra smiled, her fangs flashed, matching the hatred in her eyes. "You are part of the deal. I get to kill you." She made another swipe and advanced. "I should be queen, not some neophyte Belenus wanted to bed." She raised the dagger over her head and charged, but was tackled by one of the Fallen.

I ran for Tamara to pull the stake from her heart, but was grabbed by the scruff of my neck and thrown, like a doll, over several rows of pews and back into the middle of the cathedral. I popped up, but whoever had tossed me was gone.

Rough hands seized my shoulders from behind. I turned, placing my hands around the angel's neck, and took two quick steps, swinging myself onto his back. I savagely grabbed his wings where they joined his back and pulled. I managed to get a foot on his spine and was almost at a forty-five degree angle from the floor. I screamed out, wrenching the wings from his body with every last bit of strength I had.

When they came loose, I crashed to the ground and landed next to the motionless body of a royal from Italy. His eyes were open, and then I realized the bottom half of his body was gone. I shuddered at the lifeless eyes and scrambled to my feet.

The clash of swords was deafening, combined with the cacophony of cries and battle calls echoing off the cold stone walls. I wanted to cover my ears and tuck into a ball. The metallic smell of all of the blood was stinging my eyes. I swallowed back the revulsion and fear, readying myself to fight again. I had to find Bowen and Joshua, or at the very least, get someone out to bring reinforcements.

I started towards the east alcove, but was pulled behind a pew. The second I was about to fight, I realized it was Gabriel, his face streaked with white battle paint.

I threw my arms around his neck. "I knew you survived," I choked.

Gabriel squeezed me hard for a brief second. "Reunions later. I am with Ana. They have marked themselves and are allied with you. We are going to open a Hellmouth in the church."

"How?"

"Ana is taking care of that. We need to mark anyone that we want pulled inside with blood from both of us."

"But why—"

"You are of Michael's line, and it takes two to prevent mistakes. It must be on skin or wings; clothing will not work."

"So just rub my blood on fifty or so fallen angels without getting killed."

"Yes."

"Sounds easy," I quipped, nervous. Then I thought to tell him, "Josh is here, but Batariel stole years of his memory."

Gabriel looked relieved, but asked, "Does he know me?"

"Yes," I answered. There wasn't time to explain more.

"Missed you, kiddo." Gabriel's voice was hoarse as a fragile grin passed over his face. He turned to leave, but I grabbed his arm.

"Zahra has been working with Semjâzâ to gain the throne. Mark her if you can. I'm not sure about Icelos."

Gabriel's brow furrowed. "Semjâzâ is double-crossing whoever he promised the throne to. He plans to legitimately rule with you at his side. He waited for you to be crowned."

My heart pounded in my chest, and I felt sick. Semjâzâ had waited; his eyes had snapped open the moment my reign was official. Semjâzâ had been trying to silence me, but not kill me. Then it became clear: none of his people had drawn a weapon against me; they'd been forcing me back towards the altar. This also meant that Bowen was in more danger than just a battle.

"Go, mark them all," Gabriel ordered as he threw himself back into the melee. I watched as he left a bloody handprint on angel after angel.

I glanced around and picked up a blade from the ground. I sliced my palm and squeezed, spreading my blood. Then I decided to test my theory. Slowly, I stood and moved towards the altar as if there wasn't chaos around me. I streaked my blood on the Fallen as I passed. No one touched me. My eyes roved the crowd, searching for Bowen, Joshua, and Tyran, but I still couldn't find any of them.

Then I turned and started to head for an exit. One of Semjâzâ's men shoved me back, but I'd left a bloody patch on his forearm. Changing course to the altar again, no one touched me. I jumped up, balancing on the back of a pew, and surveyed; it was then that I caught a glimpse of blond hair. There was a battle in the hallway behind the pulpit.

I hopped down and sliced my palm again since it had already healed. Marking every enemy I could on my way to the pulpit, I glanced across the cathedral and found Gabriel doing the same thing. Two of the white-marked Fallen were fighting at his sides, keeping Gabriel from being overwhelmed.

When next I planted my palm on the wing of a Fallen, he turned to fight me, but the moment he identified me, he stopped and shoved me towards the altar as the others had done. Then he picked up the legs of a vamp from Egypt and dragged him towards the grand entrance. It was at that point that I noticed the mounting pile of staked bodies being stored in the lobby.

I renewed my effort to get to the doorway behind the altar. Suddenly, Icelos was in front of me, blocking my path. I hadn't seen him in my periphery. The stake in his hand pierced my heart before I could make a sound, though my bloody hand left a crimson streak across his neck as I went limp. I expected to fall to the floor, but was plucked from his arms. Up and up I went, giant black and white wings hoisting me towards the ceiling, the smell of Ana wafting around me.

From my bird's eye view, my sightline was directed to the spot behind the pulpit. If my heart had been beating, it would have stopped...

...I was powerless to do anything.

# 21

## MUST KILL

GABRIEL

Ana had to be almost ready to open the Hellmouth. She had Aleria high above us, but there was something wrong. Ali was not moving. I scanned between the flaps of Ana's wings to find that Ali was staked.

My heart rate increased. I exhaled and refocused on my mission, but could not refrain from looking upwards once more. Ana pulled the stake from Aleria and flicked it away. Ali sprang to life, making Ana readjust her grip.

I set a new trajectory that would get me beneath Aleria and take me through the last section of unmarked Fallen—forty feet and as many bodies. I found Aleria's smudged handprint on most of the wretched angels in this section. She had done well.

At that moment, there was a lull in the clash of metal, so I took cover with my back to a pillar to survey.

ALERIA

I sucked in a breath as I felt my heart leap to life once again. Bowen was almost directly beneath me. He was on his side, clawing at the stone floor to move himself away from Semjâzâ, Batariel, and another. Bowen's free arm was wound tightly around his torso as if he was holding his organs inside his body.

Semjâzâ approached Bowen and raised his sword above his head, readying himself to take Bowen's head. Semjâzâ wasn't going to sacrifice Bowen; he was just going to kill him to get him out of the way. I fought Ana, my emotions surging.

"Stop," she demanded.

"If you want my help, drop me on Semjâzâ—Now!" I retorted in a low voice, trying not to draw attention.

Instantly, I was falling. I landed like a rodeo rider onto Semjâzâ's shoulders. I wound my legs around his neck and swung myself around like a pendant, knocking him off balance and flipping him entirely over me until we were both on our backs and only the tops of our heads touched.

I scurried up when Batariel came for me, but out of nowhere, Joshua tackled him, driving a dagger into Batariel's stomach. I spun around, looking for the angel with Semjâzâ and Batariel, but he was no longer on the altar.

Semjâzâ was laboring to his feet; I realized that he'd landed on his sword. It had gone clean through his armor. He pulled the blade from his side and shed his damaged breastplate. He looked angry—very angry.

I placed myself between Semjâzâ and Bowen, frantically looking for a weapon. Not taking my eyes off of Semjâzâ, I backed towards Bowen and found a weapon by his side. I put my hand on him, trying to reassure him, but I was a little outnumbered.

Semjâzâ looked off to his right at the bottom of the steps leading to the altar. "Remove her. I want her secured with the priest until this is over."

I glanced to my left and right, realizing a little too late that he was speaking about me.

Semjâzâ retreated and leaned against the wall, clutching his side, as three of his underlings approached me. I crouched in anticipation, still hearing Joshua fighting Batariel and Bowen's strained breath behind me. I was afraid to take my eyes off of the three Fallen cautiously preparing to grab me.

I had one advantage: Semjâzâ wanted me alive, so they would have to hold back. At the last second, dagger ready, I ran at the leader and jumped, flipping over him. I landed on the chest of the angel behind him, knocking him to the ground, while simultaneously driving the dagger straight through his neck, severing his spinal cord. I didn't stop to ponder if that would kill him.

Turning, I launched myself, landing on the back of the leader, gripping his wings. I pulled as he cried out and thrashed, trying to shake me off. At that moment, someone put me in a headlock from behind, but I didn't let go. It was one of the Fallen, because he was attempting to cut off my air, not realizing I didn't need to breathe.

The angel, whose wings I had, collapsed to his knees, and I pitched forward with him. The weight of the one behind me crashed onto my back.

Then I felt a knife in my back break the skin and hot breath on my ear. "Release him."

I didn't reply, but pulled harder. The wings started to give way just as the blade entered my back. I screamed out, but wouldn't relent. I had to take him out, or there was no way I could escape.

Suddenly, the weight on my back was gone, and the angel smashed to the ground next to me. Before I could blink an eye, his head had been taken, and a battle-scarred Tyran stood over the headless body.

"Help Bowen. He's behind you," I ordered.

Tyran glanced in Bowen's direction and moved with preternatural speed, dragging the still warm body of the Fallen to his brother. Turning my attention back to my captive, I gave one last heave and loosed the wings from my attacker's back. When they came free, I fell to the ground and rolled to the side, instantly on my feet. I retrieved the dagger that I'd left in the first angel and put the wingless one out of his misery.

Spinning in a circle to search the area, I could find no sign of Semjâzâ—he was gone. I ran to Bowen, dragging my new kill to him so he could feed. Tyran was holding Bowen's wounds shut so they would heal faster as Bowen continued to feed. Bowen's eyes were distant; I wasn't sure if he was actually lucid at this point. The feeding seemed to be instinctual.

I dropped the other angel next to them. "Here's more. Semjâzâ doesn't want either of you to walk out of here. Did you get word to the castle?"

Tyran's brow was furrowed. "No. They had a half dozen on each of us." He motioned to Bowen with one hand and wiped at his forehead, leaving scarlet streaks. "Morpheus aided me; my brother was alone."

Motioning to the ledge above, I said, "I'm going to see what's going on and find Gabriel."

"Your Slayer is here?"

I looked out towards the crowd at two angels fighting, one marked with white. "He came with them."

Tyran tore his eyes from my face and looked at the tumultuous sea of fighting. Angels were spinning into the air and dive-bombing back into the crowd. An obvious truce had evolved; ancient vampires were working with Ana's rebels together in screaming defiance.

Bowen finally started to move. He shoved away the second angel's arm, and his breathing evened out; he opened his eyes. I abandoned my plans to look for Gabriel for a moment and rushed to Bowen. It was obvious he wasn't strong enough to stand yet.

When I touched his face, his eyes went to me, and a look of relief spread through his features. I wanted to say a thousand things to him, but the battle was still raging. Fearful that someone would hear me, I pulled Bowen to a seated position, and with my other hand, yanked Tyran to me. I whispered to both of them and explained what I could in thirty seconds: Zahra had been promised the throne by Semjâzâ, both of them were to be sacrificed, Batariel was removing my memories and visions that would jeopardize Semjâzâ's plans, and Ana was on our side and her people were going to open a Hellmouth here.

I leaned back and could see a sting of betrayal, despite having been suspicious. Quickly, I planted a kiss on Bowen's lips, told Tyran to stay with Bowen, and jumped to the ledge above before they could protest.

From my perch, I could see there were six markers in place. Large metal spears had been driven into the stone, and symbols had been painted on the floor around each of them. It appeared that Ana was trying to clear the area to set up a seventh and final marker, its markings already on the flooring. She may have been putting it up for a second time. The zone set for the Hellmouth would be in front of the pews and at the base of the steps to the altar. They were set up in a ragged circle, about the size of two parking spaces.

Joshua had found Gabriel, and they were fighting back-to-back, covering one another. Morpheus was in the middle of the cathedral; he was wounded, but holding his own. I couldn't find Icelos. I searched for Zahra and found her stalking behind Ana with a huge battle-axe.

Ana had raised her arms high above her head to drive the stake into the flooring, and Zahra sprang into the air with the axe poised for a deathblow. I coiled and launched myself towards Zahra, snatching her from the air and using her body to cushion my impact as we spilled into an alcove away from the rest of the fighting.

Zahra was immediately in a crouch, ready to engage. Suddenly, my clarity was strangled by blind rage. All I could think was that she was going to have Bowen and Tyran killed to get the throne, and then Peter's face seemed to get in the way of that. I remembered Zahra wiping Peter's blood from her chin and smiling about it.

I lunged at her with a knife. I didn't even know where I'd gotten it. Before I impacted with her, Cadeyn interfered and grabbed Zahra around the waist and tossed her to the ground —hard.

"*She* is your Queen!"

"And *she* is the one who murdered *your* brother!" Zahra spat.

Cadeyn turned and pinned me with a fierce expression. "Is it true?"

I knew this was coming and didn't hesitate. My voice was heavy with emotion as I answered. "Yes, I wasn't part of this coven, and Gareth was about to kill a member of my family, so I killed him. I'm sorry, but there's nothing I can do to fix it."

Cadeyn looked down, the muscles in his forearms flexing. I stared at him, waiting for his judgment, not sure if I should bolt. A frightful mixture of emotions filtered across his face making it hard to keep myself steady.

There was a flicker of motion from the corner of my eye, and before I could react, Cadeyn had pulled his sword, and spun in a circle. A fine spray of blood wetted my face, and I stood with eyes wide, not sure of what had just happened.

I looked to my right and watched Zahra, standing with weapons drawn and a shocked expression. Then blood poured from her neck, she fell to her knees, her body collapsed. When it did, her head rolled to my feet.

Speechless, I gazed at Cadeyn, still hearing cries of battle just outside the alcove. I'd never seen a vampire move so quickly, and I realized there was a reason he was the head of the guard. He then answered my unspoken question.

"You are my Queen, and Zahra was guilty of treason," he offered as explanation.

I nodded, mutely responding to the tentative truce.

"Where is Belenus?" he asked.

"The altar, last I saw."

"There is a concealed exit not far from the altar." Cadeyn stepped forward and grabbed my arm, moving me towards the altar, his eyes on the doorway behind the pulpit.

When we rounded a pillar, we came upon Gabriel with Joshua directly behind. Cadeyn postured aggressively, and I put myself in his path, his hand never leaving my arm.

"Gabriel is with us. He came with the white-marked angels."

Cadeyn didn't respond, but tugged me towards the altar again. Gabriel and Joshua followed.

As we approached, Ana's people were defending each of the posts she'd driven into the stone floor, marking the soon-to-be Hellmouth. I glanced around the chaos. The vampires were fighting alongside the white marked angels, but by no means were we winning. My encounters had been with the less formidable Fallen.

I spotted Icelos standing stone still next to the wall in the alcove on the opposite side of the sanctuary. Between us, there was a sea of writhing, fighting bodies, and he looked as if he were looking over a serene landscape with an expression that reminded me of Moloch. No one seemed to note his position; it was as if he was a piece of the masonry. Despite wanting to charge across the chaos and murder him with my own hands, I followed Cadeyn's lead towards the altar.

Keeping track of Ana, I noticed she was scanning the ever-shrinking crowd. Suddenly, I was jerked to the side when Cadeyn was snatched away by a Fallen. I moved to help, but Cadeyn screamed, "Go!"

Still moving towards Cadeyn, Gabriel stopped me.

"It is time. Ana needs us."

I glanced over at Cadeyn; he'd already fought himself free and was fighting back. My eyes went to Ana. All of the spear-like devices were in the floor. I wasn't sure how long her people could protect them.

Gabriel's hand was on my shoulder, urging me forward. I took two steps when ice slid through my veins. I turned towards Gabriel, managing to push his name past my lips. All I could think was *"not now"* as darkness entombed me. The last thing I saw before blacking out was Gabriel's alarmed face.

---

I was me. The adrenaline of battle drained away as I stared at the ornate ceiling—a cloudscape of the purest blues and whites, and on the far right, a hint of sunset. This was a week ago. I'd been sitting on the overstuffed couch with my head leaned back all the way, staring at the ceiling in the sitting area of the main bedroom. The painting covered the entire ceiling and was so real that I could almost feel the sun on my face and the breeze on my skin.

Bowen's face dipped into my vision, giving me an upside-down kiss.

I smiled. "I didn't hear you come in."

"I was quiet. I wanted to see how you spend your time without me when you aren't training."

"Really?"

Bowen grinned. "No. I said your name, but you were too deep in thought to take note of my entrance or my brother leaving."

"Sorry."

Bowen rolled over the back of the couch and landed with his head in my lap. I ran my fingers through his hair. He closed his eyes contentedly and exhaled slowly.

"What has you so deep in thought?" he asked.

"I'm going in circles. There is at least one more traitor in the castle and another in the Watchers. I'm wondering if it's the obvious choice, or if I'm being manipulated into thinking that."

"Who is the obvious choice in the Watchers?"

"Blackthorne was working with Ana. Even if we believe she is on our side, she was working with Semjâzâ for over a year. She will only turn on Semjâzâ if she thinks she can win. If Blackthorne knew this, he was most likely working with Semjâzâ.

"Then Rousseau is back; I can't count her out. Also, it bothers me that Sydney Sato was my Keeper for a few months, and then handed me to Gabriel, saying he could function as my Keeper. That has never been done before—like, ever. I didn't mind, obviously. But it doesn't sit right. What if she was afraid I would see through her? I tend to have visions involving people closer to me. She could've been distancing herself. I don't feel as if I really know her that well."

"There could be more than one traitor in your organization."

I huffed and let my head fall back, looking at the ceiling again. "I wish I could just run away."

Bowen became quiet and flinched so slightly that I almost missed it.

I lifted my head back up and looked down at him. "What?"

He grinned, but it didn't reach his eyes.

I tugged on his hair a little. "What's wrong?"

"You were going to run away with Joshua the night he sent you away."

I froze for a second. "How do you know that?"

"I heard you. The night before. All night." Bowen swallowed uncomfortably.

My hand dropped from his hair. "I'm so, so sorry. I didn't think you—"

"There is nothing to be embarrassed about." He paused. "I gave up that night. Tyran and I had made plans to return. I had decided to leave it to fate and not pursue you. What I had heard you say to one another that night..."

"But you were always so confident that we would be together?"

"Even those with the deepest of faith can be shaken once in a while." Bowen sat up, propping his elbows on his knees and dropping his head in his hands. This was more than my past with Joshua that was weighing on him. Bowen sighed. "I believe my own cousin desires the throne enough to kill me."

"Icelos?"

Bowen nodded in affirmation.

"Is he your obvious choice?"

"He has access to my rooms. I have a witness that heard him

encourage Cadeyn to have you captured and brought to the castle. There is another witness who was to tip him off the moment you came through the gates. He wanted you here and unharmed—just as Semjâzâ wanted. The obvious choice is the only choice in this case."

"Will you have him arrested?"

"No. I want to figure out his end game."

"And what if that is to kill you?" My voice rose in alarm.

He didn't answer, but he met my eyes and wrapped his left arm around me, pulling me close. His lips found mine, then he kissed me. His lips were soft, yet urgent. He paused and pulled me onto his lap. His hands traveled up the outside of my thighs and under my shirt until he was touching the bare skin of my waist. His fingers felt oddly warm on my cool skin.

"You will have to trust me. I won't risk this." He shook me a little so I knew he was talking about me.

He leaned forward and ran his tongue across my collarbone, ending with soft kisses on my shoulder. The burn in my belly increased, and he grinned up at me in response, feeling my desire. I shifted to straddle him and squeezed him with my thighs as I bent to kiss him, my breathing uneven—loving the feel of his lips and hands on me.

The intensity of my emotion had made me forget that this was a vision for a moment. I wanted to stay in this moment for as long as I could, fearing that this was the closest I would ever be to feeling his caress again.

Then the vision shifted. I was in a member of the Fallen. Strong wings tucked in tight against my back as I waited. Someone was approaching in an alley. It was Phineas.

I—the angel—spoke first. I didn't recognize the voice. "Were you able to procure the item?"

"You promise that every vampire in the Watchers and the

two royals from the French Coven will be exterminated?"

"That is the agreement."

"Then you have full access. The passwords will work for seventy-two hours."

"A pleasure doing business. I am sure we will see you soon."

"I'm done."

The angel laughed. "You have proven you can be bought. We will see you again." His wings snapped open with a crack, and he was soaring upwards into the black sky.

There was another shift. I was in another member of the Fallen. His thoughts darted this way and that. He wasn't coherent—not entirely sane. Then he tugged at his constraints.

An angel from Semjâzâ's inner circle appeared in front of me—him.

"Are you ready, big boy?"

I grunted, abnormally happy.

Semjâzâ's man held up a picture. It was of me. "You need to protect this pretty lady. The master wants her. Anyone else without wings—kill them."

I grunted again, rocking like an overly excited child.

The shackles were removed; I was instantly on my feet and barreling down a hallway like a bull, towards the sound of chaos. A Fallen with his back pressed against the wall handed me a heinous-looking, heavy spear before I emerged onto the back of the altar. The smell of sweat and blood filled me with glee.

I set my sights on a body. No wings. I rushed for it, focusing on nothing else. He looked important. *Kill. Must kill.* I drove the spear into his back, feeling the crunch of bone, and pleasure surged through me. I hoisted him from the ground effortlessly, shaking him and watching his body fold brokenly.

It was then that I realized the broken body was Gabriel.

## EVIL

GABRIEL

I had wrapped my hand and carefully put Aleria over my shoulder, preventing my blood from getting on her. Angel after angel turned to engage me. The moment they recognized Aleria, they backed away and started fighting elsewhere. It was obvious that she was not to be harmed, even if it meant leaving me alone.

I caught sight of Ana just as she spun into the air and landed beside me.

"What is wrong with her?" asked Ana.

"Vision." I eased Aleria off of my shoulder so I could examine her face. She looked pained. "She is still deep inside it."

"I need blood from both of you on the symbols here and here. Can you do that?" She pointed at the nearest staff.

Over Ana's shoulder, I could see both Belenus and Taranis not far away. "Yes."

"When it's done, meet me there." Ana pointed to the top of the steps on the altar. Then she took to the air again, alighting on the ledge above. It appeared as if she was searching for someone—probably Semjâzâ. I had seen Aleria knock him to the ground and had lost track of him after that point.

Without hesitation, I made for Belenus and Taranis, cradling Aleria's still unconscious body. When Belenus observed me approaching, the depth of his care for Aleria was carved on his face.

He was on me instantly, and I spoke before he could. "I need her blood on the markers." Then I explained the details. "If my blood gets on either of you—"

"I understand," responded Belenus. Aleria must have informed him.

Before I could hand Aleria over, Belenus was plucked from my side and carried upwards. Taranis suddenly relieved me of Aleria. "I heard. Do your part. I've got her. My brother will be with me momentarily."

I looked upward; though Belenus was in the air, somehow he already had the upper hand. One-on-one the Fallen were no match for Belenus. Taranis sliced Aleria's hand and started in clockwise; I decided on the opposite to spread out the targets.

Working quickly, I passed Taranis and Aleria. Despite her being unconscious, they moved with more speed. I had to fight at each marker. Semjâzâ's people were still giving Aleria a wide berth.

Just as I rubbed my blood on the third marker, something grabbed my shirt, then released me. Turning, ready to defend myself, I discovered Joshua standing over a staked vampire. Joshua had obviously recovered from some fairly serious injuries.

"Miss me?"

"Protect my flank," I ordered, grinning.

Joshua's eyes narrowed. "Which one has her?"

"Taranis."

His face went blank, and he returned to fighting stance, guarding me. It was apparent that his muscle memory remained intact; he was fighting with moves that I had taught him in the last year. With Joshua at my back, I was able to complete my mission without significant opposition.

We fought our way up the steps and met Ana next to the lectern. Her people were still involved in the broil in the nave. A few of Semjâzâ's agents became aware of Ana and I on the altar and started pushing our way. We would not have long before more would join.

## ALERIA

When the scene slowly swam into focus, a cry erupted from my throat before I opened my eyes. "Gabriel! Gabriel! Behind you!" When I could finally force my eyes open, I was in Tyran's arms. He looked away from me, and as he did, I could see Gabriel at the back of the altar in front of the doorway I'd seen in my vision.

Gabriel turned profile, just a gargantuan spear breezed by his side, just barely breaking the skin. He spun around, changing the grip on his dagger, and catapulted himself into the air at the troll-like angel from my vision. It was four times the size of Semjâzâ, who was the largest angel I'd ever seen. But there was something wrong with this one's head. It had no hair, and there was a huge scar in a rough X-marking-the-spot where its skull was partially caved in. All of the other angels could pass for human, but not this thing. It was a troll straight from *Lord of the Rings*.

It was well-muscled, but didn't have the reach to pull Gabriel off of him as Gabriel grappled up the creature. Joshua waved his arms to capture its attention.

I exhaled in relief; the spear had missed Gabriel's spine. Then I glanced around. "Where's Bowen?"

Tyran took my hand and smeared my blood on a marker. "Above us."

I looked up as Tyran moved us to the next marker. I let him move me like a puppet as I stared upwards. One of the Fallen was wildly flapping his wings while Bowen maneuvered himself onto the angel's back. The movements were quick, and I watched as Bowen severed the Fallen's head from its body. Bowen rode the body to the ground and disappeared into the roiling sea of fighting bodies. I couldn't see him, but I could feel that he was alive.

Tyran's hand went from my wrist to my elbow. "That's the last one, sissy. We need to circle back to A—" Tyran jerked forward, as he was speared through the back and lifted off the ground. He grimaced in pain. "Go!" he ordered. Then he grinned and broke the head of the spear off. He threw his legs forward and somehow slid forward off of the shaft and dropped to the ground.

I looked at the spear holder. He was one of the smaller angels. When I saw that Tyran was on him, I turned on my heel and sprinted for Ana—the spear-wielding angel would be dead in moments.


GABRIEL

Holding fast, I hooked my arm over the top of the mammoth angel's wing. It would be disadvantageous to tear or hack the wings; the bases were too large. With resolve, I dug my foot into the spine, then found the soft spot at the base of the skull and thrust my dagger into it—straight and true. The beast shuddered, its breath bellowing from its body seconds before it pitched forward. I prepared to roll off as it hit the ground.

A few of the Fallen stood aghast; it must have been anticlimactic having their ringer taken out so efficiently. And now I knew another way to extinguish them.

I began a trajectory towards the Hellmouth markers, but then I caught sight of Ali, standing stone still in a conflict. Her sights were latched onto someone. Turning, I scanned, trying to find whom she was staring at. There was a Fallen, blond, bronzed skin, tattooed face, and about my height. He was grinning at Ali. I realized he fit the description Ana had given me of Batariel.

Batariel stepped into an alcove out of sight just as Ali made a break for him. I moved to intercept, but was tackled. Ali did not know that Semjâzâ had been holding Batariel back; Batariel wanted Aleria dead, believing that Semjâzâ would not be able to control her. Batariel had learned that Ali had challenged Dagan and stood up to Moloch even when facing death.


ALERIA

I spotted Batariel, and he had the audacity to smirk at me. Tearing through the crowd, I followed him into the alcove not far from the altar. I was shocked that no one had tried to stop me when my path had deviated from the front of the church, but I'd been quick.

He appeared to be waiting for me, but there was a moment of surprise when I hurled myself into him so hard that he went crashing onto his back. I drove a knife into his shoulder.

"Can you return memories?" I demanded.

He laughed.

I pressed the blade in farther, but he threw me off so rapidly that I didn't have time to recover before he had me around the throat and immobilized against the wall. He then drove a dagger into me. He literally had me pinned to the wall—he'd driven the blade clear into the stone. My lung had been punctured. I involuntarily coughed blood into his face.

Batariel laughed again and turned his body towards the opening of the alcove. He said something in a strange language and waved his arm, palm open in the direction of the arch that I'd just come through. It seemed as if the sounds of battle in the main hall became slightly muted. After he completed his incantation and hand motion, he turned his attention back to me.

"I can return whatever memories I choose, but I will not," he scoffed. Then he rocked the blade to the side, keeping the tip in the wall, using it as a lever. There was a shock of horrible pain and a ghastly snap, then I could no longer feel my legs. I hung there helpless, grasping his shoulders, but I was doing little more than holding myself up. He shifted reaching into his pocket with one hand for a moment, then he stuck his fingers into the wound in my chest for a moment. I convulsed and had no idea what he'd done, but it seemed as if my bleeding had slowed.

He smiled at me again, the same lecherous smile he'd given me in the throne room when I'd returned with Bowen and Tyran weeks earlier. Maybe he had staunched the blood flow so he could take his time with me.

"I thought Semjâzâ wanted me alive?" I managed to gurgle.

"That has been a source of disagreement." He narrowed his eyes and grabbed my face, twisting it from side to side, examining me.

Over his shoulder, I watched as Tyran looked into the alcove straight at me, then walked off as if I wasn't here. My hopes plummeted.

Batariel glanced in the direction I was looking. "Unless someone saw you enter, no one will know that you are here."

The edges of my vision started to get blotchy; despite the decreased flow, I was still losing blood. I tried to focus on healing, but I needed to feed. I looked at the vein on Batariel's neck and felt my fangs elongate.

He chuckled. "Are those for me? I heard your bite can be very pleasurable."

I wanted to say something like, "Let me show you," and then drain the life from his body, but at this point, I was simply trying to keep my eyes open.


## GABRIEL

Still stunned by the impact, I picked myself up swiftly. But, I had not been tackled by a Fallen, it was a vampire. Suddenly, I was hurtling forwards again. Something had hit me in the back, launching me. I could smell it—the same vampire.

I sprang to my feet, instantly on guard. My attacker retreated next to a pillar. With surprise, I recognized the perpetrator. He was one of the Oneiroi, either Icelos or Phantasos. I knew they were fraternal twins, but differentiating them in person was difficult.

He glanced towards the alcove in which I had seen Ali enter. Then it became apparent: he had been stalling me. He had not engaged to protect himself.

I turned and sprinted towards the alcove. Thirty meters... twenty...ten...a Fallen dropped in front of me, and I skidded to a stop. He was large. I tightened my grip on my sword and charged.

ALERIA

Batariel pressed me harder to the wall, and then there was a blur of movement behind him. He shifted, keeping a hand on my throat, then he blocked someone coming at high speed. My eyes drooped shut for a second; I opened them when Batariel let go of me—he was fighting with Joshua. They were crashing from one side of the alcove to the other in rapid succession, bits of dust and stone filtering into the air from each impact—back and forth and back and forth. Joshua drove a knife into Batariel's gut.

Tearing my eyes away from their fight, I stared down at the hilt of the blade in me and noticed my dangling feet. I still couldn't command them to do anything. Shoving down the alarm, I drew the dagger out and immediately dropped to the stone floor. My arms barely stopped my fall before breaking my face.

Joshua and Batariel continued to fight, despite the blade still sticking from Batariel's gut. Then, I saw the flash of steel, and there was another flurry of motion. Seconds later, Joshua's body fell not far from me—staked.

I clawed my way closer to him, dragging my lower body, but Batariel dropped to his knees between us before I could reach Josh. Batariel took a moment to rearrange us, shoving our bodies parallel; he rolled Joshua on his side. Joshua's eyes settled on me once I was in sight. While staked, he could do little more than blink.

At that moment, I heard Bowen calling my name, his voice on the edge of panic. I couldn't feel him though—or Tyran or Gabriel—but I could feel Joshua. Whatever dampening or cloaking spell Batariel had created, we were completely isolated —the blood bond and visually. Joshua had obviously walked right inside.

Batariel gazed down at Joshua. "You are going to help me decide if she lives."

Joshua's eyes slowly left me, and then rested on Batariel's dark gaze.

"You know Semjâzâ wants me alive," I protested, a point worth making again.

"Semjâzâ wants many things. I support him in everything—but you. Though, when he is finished with your womb, you are promised to me. I have curiosities about Seers."

I could feel myself pale.

Batariel brushed his fingers across Joshua's forehead. "You do not remember the intensity of your desire for her." Then he pressed his index finger to Joshua's temple with his right hand and with his left, he placed a finger on one of the circular tattoos on his face. The color of his tattoos altered for a moment as he concentrated.

I looked at Joshua. His eyes were on me again, but he wasn't *seeing* me. He was reliving something. I could feel pleasure and adoration through our blood bond. It made me wonder what Batariel was up to.

"And this is how she felt about you." Batariel moved his finger to a different circular tattoo.

It was then that I realized that Batariel had more than taken my memories. He had rummaged through my brain and duplicated what he wanted. The knowledge of this new violation spread through my body and sickened me. I tried to wiggle my toes, but still couldn't feel anything. Fighting Batariel would be impossible in my present state; I decided to reserve my energy. I swallowed back all the horror that I was feeling and looked to the mouth of the alcove. The fighting continued to rage.

It was as if Batariel could read my mind. "No one is coming

to rescue you. You are supposed to be locked away with the priest for your marriage after the battle." He paused. "And battles between immortals can last a very, very long time. Hours. Even days. He let his voice linger on the word.

I knew it wasn't entirely true. Bowen and Tyran were already looking for me. I knew Gabriel would be before long, if he wasn't already, and perhaps even Ana.

Batariel's black eyes drifted back to Joshua. "And this is how she felt the very next day. I enjoyed it when you struck her."

Joshua squeezed his eyes shut. It was then that I realized that Batariel had given Joshua our last night together and the following night when he had crushed me. But I thought it was odd that he gave Joshua *my* memory of the event, and not Joshua's own memory. The hurt and betrayal I'd felt radiated from him.

I glanced up at Batariel; his eyes were closed. He looked like he was savoring the sweetest of substances. I think maybe he was—my pain.

Batariel spoke; I wasn't sure which of us he was speaking to. "You think you know what evil is? That, out there." He motioned to the bloody conflict just outside. "That is but a taste. Your people are merely a shadow of what we were." He picked his hand up from Joshua's brow and thought for a moment. Then, he clearly spoke to Joshua. "Remember, you will help me decide whether your young Queen lives."

Joshua opened his eyes as tears welled up in them. I could feel the swirl of conflicting emotions. Then Batariel placed his hand on Joshua's temple again.

"I had a visit with some of what you call familiars in this castle. When your Queen is mine..."

Fear and horror from Joshua shot through me like an electrical surge. I could feel it crackle through my body, leaving me singed and hollow. I wondered what Joshua was seeing. The tears that had been on the edge of his lids streaked from his eyes and a low keening sound escaped from his lips. Whatever Batariel was revealing, it was something I did not want to experience. I'd already known it was bad. When Morpheus had told Bowen of the attack, he'd been shaken up—and *that* wouldn't have been easy.

If Batariel was given complete control, I feared it would be the end of everything.

# CHOOSE

ALERIA

Batariel stood abruptly and paced back and forth. His eyes went from the opening to Joshua and back again. Once again, I tried to wiggle my toes, and a sense of hopelessness bubbled up when I still felt nothing. My wound had healed enough that I wasn't bleeding any longer. I worried that what he'd done to my spine was permanent. There was just...nothing.

My attention was drawn outside. Bowen was screaming my name again—he was searching for me. Batariel glanced outside, and then back to Josh and I; he seemed to think it was safe enough to do something on his phone. I waited until it sounded like Bowen was close and bellowed his name. Almost instantly, Batariel's boot met my jaw, cutting off my cry. I held my head, trying to stop the spinning. While I was reeling, it occurred to me that if Batariel was sending a text, then his phone wasn't blocked by the jamming field. We could get a message to the castle for reinforcements.

Batariel dropped to a knee. He stared at me with disapproval and placed his hand back on Joshua's temple. Slowly, he raised his hand to his tattoo. Joshua squeezed his eyes shut in reaction.

"Please," I pleaded. "I won't yell again. Stop!"

Batariel opened one eye, but his expression didn't change. To my alarm, Joshua's eyes clenched even more tightly shut.

"Please," I begged once more, dragging my way closer.

Then, to my surprise, Batariel leaned abruptly forward and pulled the stake from Joshua's heart. Josh sucked in a breath and rolled on his back. I had no idea what Batariel was up to, and I had nothing to bargain with. I prayed and tried moving my legs, but still got nothing. Not even the slightest tinge.

I clawed my way towards Joshua, pulling the dead weight of my lower body, but the moment I touched him, Batariel stood, hooked his foot under my ribcage, and tossed me thirty feet away. My arms flailed, and my legs sprawled awkwardly as I rolled the last few feet, not far from the wall, my torn gown riding up and twisting awkwardly around my waist.

Joshua started to move. He hadn't lost that much blood, so he was recovering quickly. Batariel circled with leisure so that Josh was between us. Josh rolled onto his hands and knees, but before he'd a chance to stand, Batariel grabbed Joshua by the jacket and dragged him towards me.

Batariel cooed, loud enough for me to hear. "I said I would give you the choice of whether she lives or dies. I offer you this: kill her, and she will not suffer. Let her live, and I will do to her all that I have shown you and more. And I promise that Semjâzâ will not be gentle either."

I remembered Tyran saying that whatever the Fallen had done here on Earth before had been so horrible that God had flooded the entire planet. It was hard to swallow past the lump in my throat. Joshua rubbed at his eyes and wobbled on his feet, but I felt he was more recovered than he was acting.

Batariel released Joshua's suit jacket and moved his hand to Joshua's right shoulder. With his left, he pressed a blade into Joshua's left hand, then leaned in to Joshua's ear. Batariel cooed, "Kill her. Save her from the pain and from the humiliation. Semjâzâ will degrade her, and what will come from her womb will plague this planet. Save her."

Joshua made eye contact with me for a moment, and then squeezed his eyes shut, as if trying not to see something; his emotions were like wild fire.

Batariel kept his hand wrapped around Josh's weapon-wielding hand. "Try to kill me, and I will use you as a slave." Then he released Joshua. Josh stood still like a tree leaning into wind, his hair and the torn cuff on his shirt fluttering slightly. It was then that I noticed that air was moving through the alcove like a wind tunnel into the sanctuary. It must have been from the blown out stained glass windows.

I pushed myself backwards, away from them, my heart hammering. When I hit the stone wall, I stopped, leaning against it. Looking at my motionless legs, I noticed that my dress was in tatters and my toes were sticking out of a hole in my black stockings. My foot looked bluish, it was so pale. Something about my toes sticking out struck me as funny, and I started to laugh—hard. I wiped tears from my eyes with the back of my hand. It was impossible to stop laughing once I'd started; it became sort of a gulping chortle that sounded half-crazed.

Josh stood there frozen, with the dagger in his hand. Batariel glared at me like I was poison.

It was then I realized I really had nothing to lose. "You are weak, you know that?" I scoffed. "If you want me dead, do it yourself. Are you too scared of Semjâzâ to do it yourself? You need a scapegoat to cover your cowardice?"

"I am too old to be goaded by a child."

"The vein in your neck says otherwise. Your heart is racing—it means you know I'm right. You're a coward."

Josh suddenly exploded in movement. He grabbed the front of my dress and hoisted me up, shoving me to the wall. Panic rose up, but I kept myself from crying out. I couldn't tell if my feet were on the floor or not. He was breathing hard as he pressed the tip of the blade over my heart. The pressure was great enough that it broke the skin. He sagged a little and pressed his forehead to mine. "I can't let him do that to you," he breathed. "I can't."

I cupped the side of his face, and he pulled his head back enough to look me in the eyes. We stood, locked in silent communication.

Josh tipped his chin slightly upwards and raised the elbow of his blade hand. "Ready?"

My heart rate slowed. I was calm. I was ready.


GABRIEL

My adversary was winning. Flat on my back, my arms began to quake as the angel put all his weight into pressing the blade into my sternum. Blotches of light sparked in my vision; his knee was crushing my chest, compromising my ability to breathe.

I had lost my leverage, but tried once more to throw him to the side. He did not budge, and the effort allowed his blade to press closer.

Suddenly, my vision went red, and blood choked me. I blinked. The angel, on bended knee, was still atop me, but his head had been severed. I heaved the carcass off of me and was immediately offered a hand by Taranis. He swiftly pulled me to my feet, but did not release me.

"We smell Aleria everywhere, but I can't find her."

I noticed Belenus directly behind Taranis, guarding his brother's flank. Then I pointed. "The alcove there—she followed Batariel inside. Joshua followed, no one returned." Without another word, I made for the opening, both of them on my heels.

## ALERIA

A shadow passed behind Batariel, followed by two more. But I couldn't take my eyes off of Joshua. In one movement, he released me and spun around with his dagger, slashing at Batariel.

Batariel made a swift movement, and Joshua went crashing to his side, grabbing his neck. I dragged myself towards the dagger that Joshua had dropped, still not looking to see who'd entered. I couldn't spare the time until I was armed. My fingers closed around the hilt.

The sound of fighting drew my attention. Relief washed over me when I took in Batariel outnumbered by Bowen, Gabriel, and Tyran. Within moments, Batariel was bloodied and on his knees. I continued to drag myself towards Joshua, but he staggered to his feet before I reached him, still holding the left side of his neck.

Joshua stood in front of Batariel, and the room fell silent; I could only hear the fighting in the main hall and the whir of the wind through the space. Josh held his hand out for Gabriel's sword, and Gabriel handed it over without question.

Batariel sneered. "You want more of your memories back?"

Joshua was breathing heavily, his shoulders moving with each breath. I glanced at Bowen and Tyran, but all eyes were on Batariel. With expert precision, Joshua raised his arm and took Batariel's head before I could open my mouth to protest.

"Josh! Your memories!" I cried.

He fell to his knees, dropping the sword. "He was too dangerous to live," was all he said. A volcanic eruption of emotion rolled over me, making me gasp.

Two seconds later, Bowen's hands were on my face as he frantically scanned me. "Are you all right?"

"I'm okay, but I can't move my legs."

Relief was the only expression on Bowen's face before he kissed me and scooped me up. I looped my arm around his shoulders and pressed my forehead to his jaw. It was then that I noticed the sounds of battle had gotten much louder—Batariel's magic cloaking spell had gone down when he'd been killed.

Gabriel was on a knee, talking quietly to Joshua, then he stood and walked over to me. He placed his hand on my shoulder. "Ana needs us out there, kiddo. She cannot open the Hellmouth without us. You ready?"

"Wait! Batariel's phone. I think he sent a text. We can call the castle for reinforcements."

Gabriel snatched it from the stone floor. When he saw something on the screen, he paled and immediately dialed, pressing the phone to his ear. "Raphael? It's Gabriel. Go in! Now!" He ended the call and handed the phone to Tyran. But Gabriel looked at me with worry, and I didn't miss the fact that he had used a contraction while on the phone. He looked at Josh with the same worried expression, and then back to me.

Tyran spoke up. "More Guard on the way. They'd already been summoned."

"We cannot wait. Ana's people will not be able to hold the gateway much longer."

I turned my head towards Bowen. "You okay with carrying me?"

"Yes."

Gabriel looked confused. "Can you fight?"

I shook my head. "Batariel severed my spine. I'm not healing. But, give me a weapon." Gabriel pressed the hilt of a dagger into my hand, his lips pressed into a thin line, and I felt more emotion from him than normal.

Tyran circled to us. "I'll protect your back, brother."

I disagreed. "No. They're not supposed to harm me. Batariel was defying orders. You, Josh, and Gabriel have all been marked for execution. Protect each other. We'll meet you at the altar."

There was a pause, but everyone seemed to agree. For some reason, I'd expected a protest.

Gabriel and Joshua moved towards the main hall.

Tyran gave me a look of disapproval. "You sure, sissy?" He put his hand on Bowen's shoulder, grazing my fingers.

"Protect Gabriel, as if he was me."

He didn't release my gaze. "As you wish."

I squeezed Bowen's shoulder; he paused just inside the doorway. "Bowen, I need—"

He quickly planted his lips on mine, silencing me. "Tell me when this is all over."

I nodded mutely while staring into his eyes, trying to communicate more than was possible in mere seconds.

He wore the same troubled expression I knew I was wearing. He kissed my forehead tenderly, as if he could read my mind, the last exchange taking no more than a few seconds.

And with that, we charged into the fray.

# 24

# FORGIVE ME

ALERIA

Plunging into the battle in the main hall was like being torn apart by a whirlpool. We'd only managed to travel five yards before we were knocked to the ground and ripped from one another. I had to blink a few times before I'd realized that two angels had worked in tandem to dive-bomb us, and we were now being flown in different directions. I shrieked Bowen's name as I watched him being carried towards the front doors.

After the shock wore from his face, he went to work at getting free. When I witnessed Bowen slash at the angel, opening him like a zipper, I looked away to assess my own situation.

Being unable to swing my legs to gain any sort of momentum, or even leverage, left me feeling helpless. I pried at the cretin's fingers, but the moment I freed myself from one hand, he would readjust and trap me again. I'd dropped my knife when I'd been rammed and stolen into the air.

I glanced around frantically for something—anything. It was

then that I noticed we were flapping in a slow circle over the entrance of the South alcove, the opposite side of where Batariel had taken refuge. Semjâzâ stepped to the edge of the entrance, looked upwards, made a motion, and then disappeared inside.

When we started to descend, I felt a new set of hands loop under my arms. Two wings were flapping furiously in different directions, trying to wrench me from the other. I cried out in pain when the tendons started to tear around my shoulder sockets.

## GABRIEL

Taranis, under Ali's orders, continued to protect me. He took point, blazing a path, and had taken a sword to the gut in the process. He battled on, as if unfazed, while strapping the wound with his arm.

A Fallen came from the side, aiming for Taranis' neck; I blocked with my sword and planted my dagger under the angel's ribs. Protecting the vampire that had murdered my team members and nearly broken Aleria was almost more than I could bear. But honor our alliance, I would.

Taranis turned in surprise when he realized I had saved his life. We were even now.

"Where is Aleria?" asked Ana, as she dropped between us.

I turned. Ali and Belenus were gone, as was Joshua. They had all disappeared in the moments I was protecting Taranis.

Suddenly, Joshua was back, his glowing green eyes a beacon in a mask of crimson. He looked as if he had bathed in his adversary's blood. "Bowen is near the front of the cathedral, fighting his way here. I can't find Ali. Two of them were fighting over her above us. I thought they were going to tear her in two. I lost track when I was attacked."

"Get Gabriel to the altar. I will get Belenus and use him to track Aleria," said Ana to Joshua, then she exploded into the air.

Not used to someone giving orders as if I was not present, I shrugged off the irritation. Ana lifted Belenus into the air and sped across the sanctuary. Belenus was pointing towards the south alcove.

Swooping across the nave in seconds, they dropped out of view just as Joshua ushered me towards the altar.


ALERIA

The angel carrying me was shot from the sky, and we plummeted to the ground. He landed on top of me. He may not have been dead, but he was certainly dead weight on top of me. He must've weighed as much as a cow—a very fat one. Despite the strength of my upper body, it took me a few seconds to struggle from beneath him, dragging my unresponsive lower body. I grunted as I shoved him off.

He sucked in a breath. *Nope, not dead.* I dragged myself in what I thought was the direction of the altar. My fingers were stepped on several times as I wormed my way there, not being able to rise more than knee level when I shoved myself up on straight arms and flattened palms that resembled the "cobra" pose in yoga.

At that moment, feet landed on both sides of me. Relief swept over me instantly. I rolled onto my side just as Bowen hoisted me into his arms. I wrapped my arms around his neck and pressed my forehead to his cheek.

Bowen battled his way through the crowd while Ana fought off airborne threats. He closed the distance one slash and stab at a time. I clung to him, wishing I could fight beside him. Then, somehow, we made it. All five of us were alive and at the top of the circle. Bowen held me tightly, standing directly behind Ana, with Gabriel and Bowen's shoulders almost touching.

With urgency, Ana grasped my hand and slit my palm open. Bowen's face tightened. She placed my hand around the symbols on the last marker as she instructed, "Keep your hand on this." Then she repeated the process with Gabriel. She was working with such speed that when I glanced up, I found Semjâzâ soaring towards us, wings brushing the heads of the combatants below.

As he reached us, he flapped his massive black wings and hovered just above. He opened his mouth to speak, but Ana cut him off. "It's too late, Semjâzâ!" Then Ana drove the spear into the stone floor.

A clap reverberated through the cathedral, as if lightning had struck, and then it seemed like time itself was standing still. I watched as particles hung slowly in the air, spinning away from Ana. Angels swooping in the air slowed as if caught in an unseen current. Every entity in the building looked towards Ana, and just as the recognition that something significant had happened, there was a sonic boom that threw everyone backwards.

I landed a few feet from Bowen, almost on top of Gabriel. The slice across my palm had healed, but it was still caked with blood. I swung my arm away from him to keep my blood off of him, and he was doing the same to protect me.

A surge of light poured through the room as the floor opened up. The sound that followed was like rock being pulverized with an underscore of inhuman howls, roars, and screeches. When that cacophony died down, the growing whir of air overcame everything.

At that moment, all of the particles that seemed to have been suspended in the air were drawn into the now open Hellmouth in the floor.

A Fallen who was airborne and clearly marked with both Gabriel's and my blood was swallowed so quickly into the opening, it was like sucking a moth into the hose of a vacuum cleaner. Angel after angel went flying into the chasm, shrieking as they went.

Then the unthinkable happened: an invisible force grabbed ahold of my leg, and I started sliding towards the opening. My mind spun for answers. I had avoided Gabriel's blood, so why was I being dragged towards the Hellmouth? I clawed at the ground, trying to find purchase, but only succeeded in leaving crimson streaks behind.

Bowen cried out my name, and just as his fingertips brushed mine, I watched Semjâzâ stand and thrust a broadsword through Bowen's back and into the stone floor, pinning Bowen in place. Bowen was still reaching for me, but he couldn't break free. He flailed, trying to reach the sword in his back. Semjâzâ held the hilt firmly, keeping both Bowen down and keeping himself from sliding towards the Hellmouth.

I continued getting closer and closer and still couldn't do much more to slow myself when a warm hand circled my wrist. Gabriel had managed to get a finger hold on the lectern, as well as on me.

Although everyone was being pulled towards the Hellmouth, those marked with blood faced double or triple the force. I was being dragged as if I'd been marked, too.

"Take the Queen to the chapel. Now!" Semjâzâ ordered.

I looked in the direction in which Semjâzâ spoke. Three of the Fallen nervously relinquished their grip. They were unmarked, so they'd been able to resist the pull of the Hellmouth. Two of them didn't make it far; Joshua and Tyran were on them, but the third was still approaching.

With desperation, I looked around. Ana was being pulled

into the Hellmouth; she was holding onto the marker, but was six inches off of the ground. Bowen was clawing savagely at his back and screaming, but still couldn't reach the sword Semjâzâ was holding in place. And the angels that Joshua and Tyran were fighting were formidable.

I looked up my arm. "There's no one else. You need to let go of me." Gabriel *had* to let me go in order to fight, or he was going to be as helpless as me.

"Not going to happen, kiddo."

The third angel was working his way to us, moving from one solid object to the next, keeping himself from being gobbled up by the abyss. He was about twenty feet away when he held up a gold and silver battle-axe. When he squeezed the handle, the blade on the head of the axe began to glow red with heat.

I twisted my hand, trying to loosen Gabriel's grip on my wrist. "Let go. He won't let me be pulled inside."

Gabriel shook his head. "He could miss. Stop, damn it, and reach for me." From somewhere inside, Gabriel found more strength, and he started pulling me closer, the veins in his arm bulging while his face turned red with the effort.

Crying out, I grabbed Gabriel's wrist with my free hand. I felt relief when he bent his arm and started pulling me closer. Then, in a glowing red blur, the axe came down through the middle of Gabriel's forearm, and I was sliding back towards the Hellmouth while holding onto his severed hand and half his forearm—the hot blade cauterizing the limb.

I caught a lip on some uneven stone and hung there for only three seconds before I started sliding again. Steel clanked next to me, and then an arm caught me around the waist. Joshua had driven a dagger into the floor and caught me, but now he was vulnerable, just like Gabriel had been. A hand roughly grabbed at me—the angel with the axe—but Joshua came down with his heel on the bridge of the Fallen's nose. He jerked in surprise, just enough to lose his grip, and went sliding towards the Hellmouth.

"You'd better give me that." Joshua looked at my hand, and I realized I was still holding fast to the wrist of Gabriel's severed limb. "Shove that into my coat pocket."

I looped my arm around Josh's neck and did as asked.

"Why are you being dragged in? Did you get his blood on you?"

"Maybe—I don't think so."

"Do you have an artifact on you?"

That question confused me, Gabriel must've told him something he didn't tell me. I didn't have the disks or the dagger, then Bowen's pained voice interrupted my racing mind. "In her leg—cut it out."

My eyes widened, and I looked over Joshua's shoulder. Semjâzâ was still holding the sword in Bowen's back, but Semjâzâ's eyes were trained on me. In a flash, he had spread his wings and landed on top of the lectern that Gabriel was still clinging to the base of.

Joshua blocked my view with his face. "Did you hear me?"

I shook my head.

"Can you get the knife in my belt and reach whatever is in your leg?"

I didn't answer, but robotically fumbled for the knife. As I grasped the blade, I looked towards Semjâzâ's last location—but he was gone.

Gabriel had managed to wedge himself behind the large podium, and he looked as if he was fighting with going into shock. Then I realized he was talking to Bowen. Bowen nodded at Gabriel, then put his hands flat on the floor and began to do a push up, working his body up the sword.

"Ali, I need you to stick with me." Joshua sounded exhausted.

Forcing myself to focus, I tried to pull my dress up enough to get to my thigh, but the air being sucked into the Hellmouth kept tearing it out of my hand. I decided to try to cut away the fabric and sliced as gingerly as I could.

"Stop! You're cutting yourself."

Anger and frustration rattled through my body. I couldn't feel the cut, and I wasn't sure if I could reach the gem anyway.

Joshua bumped me just as I sensed someone close. Tyran planted a dagger into the stone between my feet and used it as a foothold as he climbed practically on top of me.

"Which leg?" Tyran demanded.

I pointed to my left, and he immediately ripped a slit in my dress all the way up to waist, tucking the flaps beneath my leg. There was no sensation as he probed my leg for the lump, with a serious expression and an absence of snark.

Tyran made a motion with his hand that must've been an incision. A small piece of debris hit him in the face, and he used the back of his hand to wipe his eyes clear. I noticed his fingers were coated with fresh blood—my blood. He licked his fingers as he reached back to finish.

At that moment, I had an odd sensation, and it was as if there was a rubber band that snapped inside the middle of my brain. Tyran froze and glanced at me, releasing a shaky breath and cursing through his teeth. He furrowed his brow and concentrated, not making eye contact again.

In one, unthinking instant, he had completed the blood bond. He was feeling everything I was feeling with perfect clarity now. It was then that I noticed his emotions were clearer to me as well—as if I had been listening to one earphone, and now the other had suddenly started working.

He seemed to recover from his mistake and set to work. He excised the stone in seconds, and the moment he had closed his fist around the gem, an invisible force tried to flick him into the air like an autumn leaf. I dropped Joshua's knife, grabbed the front of Tyran's dress shirt, and pulled him roughly on top of me.

He grinned as we lay nose-to-nose. "If you wanted me between your legs, just ask, sissy." I was jolted by the anger that I sensed from Joshua.

"I hate you," I muttered.

Tyran ignored my comment. "Is the pull as strong?"

"No."

He looked around, and something changed in his expression. He reached up and grabbed the dagger, placing his hand above Josh's and keeping his feet on the blade below. "I've got her. I need you to help my brother before he tears himself apart trying to get free."

Josh glanced away, and then back at me. I nodded that it was okay. Joshua relinquished his hold around my torso and sped to Bowen's aide. Keeping a hand or foothold on one of the daggers was starting to feel like a deranged game of Twister.

Tyran was watching something behind me, and the way his jaw flexed, it made my blood go cold—well, colder than normal. He reached down and tore off a section of my skirting and wrapped it around the dagger near my head, then helped me loop my arm around the now shielded blade in my armpit so I could hold myself there without tiring.

He was still holding onto the gem that had been in my leg, and I didn't like what I was seeing. "I need you to do something for me, sissy."

"What?"

He pressed himself tight against me, his hand on the back of my head. "I need you to forgive me."

"Now?" I asked. Before I could say anything else, he kissed me, hard and demanding.

When he broke away, he said, "You take care of him."

Tyran got to a knee, coiled like a tiger, and leapt over me and tackled a Fallen in a split-second. It was Semjâzâ who Tyran had been staring at over my shoulder. They rolled and immediately started sliding towards the Hellmouth. I reached for Tyran as they slid by, but my fingers only grazed his sleeve, and without my legs, I couldn't lunge to catch him.

Semjâzâ caught the dagger towards my feet and tried to fight off Tyran with one hand. Tyran took advantage and drew a small knife, cutting away the straps of Semjâzâ's armor. The breastplate flipped away like a garbage can lid in a hurricane. Then Semjâzâ landed a blow, and Tyran faltered and lost his grip for a moment, but recovered. He planted the knife in Semjâzâ's chest and used it to pull himself back.

Semjâzâ was screaming at Tyran, but couldn't let go of the knife in the floor. Tyran was moving awkwardly, because, I realized, he still had the stone from my leg in his hand. He hoisted himself up, balancing on his elbow, and shoved the hand with the gem into the wound opened by his knife. His hand and half his forearm disappeared into Semjâzâ's chest cavity, then emerged without the stone.

The added pull to the Hellmouth could be seen immediately. Semjâzâ's arm snapped straight, and his fingers strained on the hilt of the dagger. What I assumed were curses in another language exploded from his mouth, and his fingers dug inside his chest wound.

I eased my arm into a different position, allowing my feet to droop closer to Tyran and Semjâzâ. I called to Tyran, "Use my legs."

His nostrils flared, and he looked at Semjâzâ, and then back at me. He climbed up Semjâzâ and grasped my ankle. There was some added noise in the cathedral, but I didn't look. My eyes were locked on Tyran. He reached up and grabbed my other ankle, and then my calf with the other hand. The moment I felt he was safe, Tyran cried out through gritted teeth.

Semjâzâ had rolled and driven the knife from his chest into Tyran's lower back and was using it for a handhold. Then Semjâzâ let go of the dagger in the floor that he'd been using and clung entirely to Tyran. My arm began to shake; I had been holding us up with the blade in the crook of my elbow. My arm started to slide, cutting through the fabric Tyran had wrapped around. Droplets of my blood began spattering on Tyran, caught in the wind.

Tyran's head snapped up just in time to see me lose my grip entirely when the steel hit my bone and started scraping alongside it.

Our trio slid towards the mouth, ready to devour us. Tyran caught the lower blade for a moment only with his fingertips. Semjâzâ did something I couldn't see that caused Tyran to let go. I managed to catch the hilt as we were being dragged.

My thoughts became slow and the edges of my vision blotchy. Everything was on me. I had the dagger. Tyran had my calves. Semjâzâ was clinging to Tyran. I could hold Tyran, but with the pull of Semjâzâ, it wouldn't be long. My arm was bleeding profusely, and I was so tired. I just wanted to close my eyes and let it all be over, but I didn't want to die. I'd just started my life with Bowen, and I would cling to that with every bit of strength I had. Semjâzâ needed to die—he had to go into the Hellmouth. All I had to do was let go, but I couldn't sacrifice Tyran.

I bent my head to look at Tyran. "I'm losing my grip."

Tyran suddenly slid from my calves to my ankles. "You won't."

I slipped a little more, and my eyes welled with tears. "Tyran…"

"You've got this, sissy."

A sob choked me.

There was movement at Tyran's feet. Somehow, Ana managed to get to Semjâzâ. They each had one of Tyran's legs and were battling. Ana was hacking at Semjâzâ's arm when she wasn't blocking his vicious attacks.

My trembling now encompassed my whole body. I watched my hand as my grip went from my palm, to my fingers, to just the tips. My breath went out, and we were sliding. This was it.

I jerked to a stop, my eyes flying to my captured wrist. Bowen had managed to wrap his feet around the blade, but his skin was icy cold, and he was worse than corpse white.

Semjâzâ shouted to his minions in the outskirts of the building, "Kill everyone. Kill the priest. Kill everyone left in the castle. We retreat."

We all went lurching towards the Hellmouth. Bowen's strained voice called over the whir of wind, "The dagger is bending."

I glanced up, and I wasn't sure how he was still holding onto it with his feet. At that moment, I felt a shift in Tyran's emotions. I screamed at him, "NO! Don't you dare!"

He mouthed, "Sorry, sissy," and let go.

Tyran, Semjâzâ, and Ana all slid, spiraling the last distance to the Hellmouth. Ana reached out to one of the markers, but instead of saving herself, she broke it off. Bowen lost his grip, and we went sliding towards the opening, but the second we reached the edge, it closed.

All sound, wind, and movement stopped in an instant.

I lay on the now-solid floor, slapping it with my bare palm, screaming. "No! No! You don't get to be the hero, *you bastard!*" I choked on another sob, my voice now nothing more than a pained moan. "I don't forgive you. You can't go."

But there was nothing there but cold stone and my utter agony. Seconds later, my loss was overwhelmed with the anguish of my mate who had just lost his twin.

# 25

## ERIS SEMPER IN CORDE MEO

ALERIA

Pushing myself onto my side, my focus grew to the whole room. Bodies lay everywhere caught behind pillars, making them look like seaweed entangled around the pylons of a pier at low tide. The pews were tossed and broken like driftwood, a few of them split in half, the other parts devoured by the Hellmouth. The additional noise I'd heard was from more of the Royal Guard from the castle. I wondered who'd gotten through to the castle, but then my mind skittered away. I tugged my thoughts into order and focused on Bowen. He was still on his belly where the Hellmouth had just been opened and closed.

Bowen looked like a ghost in more than one way. He was paler than I'd ever seen him. Blood was still oozing from the hole in his torso where he'd been pinned to the floor by Semjâzâ's sword. He also hadn't moved since Tyran had allowed himself to be pulled inside to save us—to save everyone. I took his hand, but he didn't respond.

I labored onto an elbow, still keeping Bowen's hand in mine, while searching for Gabriel and Joshua. Panic seized me. Several vampires were approaching Gabriel with glowing eyes. He still had one hand hooked on the lectern, and his forearm stump was around Joshua's middle, holding Josh's back to him. Joshua was unconscious and as white as Bowen.

"Stop!" I boomed.

The vamps approaching Gabriel stilled for a moment, glancing in my direction. They weren't from my coven, and they looked hungry enough to ignore a queen.

One of the vamps chuckled, and as a unit, they started moving forward, frenzy in their eyes.

I played the only card I had. "The Slayer is *mine*. I have claimed him." I could smell Gabriel from here—I didn't blame them. Just thinking about his blood made my fangs elongate. I really needed to feed.

The leader hesitated.

"Gabriel, show them."

Gabriel relinquished his grip on the lectern and used his teeth to pull up his sleeve. To the human eye, there was nothing there. To the aged vampire, there were a half dozen puncture marks from my fangs. Gabriel must have reopened up a wound when he struggled with his sleeve, because a new wave of his scent hit me.

The other vamps should've backed down the moment I'd claimed Gabriel, but they were hesitating. Keeping my face neutral, I let go of Bowen's hand and shoved myself to a seated position. I kept the effort it took hidden and leaned hard on my straightened arm.

I drew a small blade and called out to them. "I said he is *mine*. Familiars will be provided in the castle." Then, to punctuate the point, I threw the blade with everything I had. It stayed straight and true and stuck in the lectern just inches from the leader's face.

He blinked at the knife, and then at me. With a tight-lipped smile, he bowed and headed for the main entrance. The others followed him.

Bowen was still frozen in position. I wasn't feeling shock or grief from him any longer. I was feeling nothing—like there was a suspension of all rational thought.

Cadeyn limped over with a few of the guard behind him. "Secure the King and Queen." Then he addressed Bowen, "Do you have orders, Sire?"

Bowen swallowed, still staring at the floor.

I lowered my voice and answered, "Do the triage here. Escort those who have healed enough back to the castle. Summon the familiars, but make sure they are guarded. I don't want any of them drained. Do we have other humans we can call to the castle?"

"Yes, my Queen."

"Those that are staked, but not gravely wounded, leave them staked until we have enough familiars here to care for them. Call the medics."

"As you wish."

"Cadeyn, I want Gabriel to be taken to my rooms. See if Joshua still has Gabriel's hand; I want it on ice. Send a surgeon to see him. Keep Joshua with him."

I could tell that he didn't like the Gabriel part, but Cadeyn bowed and dictated orders to his men.


GABRIEL

A vampire with strange yellow eyes approached. I recognized

him immediately as Cadeyn Bradshaw. Ali had killed his brother.

"Can you walk?"

I answered with a nod, but my arm tightened around Joshua while the throb in my severed limb made me want to vomit—the initial shock was wearing off. I refused to grimace in front of my enemy.

"You will not be harmed. My orders are to escort the two of you to the Royal Suite where a surgeon will attend you."

A guard in a crisp uniform threw Joshua over his shoulder. It was obvious he had not been in the battle. I recalled Taranis saying that the castle was already preparing to send more guards. "How did the castle find out about the attack?"

"Apparently, a human came to the front gate and warned them," replied he, dismissal in his voice.

"What happened to him?" I asked.

"I wouldn't know."

I turned towards Ali's direction. Belenus was on his knees with a vacant expression. Ali was on her side in front of him whispering. I hated to interrupt, but I had to. "Aleria." She looked up. "Ian..."

Confused, she stared at me for a moment. Then, I witnessed the epiphany. "Cadeyn, who warned the rest of the guard?"

"A human male."

Belenus stood and, with barely an acknowledgement, gathered Ali in his arms and sped away, bodyguards in tow.


ALERIA

Before we were through the doors, Bowen spoke for the first time. "Where is the human who came to the front gates?"

The guard in the lobby looked nervous, and my heart sprinted. I squeezed Bowen's shoulder. "Is he alive?" I burst.

"Yes, Your Highness. He was delivered to the dungeon for questioning."

"Why?"

Seemingly dumbfounded, he answered, "The human is a Watcher."

Bowen was already on the move before I could reply. He had purpose, and I supposed he was using it to avoid the loss. I closed my eyes as we descended into the underbelly of the castle —my place of nightmares. I was startled when Bowen roared, "Cease immediately!"

My eyes snapped open, and I was looking at three of the dungeon keepers roving the maze with weapons. My heart sprinted when I saw a dead body, but realized it was a dungeon keeper. They'd been in some sort of fight. I didn't see Ian anywhere.

"What have you done with the human?"

At that moment, they seemed to realize their king was addressing them. "It was just a spot of fun, Your Majesty. Well, until he offed Giovanni, he—"

Bowen was losing his patience. "Where is the human?"

"In 'ere somewhere. He's wounded. The maze shifted, and the slippery devil made off."

"Take your man and go," Bowen ordered.

They bowed very, very low, collected the body, and fled.

Before I could request it, Bowen had already stepped to the ledge and dropped with me into the maze. I calmed myself and tried to sense him. Ian wasn't dead. I could tell now. Bowen seemed to walk straight to him in the middle of the maze.

Ian was sitting with his back pressed up against a wall, and his legs were sprawled out in front of him. He was rapidly taking small breaths. He didn't move, despite the fact that Bowen wasn't using vampire stealth.

Bowen sat me next to Ian and leaned me against the wall. Ian jostled awake and grabbed for a steal bar, but Bowen easily stripped it from him.

"Ian, it's Ali."

He seemed to focus. Ian smiled, then groaned. His face was a mess of blooming bruises and filthy cuts. "Tried to crash the party."

"You're an idiot, you know that?" I scolded, gently probing the wounds I could reach without falling over.

Bowen ripped the leg of Ian's jeans open, then his shirt. He had a stab wound in his leg, some of his ribs were definitely broken, and there were possible internal injuries. And that was besides the superficial injuries. Ian hadn't complained once when he'd been shot saving me in Germany, but he was making pained sounds now.

"I'm going to take away some of the pain, okay?"

"Can't resist me, huh?" Ian tried to laugh, but ended up yelping. He had guts flirting with me in front of Bowen.

I bit into his wrist and flooded him with the hormone. His breathing relaxed, and then he lost consciousness. Feet could be heard above. Bowen stood. "I need a stretcher down here." One of our guards disappeared.

"Love, he will need surgery or you—"

"No. I won't do it."

Bowen furrowed his brow. "It's bad."

I shook my head. "He's a fighter, and I would never turn him without asking his permission."

Just then, two of the guards rounded the corner and gingerly placed Ian on the stretcher under my glaring eye.

"Nothing happens to him. He's mine," I ordered.

They bowed, understanding my claim completely.

Once the guards had mounted the incline with Ian and were out of sight, Bowen commented, "Claiming two familiars in one day?"

"I'm greedy," I quipped.

Bowen grinned, but his grin melted into something much more serious. "I want to have you checked out."

"Not until they take care of everyone else. The medics must be overwhelmed." What I didn't say was that I was too afraid to see the doctors right now. If they told me I was going to be paralyzed for eternity, I wasn't sure I could handle the news right then. I looked down at myself. My dress was in shreds; I was crusted in blood and dirt and wanted nothing more than to be clean and to avoid all mention of my injury.

Bowen seemed to read something on my face. He swooped me into his arms once more and headed to what I soon realized was our room. There were six guards when we arrived in our hall—Gabriel and Joshua were definitely inside.

Both doors were swung wide for us. Upon entering, the clatter of the doors closing didn't distract me from the doctor examining Gabriel's arm. His hand, wrist, and partial forearm were in an ice bucket on the end table next to them. Cadeyn stood at the far wall with arms crossed.

Before any greetings could be exchanged, I blurted, "Can you reattach his arm?"

The doctor looked startled. He turned to Bowen and me, and his eyes widened slightly. "Yes, but it is beyond our capabilities. There is a replantation specialist in Paris and another in Geneva, though it takes a team of up to six surgeons."

Bowen sat me on the couch next to the still unconscious Joshua, and Bowen's eyes lingered on him a moment.

"Cadeyn, send a team on the chopper. Bring in the doctors

from Paris. Black hood them, bribe them, glamour them, or take them by force, if needed. Go."

Cadeyn sped off as ordered.

He turned to the doctor and pointed at Joshua. "I want him on a blood IV. Set up the operating room. You will have your doctors within two hours. Take care of the hand, see if you can force the circulation of bagged blood through it to keep it alive until the surgery. Is there anything else you require?"

"The patient an hour before surgery."

"Done. Dismissed."

The doctor scurried out.

Bowen then turned to Gabriel. "We can put you in Aleria's private room." He motioned with a wide sweeping motion to my door. "Would you like to clean up before surgery?"

"Yes."

"Would you like me to call an attendant to help you?"

Gabriel hesitated, indicating he needed help, but didn't want it.

Bowen didn't wait. "I will summon a nurse to assist you and have fresh clothes delivered." Bowen's tone was pleasant, but businesslike. Without another word, he picked me up and walked to his private chambers, the strain of emotion around the edges of his eyes.

Bowen called for a nurse for Gabriel, and within a minute, he had an ornate armchair sitting in the shower, not caring that it would be ruined, and placed me in it. He unbuckled his belt and strapped me to the chair to keep me from sliding out of it. After I was secure, he started to disrobe, but it was slow and labored. The events of the last several hours seemed to be crashing in on him now that we were alone.

He peeled away the last of his clothes and stepped inside the shower with me, turning on the water. The hole in his core was closed, but barely, and it was huge. He *had* torn himself apart to get free. I didn't think I would have survived that much damage.

I closed my eyes when I realized how he'd survived, and why Joshua was still out. My voice was small. "You fed on Joshua." A statement, not a question. I opened my eyes and watched the water gurgle down the drain for a second before looking at him.

Bowen frowned. "Joshua freed me and then insisted. He said to take it all if I could save you and stop the Fallen." He sighed. "I didn't. I wanted to," there was a long pause, "and not just because I needed to feed." He looked away and circled behind me, unlacing what had been left of the corset on my dress.

"Rivaling mates." I murmured the quote from the prophecy about me, and I let out a stuttering breath. He lingered behind me, his fingers making small circles on the tops of my shoulders.

When he finally came back around in front of me, he looked so vulnerable. He only met my eyes for a flickering moment, and then returned to work removing the last bits of my tattered dress, tossing them outside the shower. Then we were naked, and not just because we were without clothes. We were open wounds on the verge of something.

I grabbed his wrist and pulled him down. He complied and sank to his knees in front of me, the water swirling around him to the drain. "Hey," I whispered, in the gentlest of tones. "Hey, I chose *you*, remember?"

I caught a flash of blue eyes for a second before he looked away again. Shower water was bouncing off of his back. His hair looked like damp corn silk, the water running in rivulets down his face. His hands were on my bare thighs, but I couldn't feel them. Then I thought of something terrible when I looked at his hands on my legs. Maybe he didn't want me, now that I was broken. I'd never heard of a vampire in a wheelchair. I stifled the sob that was welling up in my chest.

Bowen sensed it and finally met my eyes. My heart hammered, and my lip quivered. "I'm broken. If you don't want me now, send me back with Gabriel after his surgery. I—"

The hurt he felt from my statement surged through me, but before I could say another word, he kissed me so hard, it almost hurt. He kept kissing me, and at some point, I started crying. And I think he was crying too, but with the shower washing it all away, I couldn't tell.

There was one thing I did know, beyond anything else: Bowen meant his vows. He wanted me no matter what. *In sorrow and in joy...In the good times, and in the bad...for all the days of our eternal lives.* He wasn't going anywhere.

"You are everything to me," he finally murmured. "I was terrified that I was going to lose you."

"*Eris semper in corde meo,* (You will always be in my heart)" I replied. They were the last words he had said to me in California. "My Latin isn't good enough to change it." I placed his hand on my chest so he could feel the rapid beat. "You *are* my heart, and I am home."

# 26

# POISED FOR CONQUEST

ALERIA

I felt Bowen approaching the medical wing before I heard him down the hall. "How long has she been here?"

Cadeyn answered, "Since the surgery started—nine hours— save the moments she watched them wheel the human into the other operating room and the doctor checked on her. He didn't finish his examination of the queen. She ordered him away."

"I know. I received a message." There was more murmuring between them, but I tuned out.

The threat of retaliation was real. Bowen had remained with me until Cadeyn had practically forced him to go and meet with survivors. Cadeyn had to speak to Bowen as a friend, not as the captain of the guard, to get Bowen's attention. Bowen left for the throne, but had ordered Cadeyn to remain with me. There was no one else to deal with the diplomats and other royals—no Tyran, and as of yet, no Morpheus.

It had been eleven hours since we'd returned to the castle. I sat in my new wheelchair with my hand pressed to the glass of the operating room in the east wing of the castle. There were two O.R.s, and both were filled with people who I cared about.

Across the hall, the in-house surgeon had already removed half of Ian's spleen and was searching for the other sources of internal bleeding. But I was frozen, watching the team try to reattach or "replant" Gabriel's wrist and hand, overwhelmed with worry and guilt. I knew Gabriel would have scolded me for beating myself up, but he had lost his arm trying to save me... and Tyran had lost his life.

I heard the snick of a door opening and closing, and then other movement behind me, but I didn't bother looking. I couldn't tear my eyes away from Gabriel. Part of me knew that I was shaking, but I hadn't realized that I'd been silently crying until Bowen wiped a tear from my cheek.

"Love, I'm sorry it took so long to get back to you. They have taken Ian to the recovery room. He survived the surgery. They said he should be awake any moment. Wouldn't you like to be there?"

In that instant, Gabriel convulsed on the operating table. Buzzers and lights went off, and a strangled cry escaped me. I leaned forward, my instinct to stand, and nearly toppled from the wheelchair.

"Aleria." Bowen's hands framed my face, forcing me to look at him and not the crisis. "They will do everything they can for Gabriel; it will be another three or four hours. Ian will need a friendly face when he wakes."

I nodded mutely and smudged the rest of the tears away, knowing that Bowen was giving me purpose—and distraction. The blare of alarms in the O.R. ceased, so I allowed Bowen to wheel me into Recovery. He stopped at Ian's bedside and took a knee. Bowen peered at me. "How are you?"

I shrugged noncommittally. Part of me wanted to rage. I had no use of my legs. I hadn't seen Joshua in hours. I didn't know if he was still unconscious in my room or not. Morpheus was still unaccounted for, as well as, Icelos, who I firmly hoped was dead. Something was still nagging me about Gabriel's abrupt phone call to Raphael on Batariel's phone. But what came out was: "I'm fine." I smiled feebly. "I know you need to be meeting with the delegates who survived. Cadeyn won't let anything happen to me. And I'm guessing there are at least several guards outside the hospital wing."

The edge of Bowen's lip twitched. "Or an army." He stood and gazed at me for a full thirty seconds before he made his decision, then bent and kissed my forehead. "I will be back as soon as possible. Send word if you need me." He stared at me until I replied.

"I will." Once Bowen was gone, I wheeled the last couple of feet to Ian's bed and took his hand.

"Your hand is cold," he slurred through the medication.

"Eavesdropper."

"Reconnaissance," Ian countered. There was a pause, and he cracked his eyes open. His gaze dropped to the wheelchair, and then back up to my face. "How are you really feeling?"

"You just got out of surgery—you answer first."

A shallow sigh billowed from him. "Do I have all my bits and pieces?"

"Minus half a spleen, yes."

"I was kinda passing out. Did you claim me as a familiar?"

I twisted my mouth to the side. "Yes."

Ian grinned. "Never thought I would be a queen's bitch."

"You are so drugged right now."

Ian closed his eyes. "I need to enjoy it. I have a feeling that once this stuff wears off, I won't be so happy."

I squeezed his hand. "Just get some rest. You will be back in your shiny club shirt in no time."

His grin widened a little more. "Thanks for being here." Then he drifted off to sleep almost instantly.


## GABRIEL

Swimming to the surface, I could taste the acrid heaviness of the sedatives. I remained still as death to gather information. There were straps on my arms and chest, an IV in my left arm, and a weight on my leg. Someone was in the room. I drew in more of a breath—Ali. I curled my toes, and the weight on my leg moved.

"Gabriel?"

Answering was difficult, my body not fully under my command. "Mmmm," I forced, while prying my eyes open.

Ali appeared to be exhausted. There were dried tear trails down her scrubbed cheeks. She needed to feed; her skin was alabaster and the veins beneath a maze of blue. I was surprised that Belenus had not made her feed. Unless... "Belenus?"

"He's fine. Well, as fine as could be, with a war between the covens on the verge of breaking out. Ian was in surgery for almost four hours. He had a lot of internal injuries, but is doing well now. He lost half his spleen, but he has a second one. Did you know that thirty percent of people have a second spleen? So, it shouldn't impact his immune system enough to keep him from traveling with you. Joshua has recovered, although he has requested to be alone, but with text updates on you and Ian. I think that's it," ended Aleria.

"How long was I unconscious?"

She hesitated. "It's been two days. It seems that my claiming a Slayer and a Watcher as familiars caused a bit of a stir. If you were unconscious, it was better. And you needed to heal. It's fine now." A nervous laugh escaped her. "It seems that you ordering me to feed on you all those times saved your life. If there hadn't been evidence of it happening for a prolonged period, they would've demanded your death."

My wits were coming into focus. "It is hot in here."

"Keeping the room at eighty degrees helps your arm," she stammered when she saw me stare at the wheelchair she was seated in.

"Why are you not healing?" I asked.

"Everyone else first. Then me."

She was scared and putting on a brave front, but there was more. Wanting to place my hand on her shoulder, I tried to lift my left arm.

"Straps. Sorry." She wheeled around, unfastening me. "They hadn't anticipated your accelerated healing; you started to wake during the surgery and thrashed. In a panic, one of the doctors accidentally pulled out some of your vital sign monitors. I thought you were going into cardiac arrest." Her voice broke. "You are not allowed to die until you are a very, very old man," said she, her lip aquiver. "At least 150 years old. At least."

When she rolled back to my left side, I held out my hand to her. She immediately took it. "I wish I could help you more, kiddo."

She cleared her throat. "Your surgery went well. It's been long enough that they think the replantation will take. It's your arm, so you don't need anti-rejection drugs. But, Gabriel, there's a chance..."

"I will not have full use of my hand," I finished. I glowered at my bandaged arm. "So war, your legs, my arm." I stared at her until she met my eyes. "What else is bothering you?"

She sagged. "Did you see Tyran in the battle?"

I shook my head and worked to focus on the events after my

arm had been severed. "You were sliding away from me towards the Hellmouth. Shock was setting in; I worked to get a grip on the lectern. I remember trying to calm Belenus down. Black wings enveloped me when Semjâzâ landed on top of the lectern. I had no weapons; I thought I was done for. I blacked out for a moment and woke with my head throbbing. Then Belenus was trying to secure Joshua with me. It took all of my strength to stay conscious and hold onto Joshua." The shock had mottled my memory. I knew I had tried to do more.

She swallowed. "Tyran asked me to forgive him, then he attacked Semjâzâ. He...he allowed himself to be pulled into the Hellmouth with Semjâzâ to save Bowen and I. To save everyone from Semjâzâ."

"You loved him."

"No! I was not in love with him!"

"Not *in* love, but you loved him."

"He killed my friends and tortured me. How could I love him? How could I forgive him?"

There was a long silence as I chose my words carefully.

"Forgive him."

Her mouth popped open in shock. "It will eat you up if you do not, kiddo. You sparked genuine change in him. I know you have been guarding your heart after we have lost so many, but the reason you have made changes in other people is your ability to care and to hope. Do not let that be destroyed."

"But I still want to hate him," she protested.

"Hate eats up hope and leaves sickness and ruin behind. It is a waste of energy."

She looked at me dubiously.

"It keeps you connected with the object of that hate. It is not worth it."

"Can *you* forgive him for killing Gentry, Leslie, and Winslow?"

I let go of her hand and drew her eye to the scar on my face. "Actively hating causes stupid mistakes." I took her hand again. "It is your choice. If we mourn the losses, we can be healthy enough to appreciate that which makes us whole."

She squeezed my hand and remained quiet for over a minute before she finally spoke again. "Martin Luther King Jr. said, 'Only in the darkness can you see the stars,'" replied she, thoughtfully.

ALERIA

The castle had one elevator used by the human staff to move supplies. It was off of a hallway between the throne and largest ballroom. After seeing Gabriel, Cadeyn wheeled me towards the main wing to take me upstairs. As we neared the throne room, raised voices boomed down the hall. The doors were flung open, and one of the dignitaries came storming out. He stopped short at seeing me and pivoted towards the throne room again. Bowen appeared in the doorway.

"And this is what I mean: the Queen in a wheelchair to elicit some sort of sympathy and garner grace from those who have lost so much."

I was taken aback. "This isn't fake," I declared, a little too softly.

The dignitary approached me, but Cadeyn was instantly in his path. He put his hand on the man's chest.

Bowen grabbed the man's collar and shoved him back towards the throne room. "Vasile, attack my wife, and I will end you."

Vasile argued, "If she was really injured, why was the Queen not attended to first?"

"Because I wouldn't allow it," I answered, though he asked Bowen.

"Why?" he turned pointedly.

"My life wasn't in danger—others were."

Vasile slowly circled towards me. Bowen and Cadeyn cautiously allowed it. "By allowing the slaughter of seventy-eight members of other covens, your coven remains poised for conquest."

"By setting us up, the slaughter undermines the peace that Belenus has been negotiating," I countered. I was afraid to look to Bowen and have Vasile think I was looking for answers. I exhaled and shifted the skirt I was wearing so that the slit exposed my leg.

Vasile raised a brow.

I pulled out a blade I had strapped to my thigh. "Don't believe I'm injured?" I came down with force and stabbed my leg, driving the blade all the way to the small hilt. I raised my hands, palms open, still completely calm. "I don't feel a thing."

He stared at me with unwavering attention, waiting for some flinch or giveaway, I was sure.

"Need me to stab the other leg? Or are you satisfied?"

"An arm will do," was his icy reply.

Without hesitation, I impaled my forearm, not breaking eye contact. My heart stuttered, and I gritted my teeth, controlling the scream I wanted to release. There was no hiding my pain. I withdrew the blade and risked a glance at Bowen. His expression was unreadable.

Vasile pulled a crisp handkerchief from his pocket and offered it to me. I took it and put pressure on the wound in my arm and used my skirt for the leg, making sure that none of my blood spilled to the floor. Neither would take long to heal. Vasile didn't say anything to me, but his shoulders relaxed. He gave Bowen a long look, and then returned to the throne room instead of leaving. I hadn't realized that we'd drawn a crowd. Those loitering in the hall filed back inside after Vasile.

Once it was down to Bowen, Cadeyn, and me, Bowen approached me. I still couldn't read his emotions. He bent at the waist and used his index finger to raise my chin. He gave me a soft kiss, his warm breath cascading down my neck.

"I will see you in a few hours." Bowen's blue eyes filled with some sort of restrained emotion.

I nodded wordlessly and watched him return to the throne room. I still didn't know if I'd helped or hindered. As soon as the door shut, Cadeyn started pushing me towards the elevator again.

"Cadeyn, did I do the right thing?"

He was quiet for a long moment as the elevator doors clunked shut. "Belenus did not stop you, so it was not wrong."

His diplomatic answer didn't help ease the knot in my stomach. And honestly, I wasn't sure what would.

2 7

___

FLOOD

GABRIEL

The soft squeak of rubber soles on the sterile floor drew my attention. The same nurse whom Belenus had summoned to help me the night of the battle entered with a clipboard. There was a hitch in her step when she realized I was awake. I had to search my memory for her name: Mireya.

"How are you doing today?" asked she, her face becoming a mask of professionalism.

I met her eyes, but did not answer, moments ticked by.

She exhaled. "Did you hear that?" She was not referring to her question, but the conversation she had just had at the end of the hallway moments ago.

I answered in a single nod.

She fidgeted, starting to take my vital signs and checking boxes on her list. "You are safe in here," assured Mireya.

"Is the *Queen* safe?"

Her hands trembled as she began to attend to the dressings on my arm. "Few inside the castle would harm her," answered

I did not miss the fact that she had said *inside* the castle. She wanted to tell me more. I waited.

She stopped, gauze hanging loosely between her fingers. Her breath became uneven as she turned and closed the door, but she did not speak until she had stared out the window into the hall for a several seconds. "Before my shift, I overheard a conversation outside the medical wing. Icelos fled during the end of the battle, but he has gathered some forces. He intends to return and use the anger of the surviving royals to oust King Belenus and his wife." She returned to my bandages. With hesitance, she added, "Queen Aleria has claimed two familiars who are enemies of this coven, yet she has not fed on them once since the attack. Claiming a familiar is something that is rarely done."

"But—"

Mireya held up her hand. "I know, you are both recovering from surgery, but for those looking to undermine the throne, it appears as if she is moving Watchers into the castle and a Slayer of all..."

The door swung open, behind her. "Mireya, you are needed in the in the North Wing; a familiar has been injured." The guard kept his eyes on me.

"I'll be right there," replied she. Then she spoke to me, "I'll be back to check on you again before the end of my shift. Please keep drinking fluids. You are healing quickly, but you are mildly dehydrated."

"Thank you," responded I.

She turned quickly with the excess supplies and followed the guard, leaving me alone, with a sick feeling in my gut.

ALERIA

Bowen entered our room. Well, his private room. Joshua was still in my private room, so we left the main bedroom as a spacer. When Bowen saw me, he smiled, but it faded when his eyes drifted to the wheelchair. Emotion clutched my throat, and he closed his eyes.

He walked towards me, untucking his shirt. Then he ran his hand through his hair, and it stuck up irregularly. I normally would've teased him about it, but not at this moment. When he reached me, he dropped to his knees and grabbed the arms of the wheelchair. He took a deep breath and exhaled through thin lips before he finally met my eyes. "I need you to promise me something."

I swallowed hard and waited.

"I need you to promise to never doubt my feelings for you again. I can't bear it. If I dare to glance at this chair, I feel your doubt. My only desire is that you are well. I would never *ever* discard you because you are injured. I want you with me. I would have you in the throne room if I thought you were up to it." His fingers glided to where I'd stabbed my arm to prove my injury to Vasile; there was no trace now.

"Are you angry with me?"

Bowen eased back and sat on his feet. "I want you to let the doctor finish his examination."

"I let him poke and prod me, and I didn't object to the ultrasound, but he wanted to make me leave the hall and take me away from Gabriel. He wanted to cut me open. I just couldn't." I looked away. "I just kept thinking that if he gave me bad news—if he said it was permanent, that I couldn't handle it, not with everything else."

He was quiet for a long moment. "Vasile backed down after his encounter with you. I pray it will be enough."

"Others aren't happy?"

Bowen dragged himself from the floor. "I'm afraid tomorrow will be another long day."

"Any news about Morpheus?"

His shoulders sagged. "None."

"And he wasn't sucked into the Hellmouth?"

"One of Ana's people was commissioned with recording every being that was pulled inside—no Morpheus."

I hadn't even thought of Ana since we'd returned to the castle. "Ana's people?"

"A half dozen survivors have retreated. We don't know where. They left word that they would be in contact, and that they expected Gabriel to be returned to the Watchers unharmed."

That made me like them just a little bit more—that and turning the tide of the battle in our favor.

"I need a shower to wash off the stench of diplomacy," he winked at me. "Can I do anything for you?"

"Just get cleaned up and take me to bed."

I felt a breeze in the room and was abruptly lifted from my chair and carried to the bed. He placed me on the sheets and slid in next to me.

"Is it even possible to get clean that quickly?"

"All I want is to sleep holding you."

I exhaled. "Sounds perfect."

He pulled me to my side and wrapped his arm around me. We lay nose to nose for a long while in comfortable silence. I nuzzled up closer. He kissed my nose, then my cheek, and then buried his nose in my hair, breathing deeply. Lazily, he started running his fingers up and down my back. I lost sensation of it the moment his fingers drifted below my shoulder blades. Like those brief instances before, I felt something, and then it was quickly gone.

"I felt your hand," I gasped. I was so caught up in tracking down the sensation that it took me a moment to realize that Bowen had completely let go of me and lost all hint of color.

He backed off the bed, looking terror stricken—irrational fear in his eyes.

"What is it?" I pleaded.

"There is something inside you. You reacted to my touch, and something moved beneath your skin."

A horrible feeling of dread washed over me. It was so strong, that for a moment, all other thoughts were blocked out. Batariel had had me pinned to the wall. He'd broken my spine, and I was going to bleed out. While he held me against the wall, he had reached into his pocket, and then put his hand inside the wound. The bleeding had stopped, so I thought he'd done something to stop the flow of blood.

He may have stopped the bleeding, but he had done something else—he'd put one of those beasties inside me; it was simply programed to do something different to me.

My focus went from my memories, back to Bowen. I wanted to panic, to drive a knife in and rip the thing out of me, but I forced myself to calm down. "The beasties, they are able to try to preserve themselves. They avoided the ultrasound when we used it on you. When we figured it out, we used it to our advantage to chase it to where we wanted it, and took it out of you."

"Then let's get it out."

"We need some sort of bomb safe or something first." I had to work at not panicking again. If Joshua hadn't grabbed the thing and thrown it into the alley and shielded himself with the metal door, Bowen, Tyran, and I may not have survived the blast.

I didn't think Bowen could pale any more; this had to be reaching some sort of primal level of fear in him. He had been sentenced to a thousand deaths and had died over a hundred times before we had pulled that thing out of him.

"Bowen, I'm sorry, but Josh was the only other one there. I don't know if he remembers or not. Would you get him?" There was tremor in my voice.

Bowen left without a word. A second later, I heard a knock on the door to my private chambers and the low rumble of speaking. Then Bowen returned with Joshua. Joshua was recovered, but looked as if he hadn't been sleeping or feeding nearly enough.

"Als, what do you want me to do?"

At that moment, I realized that I could wiggle my toes. "It knows," I cried.

"How could it know?" Bowen asked.

I pointed to my bare feet, my toes twitching. "I'm healing," I said, my voice rising. "I can't feel where it is though. What if..." I couldn't bring myself to say *explode*.

Bowen spoke. "I will get the ultrasound. Joshua, punch a hole through that window. We will throw it into the ocean. There are knives in my closet." Then in a flash, he was gone.

Joshua said, "We'll get it out. You'll be fine."

A nervous laugh escaped me. "Wouldn't it be ironic to survive the battle only to be blown up in my bedroom?"

"It's not your time, Als. You are a creature of prophecy. You won't bite it in your bedroom."

The haunted look in his eyes made me want to believe him and to wonder how much of his memory Batariel had returned.

## GABRIEL

"Raphael?" I questioned, after someone picked up, but said nothing.

His voice was thick. "Gabriel, I'm sorry. I got the kid out, but no one else survived. There were two of them—dead now. Cleaners have fixed the scene. What do you want me to do with the kid?"

"Bring him in—there is no other choice. He is one of ours now. Take care of him."

"Affirmative, moving east. Contact in seventy-two hours."

"Be well, Raphael."

"Be well." The line went dead.

Before I could digest the news, I was shocked to see Belenus' face in the doorway. "You strong enough to get out of bed?"

"Yes."

"I need you." Belenus turned to the guards in the hall. "Escort him to the royal suite immediately."

I threw the covers off and stood. I could hear Belenus not far off, asking for supplies, including high doses of painkillers. He was in a controlled frenzy; something was wrong with Ali.


## ALERIA

An agitated Gabriel entered, surrounded by guards. He was wearing grey sweats and a hospital gown. Gabriel met my eyes. There was some shadow behind his eyes that made my stomach turn to stone.

Bustling in behind him came the ultrasound and various members of the medical staff, carrying vials and towels and whatever else Bowen had ordered up. I didn't want the medical personnel in here.

I had some throwback memory of being trapped on the operating table after being poisoned by Rousseau. The mercenary Lazare had loomed over me after being sedated for surgery—I'd been helpless. I'd woken, not knowing that Lazare had stolen my blood and one of my ovaries and implanted a tracking device. This time, I wanted to be awake and did not want anyone I didn't know touching me.

Our room was located at the edge of the castle over the sheer cliff. The view of the ocean was spectacular. They positioned a gurney and all the supplies next to that window where the beastie could be safely tossed from our room and over the cliff. Everything was in place. I explained to Bowen that I didn't want the medical people here. He disagreed, but allowed my request.

Gabriel was quietly talking to a nurse near the doors. When the last of the staff left, she followed. Bowen and Joshua worked quickly to strap me down.

Joshua pinned me with an intense look. "Do you still think that thing knows?"

I concentrated and managed to draw a leg up from the gurney a few inches. Bowen started to smile, then he must have come to the same conclusion I had. We needed to get it out—now. He came towards me with a syringe of something.

"No, I want to be awake."

"Painkillers," Bowen replied.

"Please, just get it out now. I don't want anything. I don't want to let it know."

"Als," Joshua said, disagreeing.

Bowen pleaded, "We may have to open you up completely."

Gabriel's hand rested on my shoulder. It was the bandaged one. Then, there was a needle in my neck.

I opened my mouth to curse at him, but my tongue already felt huge, and things seemed to slow down.

The fog began to lift, and I had the feeling that it hadn't been that long, but I couldn't be sure. The smell of my blood was everywhere, and the bedding I was on felt damp. I could smell Gabriel's blood, too. There was a tugging sensation as I forced my eyes open a little. Six blood bags were hanging above me —*six*—and I was pretty sure my body only held around ten. Something had gone wrong.

Without moving my body, my eyes wandered to the scene around me. I wasn't on the gurney; I was on the floor, and the hospital bed was on its side next to me, looking charred and mangled. Gabriel was beside me on the floor. He sucked in a breath, biting back some pain as Joshua pulled a huge shard of glass from Gabriel's side.

My eyes drifted back around to my own body when I felt the tugging again. Bowen was on his knees, stitching me closed, black smudges and blood on his face. Nausea rolled through my body, not only from my injuries, but from the invading of dreams while I was out.

I managed to lift my hand and put it on top of Bowen's, who was tying a knot over my sternum. He made a strangled sound that I'd never heard him make, and he pulled me into a sitting position, holding me so tightly that I thought we might meld into one being.

Forcing my lips to work, I uttered, "Morpheus. He's staked in the cave."

Bowen leaned back and looked at me with confusion.

I pointed towards the window that I now realized was blown open. Salty air was streaming inside, and the crash of waves on the cliff came into sharper focus. "The half underwater cave that

Dagan had put Joshua in. Under the stone platform." I didn't know if he needed that much explanation, but my eyes had closed at some point. I was going to pass out again—no, it was a vision. I pushed out a few more words. "Icelos is coming."

---

I was standing on top of a stone platform—this was a vision. The platform began to rise, and along with it, a garden of headstones nested in a hundred colors of green grass.

Semjâzâ appeared before me. He spread his black wings and braced as if he was going to take flight, but black suddenly oozed from the middle of his belly. Without any sort of ceremony, he turned to ash that fluttered away in swirling wind, leaving Icelos in his place.

Icelos stood like a sculpture, staring at me, a knife in his hand dripping with black. The sound of wind and water rose and salt water flooded the surface, drowning the beautiful grass. Then the tombstones started to grow, rising and stretching until they were pillars extending into the sky. There were so many that the expanse became a faceted wall of stone.

Icelos disappeared beneath the water, but like a predatory sea monster, I could see a small wake as he moved towards the cliff. When he emerged, he climbed upwards, leaving claw marks in the stone that dripped black all the way down to the sea. When the liquid made it all the way down to the water below, the sea began to bubble and roil. Dozens of hands breached the surface of the turbulent water as bodies rose from the depths, and they too, began to claw their way upwards towards the dim light at the top.

Icelos reached the peak, and soon after, there was a cry

carried in the wind, like that of an eagle. When it was silenced, the black liquid running down the pillars was mixed with a flood of red from the top of the cliff. Then the entire world fell into darkness.

2 8

---

COWARD

I woke. I didn't think it had been long. I was on the couch in the sitting area with a blanket tucked tightly around me. Gabriel was in the chair next to me with his head leaned back, his hand from his good arm outstretched and on my shoulder. The second I moved, his eyes popped open.

There was no greeting; Gabriel got straight down to business. "Kiddo, what did you see?" I could feel everyone's attention on me.

Rubbing my eyes, I stretched and drew my legs up towards me. The deliciousness of the movement distracted me—I gasped. *I could move my legs.*

In celebration, I sat up, then bent and straightened my legs several times, rotating my ankles and pointing my toes. Tears came to my eyes.

Then Gabriel's question caught up with me, and I shook my head to focus my thoughts. "I watched Semjâzâ turn to ash, and Icelos took his place. At first, we were in a graveyard; then a flood of salt water enveloped us. The tombstones grew and became a cliff. Icelos and his minions climbed it, leaving behind a trail of black ooze.

"When they reached the top, there was a struggle, and I heard the cry of an eagle. Even though it was dark, everything was crisp and clearly visible. It was as if I had been watching everything during a full moon. Then the eagle went silent." I thought for a moment. "Correction: I think the eagle was *silenced*. When that happened, the moon itself was snuffed out, plunging everything into darkness."

Behind me, Bowen had obviously gotten on the phone. "Cadeyn, I want spotters on the cliff. Have them keep an eye on the water...Yes...yes...*now*. At sunrise, I want humans there as replacement."

I looked over my shoulder. "You think that's what it means?"

Gabriel asked, "Do you have a cemetery on the grounds?"

"Yes, not far from the cathedral," Bowen answered.

All of us fell into silent thought for a few minutes.

Then Bowen's voice broke into my reverie. "Aleria, what does your name mean?"

Before I could answer, Joshua did. "Eagle."

Gabriel cursed under his breath, and Bowen sat next to me, putting his arm protectively around my shoulders.

"That doesn't mean the eagle in the vision was me," I protested. But even as I said it, my gut told me that I was wrong.

Bowen stood, pulling me up with him. "We should move to an alternate secure location. Icelos will expect us to be holed up in here or in the throne room."

"How about the library on this floor?" I offered. "It's defensible."

Bowen thought for a moment, sadness flickering on his face. "That will work."

"What is it?"

His voice was hoarse. "I could always rely on my brother in situations such as these."

"I'm sorry," I whispered, and my grief over Tyran's loss came soaring to the surface once again. I knew it could only be a fraction of Bowen's.

He gave me a brittle smile. "I'll go with all of you now, but I will need to meet with Cadeyn. Gabriel, I will trust you to plan defenses within the room."

We filed down the hallway with purpose and arrived at the library. Bowen pointed out some of the features of the room for us, including hidden panels that I'd been unaware of. He paused briefly before leaving and brushed a kiss across my lips. He didn't need to say anything else. I felt a rush of love swirling with protectiveness, the depth of which was overwhelming.

I watched Bowen leave and turned. The expression on Joshua's face was controlled. It was then that I knew he'd felt everything that had just passed between Bowen and I through the blood bond. It made me wonder once again how much of his memory Batariel had given him back. I tore my eyes away from Joshua and looked to Gabriel.

"What's the plan?"

Gabriel's expression was thoughtful. "What would you do?"

I turned, exhaling, and examined the space. "If I were them, I would attack just before sunrise so that no one could escape."

"I believe Belenus is acting on that assumption as well," Gabriel agreed.

"As far as the room goes, I would move all the bookcases across here and force them to pool together and bottleneck to get to us. I would wear Daylight Gear, and once the bulk of them were through, I would blow the windows and let them burn.

That would thin the ranks enough that we would be able to fight the rest hand-to-hand."

He grinned and looked at the windows appreciatively. "Good."

"Glad you like it. You sit there, and Josh and I will move everything."

"You—"

I cut him off, holding up a hand and raising a brow. "The surgeons just spent twelve hours putting that back on, and you just pulled a six inch shard of glass from your side. You are going to save your strength. You may have to fight, but you don't have to move shelving." I stopped myself from pointing out how terrible he looked. Gabriel's skin was sallow, he had dark circles under his eyes, and his shoulders had an exhausted slump.

Joshua and I worked in silence, which I could only describe as a comfortable electricity.

A sick feeling came over me, and I started thinking out loud. "The black liquid from my vision...I—" Turning towards the door of the library, I stared at it, trying to capture the memory on the edge of my vision. I turned and looked at no one in particular. "No. No. No!" I shouted, then sped out of the room.

The cliff was just part of their plan. I knew exactly where Icelos would surface. I vaguely realized that Joshua was behind me as I threaded my way through the maze of hallways. When I came within a hundred feet of my suspected target, Joshua grabbed my shoulder and turned me to look at him.

"You figured something out," he stated, although it sounded more like an accusation.

I met his piercing, green stare. "When I escaped, Dagan sent me through the aqueducts and sewers. I climbed down a long stone shaft—like a well. It was so old that water seeped from the sides and ran down the walls. It looked black in the lighting. The black ooze wasn't symbolic. Icelos is coming up through that passageway with a group of his people. I *know* it."

"And you are going to fight them off all by yourself?"

"I..." I looked around and realized that Josh and I were alone. Gabriel wasn't well enough to keep up. I faltered. I could be wrong.

"I'm in, but we stop for weapons," Josh necessitated.

Then, I felt a little dimwitted. There were no guards, and I hadn't heard from Bowen. I pulled my phone from my pocket and sent him a text: "Think I know what the black liquid is." I shoved it back in my jeans and led Josh towards the practice room. It was on the way to my former escape tunnel and fully stocked. Urgency was nipping at me. I still hadn't seen a guard.

We rounded the corner and almost barreled into Morpheus. He came to a halt and stood with the same stricken expression I'd seen when Phantasos had betrayed us and helped Batariel invade my dreams. Part of me wanted to run. I didn't know if he could handle losing another brother. But before I could let fear seize me and question his loyalty, I threw my arms around him, hugging him hard.

Morpheus hesitated for a moment, and then returned my embrace, whispering, "You are the reason they found me."

I nodded against his chest. "I had a vision."

Holding my shoulder, he stepped back from me, his eyes their normal stormy grey. After a long moment of examining me, he finally spoke. "My brother is coming, isn't he?"

I started moving down the hall again, forcing him to release me, Joshua still at my side. "I don't expect you to come with me, Morpheus."

Josh and I entered the practice room, and a few seconds later, Morpheus joined us in silence. Morpheus took a sword and a few blades for close-quarter fighting.

Once we were fully armed and heading to the door, Morpheus grabbed my elbow and pulled me to a stop. "Where is Belenus?"

I pulled my phone from my pocket—he hadn't answered my text. I hit the call button and put it to my ear. It rang and rang, but Bowen never picked up. Worry fluttered somewhere inside me, but I couldn't let it take root. I needed to head off Icelos if I could, then I would check on Bowen. Part of me wondered if Icelos was already inside, although it could have simply been that Bowen was in a meeting, and it would have been offensive to pick up his phone.

I shook my head. "He isn't answering, but we need to go."

I shouldered past him and Josh and headed for my former escape route. We traversed several staircases and a few more hallways until we came to the reinforced door closing off the shaft. When I had used it, Dagan had given me a key. Now, the lock had been broken.

Turning, I whispered, "Do you think they are inside, or was this just prepped for their entry?"

Morpheus stepped forward and opened the door with caution. We crept inside the space that was no larger than a small bathroom and closed the door behind us without latching it. Then we listened to the noises coming up the long stone shaft. There was a flicker of sound amidst the trickles and drips of water. In the distance, not in the shaft, it felt as if there was a tremor in the building itself.

I started to speak, but there was a flurry of movement, and I was knocked backwards as the door was smashed open, tearing it from the hinges. Morpheus tumbled across the floor, locked in battle with his brother, Icelos.

Sensing something coming up the shaft, I spun around, but Joshua had already taken the head of Icelos' follower. There was a splash far below when the headless body hit the water. As I stood beside Joshua, I readied myself for the next conspirator to emerge. This time, as another came catapulting out, I was quicker. He fell dead before Joshua moved.

"Is this a competition?" Josh grinned.

"Wanna make it one? It'd be like when we were kids."

"I always won when we were kids," he taunted, a little smug.

"You were older. It doesn't count."

"It always counts," he crooned, as he lunged forward and engaged the next vamp that surfaced. Unfortunately, two more were on that vamp's heels. It got real very quickly. But we had two things going for us: we still had the advantage of the higher ground, and they entering through a bottleneck. There was a maximum of two that could surface at a time. We fought with ferocity, and the bodies started to pile up.

Despite the noise, no one from the castle came. I could hear Morpheus behind me and kept part of my attention on him. If he became overpowered, I didn't want Icelos attacking my or Josh's back.

Sunrise was not far off. I was still worried about Bowen, but I didn't sense anything through the blood bond—whatever he was doing, he was controlled.

Joshua and I stood side-by-side, waiting for more to crest the top of the shaft, but there were no more. Cautiously, I tiptoed towards the opening, but Joshua caught my elbow. He shook his head and motioned me back. His chivalrous gesture made my inner feminist rise up and want to object, but he was faster than me.

He leaned in over the shaft, ready to retreat, but then he relaxed. He glanced back. "Empty."

I immediately turned on my heel to help Morpheus, but

both he and Icelos were gone. In that second of distraction, I had lost track of them.

"Josh," I called as I started to follow the trail of damage. He was immediately by my side. My throat tightened with the memory of all the missions we had been on together—memories he no longer had.

We came around a corner and found Morpheus, breathless, and pinning his brother to the floor. He had a knee in Icelos' stomach, a hand on his chest, and a blade buried in his shoulder. Icelos looked defiantly at Morpheus as he murmured something.

Josh and I hung back and listened, but Icelos caught sight of me.

Icelos spat, "You traded me for that pretender—you were my brother."

"Not for her—for Belenus—the rightful heir who has been our family," Morpheus argued.

Icelos struggled beneath his brother, and Morpheus pressed the knife in farther. Icelos panted, "Distant cousin."

Morpheus' voice was thick with emotion. "He *has* been a brother. You are blinded by your desire for the throne."

"Easy for you to say. You gave up your right to the throne for a woman."

"I never wanted it."

"That is my point. *I* do—and I won't stop."

"Agrona was wrong. We aren't meant to rule the humans."

I noticed that blood was soaking into the carpet, the ring growing ever wider. Icelos' was growing more cadaverous by the second.

"I won't stop," Icelos repeated as he wrenched himself upward until the knife was sunk in to the hilt.

"Don't make me do this, *please*," Morpheus begged.

"No tribunal for me." The look on Icelos' face was defiant and broken at the same time.

I wasn't sure how, but Icelos bucked and threw Morpheus off. They were both on their feet, then Morpheus was spinning, his leather coat billowing as his sword arced through the air and found its target. Icelos stood still as stone for a long moment, staring at his brother—no judgement on his face, only resignation—then he collapsed gracefully onto the floor.

Morpheus fell to his knees, a wail of pain bellowing so loud that it shook my core. Instantly, I was on my knees in front of him, wrapping my arms around him. I glanced at Joshua. He was on alert, sword drawn, keeping watch. I needed to find Bowen and Gabriel, but I couldn't leave Morpheus like this. Icelos was a coward for making his brother kill him, and it made me sick.

I held onto him as he shuddered with convulsion-like sobs. He heaved as if trying to catch his breath while grabbing onto me. He quieted for a moment and leaned back and grasped my shoulders, his grey eyes a tempest.

"The quake we felt a few minutes ago. It must have been my brother's diversion. We need to find Belenus."

Morpheus took point as we three trotted down hallways towards the throne room. We rounded the last corner before the lobby and were met by the blinding pain of sunlight. We dove back into the hall in what seemed like a coordinated movement.

I pressed my back against the wall and concentrated on the smells—dust, rubber, oil, and...antifreeze. A memory of lying on my back next to my dad under our family car surfaced. I had to squeeze my eyes shut to chase away the thought; missing my family right now couldn't distract me. But the pain of separation had already taken root.

"It smells like a wrecked car," I finally forced out.

Josh agreed. "They must have rammed through the front doors. Was Bowen down there?"

"I don't know. Maybe the throne room. There is a long hall before you reach it; I doubt the vehicle made it that far." At least I hoped. I looked over at Morpheus, but his mind was elsewhere. "Morpheus?" His attention refocused on me.

"Yes?"

"What is the best way down there? I don't think we want to take the elevator. I don't know this place like you do."

He processed my question slowly, but then was on his feet and moving quickly while he beckoned. "Follow me."

He led us to what looked like a service stairwell that I had never seen. When we reached the bottom, I realized we were in the kitchen that serviced the throne room and ballroom. My anxiety kicked up, and I checked my phone again. No messages and...no service. My heart started racing as I pushed ahead of Morpheus into the throne room.

There were bodies everywhere. Bowen was hunched over Cadeyn, grabbing onto the lapels of his jacket. "...lie still."

Cadeyn smiled, but his teeth were bloody. "I'm going to have to take the day off, Your Highness."

Bowen released an emotion-filled chuckle. Cadeyn looked bad, but if he was joking, he'd be fine.

Cadeyn noticed me and pointed. "Go."

Bowen turned and saw me flanked by Morpheus and Joshua. Relief washed over his face, and he was instantly across the room. He picked me up, encircled me in his arms, and crushed me to him.

After a long moment, he eased my feet to the ground and captured my face between his hands. A half-sob came out now that I knew he was okay. I pulled him down for a quick kiss and stepped back.

"I need to find Gabriel."

"He's not with you?"

"We left him in the library." I glanced back at Morpheus. The lines on his face were tight. When I looked back at Bowen, his eyes were on Morpheus.

"Icelos is dead," I whispered. "Morpheus. He..."

Bowen strode to his cousin and embraced him. For a few seconds, it looked like Morpheus would crack again, but he shored in his grief, taking Bowen's strength.

Joshua cleared his throat, getting my attention. He mouthed, "Gabriel."

I nodded, and we started back towards the kitchens. Cadeyn's labored voice called out, "Stop. The castle isn't secure."

I wanted to balk; it wasn't like he could stop me. At that moment, some of the guard filed in from the kitchen. Judging from the state of their uniforms, they'd been in a fight, too.

Bowen and Morpheus had some sort of silent communication and started walking towards me. "We are with you."

Cadeyn grimaced in frustration. "Your Majesties, please."

Bowen addressed the guards who had just joined us. "Half of you take your Captain to medical. The rest of you with me."

Within seconds, we were in the hall by the library and were greeted with the distinctive smell of salt air. Sunlight was streaming through the doorway, and I knew, without a doubt, that Gabriel had broken the windows—and that he'd been alone.

I shoved my way past everyone and came as close as I could to the door without entering the sunlight. "Gabriel! Are you in there?"

"Yes," he replied, his voice labored. "I am pinned."

I took a deep breath and stuck my head inside the doorway

to find him; he was in the back corner. Bowen yanked me back and scowled at me. The burn healed within seconds. Seeing this, his disapproval waned. "Let's get the daylight gear from our room."

"You're telling me that there isn't an ambush waiting for us in our room? I'll be quick. I can take more sun than any of you."

Bowen opened his mouth, but it was my time to scowl at him. He stared back at me and pressed his lips into a hard line, then finally nodded.

I turned and darted into the room to the corner that was straight across from the door. There was a small triangle of shade to stand in. Pressing my back to the wall, I counted ten piles of ash and felt even guiltier that I'd left him.

I examined his position, trying to figure out the easiest way to help him. He was on his back, immobilized with his two colossal bookcases at least partially on top of him. Beyond that, I couldn't see from where I was how much help he needed.

"What are you doing in here without protection?"

I rolled my eyes. I couldn't help it. "Are you pinned beneath one or both shelves?"

"Both. My arm under the lower case."

"I smell blood. Is the bleed excessive?"

"No."

"Anything else I need to know?"

"No."

"Since you are my captive audience, I will remove the bookcases if you will talk to me later and tell me what you have been keeping from me."

Gabriel audibly exhaled, and I could feel the conflict, but more than anything, sadness. "I was going to tell you, kiddo."

The confirmation that he *was* keeping secrets from me caused a lump in my throat. Whatever it was—it was bad. I heard Bowen speaking softly in the hall. I wanted to know what was going on, so I decided to get this over with. I wasn't exactly looking forward to the pain, but I knew what to expect, so I knew I could control it.

I dashed out into the light, ignoring the sizzle of my skin. Clamping onto the heavy casing of the top shelf, I lifted it, flipping it over like the page of a book. Leather hardbacks spun through the air, burying him further. Then I picked up the second one long enough so he could pull his arm out and flashed back to the corner to recover for a moment.

I concentrated on pressing my head against the wall as my skin renewed itself.

Bowen yelled around the corner. "Aleria, are you all right?"

"I'm good," I managed. The blistering started to disappear, and I could breathe more easily.

Gabriel grunted, and books started falling away. Watching him struggle was killing me. I'd seen him with multiple stab wounds, but this was far worse.

I could hear movement in the hall, then the words, "This floor is secure."

I exhaled away some of the tension and closed my eyes. That meant our bedroom had been cleared, too. A few more books tumbled near Gabriel, and my eyes snapped open. He had gotten to his knees and was cradling his arm to his chest with much concentration.

"Please tell me your arm is okay." I leaned towards him, ready to help again.

Gabriel responded, "Stay there. Just some broken ribs." He stood woodenly and swayed, a fine sheen of sweat breaking across his forehead. "I need to make a phone call before I talk to you. And I want Joshua there too."

Suddenly, my mouth had no moisture, so I nodded in agreement.

"After you." He motioned to the door.

I flashed by him into the hall to the expectant eyes of Bowen and Joshua. It was apparent they had the same sinking feeling I did. Gabriel limped out of the library, and then I realized that our entourage was hungry, and we had a bleeding Slayer dangling in front of them.

Bowen spoke. "Joshua, would you please assist the Queen's familiar to her rooms? I would like to speak with Morpheus and the guard." Bowen gave me a knowing look. "I'll meet you in a few minutes, love."

As our trio made our way back to my room, part of me wished that I hadn't forced the upcoming conversation. Maybe it was better I didn't know what Gabriel was keeping from me.

Then I realized I was being a coward. I sucked it up and prepared myself for whatever was coming my way.

# 29

# I AM NOT RIGHT

GABRIEL

Joshua helped me onto the couch. I knew Ali was behind me, but she was silent. Finally, she stepped around in front of me, but instead of boldly asking me for answers, she sank to her knees in front of me and sat on her feet.

"Are you in pain?" asked she.

She knew I was. My heart rate was elevated, and I had seen her cock her head to the side as she listened in the quiet room. I realized I had not answered her question. "Yes."

Despite her anger with me for withholding information from her, she took my uninjured arm gently. She rubbed her fingers thoughtfully over the pulse point at my wrist. There was a hesitation—she met my eyes, asking permission, and I gave her an almost imperceptible nod.

Aleria bit into my wrist, and as the hormone surged through my system, the pain vanished. My heart rate slowed to normal, and my breathing eased. She did not feed after alleviating my pain; she simply sealed the wound, stood up gracefully, and moved to the chair straight across from me.

I realized that she had grown up in that moment. She had been a kid when we had found her unconscious in that apartment. She had always been strong, but had been so innocent and trusting. She was no longer a child—but a woman —a queen.

Belenus entered in a whisper and appeared on the arm of the couch next to Ali, as if he had been there since we had returned. I did not like my back to the door; it was counter to my instincts and training.

I made a sweep of the room with my eyes. It was just the four of us—no guards. I knew everyone was waiting on me. "Before I tell you, I would still like to make a call to check the status on someone."

Aleria stood. "I'll grab a quick shower." She looked down at her soot and bloodstained clothing, but avoided me. There were her nerves again. Belenus touched the side of her face with affection. She smiled up at him, then fled to her room.

Belenus looked towards Joshua. "If you would like to clean up, feel free to use my rooms. Take what you need from the closet."

Joshua glanced at me and then nodded at Belenus. "Thank you," he whispered as he left the room.

Belenus handed me a cell phone and angled his body towards Ali's room. "I'll leave you to make the call."

"Wait."

He froze like a burglar caught in police spotlights.

"I want you prepared for her reaction."

A curse slid through his lips, and he reluctantly sat back down.

ALERIA

I toweled my hair and pulled on comfortable clothes. Even for a vampire, I was sure that was record speed. I wanted to hide in my room to avoid reality, but that just spurred me to get it over with. Just as I reached for the door, a wave of emotion from Bowen caused me to miss the knob.

The blood in my body seemed to pool in my stomach as I made my way out to the main room again. Judging from Bowen's change in expression, I looked as pale as I felt.

When I sat next to Bowen, he took my hand and squeezed it reassuringly. Joshua came in from Bowen's room smelling of soap, his jeans and t-shirt slightly too large. He sat on the other side of me, so that all three of us were facing Gabriel. It felt like I was waiting for a cancer diagnosis.

Gabriel cleared his throat. "We received some intel recently and sent Raphael to investigate. He reported that nothing was out of order, but that his gut told him something was wrong. So he stayed."

"Where?" I asked.

"California."

The blood in my veins crystalized. My heart stopped beating. The world stopped spinning. All existence splintered into a million irreparable pieces. There was only one reason Gabriel would...

"Ali—"

"Don't say it," I moaned.

"Batariel sent two of them into your parents' home—"

"Please. Don't say it." I could feel Joshua's emotion layered with my own.

"They split up once they entered the house—"

"Gabriel," I pleaded, my voice rising. "I did everything right. I left. I let them think I was dead. I stayed out of their lives to protect them. I did everything right. It's not fair!"

"Raphael saved your brother."

Tears burst from my eyes. "Cameron is okay?"

"Yes," he paused. "He saw everything, though. He knows our world exists. Raphael managed to kill the Fallen, and then called cleaners. As far as the world knows, your entire family perished in a fire."

A sob lodged in my throat, and my mind started to sprint through the possibilities. I tamped down the loss of my parents and focused on Cameron. If I didn't, I was afraid I might literally fracture. Could grief break bone and collapse bodies? It felt like it could.

I stood and started pacing back and forth, shaking out my hands.

"Where is Cameron now?" Joshua asked.

"He was smuggled into Geneva. Raphael is getting papers for him there. It will take another two days. He is awaiting my orders."

My voice was weak. "I want him with me, but if he comes here, he will end up—"

Bowen finished, "Being turned or becoming a familiar."

"I can take him. Train him. He's my family too," Joshua offered.

Gabriel sighed. "I am sorry." He covered his eyes with his hand and rubbed his temples. He looked like he had aged ten years in the last ten minutes. "I am so sorry," he repeated under his breath.

GABRIEL

Belenus took Ali back to his room and left us use of the others. He had picked her up like a babe, and she had practically collapsed into his arms. Joshua had gone to sleep in Ali's room. Hours passed, and I sat staring out the window. The sun turned from yellow to gold to red, and I watched it melt into the horizon. The dark waters of the ocean seemed to swallow it.

Joshua entered and sat next to me, his aura solemn. "Do you think she will stay here?"

"She needs to," I replied, not without compassion.

"Her brother..."

I changed the subject. "How much do you remember?

"Fragments. Batariel returned some of my memories and gave me some of Ali's."

"Some of hers?"

"I hit her. I just...I can't imagine doing that. But I saw it. I felt it. What sort of monster am I?"

I wondered if I was making a mistake. I exhaled long and slow as I considered. "You are not a monster at all. You were being blackmailed. You left her to protect the Hayes family."

"But the Fallen killed them."

Joshua's sense of justice could not comprehend that there was nothing fair about evil. It betrays and corrupts, and that was what we were up against.

I tried to explain. "Batariel lost—he lashed out, destroying what he could." I waited. I knew what his next question would be.

"Does Ali know?"

"No."

Joshua fell silent.

After several minutes, I finally asked, "Do you want her back?"

ALERIA

Bowen kicked the door closed behind him after he carried me into his room. I was concentrating on my breathing. In. Out. In. Out. In. Out.

He stood by the bed, swaying a little, dropping kisses onto my hair, my temple, and my cheek. I couldn't tell what he was thinking, but I could feel his strength.

After a long while, he dropped my feet to the floor, holding me steady until I was ready. I grabbed onto his shirt, pressing my forehead against his sternum, feeling so small.

I choked on my words. "I go through things, and I think that nothing can be worse than what I have just gone through...and then it's like the universe is laughing at me and makes it worse. I don't understand. Why?"

"Give me your pain," he whispered.

"You have your own pain; you just lost people you love."

Bowen chuckled, but there was no humor in it. "Gabriel said you would do that."

"Do what?"

"Think it was selfish to rely on me. He told me not to let you get away with it."

"Damn traitor."

This time, there was some humor in his chuckle, but I immediately felt guilty for finding anything humorous.

"Hey." He kissed me, slow with soft lips. His voice grew more serious. "Give me your pain."

"I don't know how," my voice cracked.

He ran his nose down the side of my face until his mouth was in the hollow behind my ear. "Give me your pain," he whispered one last time, and then I felt his teeth in my neck. I sagged against him as the hormone flooded me. My eyes closed, and then fluttered open when he closed the punctures.

He cradled my face between his hands. "It is incomprehensible how much I love you."

I was swirling in the euphoria and somewhat confused by the tone in his voice as I returned each kiss. I needed him. I yanked my shirt off and unzipped my pants. He pushed them over my hips as helped him with his clothing. A few more tugs, and there was nothing left but skin between us.

A feral sort of energy took over. I didn't understand why, but I felt like each touch and caress he gave me was a goodbye. It reminded me of my last night with Joshua. I didn't understand.

I pulled him onto the bed and on top of me, desperation fueling me. I loved every angle of his body. Many had worshipped him, and that was exactly what I wanted to do now.

His hands glided over my body as his mouth claimed mine. I felt guilt again for feeling pleasure. Then I realized that Bowen was taking my pain. Somehow, he was taking it all on himself.

I arched as he took all of me.

I couldn't bear it, so he was carrying me. His strength was mine.


GABRIEL

Joshua eventually went to bed, but despite it finally being dark, I could not sleep. I lay in bed with my good arm behind my head and my eyes closed. I did not sense Belenus, but I smelled him.

"You are leaving her alone?" I asked.

"She will be asleep for a few hours," answered he.

I closed my eyes again, but when I did not hear the door open, I opened them again. He was standing with his hand on the knob and his head pressed against a panel of the door.

"May I help you with something?" I asked.

He rolled his head to the side. "Joshua threw her away like that to save her family?"

"Yes." I noted to never underestimate vampire intelligence.

He did not reply, but left the room. I caught a glimpse of Morpheus just outside the door. I wondered what he would do with that information.


ALERIA

I woke. Bowen's side of the bed was cold. I rolled onto my back and pulled his pillow to my chest, breathing in his scent. I couldn't help but think about the way he had kissed me until I fell into a deep sleep.

Sadness started to creep its way through my limbs, beginning with my toes and fingers. I would grieve, the storm was imminent, but I wanted to talk to Gabriel more. When I opened the bedroom door, he was seated on the couch, facing my room as if he was expecting me. I suppose he was.

"Where is everyone?" I asked.

"Bowen left, looking at his phone. Morpheus met him at the door. Cadeyn has escorted Joshua to Medical to visit Ian. He should be released today."

I realized Gabriel was sitting a little stiffly. "Are you in pain?" I asked.

"Only if I breathe," Gabriel replied with a wry grin.

"Your super Slayer abilities didn't heal your ribs in eight

hours? You might want to have that checked out." I sat next to him and took his wrist.

"I do not need it," Gabriel resisted.

"You are my familiar now, and if for no other reason, we need to keep up appearances." Then I added, "I guess you will be leaving in the morning, so you should take advantage."

He relaxed his arm and allowed me to help him. When the tight lines of tension around his eyes softened, I stopped. It was hard not to feed. I was way overdue, and he tasted amazing. The only thing better was the blood of a mate.

"Have you decided where to send my brother?"

"Some of that is up to you," he replied, not giving away anything.

"I can't bring him here. This is no life for him. He's sixteen." I leaned back and examined the mural on the ceiling. "I have missed so much of his life. He was in junior high. The pictures I saw, he was a sophomore on the varsity soccer team."

"He quit soccer."

"Really?"

"There was a school shooting during practice. He was shot. He is fine, but he quit the team."

I took a minute to digest that information. "Was the shooting random?"

"Semjâzâ and Batariel were responsible."

I felt ill. "Was I responsible? Did they find my family because I had asked for pictures of them?

Gabriel answered. "No, Phineas had betrayed us. He had given the Fallen their address."

Hatred. That was all I felt. "I'm going to kill him."

"Joshua already did. He snapped his neck the moment he admitted it."

As if on cue, Cadeyn opened the main door and Joshua

entered, pushing Ian in a wheelchair. Cadeyn bowed and excused himself.

I turned to Joshua. I didn't say hello, but questioned him, "You killed Phineas?"

He looked puzzled, but nodded in affirmation.

There was an epiphany looming in front of me, but I still couldn't quite put the pieces together. I asked Gabriel, "When did you find out about the shooting?"

"Days after you left with Belenus. I had no means to contact you."

I felt a little better knowing he hadn't kept it from me.

Ian looked pale, but he was in good spirits. "I hear I missed all the fun."

"Yeah, it sucks healing like a human. You don't get in on the post-battle attempted *coup d'état*." Then I looked at Josh, and the last of the puzzle pieces became clear. Click. Click. Click. I stood; he froze in the intensity of my stare. My gaze moved to Gabriel.

"Ali," Gabriel whispered, but his tone was cautionary.

I stalked towards Joshua. "You killed Phineas for my family. You broke me to pieces to save them." It wasn't a question.

Josh held up his hands in surrender. "I'm sorry, Als. I just figured it out. I don't remember."

"You didn't trust me to know!"

Joshua reached for me, but I evaded him.

I turned around, fixing my gaze on Gabriel again. "Does Bowen know?"

"He asked before he left a few hours ago."

From the expression on Ian's face, he knew too. "So I am the last to know?" Anger thrashed around inside me intermingling with violence—my grief and disappointment raging into an unstable mix. I needed to leave and get my head straight. I didn't bother saying anything else as I stormed from the room.

Hours passed. I sat on a stone bench of the veranda, a statue myself. I searched the ocean, the stars, and the night—for some sort of answer. I was praying for clarity and wishing for a light to shine down from heaven and a list of instructions to magically appear in front of me.

Every once in a while, I could sense eyes on me from behind. I didn't know if it was just the guard or one of the boys. When dawn was no more than an hour away, I broke from my position and headed back to my room.

When I entered, I was surprised to find everyone present—even Bowen was sitting with Gabriel, Joshua, and Ian. But it seemed as if they'd all been sitting in silence for a while.

I hesitated, then asked Bowen, "May I speak with Gabriel alone?"

He stood and walked over to me. He gave me a whisper of a kiss on my forehead before going to his private chambers. Ian and Josh retreated to mine.

My discussion with Gabriel lasted almost a half hour. Then I asked to speak with Josh. I felt drained after all our talking.

It was an hour before I went to Bowen's room. I felt bad making him wait so long, but I had to settle some things first. When I entered, the room was dark except for the light from a fire. He was sitting on the bed, leaning against the headboard. When he met my eyes, there was only a flicker of a smile on the edge of his full lips.

I crawled onto the bed and sat cross-legged, facing him. I pulled one of his hands onto my knee and laced my fingers through his.

"Are you leaving to be with your brother?" he asked.

"Is that why every kiss has felt like a good-bye since yesterday?"

He swallowed and didn't answer.

I picked up his hand and pressed my lips to the back of it. "I'm not going anywhere—I'm not leaving you—ever."

The spark in his blue eyes returned, but he still looked cautious.

"I spent all night trying to figure out what is best for my brother. I'm not right for my brother right now, but Gabriel is. He's agreed to take him on like he did me. Joshua is the family he will need; he will also help with training. When Cameron finds out that I'm alive, he's going to be angry, but if he knows our world, I think he'll understand." I smiled. "In a few months, maybe I can see him. Even if it is limited, I can still be part of his life."

"And Joshua?"

I crawled onto Bowen's lap, straddling him. "What he did was for a good reason, but it doesn't change my decision." I leaned in, my hands immediately in his hair, and kissed him—heat coiling in my belly. His hands went to my waist.

"Aleria," he breathed into my hair. It sounded like an answered prayer.

"I'm going to cry very soon, and it's going to be ugly. I can feel it coming. I lost my parents. But right now, I need to be selfish. I need your hands on me. I need to know that we are okay—that I have one stable thing in my life."

It was as if a dam broke. He shifted and pushed me onto my back, lying on top of me. He propped himself on his elbows to look at me.

"You woke a part of me that had been asleep for centuries. You are the blood in my veins. I lived before, but now I am alive.

You have given a husk a soul." I could see that last vestige of doubt about my choosing him leave his eyes.

"I will love you until I am nothing but ash," I repeated from our vows, and our lips crashed together.

It was then that I felt his unrestrained love envelope me.

I was exactly where I should be.

I had found my true home.

# 30

# EPILOGUE—MAN ON FIRE

ALERIA

Propped with pillows against the headboard, I was enjoying the fading light outside. I had made watching the sunset part of my routine. I didn't want to let a day go by without being thankful for the life I had.

Bowen's voice startled me. "You look nervous."

I grinned at him. "I guess I am." I took a deep breath. "I'm nervous *and* excited."

"Maybe you shouldn't go?"

I cocked my head in disapproval. "I will be gone for four *days,* and I have waited six *months* to see Cameron, Gabriel, and everyone else."

"I know," he groaned, snaking his arms around my waist and pulling me nose-to-nose.

"Pouting and eye rolling—I don't think I've ever seen such behavior, Your Majesty," I teased and caught his bottom lip with my teeth. In reality, I thought this really was the first time I'd seen him pout. I released his lip and gave him a soft kiss; his lips parted and desire filled me.

His blue eyes feverish, he kissed me beneath my jaw. "I like to be able to worship *this* whenever I want." He tugged the strap of my nightgown off of my shoulder and kissed my collarbone. "And this." He moved down my body, lifting up the silk and kissed my hip.

I gasped. "You aren't going to make this easy on me."

He grinned up at me. He shoved the fabric up over my belly and kissed it with added affection. "Did you tell them?"

"No. Gabriel is not going to let anything happen to me. Neither will Morpheus or Cadeyn."

"I am regretting not going."

"Then everyone will know I've left the palace."

He spoke to my belly, "If you are as stubborn as your mother, there is no hope for civilization."

"For civilization? *Really?*"

"For me, anyway." He gave me one of his radiant smiles that always made me melt.

"You have thirty minutes before I have to gear up and go for a swim with Morpheus. Cadeyn should be ready at the rendezvous location in an hour." His smile began to smolder. "Thirty minutes…"


GABRIEL

Sitting across from Cameron, I observed him staring at the front door, knees bouncing in anticipation. The outer perimeter sensor beeped, and my eyes flicked to the monitor. A black Mercedes with tinted windows was prowling down the private driveway half a kilometer away.

Ian's voice came over the comm: "Heat sensors show three at

sixty-five degrees. Size indicates two male, one female with a heartbeat."

I turned back to Cameron only to see his mop of red hair disappear around the corner at the end of the hall. The kid was stealthy and *still* angry, but he had finally asked to see his sister.

"Joshua," I started, but he was already on his feet, moving down the hall.

"On it," he answered behind him as he went after Cameron.

"Jess, would you wait downstairs with Uriel?"

"My pleasure," Jess answered. Then, as she started towards the stairwell, she hesitated.

"Ali will be happy to see you," I reassured.

"Even with—?"

"Yes, now go."

I stepped out onto the portico between the columns. The evening was warm, and the night air fragrant. Samael stepped around the corner; I nodded and flicked my chin back towards the rear. He was to remain out of range of both Morpheus and Cadeyn. He wanted to see Ali–his insistence had surprised me– but he had been there when Joshua had broken her and changed all of our worlds.

The car came to a stop in front of me, and Cadeyn emerged from the driver's seat, looking none-too-friendly. He came up the steps, his eyes moving as mine would have, searching for threats.

I held out my hand in greeting. "Mr. Bradshaw, pleased you arrived safely."

Cadeyn hesitated, then shook it briefly, his yellow eyes suspicious.

I pulled the tablet from beneath my arm. "This is yours. You have access to the cameras on the entire property, which is quite extensive." I tapped through the controls to show him. "Outer grounds, base of the walls inside and out, living spaces, hallways, and bedrooms—including mine. Everything except the bathrooms are under surveillance. We have complete transparency.

"Including myself, we have three Slayers on site—all personal friends of your Queen—four humans and one vampire. We have brought in blood for you, but if you choose to go off site, I understand. Is there anything else I can do for you?"

"The bedrooms we will be occupying?"

I pulled up the blueprints on his tablet and highlighted them. "Upstairs, the three at the end of the hall. Feel free to make a security sweep," I offered.

He was nothing but a blur of movement. I stood, waiting for Cadeyn to return. There was no movement in the car, and it made me uneasy.

Suddenly, Cadeyn was back in front of me. Ali had warned me that he was faster than anything she had ever seen. "Who is the child?"

"Which one?"

"I assume the boy is the brother. The female."

"I think you know."

Cadeyn's light brows raised in surprise.

"I am trusting you as well."

He turned on his heel and descended the few steps to the car and opened the rear door. Morpheus emerged, then offered his hand to the person inside. When Ali came into sight, I had not expected to have such an emotional response. I took two steps forward and had to force my own restraint.

She took three very dignified steps to get around her sentinels, and then ran to me. She flung out her arms, and we embraced. I held on tight, wishing that I was greeting her back permanently. I had missed her more than I had thought.

I released her, but still held her shoulders, my eyes going to her stomach. She was dressed to cover the evidence, but there was no mistaking her pregnancy when I held her.

"I'm five months along." She answered my unspoken question.

"You did not say anything."

She shrugged. "You're already nuts about security. I didn't want you to have an aneurism."

I glanced at Morpheus and Cadeyn. I took my right hand away from her shoulder and offered it to Morpheus. He shook it without hesitation.

Cadeyn spoke, "Your Highness, I will make a sweep of the grounds."

I hit the comm unit. "Samael, that Captain of the Royal Guard is making the rounds."

"Affirmative."

Ali smiled. "Samael is here?" Then she frowned. "Is he okay with my escorts?"

"Yes." I slid my arm around her shoulder and encouraged her inside. "Get settled. I will see if Joshua can coax Cameron back out."

"*Back* out?"

"He got nervous; just be prepared, kiddo. He is doing really well, but he has a ways to go."

"But you think he will be okay?" Her eyes were fraught with worry.

"Tough runs in your family. He was pretty beat up from the attack when Raphael first brought him in. He went after the Fallen with a baseball bat, even after Raphael had killed one and told him to run. With Cameron's injuries, I called in Jess. She had helped Joshua transition into our world and is still with us."

Ali smiled. "I like Jess."

I pointed to the stairs. "I have you in the master."

"Really? I never really want to be in *that* room ever again."

"Petrescu is not using it. This was the most secure venue available."

She shuddered and looked off as if seeing through the walls. "You just don't forget being tortured in a basement, escaping through secret tunnels, and almost burning to death."

"Sorry you had to do that." It had been almost impossible to let her go on that mission.

"We wouldn't be here if I hadn't. The Fallen would've gotten into this place eventually. We wouldn't have been able to stop them. I would do it again," admitted she.

Ali vanished up the steps to clean up, but I caught Morpheus' elbow before he followed. "How is she *really* doing?"

He deliberated a moment. We were not friends, but we had had some honest conversations before I had left the coven. He did not like me, but respected me and had thanked me for protecting Ali for years.

Morpheus finally answered. "Claiming a Slayer as a familiar *and* her association with you in general hindered her at first. But the alliance to hunt down the escaped Fallen has helped. She is proving formidable. And as with any royals, the heir will help. That is all I will disclose."

"Understood."

He nodded and went upstairs. I was glad that Ali had him as a confidant and friend. I shook my head, wondering how I had come to the place where I was thankful for one of the Oneiroi and approved of the King of the French Coven.


ALERIA

Thirty minutes later, I was still in my room—petrified. Bring on a hoard of mindless Strigoi monsters—the sixteen-year-old boy downstairs was more terrifying. During my conversation with Gabriel on the phone, he'd told me that when Cameron had first found out I was alive, he'd been so angry that he'd wished me dead.

Joshua had not escaped his rage either, not with Josh flying home and attending the funeral. When Cameron had found out that everyone thought I was truly dead—that I'd actually died from a sword through the chest—he'd promised to work on forgiving. But Cameron still didn't understand why I had stayed "dead." He couldn't understand that every time I forced myself to not think of them, I was trying to save them.

There was a knock at the door. "Come," I responded.

Morpheus casually leaned against the frame. "They are waiting for you, Your Worship."

I narrowed my eyes. "*Your Worship*?" He knew I hated all flowery titles.

He opened the door wide and motioned to the hall, prodding me into action. I walked down the main stairwell at human speed, feeling Morpheus right behind me. But when we reached the ground floor, he remained at the bottom of the steps. I turned to see why, and he gave me an odd smile.

"This time is for you. I am not part of this world. Go," he whispered.

I grabbed onto his shirt and leaned my forehead against his chest, trying to tamp down the last of my nerves. In the coven, he'd become my best friend. He was my sounding board that was never swayed by my Lux Casta blood.

"He loves you. No matter how angry." Then he gave me a little shove me towards the living room.

I entered. I'd had dinner with Petrescu on the far end of this room, which overlooked the gardens. Gabriel was leaning against the wall in the corner, looking at a tablet. He'd positioned himself where he could see everything in the room and outside. My bet was that he was looking at camera feeds from outside.

Joshua was on the couch facing me, and I could only see the back of Cameron's head over the chair he was in. When Josh's eyes flicked up to me, Cameron's shoulders stiffened. He whipped out of the chair, flinging around to face me.

I froze, my hands partially raised in greeting.

Cameron stared at me, a hundred emotions dancing across his face, with anger settling in.

My heart constricted, and all I could do was be thankful he was here. His hair was darker, more auburn than the red it had been. He was almost as tall as Josh now. When I'd left, Cameron was gangly and shorter than me. Now he had more weight on him, still a little gangly, but obviously the lean, athletic body of a soccer player like Josh.

Tears flooded my eyes. I finally managed a choked, "I missed you so much."

Cameron stood for a long moment like a statue, but there was a crack in the anger. He trembled, the conflicting emotions warring inside him, then he closed the distance and grabbed onto me. We wrapped our arms around each other, clinging like vines to something ancient.

The loss of my parents became real again, and the pain mingled with my joy of being reunited. I started to sob. Words poured from each of us, but over everything, I just kept saying, "I'm sorry, I'm sorry, I'm sorry."

For a long while we stood there, then I spied Joshua standing not far off, watching us. I raised my arm, motioning him towards us. He wrapped his arm around both of us. Joshua wasn't my husband any longer, but he was still my family. The three of us were all that was left of the past.

Sitting, relaxed on the couches, we talked for hours—Cameron filling me in on all of his training. I quizzed him about my friends from home, and was pleased to know that they'd been looking out for him. Josh told stories about the items he was allowed to tell me about the Watchers.

Gabriel had joined us for a long while. He was quiet and listened mostly. Then he'd disappeared downstairs a half hour ago. I knew other people were here, but I hadn't seen them.

Despite the guilt of not taking Cameron, I'd made the right decision. He was happy and thriving here. And no one here would want to turn him or drink from him—not even Josh.

I sensed Gabriel before he appeared in the doorway. When I looked up, I gasped, my hands flying to my mouth. Nuzzled against his chest was a baby girl of about a year and a half. Her lips were parted in sleep, her small hand holding a fist full of his shirt. She had dark waves that curled around her tiny ears, and her skin was a creamy olive, a shade lighter than Gabriel's.

I'd never seen our daughter—ever. I didn't even know her name. Gabriel had only seen her a couple of times. But the way he was holding her now, it was apparent that they had bonded. I felt both jealous and amazed. He'd taken a step back from his duties to be in her life. Then I realized that maybe he hadn't. The French Coven was the main reason we had isolated ourselves from her. Even after Agrona's death, outlying members of the coven had been hunting us—and now that coven was me. Gabriel was safe to have a relationship with her as long as I was on the throne.

"You are part of her life," I whispered.

The warmth of Gabriel's smile made my heart grow. "Yes. Meet Rosemond Cassiel," he cooed.

I looked up at him, shocked; she had my great-grandmother's first name.

"The name seemed appropriate." He paused when she stirred and stretched. "Cassiel was my mother."

"Why didn't you tell me her name?"

"She didn't have one. We don't name Slayers until their first birthday, when they exhibit characteristics of their bloodline."

The baby stretched once again, and her eyes fluttered open. She tilted her heavy head back to look up at Gabriel. He smiled back at her with an expression I'd rarely seen on his face. Then his words sunk in: "exhibit characteristics of their bloodline."

I gently ran my finger down the side of her face, hoping she would look at me. She squeaked at my cold fingers and swiveled her head of dark hair. A pair of lavender eyes met my own.

"Agrona did it. She is a Seer," I said, almost in disbelief.

"She is both."

"But I thought the Slayer gene was dominant?"

"Apparently, our daughter is both. You retained your gifts after being turned. Seers that had been turned in the past had lost their abilities, but you did not. So, little was documented about the Lux Casta; perhaps part of your gift is retaining the traits of two dominant genes."

My hands went to my stomach. "So..."

"So, we have a burden to raise these children properly. They will be more powerful than us."

With my hand still on my belly, I added, "I want them to know each other."

"As do I," Gabriel replied.

I wrapped my right arm around Gabriel's back and rested my head against his chest while gazing at Rosemond Cassiel. She reached out and planted her little hand on my cheek and leaned in, holding me with her lavender stare. "Your daddy should have named you Hope. You will make this world a better place."

I felt a hand on my shoulder. I immediately turned and threw my arms around Uriel.

"Awwr, biscuit, I missed you. Though I guess I shouldn't call you that anymore, Your Queenship," she drawled in her Aussie accent.

"No titles. It's just me." I frowned. "Though, you're not allowed to throw me over your shoulder and dump me into showers anymore." I pushed her teasingly.

"Done, chickie. Glad you haven't outgrown us lowly folk." She winked. Uriel was anything, but lowly.

Jess was behind her, and I promptly hugged her, too. I'd met her when she had pulled the tracking chip out of me after I'd been poisoned. Over the last few years, she had tended to my wounds many times. But something was off today. Her heart rate was elevated, and she seemed skittish.

She stepped back, and I looked her up and down, trying to place what was off. I'd been envious of her the first time I'd met her. She was everything I wasn't. She was tall, long, and lean. She had straight hair that always looked perfectly kept, not unruly like my waves.

Joshua joined our grouping, stepping up behind her. The slight tightening in her eyes gave it away, even though they didn't touch or anything. Before I could sensor myself, I blurted, "You're dating?"

They both looked alarmed for a moment, and I realized I'd sounded accusatory. Josh put his hand on the small of her back, and I *did* feel a pang of jealousy. I had sensed chemistry between them the first time I'd seen them together and had felt jealous until Josh had proudly claimed our relationship. As quickly as it had risen, my jealous feelings were washed away by ones of joy. I wanted Joshua happy, and Jess met my approval in every way.

"I'm glad," I finally managed, my voice choked. "Sorry, pregnancy hormones wreak havoc in vampires, too," I added.

Rosemond started to fuss and let out a long string of baby babble that included "food."

"Can I feed her?" I asked.

A few minutes later, she was in a portable high chair, and I was spooning into her organic puree that smelled disgusting, but she seemed to like it. After I'd wiped her down, lifted her from the chair, and rested her on my hip, I then realized I needed to feed.

I closed my eyes, shoving away the sensation—as twisted and wrong as it seemed, babies *did* smell amazing. I quickly handed her to Uriel and sped out the front door for some air.

"You okay, Als?" Joshua leaned against the pillar next to me.

"I haven't fed since we left. I was too nervous while we traveled here."

"You aren't upset?"

I exhaled in a long stream. "About you? I have no right to be upset. I'm married to someone else, remember?"

"It doesn't mean it isn't weird," he replied, the look of worry still on his face.

"I don't want to see you make out with her or anything, but I approve. And things aren't the same between us anyway–you don't remember most of our marriage."

He nodded, his voice rough when he replied, "I remember enough. We had something...extraordinary, didn't we?"

"Yes." I reached out and took his hand. "We still do. It's just different. You are still my family. I'm thankful every day that you are with Cameron."

Joshua encircled me with his arms and rested his chin on top of my head. After a few minutes of holding me, he kissed the top of my head and murmured, "I'm gonna go grab Gabriel. I can feel your hunger radiating off of you."

"You don't nee—"

"You made him your familiar. It will be a few minutes. He headed to his room for a video conference," Josh firmly replied.

I rocked back on my heels. I had. I needed to feed on both Gabriel and Ian. Both of them were high profile now and needed to appear the part to stay safe.

I strolled around the side of the house to a sitting area with cushioned wicker furniture. But before I could even sit, Cadeyn had to check on me during his perimeter sweep. Then a few moments later, Samael came around the corner. He grinned.

"Hey," I greeted. "I am surprised you're here," I admitted.

He shrugged, his abnormally square jaw flexing at the same time. "Gabriel told me you are doing well. Are you really?"

"Yeah, I can't believe it, but I am. I think I'm making a difference."

Samael seemed to relax a little. "I just needed to see you with my own eyes and make sure. The last time I saw you, you were leaving with those two..." He caught himself before he insulted Bowen and Tyran. Part of me cursed him for making me think of Tyran.

"Thank you for being here." It meant a lot. Samael putting himself near any vamps he wasn't allowed to kill was not easy for him.

He shifted awkwardly on his feet. "I should get back to my rounds." He moved off before I could say another word.

I finally sat and propped my feet on the marble top coffee table. I leaned back and watched the night sky. The moon was especially bright and lit the edges of the occasional cloud with silver that drifted in front of it. I caught Gabriel's scent in the breeze. He rounded the corner, looking a little more on edge than he'd been a while ago.


GABRIEL

"Is everything okay?" asked Aleria.

I drummed the small manila envelope in my hands, wondering the repercussions of what I was going to share with her, but not until she had fed.

"Gabriel?"

I realized I had lost myself in the reverie. "I apologize. You need to feed."

She sighed, her face twisting into distaste.

A grin crept onto my face. "I always wonder if I should be offended." I took a seat next to her.

She remained in her relaxed position with her feet up, looking towards the night sky. "I can just use the bagged blood. It wasn't in the fridge."

"It was a conscious choice not to put it there."

She rolled her head to the side and gave me a dry look. "You mean you hid it from me. I think there is a law against starving me."

"I had extensive conversations with Belenus about familiars. He made—"

"You did?"

"He made it clear for your safety, as well as mine. It needs to real and that you need to feed from the neck. No claimed familiar would be fed on exclusively from the wrist."

She leaned forward and dropped her head into her hands. "He told me the same thing. I'm sorry, Gabriel."

"I got over you feeding on me years ago when I almost killed you. Now get on with it."

She parted two of her fingers and glared at me a moment before she dropped her hands from her face and sat back up. "Okay, bossy. Turn a little so your back is to me."

She pushed at me getting me to sit how she wanted. I placed the envelope on the opposite side of me. She moved my left elbow to the back of the couch and nudged me to lean in that direction before she got on her knees in back of me. Then she placed a throw pillow on my left shoulder.

"Tilt your head and rest it to the side."

She ran her cold fingers over the side of my neck a few times; she was hesitating again.

"Do it," I ordered, though she was not mine to order. I understood her reluctance, but she made it worse than it was.

We were already bound. She had been more than my student or apprentice for a long time. She had become my surrogate younger sister, filling the chasm Laylah's death had left and the niece I would never have.

I had been on a path to bitterness, and it was Joshua's heart and Aleria's spirit that had brought me back and given me hope. I had never told her that. Maybe she knew; she had been afraid of me when we had first met and rightfully so. I had been training Joshua, but had been ready to kill him with a simple order from Sebastian. And now I would have died for either of them. The irony was not lost on me.

Ali grabbed my head, placing her palm on my forehead, and hooked her other beneath my right arm, wrapping it around my torso. I did not flinch when her teeth punctured my neck, before I felt the relief of her chemical secretion. Then it became apparent that the neck was different—more powerful —more connected. My senses dulled, and I was no longer acutely aware of my surroundings. I was no longer keeping track of Cadeyn as he stalked by in the shadows near the garden wall—or anything else. It felt odd not being on alert, but I simply did not care.

She stopped, sealed the wound, and repositioned her jaw, making another bite. I knew at that moment: she was not planning on doing this again during her visit. She was creating all the evidence at once. She made two more sets of bite marks afterwards, a total of four, before she finished. Then she leaned her head against my shoulder blade, hugging me to her.

"I really wish you wouldn't taste so good. It's hard not to kill you."

I chuckled.

"I'm not joking, Gabriel."

"I know."

She backed up and sat, twisting her legs beneath her and unconsciously rubbing at her belly. I shifted to a normal sitting position and put my arm around her. She did not resist and leaned against me, her head against my chest.

"Are you happy? Is he treating you well?"

There was no hesitation in her reply. "Yes, and he is. Sometimes I don't feel like I deserve him."

"You do. I do not know why you would feel otherwise."

"Are *you* happy?" asked she.

I did pause. "I am. I have a balance in my life that I have not had since my sister was alive."

"I'm glad," replied she. She ran her fingers over the scar from my replantation surgery. "How is your arm?"

"I have eighty-five percent mobility. Doctors consider anything over fifty percent highly successful. I may gain another five percent with continued therapy, but even with my advanced healing, I will never be the same."

A pained look came across her face.

"Do not apologize again. I do not blame you."

She wilted. "I know."

We were silent for a long while. I pulled her closer; after this visit, it would be many months before I would see her again.

She broke her silence, her voice thoughtful. "We have given so much and lost so many. There was a while where I had wondered if I could ever be happy again."

It reminded me of the envelope. I picked it up and handed it to her. She sat up and removed the stack of papers, seeming confused when she examined the report on top. "Is this Spanish?"

"Yes. There is a translation on the back."

"A report about an earthquake?" asked she, confused.

"It is from a small town in South America, not far from a Hellmouth. This was an eyewitness account written in a rare dialect, so it was not flagged and forwarded to me until a few days ago."

"But this happened the day after Semjâzâ..." Her voice trailed as she began to read again, but this time, she read aloud. "A large tremor shook the area not far from the Hollow of the Spirits. Is that—"

"What the locals call the Hellmouth in that area. They believe it is possessed by evil spirits."

She continued. "A sink hole opened at dawn, and from it, a winged man clawed his way out. His wings and hair were black, and he held a wound in his chest. A second quake hit, opening the rift farther, and two more emerged from the chasm: one red-haired female with wings and one male with glowing blue eyes and no wings. The new arrivals attacked the larger winged-man, tearing him to pieces. The glowing-eyed man began to smoke with the rising sun, but continued to fight until the winged man was dead. The female picked up the burning man, flying into the mountains and leaving the corpse behind."

Ali stopped reading aloud and went back over the report again. I watched as her finger moved down the page, and her lips moved.

"Ana and Tyran are *alive*? It's been six months. Where are they?"

I motioned to the stack of papers. She looked over the next report. "Keep going."

After reading it, she met my eyes. "They think a demon started living in the mountains. Dead animals drained of blood and a search party returned with no memory of what had happened."

"We hacked into an intelligence agency and used their facial recognition search of stored images. We got one hit."

Ali shuffled through the papers and pulled out a photo. The picture was of a member of a drug cartel, but in the background, there was a clear picture of Taranis. His hair was dyed brown, and skin had been darkened with bronzer, but there was no mistaking him.

She was quiet for a long while, staring at the picture. "I...I just don't understand why he hasn't come home or at least called."

"Kiddo, is it really not obvious to you?"

"No," she whispered, hurt.

She was whip smart, but still not aware of her allure. "He is in love with his brother's wife. I think it is probably easier for him to stay away—and to give you and Belenus a chance. His presence would complicate your marriage. I think he loves both of you too much."

"But it wouldn't," she protested.

"Would you be able to sit back and watch?"

There was a long pause. "Probably not. I guess. I know

Joshua and Jess are together, but I'm not really ready to see them touch—like, at all."

"And there you have it."

She shuffled through the remaining items, and then tossed the stack onto the coffee table, leaning back onto my arm again. A smile crept onto her face.

"What?"

"Tyran would have been in bad shape after the sun exposure. He didn't kill anyone like he would have in the past. He would have eaten his way through a town a year ago just to save himself. He glamoured the locals, took what he needed, and sent them home to their families."

My eyes drifted to Aleria's growing belly. I found myself smiling at her epiphany. The future suddenly seemed brighter than it had a few moments ago.

If a creature such as Taranis could change this much—then this was a world worth fighting for.

# 31

# AN EXCERPT FROM ALLURE: THE WATCHER SERIES PREQUEL

READ ABOUT THE ADVENTURES OF ALERIA'S GREAT-GRANDMOTHER, ROSEMOND, AND FIND OUT WHAT HAPPENED WITH CADEYN BRADSHAW, THE CAPTAIN OF THE ROYAL GUARD IN THE 1920S.

## ROSEMOND

"What are the chances that neither of us breaks anything or dies?" I asked.

"I'm an optimist by nature," George replied, looking out at the tracks spilling behind the train being swallowed up by the darkness. His face was smooth without a trace of worry. I wondered how he did that.

A small nervous laugh gurgled out of me and he met my gaze. His dark hair was whipping around in the chilled night air. "You, sir, are not an optimist. You are a realist, who is trying to ease my fears."

He didn't argue, but his eyes seemed to soften for a moment before he looked out at the tracks again. "It is starting to slow."

After a moment of concentration, the reduction in speed was discernible. Taking an inventory of myself, I had on a pair of George's pants under my dress to protect my legs and his spare coat over the top of everything. I felt ridiculous but thankful. A few long minutes passed as the wind continued battering us.

"It is almost time," he said, without taking his eyes from the tracks.

I nodded in acknowledgement, though he wasn't looking at me. I was jealous of how calm he appeared. I was too frightened to utter a word but tried to be more like him and to fix my face with something that might resemble words like 'brave' or 'fearless' or at the very least, 'plucky.' But it probably resembled something more like 'has-horrible-food-poisoning' or 'about-to-tame-a-lion-whilst-covered-in-meat.'

Perhaps he sensed my bubbling anxiety, or I may have made a sound, because he turned towards me and gave me a most comforting half-smile. His eyes looked almost black against the night landscape.

He raised his hands and buttoned the top button of his coat that I wore. Strangely, this small gesture made me feel so safe, as if I could fly from the train and not be harmed.

Taking a steadying breath I said, "You are a good man, George Yates." I felt a little embarrassed that I had said it but at the same time, knew it was true.

The smile faded from his face. It appeared as if he wanted to say something. He cleared his throat, "Almost slow enough. The luggage, then us. Remember everything I told you. Roll when you hit the ground."

"Roll when landing, avoid large rocks and trees and also dying. Was that all?" I managed to quip.

"Farm animals should also be avoided," he replied, deadpan.

The train had slowed to a little faster than a man could run. I had asked him why we couldn't unhitch the caboose, but he said if someone was looking for us at the next stop, it would be immediately obvious. He wanted to allow for the possibility that we slipped by them at the station—to spread their forces thin.

It made sense, and jumping was probably the better option. But I didn't care for pain, especially if it involved large amounts of it. I groaned internally.

"It is time," he said, then we jumped.


Find out what happened by reading ALLURE.

# ACKNOWLEDGMENTS

First, I have to thank my amazing husband. I dedicated my first novel to him, saying that he is my rock. That has never been truer.

Beth, you are my frontline, and I can't thank you enough for bravely hacking through my first draft. You have a tremendous gift and are still my number one fan. ;)

Tamar, you started as my proofreader, evolved into an editor, and now you are my writing partner. I can't thank you enough for all of your support. You make the journey a heck of a lot more fun. You are my writing soul sister. xoxo

Without Alexis, Rebecca, and Rachel pushing to "write more!", I wouldn't have gone back to the series.

Rachel and Roy, I appreciate that my weaknesses are your strengths. Thanks for always being supportive and being willing to help me out.

I want to give a shout out to my beta readers for being willing to drop everything and give me feedback when I have needed it. Your input is so incredibly valuable, and you have my eternal gratitude. Thanks to Alexis, Judi, Rachel, Rebecca, Jessie, Barbara, and Mom and Dad.

Vera Walker, you overflow with talent and always deliver. Thank you for using your graphic design wizardry once again. You always surprise me. You are a beast (in a good way).

**Fiction Books**

Allure: A Watcher Series Prequel

The Unintended: Book One

The Nexus: Book Two

The Sacrifice: Book Three

The Fallen: Part One: Book Four

The Fallen: Part Two: Book Five


Coming in 2020:

Light & Shadow: The Watcher Series Shorts & Extras


Thank you for reading. If you enjoyed this novel, please take a moment to write a review. It is the best way to help authors you love. Blessings!

**Creative & Fiction Writing Books**

Prompt Me Novel: Fiction Writing Workbook & Journal

Prompt Me: Creative Writing Workbook & Journal

Prompt Me More: Workbook & Journal

Prompt Me Again: Workbook & Journal

Prompt Me Sci-Fi & Fantasy: Workbook & Journal

Prompt Me Romance: Workbook & Journal

Prompt Me Horror & Thriller: Workbook & Journal

Prompt Me Reading Log & Analysis: Workbook & Journal

Coming in 2020: Prompt Me Mystery & Suspense

## ABOUT THE AUTHOR

Robin Woods is a former high school and university instructor with two and a half decades of experience teaching English, literature, and writing. She earned a BA in English and an MA in education.

In addition to teaching, she has published six novels, eight creative writing books (and counting), and has multiple projects in the works, including writing for a Hollywood producer.

When Ms. Woods isn't chasing her two elementary school kids around, she's spending time with her ever-patient husband, or sitting in a coffee shop wondering how vampires like their lattes.

For more information, an extended bio, free writing resources, links to social media, and free extra scenes, visit her website at www.robinwoodsfiction.com